JAIMIE ADMANS is a 32-year-old English-sounding Welsh girl with an awkward-to-spell name. She lives in South Wales and enjoys writing, gardening, watching horror movies and drinking tea, although she's seriously considering marrying her coffee machine. She loves autumn and winter, and singing songs from musicals despite the fact she's got the voice of a dying hyena. She hates spiders, hot weather and cheese and onion crisps. She spends far too much time on Twitter and owns too many pairs of boots. She will never have time to read all the books she wants to read.

Jaimie loves to hear from readers. You can visit her website at www.jaimieadmans.com or connect on Twitter @be_the_spark.

D1137955

Also by Jaimie Admans

The Château of Happily-Ever-Afters
The Little Wedding Island

It's a Wonderful Night

JAIMIE ADMANS

ONE PLACE. MANY STORIES

HQ

An imprint of HarperCollins*Publishers* Ltd
1 London Bridge Street
London SE1 9GF

This edition 2018
2

First published in Great Britain by
HQ, an imprint of HarperCollins*Publishers* Ltd 2018

ISBN: PB: 978-0-00-832106-2
EB: 978-0-00-829689-6

MIX
Paper from
responsible sources
FSC   FSC® C007454
www.fsc.org

This book is produced from independently certified FSC™ paper
to ensure responsible forest management.

For more information visit: **www.harpercollins.co.uk/green**

Typeset by Palimpsest Book Production Ltd, Falkirk, Stirlingshire
Printed and bound by
CPI Group (UK) Ltd, Croydon, CR0 4YY

For everyone.

You are good enough.

No matter how impossible things seem, you truly have a wonderful life, and the world will always be better with you in it.

Chapter 1

I'm in the cupboard under the stairs trying to wrangle a naked mannequin up the narrow steps to the back room when I hear the phone ringing. I groan. It's only going to be a telemarketer, isn't it? It's eleven o'clock on a November night and I'm working overtime because, as the manager of the One Light charity shop, it's my responsibility to get the Christmas window display finished before morning. I don't have time for discussing 'an accident I've had recently that wasn't my fault', mis-sold PPI, or my solar panel needs. Don't they even stick to normal working hours now?

I'll ignore it. I take a defiant bite of the fun-size Crunchie I've just found a bag of in the cupboard under the stairs. Who put chocolate down here? Maybe the volunteers were trying to hide it from me? It's obviously leftover from Halloween and that was over a month ago. There's not usually chocolate hanging around that long if I know it's there. A day would be pushing it. Maybe it wasn't such a bad hiding place after all.

The ring is insistent and I have a conscience about ignoring a ringing phone. It could be an emergency. It could be my dad saying he's fallen and can't get up, or paramedics who have been called out because he's had another heart scare.

I look at the mannequin's blank face. 'Sorry,' I mutter to it as

I try to prop it against the wall, shove the last half of the Crunchie into my mouth and rush through the back room and out onto the shop floor, leaving behind a series of thuds as the mannequin slides back down the steps I've just dragged it up.

I've forgotten to hit the light switch so the shop floor is in darkness and I trip over a clothing rail and nearly go flying.

'Hello?' I say with my mouth full as I grab the handset from behind the counter. It's far from the polite 'One Light charity shop, how can I help you?' that we're supposed to answer the phone with, but I fully expect the caller to have rung off by now anyway.

'Do you think it will hurt?'

'What?' I say with all the eloquence of an inebriated badger, hopping about with the phone in one hand, the other clutching the toe that collided with the clothing rail.

'If I jump off this bridge?'

I choke on the Crunchie.

'Are you okay?' the man's voice on the other end of the line asks.

'Yes, thanks.' I clear my throat a few times, trying to dislodge rogue bits of honeycomb. Only *I* could greet a suicidal man by choking at him. 'Shouldn't it be me asking you that?'

He lets out a laugh that sounds wet and thick, like he's been crying. 'I'm not the one choking to death. Do you need a glass of water or something?'

'No, no, I'm fine,' I say, wondering if swallowing actual sand-paper might've been more comfortable. 'I'm so sorry, I'd just shoved an entire fun-size Crunchie into my mouth and then tried to speak. If that isn't a recipe for disaster, I don't know what is.'

I don't know why I said that. A recipe for disaster is not me choking on a chocolate bar – it's a guy about to throw himself off a bridge who doesn't realize he's phoned the charity shop for a suicide prevention helpline rather than the suicide prevention helpline itself.

My heart is suddenly pounding and a cold sweat has prickled my forehead. I don't know what to do. I've always been petrified this would happen but never really thought it would. I've always thought that the two numbers are printed worryingly close together on our leaflets. Head Office told me I was worrying too much, but I've often wondered how easy it would be for someone to get our number muddled up with the helpline number and phone here by mistake. And it seems like the answer has just rung.

What am I going to do? I can't take this call. I don't know how to talk someone down off a bridge.

'Oh, I love Crunchies. Don't tell me you still have fun-size ones leftover from Halloween?'

'I think they were hidden from me. I've only just found them.' I'm rambling about nonsense but I don't know what else to say. I know people think chocolate is the answer to most things, but I doubt it's likely to help in this situation, and as much as I'd like to keep talking about Cadbury's honeycomb treat, I can't keep avoiding his first question.

I go to speak but he gets there first. 'Can we just keep talking about chocolate? This is the most normal conversation I've had for days.'

I let out a nervous laugh. 'We can talk about anything you want. Chocolate's always a good topic.'

'Where's your hiding place? I never manage to hide mine successfully; I always remember where it is and scoff the lot. I bought boxes of Milk Tray for the family when they were on offer a couple of weeks ago, and let's just say I've now got to go and buy more before Christmas. You can guess what happened to them, right?'

Another nervous laugh. 'Well, this time, my staff bought them in case any trick or treaters came round before closing time, but none did, so they must've hidden them in the cupboard under the stairs of all places. I was just wrestling a naked mannequin out when I found them. Safe to say there aren't many left now. And I feel a bit sick. Those two points are probably related.'

'Well, if they've been there for a month, you're only testing them for quality, right?'

I giggle again. How can someone about to throw himself off a bridge make me laugh? 'Yes. Testing them *vigorously*.'

He laughs too and the laugh seems to go on for much longer than for anything that was actually funny. 'God, I haven't laughed in so long,' he says eventually, sounding out of breath. 'So what are you doing naked wrestling mannequins under the stairs at this time of night? Aren't you in a call centre?'

'Um…'

'Oh God, please don't tell me I phoned the wrong number.' He must be able to hear my hesitation because he suddenly sounds distraught and I hear paper rustling down the line. 'I have, haven't I? There are two numbers on here and the leaflet's all wet and the ink's blurred. God, I'm such an idiot.'

'No, you're not. You're *not*. Trust me, it's our fault; I've been trying to get those leaflets redesigned for years,' I say, feeling panic claw at my chest. What if he's going to hang up and go through with the jump because of a silly mistake?

'I'm so sorry.' He makes a noise of frustration. 'I'm so, so sorry to have disturbed you. Please forget this ever happened. I'll leave you to your naked mannequin wrestling.'

He says the words in such a rush that I can't interrupt him quickly enough. 'Please don't go,' I say, my voice going high at the fear of what he might do. I need to give him the number of the real helpline. There are business cards on the counter right in front of me. It would be easy enough to read out the number and tell him to phone there instead, where there are people who do this all the time and have a lot of training in dealing with these situations. But what if he doesn't phone them? What if he feels stupid for phoning the wrong place? What if he decides to jump rather than make another phone call?

4

I can't tell a suicidal man to hang up and try again, can I?

'Please stay and talk a minute,' I say cautiously. Surely the best thing I can do is talk to him? There are testimonials on the One Light website that say the most important thing in deciding not to go through with a suicide attempt was having someone to talk to, and the charity have run campaigns about how important making small talk with a stranger can be. 'I don't have enough people to talk about chocolate with. And I feel like I shouldn't let you go without clarifying that it's the mannequins who are naked, not me. It's way too cold for that.'

He lets out a guffaw. 'Ah, so if I'd phoned on a summer night, it would have been a different story, huh?'

I laugh too. 'What did I expect from a conversation that's revolved entirely around chocolate, naked mannequins, and wrestling?'

'I think I'd be letting the male species as a whole down if I didn't derive something dirty from a conversation like that.'

'I think we've both done our duty with weird conversations so far tonight,' I say. I need to end this and get him on the phone to an actual counsellor who can help him talk things through, but I don't know how to broach the subject. I can't just say, 'Right, here's the number, off you go'. It's too abrupt, it could make him feel rejected, and it could make him more likely to jump.

'Where are you?' I ask instead. Maybe getting back onto the subject is a good start.

'The suspension bridge over the Barrow river. It's on the outskirts of Oakbarrow town.'

He's local. I know exactly where he is. Turn right at the end of the high street and go past the churchyard, it's a ten-minute walk away. The old steel bridge on the road that leads out of Oakbarrow. I was up there two days ago putting One Light leaflets out. I leave a few of them weighed down with a stone in the corner of the pavement, next to the safety barrier that was replaced after an accident a few years ago. The replacement part is just a

5

bit lower than the rest of the barrier; the part where anyone thinking of jumping would be most likely to climb over.

'What are you doing up there at this time of night?'

'I don't know. God, I don't know. It seemed so clear when I walked up here, but I got to the edge and looked down, and I couldn't see the water, just blackness in the dark, and I went dizzy so I sat down on the pavement, and I just… I don't know. Sorry, I'm rambling.'

'Not at all,' I say, thinking his voice sounds familiar. He's got an English accent but he puts a little emphasis on his 'r's. It's typical for this part of Gloucestershire. That must be why I think I recognize it.

'I walked across the bridge yesterday and saw a stack of your leaflets. The thought of … you know … jumping … has been in my head for a while and I grabbed one and stuffed it in my pocket. As I stood there and looked over the edge tonight, I put my hands in my pockets and my fingers brushed it, and it was like I didn't even remember putting it there.'

That must've been one of the leaflets I put out the day before. It makes me feel weirdly connected to him. This man has reached out in his darkest moment because of something I did. I have a responsibility to help him.

'I sat on the pavement and unfolded it and thought about my dad – he died on this river – and I just felt … compelled to ring you. He'd be so disappointed if he could see me now. He thought life was the most precious thing any of us have.'

'You didn't jump. That's the most important part. Life *is* precious and you chose to sit down and call me instead of throwing it away. That's the first step to making things better.'

'I didn't choose to sit down, I thought I was going to pass out.'

'That's okay too. The only thing that matters is that you're here and talking. It's got to be better than the alternative,' I say carefully, trying to sound as neutral as possible.

'I shouldn't be talking about this to you though, should I? I

6

phoned the wrong number. I wouldn't mind betting this is definitely not part of your job description …'

'It's okay, it's absolutely fine.' I'm glad he can't see the expression on my face because it definitely doesn't match the lighthearted tone in my voice. 'It's just the people on the helpline are properly trained counsellors, and I'm not. I don't want to say the wrong thing and make this worse,' I say, deciding honesty is the best policy.

'Please don't hang up,' he says after a long moment of silence. He sounds so cautious, almost afraid, and kind of hopeful, that there's no way I could refuse. 'I know I shouldn't be asking you to talk to me but I don't know what to do, and you're reminding me of normal people and normal conversations and feeling normal and you've already made me laugh and it's been so long since I …' His voice goes choked up again and I can hear him sniffle.

'I'm not going anywhere,' I say quickly, trying to reassure him. My hand tightens around the plastic of the handset. In my head, I'm wondering if I could somehow get in touch with the helpline while he's still on the line and try to transfer the call without hanging up on him, but I can't think of a way to do it. The phone in the shop that I'm talking on is an old corded one that's attached to the wall behind the counter so no one can accidentally sell it – been there, done that – and my mobile is in my locker upstairs. I'd have to leave him for a few precious minutes to dash up there and get it. It would be too obvious what I was doing. What if he felt like I was just shafting him off onto the next person because I didn't care? If he feels like I can't get rid of him quick enough, it might make this situation worse. Even if I could get my phone and text the helpline and ask them what to say, I'd still have to leave him hanging here in silence while I got right the way across the shop floor, through the back room, up the stairs and into my locker and all the way back again, and who knows what he might do in that time? He phoned because he needs someone to talk to *now*. I can't just leave him.

7

I wind the cord of the phone around my fingers and sink down into a sitting position. I thunk my head back against the wall behind the counter and listen to the rain pounding on the shop roof. Even Bernard, the homeless man who lives in the churchyard, will have found shelter tonight. 'Aren't you soaked?'

I hear movement and can imagine him lifting an arm and looking at it. 'I am, actually. I hadn't even noticed.'

I don't know what it's like to be in that situation, to feel so bad, so desperate, that there's no way out, but I imagine a little fall of rain is the last thing he's worrying about. I hate the idea of someone sitting on the pavement outside in this weather though. He must be drenched and freezing. I could go up there, take him a warm blanket and a hot cup of tea, but that too would mean leaving the phone, and it would eradicate our anonymity.

Privacy and anonymity are the foundations of the charity. The helpline exists so people in a crisis can open up to an unbiased stranger. Callers are routed through a server that hides the number from the person on the other end. Helpline staff are not allowed to ask the caller's name if they don't share it, and not allowed to give their own name unless asked. He knows I'm not proper helpline staff, but I still work for One Light. Those rules must still apply to me, even if this is a situation that's never happened before.

'Talk to me,' I say gently, terrified that I'm saying the wrong thing. 'Why were you thinking of jumping?'

'We'll be here all night if I start listing the reasons.'

'That's okay. We can be here all night. There's no time limit. What's going on?'

'Everything. I'm a failure at life. My business is going under and I've done everything I can to try to save it, and I don't know what else to do. It was supposed to be a way of honouring my father, but it's taken every bit of money I had, and it's dead. I have no customers. My mum is seventy-seven years old and on her feet at seven o'clock every day to help me out because I can't afford to pay any staff. I'm in debt up to my eyeballs and I got my business rates bill this morning, and I can't afford to pay even a fraction of it. And just to ice the cake, the rates are going up in January and there's *no way* I can pay them.'

Because of the anonymity rules, I can't ask him outright where he works, but if he's in Oakbarrow then chances are it's somewhere nearby. It might even be on this high street.

I sit up on my knees and look over the counter at the darkened road outside. Even the streetlamps have flickered their final death and no one's bothered to mend them. Oakbarrow High Street used to be a hive of activity, especially at this time of year, but now it's deader than the burnt-out bulbs in the streetlights. The truth is that I know how quiet things are. I know how difficult it is to get people through the door. Every day, I expect a phone call from Head Office saying they've decided to shut our branch down.

'Well, it's nearly Christmas,' I say. 'People are out shopping in the big towns at this time of year. Maybe things will pick up in January?'

'There's a new retail park on the roundabout outside of town. It's easy to get to, there's plenty of free parking, and it's got every kind of shop you could imagine. No one needs to come to high streets anymore, no matter the time of year.'

'Yeah, but the retail park is a bit … soulless, isn't it? These business parks are all the same – if you've seen one, you've seen them all. I'd rather go to a little high street full of independent shops that actually mean something to the people who own them. That comes across to shoppers, you know?'

'Well, you must be one of about ten people left in the country who think that way.'

I suddenly feel incredibly sad because he's so right about the high street. I've lived in Oakbarrow all my life. This high street used to be the centre of the universe, especially at this time of year. I remember going Christmas shopping with my mum when

I was little and being amazed by it; the sights, the sounds, the smells. The giant tree they put up in front of the churchyard, always at least ten-foot high, lush green branches weighed down with twinkling lights and ornaments that local school children had made. It was magical back then. Shopkeepers would stay open late, decorations of reindeer pulling Santa's sleigh ran across the road above our heads, snowflakes twinkled on hangers outside every shop, lampposts were wrapped with tinsel and bows and had bright bulbs that still worked.

I look out the window again. The shop across the road is empty, its windows painted white from inside, the shop next to that has a 'for sale' sign nailed to its front though the 's' has worn off, and the one on the opposite side has had 'closing down sale' notices in its bare windows for the past three years.

Just about the only shops still in business are the charity shop and the bank next door, a coffee shop, a tanning shop, a lingerie shop, and a television repair shop at the upper end of the high street. Even the only pub, that used to be the heart of all village gatherings, has closed in recent years. It used to be called The Blue Drum but some clever vandal has removed the middle five letters, so now it's just The B um. I hear a lot of regular customers talking about wishing The Bum was still open so they could go up it.

It feels like every one of us is only here to await the death knell. Even the mini supermarket that put the independent green-grocer out of business and contributed to the market closure has shut up shop and run for the hills. Or, more specifically, run for the retail park to be with all the other convenient and cheap shops that make high streets everywhere irrelevant.

'I wish there was something I could say to make you feel better, but there's no denying what a state high streets everywhere are in.'

'At least you're honest. Somehow, even hearing that makes me feel better.'

Well, I want to make him feel better but I'm not sure commiserating over the state of things was quite what I had in mind. 'How are you feeling now?'

'Cold. Wet.' I can hear his teeth chattering. 'Stupid for being up here. Stupid for thinking this was the answer. Pathetic for crying down the phone to a stranger.'

'Hey, that's not pathetic.' I wonder if we are strangers. If he works around here, I might know him in passing. I've had this job for four years now; you get to know people who work nearby, and his voice *does* sound familiar. 'When you need help, the bravest thing you can do is reach out and ask for it.'

'Or phone a stranger and talk about naked mannequin wrestling.'

The laugh takes me by surprise. 'Or make them choke on a Crunchie.'

'Or that.' His laugh turns into a sob. 'I shouldn't be up here. I feel like I've let everyone down. My family would be devastated if they knew it had come to this.'

'You haven't let anyone down because you're still here. The only thing your family would care about is you being all right. I know what it's like to lose someone you love. I promise you, there's nothing in the world worse than that. Any business that's failing is just a business, a building, a job. Losing that can be recovered from. *You* are irreplaceable.'

'Thank you.' His voice breaks and I can hear the thickness of tears welling up again. My heart constricts in my chest and I want nothing more than to hug this man I don't even know.

'None of us know how much we matter until it's too late. No matter how bad you feel, you're so important to so many people. One person's life touches so many others.'

'Do you know *It's a Wonderful Life*?'

I feel myself sitting up a bit straighter because he obviously recognized the quote. *It's a Wonderful Life* is not just a film to me. It was my mum's favourite, so much so that she named me

Georgia Bailey after it. 'I would be seriously concerned for anyone who *didn't* know *It's a Wonderful Life*. It's an amazing film.'

He makes a noise of agreement.

'It's kind of life-affirming,' I say pointedly. 'It really shows the importance of every life. No matter how insignificant we think we are, our little lives still make a big difference.'

He considers it for a moment. 'You have no idea how much I needed to hear that tonight.'

We sit there in silence for a while, neither of us speaking, and I realize I'm holding the phone handset so tightly that the plastic must be in danger of cracking by now. It feels like a lifeline to him and I could sit here all night just listening to him breathe. His breath has got that shuddery hitch you get after a long cry, and I have never wanted to hug someone so badly in all my life.

At the end of the high street, the church bell dongs for midnight.

'Every time a bell rings,' he murmurs. 'Did you hear that?'

It makes my heart pound harder. It's what I say every time I hear a bell ring too because they make me think of my mum. I love that he knows the film so well because it means so much to me and not many people get that.

'I heard something,' I say, because I don't know whether he's asking if I heard it through the phone or if he realizes I'm just down the road.

'That was the Oakbarrow church telling us all it's officially December.'

'Christmas month,' I say.

'Don't remind me. I can't deal with Christmas this year.'

'Why not?'

'It makes me realize that another year has gone by and I've done nothing with my life. You're supposed to be all happy happy, joy joy at Christmas and I've got nothing left in me to give.'

'I wouldn't mind betting that the only reason you've got nothing left is because you're so busy looking after everyone else that you forget to take care of yourself,' I say, because so many men are the same. He's probably a guy who's grown up thinking men must always be strong and never let their feelings show. It's a toxic masculinity that's dangerous to men's mental health. It's why suicide is the biggest killer of men under fifty. Men bottle things up inside and don't let it out until it's too late. I don't know the exact figures off the top of my head, but I do know that a majority of One Light's callers are male because of this exact reason.

'My mum always says that.'

'Mums are always right,' I murmur, wishing mine was still here.

'Sometimes I feel like I'm frightened of being alive.'

My breath catches in my throat. 'Me too.'

'Really?'

'Yeah,' I say slowly, nodding even though he can't see me. 'No one's ever hit the nail on the head like that before. That's exactly how I feel too.'

'I've always wanted to travel but I never have.'

'Me neither. I've never told anyone this but my ultimate dream is to go backpacking around Europe,' I say wondering what it is about him that makes him so easy to talk to.

'Really?' he says again. 'I'd love to do that.'

'I think I'm a bit old for it now, it's kind of a "gap year" thing, isn't it?' I shake my head at myself. I'm too old for daydreams like this, I should've forgotten it years ago. 'It's just a dream anyway. I have responsibilities that I can't just leave.'

'Me too. I was going to travel after college, but family stuff happened and I couldn't leave, then I was going off to uni but more family stuff came up, and it made more sense for me to get a job and stay here, so I'd been saving up for years to do one big trip somewhere, and then my dad died, and I bought the business, and now … well, I'm still here. I keep feeling like there has to be more to life than this.'

'Me too,' I say.

'Wow, really? Sorry, I keep saying that, don't I? I've never spoken to someone who knew that feeling before.'

'Me neither. And there you go, I just keep repeating some variation of "me too" and "me neither". It doesn't make for the most exciting conversation in the world but I've never said this to anyone before.'

'Me neither,' he says, making us both laugh. My grip on the phone tightens, like if I hold it tight enough he'll be able to feel me squeezing his hand through the handset.

'This isn't what I thought my life would be like,' I admit. 'And I know I can't really complain because I'm so lucky compared to others, but I feel like I'm still waiting for my life to start.'

'I think we might literally be the same person. I'm thirty-seven and I feel exactly the same. I'm too old to still be waiting for my life to begin and too young to be this jaded, but I don't know what to do about it.'

So he's only three years older than me. I couldn't possibly know him, no matter how familiar his voice sounds. I can't think of anyone around that age who could be in such a dark place and hiding it so well.

'Me too,' I whisper.

'We grow up thinking life will be wonderful and amazing and exciting, and it's just quite dull really, isn't it? I keep thinking what if I die before anything wonderful or amazing or exciting happens to me?' He gives a self-deprecating snort. 'And yes, I know throwing yourself off a bridge isn't exactly conducive to that.'

At least he hasn't lost his sense of humour. He lets out a wobbly little giggle and I feel something like butterflies in my tummy. How can I possibly have butterflies over someone I don't even know? Someone who phoned because he was about to jump off a bridge?

'Okay, so … I should go, shouldn't I?' he says after a few moments silence.

'You don't have to. We can carry on talking.' I kind of want him to stay on the line for my sake now. I *love* talking to him. There's something about him that's so easy to chat to and a familiarity that you'd only expect to feel with a friend.

I can hear the smile in his voice. 'As tempting as that sounds, I think I should go home. I'm so cold that I might actually die from hypothermia and, thanks to you, I've realized I don't want to die tonight.'

'Or any other night, right?'

'Nah. I'll stick to killing myself only in daylight hours.'

'I'm glad you can joke about it, but it's not funny. You were really going to –'

'I know,' he whispers. 'But I feel better already just from talking to you, getting it off my chest, feeling like I'm not alone.'

He pauses and I can almost sense how ashamed he feels. I want to tell him that there's no reason to be, but I'm out of my depth and don't know how to word it.

'I can't thank you enough for staying on the line with me. I shouldn't have asked. I'm sure I've totally ruined your night.'

'Oh God, not at all. I've loved every second of talking to you. It's been a wonderful night.'

I can hear a smile in his voice. 'You just sounded so normal, it made me forget everything that's been in my head and just feel normal for a change. I can't remember the last time I felt connected to anyone. As daft as that sounds in our modern world of technology and the internet and being connected *all* the time.'

'It doesn't sound daft at all. It sounds exactly like what I was feeling too.' I wonder how many more times he's going to surprise me tonight. He seems to understand thoughts I've had but never put into words before. 'I think it's something that's easy to forget sometimes. We get so caught up in social media and being as good as everyone else that we forget we don't really "talk" anymore. And if you want to know about the modern world, I'm on an old corded phone that's screwed to the wall, rarely seen in Britain

15

since the Seventies. David Attenborough should be doing a documentary about something so ancient.'

He laughs and I'm glad he got a kick out of that because there's something about his laugh that I just want to keep listening to.

'Thank you for reminding me what it feels like to be alive,' he says.

'I think you might have reminded me a little bit too.'

'I keep thinking I know you. Your voice sounds so familiar,' he says softly. 'I don't even know your name.'

My breath catches in my throat, but I think it's probably best not to tell him that he sounds familiar too. If he *is* someone I could one day come across in real life, he's not going to want to be reminded of this night, is he? People can be more open with a stranger. They can tell them things they wouldn't tell a friend. If he thought we might run into each other somewhere, he probably wouldn't have said half the things he said tonight. No matter what connection we have here, it has to end when we put down the phone. 'I don't know yours. And that's the way it's supposed to be. It's often easier to talk to an anonymous stranger. Someone completely non-judgemental and impartial, who's not involved in your life in any way at all. Like ships passing in the night, honking their horn at each other and continuing their journey.'

'Consider your horn duly honked.'

It makes me laugh. 'And yours too.'

'I like that, you know?'

'Horn honking?'

'No, being anonymous. It makes it seem all mysterious and romantic, like the start of a great story. Well, and horn honking. Honking is a good word. People don't honk enough these days.'

'They leave the honking to geese and old-fashioned car horns.'

It makes us both laugh again and I realize I've gone from panicking when I picked up the phone to relaxing with his company. He really is easy to talk to, and now I don't think he's about to do anything stupid, I'm just enjoying the chat.

'You can hang up, you know,' he says. 'I feel like I've wasted your time tonight.'

'Are you kidding? I've really enjoyed it. I didn't think anyone understood half the things I've said to you tonight. *You* made *me* feel more normal too, you know.'

I hear him swallow.

'And I'm not going anywhere until I know you're okay.'

'Okay, okay.' His chuckle gives way to a grunt and a series of groans as I hear him moving. 'God, I've sat here for too long. I think I need oiling. Got any WD40 handy?'

I smile but his attempt at humour is not going to deter me from what's really important here. 'How're you feeling?'

'I don't know. I'm so cold that I can't feel anything from the neck down.'

I wish I'd taken him a coat or something. I should've just gone as soon as I knew where he was. Anonymity be damned.

'I'm okay,' he says before I have a chance to push him any further. 'Really. I'm not going to do anything stupid. I feel better just for having let it all out. I don't think I've ever cried that much in my life, and I watched *Titanic* fourteen times when it came out on video. How can one set of sinuses hold so much snot?' He does an exaggerated sniff as a demonstration.

It makes me smile. 'When you get home, do me a favour and take care of yourself, okay? Apart from cold and wet, you must be drained. You've been through something traumatic tonight.'

'Ah, I wouldn't call talking to you traumatic.'

'Make light of it all you want. Do whatever you need to cope. But you and I both know that trying to brush things under the carpet is how you ended up on that bridge in the first place.'

I think he's going to say something else sarcastic, but he swallows. 'I know.'

'So take care of yourself. When you get in, have a long hot shower or bath. A long cry is draining, so drink a really big glass of water and get something to eat. I don't care if it's healthy or something made of chocolate, but make yourself a cup of tea and eat some biscuits, and snuggle up into bed with a book or a movie or something. Please? You deserve some TLC too.'

'*Waterfalls* or *No Scrubs*?'

'Oh, ha ha,' I say, even though it does make me want to laugh. There's never a bad time for a Nineties music reference.

'Hot shower, warm pyjamas, drink of water, bed, book, tea and biscuits. The Great British cure for everything.' I can hear that he's smiling as he repeats my instructions. 'I wish I knew your name so I could thank you properly, but at the same time, I kind of like not knowing it. So thank you, mysterious stranger, for saving my life. And for the interesting mental images of mannequins wrestling naked in chocolate. Or something. That *is* what you were doing when I called, right?'

I giggle. 'Thank you for a night I'll never forget.'

'Even the rain's stopping,' he says. I can hear him walking now, the wet flop of something against his phone. Maybe his hair? 'What a wonderful night.'

I smile because, in a weird way, it was.

I've never spoken to someone who understands me the way he seems to. It feels kind of magical to speak to someone who you can never speak to again; a connection with a stranger I'll never meet, on a night I'll always remember.

'Thank you for everything,' he whispers, his voice catching again. It makes me want to hug him even more than I wanted to hug him anyway which was already immeasurable on the wanting-to-hug-someone scale. 'Goodnight, lovely.'

The phone clicks off and I sit back on my knees, staring at the handset in shock.

Lovely. That's what Leo from It's A Wonderful Latte up the road calls me. I mean, I'm sure it's what he calls every customer but it still makes my heart beat faster every time he says it.

The thought that it could've been him flits across my mind

18

but I dismiss it instantly. There must be millions of guys who use endearments like that...

It couldn't be, could it?

No way.

No way could someone be suffering so much on the inside and hide it so well on the outside. Leo is the happiest person I know. He's the one bright spot on a dull winter day. He's the reason I buy a coffee every morning on the way to work. His smile makes every overpriced cup worthwhile. He's the brightest, happiest, smiliest, most cheerful guy in town.

No way in a *million* years would he be considering taking his own life.

No way was the guy on the other end of that phone Leo.

Chapter 2

'Puss puss puss puss,' I call, standing in the front garden and shaking a box of cat biscuits.

A black cat immediately appears on the gatepost and starts rubbing around my hand, a tabby cat peers cautiously out of the hedge, a ginger cat jumps onto the fence from the other side, and there's a meow from up the street.

'Good morning, kitties.' I pour cat biscuits into a row of dishes and stroke the cats brave enough to come over. I put a handful of biscuits down in the hedgerow for the little tabby cat who's too scared to come out.

'Morning, George!'

My dad makes me jump, peering around the side of the house from the top of a ladder and giving me a wave. I thought he was still in bed. He deserved a lie in after he waited up for me to come home last night. When I eventually got in, he had dropped off in front of the TV with a blanket over him and a cold cup of tea beside him. A cold cup of tea is enough to ruin anyone's night.

'What are you doing up there? You're nearly eighty!' I try not to cringe at the sight of him up the ladder, merrily waving with one hand while stapling his Christmas lights up with the other.

He's not even holding on. 'Please will you get down? I can do that after work!'

'It'll be dark by then and you won't be able to see what you're doing. Besides, I like doing it, and I'm being careful. Reminds me of being a young lad again and you wouldn't deny an old man the pleasure of remembering his youth, would you?'

'You're not young anymore,' I mumble to myself. I often feel like I'm the only one who notices my dad's age. He's had a couple of scares with his heart, and some nights his arthritis means he needs help getting out of his chair, and then other days, he'll be outside washing the car, painting the shed, and stapling Christmas lights up from the top of a very high ladder. Possibly all three at the same time. You never know with my dad.

He's retired now but he used to work for the council. He was solely responsible for the Oakbarrow Christmas tree that stood outside the churchyard every December. He's fearless when it comes to decorating. The other workers used to stand back and let him get on with it. I remember many an enchanting walk to school with my mum when we'd stop for a few minutes and watch him putting the first decorations up, and then we'd be late so we'd have to rush, but it wouldn't matter because everyone who walked to school down the high street would've stopped to watch too. And then, like magic, on the way home, we'd stop and admire the newly decorated tree. His retirement was the beginning of the end for the Oakbarrow Christmas tree. No one else on the council cared about it as much as he did. Now the only thing he decorates is our house, and he manages to put the same amount of magic into it as he always used to with the Christmas tree.

I give the ladder a wary glance, trying to assess it for rickety-ness, and Dad gives me another reassuring grin from the top of it, like he can tell exactly what I'm doing. I could try to argue with him about getting down, but I know that even if he gets down to appease me, he'll be back up there as soon as I've turned the corner at the end of the street when I leave for work.

After the phone call last night, I tried to go back to doing our first Christmas window of the season –

showcasing our brightest, sparkliest eveningwear ready for Christmas party season – but I couldn't concentrate on a thing, and it was about half past one when I finally gave up and went home, leaving the windows unfinished. If Head Office pop down for a surprise spot check today, I will be in serious trouble. Thankfully surprise spot checks are few and far between now. Things have been so quiet that there's not much to spot check on.

I grab my bag from beside the door and tell Dad again to be careful as I go out the gate in the bright December sunshine. It's a beautiful morning, surprising after the downpour of last night, and I'm earlier than usual because Head Office consider it unprofessional to dress windows when customers are around, so I need to get them finished before we open at nine.

There's something niggling me about Leo from It's A Wonderful Latte too. I haven't been able to stop thinking about him all night. All right, he's so gorgeous that I tend to think about him quite a bit anyway, but there's definitely been an abnormal amount of thinking about him since that 'lovely' last night. It *couldn't* have been him on the phone, and yet the thought won't leave my head.

My pace quickens as I walk through the residential streets towards the upper end of the high street. I don't even know why I'm going so fast. I tell myself it's just because I really shouldn't have left naked mannequins on display in the window and sequinned backing paper only halfway up, and I've actually got quite a lot to do before the shop opens – not least because if Head Office do find out about the windows and question *why* they aren't done, I will be in huge trouble. Taking that phone call last night goes against every rule the charity has. It was a call meant for the trained counsellors on the helpline. By taking it, I could have been responsible for making the situation worse. I should have immediately redirected him to the correct number, and the fact that I didn't is probably a firing offence. If anyone notices the windows, it will open a can of worms about why I clocked a few hours of overtime last night but apparently didn't get anything done.

My chest is tight and I'm walking so fast that sweat is beading on my forehead even though the morning air is so chilly. I pause outside what used to be a toy shop next door to It's A Wonderful Latte and try to mop it up with my sleeve and calm my heart rate. I take a deep breath, count to five, and carry on, glad all the surrounding shops are shut so there are no shopkeepers to watch me trying to remember how to breathe outside the old Hawthorne Toys building. Even I don't understand what I'm getting so worked up about. I love coming here every morning. Leo's mum works in the kitchen, baking sweet treats to tempt customers, and Leo makes the best coffee I've ever had. The shop has a real homely, family feel, with a big open fire in one corner surrounded by cosy sofas, mismatched tables and chairs that make it easy for customers to take a liking to and always sit in the same place. There are lots of natural wood fittings and fixtures, the lighting is soft and warm rather than blindingly bright, and it always smells of roasting coffee and cakes baking.

'Ah, my favourite Georgia.' Leo looks up and gives me a wide smile when the bell above the door tinkles as I go in. His curly hair flops across his forehead and he shakes it back. 'You're early today. Morning, lovely.'

And I just know. No one says 'lovely' in quite the same way he does. No wonder I thought his voice sounded familiar. I speak to him every day.

My mind is suddenly reeling. How can he have been the person on the other end of that phone? How can he have been thinking of taking his own life? How can things be so bad for him underneath the happy face he shows to customers?

'Yeah. Er, couldn't sleep. Thought I'd get an early start,' I stutter. I'd be less shocked if I'd just walked smack bang into the back end of a hippopotamus. It's like I'm having an out of body experience. My brain can't comprehend that the man on the phone was Leo. That *he's* the guy I felt such a connection with. That his bright smile is hiding so much pain.

Maybe I'm wrong. I *must* be wrong, and at the same time, I know I'm not. I have absolutely no doubt that it was him. Everything suddenly adds up. Leo named his shop after *It's a Wonderful Life*, so he obviously knows the film we talked about last night. He's definitely in his late thirties. The man on the phone even said his mum works with him and Leo's mum does. Leo often talks about funny words and the man last night said that honking was a good one. Which it undeniably is. And I get the feeling it's one Leo would appreciate too.

'Me too, on both fronts,' he says. 'What can I get you? You're just in time for the start of the Christmas menu. The festive coffees I've been teasing you with for weeks are finally available if you want to try something different?'

His smile doesn't falter and the expression on his face doesn't change. He looks at me exactly the same way he looks at me every other morning. He doesn't realize it was me.

And I can't tell him.

How can I say that the 'stranger' he opened up to is someone he sees every morning? I can't tell him that I work on the same street, that if I walk to the bend in the road just past the bank, I can see the duck-egg-blue and mocha-brown frontage of his coffee shop. I can't tell him that he's the sole reason for my caffeine addiction, or that seeing his smile brightens my day, or that he shared his deepest feelings, something he obviously works hard to keep hidden, with someone he actually knows. He'll be embarrassed. He might be scared that I'm going to tell someone. People can be more open with a stranger. They can tell them things they wouldn't tell a friend. Not that I'm exactly a friend of Leo's, but we share two minutes of conversation every day. He wouldn't have said half the things he said last night if he knew I'd be buying a coffee from him in the morning.

It was a private conversation between two strangers. It was a magical connection on a wonderful night. It's not my place to drag it into the real world. It will change everything, and it would certainly breach even more anonymity rules than I've already broken. If he'd phoned the helpline like he intended to, if I'd given him the right number and made him phone there like I *should* have done, we wouldn't be in this situation.

If he doesn't know, which he clearly doesn't, I can't tell him.

'Go on then, what have you got?' I suddenly realize that if I recognized his voice then he could recognize mine. He did say he thought I sounded familiar too. I clear my throat and put on a lower voice to disguise my own. I'm going for low and sultry but probably sound more along the lines of flu-ridden moose. 'I still think you could've given me an early preview. You've had that countdown to Christmas coffees on the counter since mid-October, and everyone knows your Christmas coffees are the best thing about this time of year,' I say, referring to a joke we've had every morning lately. He's had a hand-drawn chalkboard by the till counting down the days to Christmas coffees for weeks, and knowing I love all things festive, he's been teasing me about them every morning.

It's a shred of normality in what has otherwise been a completely abnormal morning.

I search his face for some hint of what happened last night, but I don't know what I expect to find. He's wearing his usual plain black T-shirt and baby blue apron with 'It's A Wonderful Latte' embroidered on the chest in brown thread. There's no hint of how cold he got. His denim-blue eyes aren't bloodshot from crying, his face isn't red or puffy, and his mop of curly hair is styled and quiffed at the front. If I think the man in the shop this morning will show some hint of the truth revealed by the man on the phone last night, then I'm sorely mistaken. His mask is firmly back in place.

'So …' he says, sounding like he's waiting for an answer.

'Oh, I'm sorry, I was miles away. Can you tell me again?' My face flushes bright red. I must've been staring at him without listening to a word he was saying.

'You okay?' he asks in such a genuine way that it makes me feel like I really could tell him if I wasn't.

'Absolutely fine, thanks. Sorry, the early start clearly doesn't agree with me. Better add an extra shot of espresso to today's drink. What have you got again?'

'I was saying my Christmas coffee syrups are out today because it's the first of December. I was thinking about you when I put them out this morning because I know you've been waiting. I've got warm apple pie, caramel pecan, chestnut praline, gingerbread biscotti, peppermint, orange and cranberry, mince pie, and unlike the big coffee chains, my pumpkin spice will stay available until January.'

'Mince pie flavoured coffee?' I pull a face involuntarily. 'Yuck.'

He grins. 'I knew you'd say that. It's really nice though, trust me.'

I'm sure he knows as well as I do that I'll try one flavour a day until I've decided on a favourite. I love seasonal coffee and he always has the best selection. 'How am I supposed to choose out of all those? They all sound delicious. I'll try the –'

There's a clatter from the kitchen and Leo looks panicked for a second. 'Hold that thought.'

He rushes out the back and I hear him talking. I sidle along the counter to the one spot where, if you squint, you can see through a gap in the sliding door and straight into the kitchen.

'I'm fine, dear, I just dropped an oven tray.' Leo's mum pats his arm. 'You don't have to worry, I'm quite capable of managing. It was all vibration and no damage.'

Maggie is a tiny, frail woman who I sometimes see sitting in the kitchen of the coffee shop with her feet up and an oven timer on the unit beside her, always looking so happy to be there. She's just as cheerful and friendly as Leo is, with the same bright eyes and curly hair, and never without a smile.

Leo comes back looking slightly more het up than before. 'Sorry, just my mum clattering around with the morning muffins. Have you decided yet?'

To be honest, I'm so distracted that I've already forgotten what his new flavours are, but an idea comes to me. 'What would you have? If you were going to have one, which would you go for?'

'Mince –'

'And not mince pie, I'm not brave enough for that this morning.'

His face lights up with his wide grin, the one that makes it impossible not to grin back at him, letting me know he was only saying it to wind me up. 'I'd go for the peppermint.'

'Okay, peppermint latte it is. I'll take two of those, please.'

'*Two*?' He doesn't hide the double take. 'You must be really tired. How many years have you been coming in here and I've never made you two coffees before. Rough night?'

Oh, if only you knew. 'Something like that. How about you?'

'Me?' He's already gone over to the espresso machine but he turns around with a raised eyebrow that makes me wish I'd kept my mouth shut. 'Nah. I was tucked up in bed with a hot water bottle and a hot chocolate by ten o'clock. Snug as a bug.'

What did I expect him to say? I'm a customer. We might have a few minutes of friendly banter every day, but we're not friends. I didn't really think he'd turn around and say, 'I nearly threw myself off a bridge last night', did I?

He slides one peppermint latte onto the counter and goes back to the chrome coffee machine to make the other one, the milk frother hissing on the unit beside him. I look at him while his back is turned and wonder when he lost so much weight. I've never noticed how loosely his apron is done up at the back, as if to hide his waist that hasn't always been that narrow. His bare arms are pale, having lost the tan they had in the summer, and although muscular, there isn't an ounce of fat on them and I'm certain there used to be. His hair is short at the nape of his neck but straggly, like it needs a trim, and the curls on top are light brown with a few natural highlights left from the late autumn sun. He reminds me of a cross between Patrick Swayze in *Dirty Dancing* and the Hollywood stars of years gone by, a lovechild of Steve McQueen and Paul Newman, with his sharp jawline and bright blue eyes that are always smiling.

He carefully writes my name on the first cup, complete with fancy scrolls underneath and a star above the 'i', and it makes me smile like it does every morning. Even though the shop has been gradually getting emptier in the last few months, even when I'm the only customer, he still writes my name on the cup, and I don't know why it feels as special as it does, or why I try to imagine what he's like outside the coffee shop as I walk to work sipping my latte. I think about what his life might be like, if he might be single, and how much I wish I had the courage to ask him like my best friend, Casey, would. She'd just march in and say 'Are you single? Do you want to sleep with me?' I'm not that brave. I just chat to him while he makes me a latte and think about how much I'd like to run my fingers through his curly hair.

'Seven quid, please, lovely.' He puts the second peppermint latte down as the coffee machine gurgles itself to completion with a puff of steam behind the counter.

Why is my hand shaking as I go to hand him the money? I fish a note and two coins out of my purse and try to brace my elbow against my stomach to hide the trembling as I put them into his hand. I might have a teeny tiny crush on the man but I've never trembled when talking to him before. It's because of how much I want to grab his hand, I tell myself. I want to take his hand between both of mine and squeeze it and tell him he's appreciated, that he's lovely, and funny, and the world would be a much darker place without him in it.

'Thanks, beautiful.' At least he's enough of a gentleman not to mention the shaking hand if he notices it. 'Here, let me get the door for you, you'll have your hands full.'

'Wait, actually …' I push one of the peppermint lattes back across the counter towards him. 'This one's for you.'

'What?'

'It's for you.'

'Why?'

I shrug. 'I don't know. I just thought you might like one.'

He looks at me like I've asked him if he'd like to exfoliate with someone else's toenail clippings. 'You do realize I work in a coffee shop, right?'

'Yeah. And I bet no one's ever bought you a coffee before.'

'Well, no, but …'

'There you go, then.'

'Yeah, but … why?'

'I don't know. Because it's December. Because it's nearly Christmas. Who doesn't deserve a peppermint latte to kick off the best month of the year?'

He grunts.

'Oh, come on. You're not a Grinch, are you? Because I distinctly remember seeing you in here last year in your tinsel reindeer antlers and your red apron with Santa's belt on it. Tinsel reindeer antlers are very un-Grinch-like, Leo.'

I know that Leo loves Christmas usually. He always goes all out in December. He gets in purple cups with sparkly silver swirls on them, he's always got loads of festive coffee flavours, more than the big coffee chains get, and the shop is always decorated beautifully.

'You have a good memory.' He looks down at the coffee and shakes his head. 'This is really sweet of you, but I can get a coffee literally twenty-four hours a day, I don't deserve … at least let me give you the money back.'

The vintage till rings as he goes to open it, making me think of angels getting their wings, and I slap my hand on the counter. 'Don't you dare. I asked you what you'd go for, end of story.' I pick up my own cup and tap it against his. 'Cheers. Have a good day.'

'At least stay and drink it with me,' he says as I go to walk away. 'Unless you're rushing to get to work or something?'

I make a show of checking my watch even though I've got bags of time. It's not even half past eight, I've got twenty minutes before I need to open the staff entrance. 'I've got plenty of time, I'm really early this morning.' I go back over to the counter, trying not to think about the unfinished window displays. I'm going to have to get the volunteers doing the take-offs this morning while I finish them in opening hours.

I lean against the counter and let my bag slip off my shoulder to the floor as I look around. I had no idea It's A Wonderful Latte was in trouble. I mean, I know Leo doesn't have as many customers as he used to, but I still thought he was doing okay. He always seems like he's doing okay. If it wasn't for what he said about his business going under last night, I would never have known.

'Thank you,' he says quietly. He leans his elbows on the counter and lets his head drop, and for just one second, his mask slips. In that moment, the lighting shows up the grey bags under his eyes, the taut lines around them, the stubble darkening the jaw of his usually clean-shaven face. I wish I'd looked at him more closely before. I've been so caught up in his infectious smile that I've never tried to see what it hides.

He covers it quickly, too quickly, and looks up at me with the same pasted-on smile. 'Now I know why I call you my favourite Georgia.'

'I'm sure you say that to all your Georgias.'

His laugh makes me smile. 'Nope, you're definitely my favourite. Gotta say, being bought a coffee is kind of a novelty. That's never happened before.'

'Well, you do make wonderful lattes.'

'Hence the name,' he says with a tight grin.

'And I bet that's the first time you've ever heard that joke, right?'

This time his smile reaches his clear eyes, making his eyelids crinkle. 'It's the first time this week, I'll give you that.'

'I always thought it was a play on *It's a Wonderful Life*?'

'It is. It's named for my dad, it was his favourite film of all time, and he loved a good pun. It took me ages to come up with a clever name when I bought the place.'

'It was my mum's favourite Christmas film. I'm named after it too.'

'Georgia. After George Bailey?'

I nod. 'It helps that my surname is actually Bailey. My mum thought she'd hit the jackpot when she married my father and took his name. She knew what their first child would be called before the end of the first date.'

His jaw drops in surprise but he's smiling too. 'Wow. You should be, like, my mascot or something. What are the chances of a Georgia Bailey and a coffee shop called It's A Wonderful Latte living in the same town? That's like fate or something, right?'

Fate. Like Leo finding the leaflet I put on the bridge. Like him accidentally phoning the shop on a night I just happened to be working late.

'That's why I come in here. Couldn't walk past a shop named after the same thing as me. It's like fate is calling me in. Fate and caffeine addiction.'

I don't add that I didn't even like coffee until I peered in the window on the day it opened to see what it was like inside, unable to ignore it because of the *It's a Wonderful Life* connection, and he flashed me that smile through the glass.

'Oh no, really? I've always thought it was my scintillating charm and incessant wit.' He pushes his bottom lip out, pretending to pout, and I force a smile, but all I can think about is the man on the bridge last night who was at rock bottom. Leo's false confidence doesn't seem as funny today.

'That and your impressive coffee flavours,' I say, because all I want to do is wrap my arms around him and whisper 'I know' in his ear, but I can't. 'Speaking of Christmas films, you're late putting your decorations up this year,' I say instead. I know from our conversation last night why he hasn't, but he doesn't know I know that, and even though I can't tell him it was me, I can try to get him to open up to the real me in the real world. Now I know how bad things are, I have to help him. I have to show him how much he matters to people, like Clarence did for George in *It's a Wonderful Life*. He needs a friend and he's going to get one, whether he likes it or not. I don't know how to make more customers come in, but I do know that Leo needs someone to talk to, someone he doesn't have to put on his happy face with, and it's going to be me. He has no choice in the matter now.

'I'm already done.'

I look around for some hint of these decorations and Leo points to the front window. There's a narrow ledge running along the inside of it; usually it's decked out with holly garlands with bright red berries and twinkling lights and the tops of the window are draped with sparkly paper chains, but today, only a gingerbread house sits on one side of the window ledge, facing the street outside.

'That's it? Usually this place is …' I wave my hands above my head to demonstrate the amount of decorations he usually has up.

'Festooned?' he offers. 'Festooned doesn't get nearly enough usage these days.'

'Festooned is a good word.'

'So?' I prod when he doesn't make any attempt to answer the question.

'Oh, my mum made the gingerbread house. It's an excellent gingerbread house.'

'I wasn't debating its merits. If the witch from Hansel and Gretel was real, she'd hire your mum as chief house builder. It's just … usually you go all out.'

He's quiet for a few moments and then he throws his arms

out to the sides and gestures towards the empty shop. 'What's the point? As you can see, this place is absolutely crawling with customers to appreciate it. Honestly, I just couldn't be bothered. Seems pointless this year.'

'But people like festive things. We're always told to make a big deal of our Christmas windows to attract customers.'

'There are no customers to attract,' he says with a shrug.

I glance out the window again. He's got a point. Oakbarrow High Street is silent out there. Even the sky has gone from blue to dark grey, almost like it's reflecting the mood of the few people left working on this street. 'I remember a time when you'd be dodging delivery lorries and shopkeepers displaying their goods at this time of morning.'

His face replicates the forlorn feeling as he looks towards the window. 'Those days are gone.'

I want to say something positive, but it's impossible to ignore the feeling of desolation that this street bleeds out of the cracks in its concrete.

He puts his upbeat voice back on. 'But my mum loves Christmas baking so the least I could do was display one of her gingerbread houses. She could give Mary Berry a run for her money any day,' he says loudly, angling his head towards the kitchen so she hears.

Maggie sticks her head round the door. 'He's not talking me up in front of the customers again, is he?'

'He was just telling me about your gingerbread house,' I say with a smile. 'It's absolutely stunning. It must've taken you ages.'

'Oh, I don't mind things like that, lovey. The fiddly bits are my favourite part of baking. I can sit down with my feet up and take my time over it. I wanted to make some miniature ones for the shop this year, but it seems such a waste of energy. We don't sell enough to warrant more than a batch of pumpkin spice muffins. Even my batch of decorated shortbread robins went to Bernard last week. Not that that's a waste as he deserves food, but I like to make him something more substantial than twenty-four shortbread birds.'

Maggie is standing in the kitchen doorway looking between us sipping our coffees. 'I must say, it's nice to see a customer in here enjoying one of his creations. People never have time to stop for anything these days. Most of them barely look up from their phones as they order, let alone have time to read the menu or look at the bakes on offer.'

'People don't see what's right in front of them nowadays,' I say, knowing I'm just as guilty as everyone else. Maybe not with my phone because talking to Leo is more interesting than anything that could be happening online, even on the days that John Lewis premiere their Christmas advert, but I've always taken him at happy, smiley face value, never talked about anything deep or meaningful, and never hung around long enough to let him suspect I've got a crush on him. I've never asked him how he is. Not really, anyway. Not in anything other than a polite way, expecting nothing but a bright smile and a 'Fine, thanks, and you?' in return. No one would ever, ever think things were anything but fine.

Maggie's wrists are bony and her fingers curled with arthritis, and her thinning white hair is covered by a hair net. Even at this time of day, her apron is already splashed with flour. She looks small and frail, and I get the impression that she hasn't got much energy to waste.

I wish I could make her sit down and take over her duties. Although, if they don't have any customers now, they can kiss the last one goodbye after I've got my mitts into the muffin recipe. The extent of my cooking ability is 'three minutes on 800 watts'.

'Ah well, onwards and upwards,' Leo says, his cheery words sounding rather false. 'I'm sure my new mince-pie-flavoured coffee will attract customers in droves.'

I know he isn't going to drop the act that easily, but I wish he would.

'Don't listen to him,' Maggie says. 'I don't drink coffee but I tasted a spoonful of the syrup, it's frightful.'

The giggle takes me by surprise and I point at him accusatorily. 'And you almost had me taken in this morning too. I *knew* it would be awful.'

'It's not,' he says with a grin, holding up his hands in a surrendering gesture. 'It's not supposed to be tasted by itself, *Mum*. It needs the coffee to bring out the flavours. Just because you wouldn't even try a decaf with it doesn't mean you can go around telling my customers it's awful.'

His tone is light and Maggie is smiling the whole time and I like the easy teasing relationship they have. 'Oh, I think all your coffee's awful, dear. You do make a nice cup of tea though, I'll give you that.'

'You can't say that in front of a customer.'

'Georgia knows I'm joking, she's your best customer. If she hasn't figured out your coffee's awful by now, there's no hope.'

'One cup! That's all I've ever made you, and it was back when I was learning how to use the machines.'

'I know. I was picking coffee grounds out of my teeth for a week.' She grins at me. 'He has improved now though, don't you worry, lovey.'

'You don't have to tell me, he makes the best coffee for miles around. Even if he does try to force mince pie flavouring on unsuspecting customers.'

'Ah, but you're still going to try my mince pie coffee one day, aren't you?' He waggles his dark eyebrows at me. 'I know you, Georgia, you'll try them all eventually. I'll even throw in an actual mince pie for free. As compensation.'

'Wanna know a secret?' I lean across the counter towards him. 'I know they're a British festive tradition but I don't actually like mince pies.'

He steps back and gasps in horror. 'Oh no, I think an elf somewhere drops down dead every time a British person says

35

that. Next you'll be telling me you don't like Brussels sprouts either ...'

I pull a face. 'To be fair, who *does* like Brussels sprouts? I mean, we always have them on our Christmas dinner and I appreciate the tradition of them, but no, like ninety-nine percent of the country, I don't actually like them.'

'Ah, Christmas. The annual time we torture ourselves with food we wouldn't eat if someone paid us the other three hundred and sixty-four days a year.' His wide grin offsets the wistful tone in his voice.

'All part of the fun, Grinch,' I say, grinning back at him.

'Do you know, when someone tells me they don't like mince pies, I take it as a personal challenge?' Maggie says. 'You'll like mine, Georgia. I'll make you some and change your mind on the humble mince pie.'

'Oh, please don't go to any trouble for me. I'll buy a box in the supermarket and try them again. I'm sure –'

'Blasphemy!' she cries, smiling so wide I'm sure her teeth are going to fall out. 'Mass-produced supermarket pies that have been pumped full of preservatives since August won't help. Homemade mince pies are Christmas in a bite. They were my husband's favourite, and he wouldn't stand for anyone running them down in his shop.'

I glance at Leo for help but he holds his hands up. 'Don't look at me. My mum has never left a mince-pie-hater unconverted. And if she fails, free coffee for a week.'

'Don't be daft, you're not doing –'

There's a crack of thunder overhead, making us all jump, and the sky that's gone from grey to black suddenly opens, rain pouring down, splashing off the coffee shop's striped awning and pounding against the pavement, as the world outside lights up with a lightning flash.

'Flipping heck, it was sunny just now.' I glance at my watch, having completely lost track of time. The 'bags of time' I had earlier have turned into minutes before Mary and the volunteers due in today will be banging on the back door, and they aren't going to want to be kept waiting in this rain. I slurp the last of my peppermint latte and deposit the cup into the recycling bin beside the counter. 'Thanks, Leo, that was gorgeous,' I say, meaning the chat with him and his mum just as much as the coffee. 'And now I'm late. Have a good day. See you tomorrow.'

'You got an umbrella?' he asks as I throw my bag over my shoulder and pull my hood up at the door.

'Yeah. At home, on my desk. It was a beautiful day when I left the house.'

'I can't send a lady out into a thunderstorm without an umbrella.' He puts his cup down on the counter and slides his arm round the kitchen door, feeling around until he pulls out a tall umbrella and thrusts it into the air in victory. 'Come on, I'll walk you. You only work down the street, right?'

I nod.

'Mum, you all right on the counter for a few minutes while I make sure my best customer gets to work safely?'

'Of course, dear. Have a good day, Georgia. Don't forget, no supermarket mince pies.'

'I'll try to restrain myself,' I say, watching as Leo disappears into the kitchen and comes back shrugging a coat on. 'Leo, you really don't have to do that. I'm literally just around the corner.'

'Do you see how heavy that rain is? You'll be soaked in less than a second. My conscience won't let me hear the end of it if I stay here in the nice dry shop and watch you go out in that without an umbrella.' He walks across the shop and pulls the door open, peering out and making a face. 'Come on, it's for my peace of mind rather than your dryness. Your carriage awaits.'

I can't help smiling as he leans out to open the massive umbrella and gestures for me to walk out underneath it.

'Thanks.' I squeeze past him in the doorway, lingering for just a second too long because it's the closest thing I can get to the hug I wanted to give him last night, and then I step straight into a puddle. No one maintains this street anymore so the pavement is cracking up and there are more potholes than in a block of Swiss cheese that a family of toothy mice have had a nibble of. Cold water seeps into my supposedly waterproof winter boots, freezing my socks against my skin.

Leo steps out behind me and pulls the door closed and I give Maggie a wave through the window as he holds the huge umbrella over both of us.

'I didn't mean to get her making mince pies too,' I say. 'I don't want her to go to any trouble for me. I'm sure she works hard enough as it is.'

'Don't worry, she loves baking and it's December, she'll be making them for all the family anyway. And you don't have to like them. I'll happily scoff anything you don't want and you can go on in your narrow-minded tradition-hating anti-Brit Christmas forever.'

'Says the man with no Christmas decorations up.'

'Even the street isn't decorated anymore. I don't think one shop will make much of a difference, do you?'

'It might attract more customers. When they're cold and wet and tired and it's dark outside and they see the warm glow of your fire and the twinkling lights, it's going to draw people in.'

'Well, the warm glow of the fire will just have to work alone this year.'

Huge drops of rain are splashing down on the umbrella and water is running in rivulets along the gutters, and I can't believe Leo is so caring that he'd willingly come out in this just to save me getting wet.

'It's miserable, isn't it?'

'Yeah,' I say as we walk in the middle of the road to avoid the puddles on the pavements. There was a time when that would've been impossible because of the traffic, but now, there's less chance of being run over by a passing car than there is of us coming face to face with a flying red-nosed reindeer. 'It doesn't really get any brighter on the high street though, does it?'

'Tell me about it.' He turns around, spinning the umbrella as he moves to make sure we both stay dry, walking backwards as he looks at the shops behind us, not even worrying about tripping over. 'This place used to be the life and soul of everything. I remember coming here at Christmas and feeling it pulsing with life, and light, and sound. Did you grow up here?'

I nod.

'Do you remember Christmases on Oakbarrow High Street? I was telling my niece what it used to be like and she thought I was pulling her leg.'

'It was amazing, wasn't it?' I feel myself light up at the memory. 'The lights, the decorations, the window displays. There were always carols playing and it always seemed to be snowing.'

'And now look at it. Even Hawthorne's, the one shop I thought would always be here. One look in that window would leave you convinced that Santa's elves were working out the back.'

I glance behind me in the direction he's facing, at the sad old building next door to It's A Wonderful Latte. It used to have bricks of the deepest burgundy, green fascia boards, and gold lettering. Now the bricks are sun-bleached to a dirty salmon pink, the green boards are grubby and cracked, and the gold lettering has faded beyond recognition. There's moss spilling from the guttering and some form of black mould crawling out of every crack.

'What's it got to offer now?' Leo says. 'Graffitied windows and a solitary cobwebbed teddy bear looking out. It makes me sad every time I walk past it.'

'Me too.'

'What have we got left, eh? A coffee shop, a bank, a charity shop, a tanning shop, a television repair shop with an old CRT TV in the window to really attract modern day customers, and a lingerie shop called Aubergine.' Leo laughs. 'Aubergine. I mean, of all fruits and vegetables to name a lingerie shop after. It's not even a distantly sexy vegetable, is it? Even cucumber has a vague phallic connotation, but aubergines? They're not quite the first thing you'd associate with sexy lingerie, are they?'

'Maybe she meant the colour, not the vegetable?'

'Call it Deep Purple then. Even that's sexier than Aubergine.'

'You've clearly spent an abnormal amount of time thinking about this. You don't strike me as a sexy lingerie type of guy. Do they do plunge bras in your size?'

'I've never been in there,' he says with a grin. 'I just don't get it. It makes me laugh because it's so random. Why not Pomegranate, or Celery, or Granny Smith?'

'Well, it doesn't get much more seductive than Granny Smith, does it?'

'See?' he says. 'You get it. Shops called Aubergine are a testament to Oakbarrow as it is now. It looks more like a brothel than a lingerie shop and its name doesn't make a blind bit of sense. No wonder no one shops here anymore.'

'Say what you want, but Aubergine are still open. Poorly named vegetable decisions or not, they're still going when most other shops have closed.'

'I reckon it's a cover for a drug cartel or something. Maybe it is an actual brothel.'

I raise an eyebrow and it makes him grin again. 'So where are you? All this time we've known each other and I can't believe I've never asked you where you work before.'

I meet his eyes and try to keep a straight face. 'Aubergine.'

He stops walking so abruptly that he nearly falls over his own feet, and my shoulder knocks into his arm as his eyes flick between mine and my mouth.

'I might believe you if you could keep a straight face.' He grins. 'Nice try, though. You nearly had me there.'

I burst out laughing. 'Sorry. Couldn't resist.'

'I'd have done the same.' He knocks his shoulder into mine

again, deliberately this time, and it makes a little shiver run up my spine. At last he turns around and walks forward again so he can see where he's going. 'Where are you really?'

I go to answer and suddenly realize that I can't. I hadn't even considered that he might walk me to work. What on earth am I going to tell him? If I say One Light, he's going to make the connection straight away.

'The bank!' I say as a moment of blind panic combines with a moment of inspiration. If I was a cartoon character, a lightbulb would've just pinged above my head.

He laughs. 'Well, if that isn't life imitating art, I don't know what is.'

I look at him in confusion.

'The real George Bailey worked at a bank too, didn't he? Well, the Building and Loan, that's close enough.'

'Oh, right! Yes!' I laugh but end up overcompensating and come across as marginally hysterical.

'So was your career mapped out based on *It's a Wonderful Life* or is that just coincidence?'

I look at the One Light sign sticking out from the charity shop in front of us. 'Just coincidence.'

'Maybe fate has more of an *It's a Wonderful Life*-shaped influence than you think.'

'Yeah. Maybe.' I bite my lip as I look at him. I don't want this to end yet. I could stay here and talk to him all morning but we're nearly at the door of the bank and if we get much closer, he's going to expect me to go inside.

'Well, thanks for walking me,' I say breezily. 'You should get back to your mum. See you tomorrow!'

'It's chucking it down. Go on, get someone to let you in, I'll wait.'

He's too nice for his own good. And mine.

I don't work here and if I knock on the door, whoever answers is going to say exactly that. I peek in the window of the bank as

I hesitate over what to do and see Casey setting out leaflets on one of the tables in the waiting area. Casey! My best friend, and now, a godsend. She'll play along.

I knock lightly on the door just in case anyone else comes to answer it.

'George!' she says, sounding surprised and confused in equal measure. 'And Coffee Man.'

Leo nods to her. 'I've been called plenty worse than that.'

'Hi, Casey!' I say, wondering if anyone will notice my voice has suddenly gone up three octaves. 'Just come to work! In the bank! Where I work!'

'Right …' Casey says slowly, her eyebrows rising up towards her hairline where her blonde hair is pulled back into a conservative bun.

'Are you going to let me in before we need an ark out here?'

'Of course,' she says smoothly, stepping back and pulling the reinforced glass and sturdy metal door fully open. 'Come into the bank where you work.'

I knew I could rely on Casey.

Leo shuffles forward until the huge umbrella is pressed right into the open doorway so I can go through without getting a drop of rain on me. As I turn to thank him, I don't miss the way he's looking up at the sign for One Light next door or the way his eyes have gone distant.

'Thanks, Leo. You're my knight in shining … coffee apron.'

He looks back at me and blinks, looking like he was lost for a minute, then he pastes a smile back on his face, steps back and twirls the umbrella so raindrops spray from it in a perfect spiral. He does a curtsey. 'Always a pleasure to serve you, Madame. And thanks for the coffee. Have a good day, lovely, I'll see you tomorrow.'

'Hey, Leo?' I say as he goes to walk away. When he turns back, I make a point of looking him in the eyes. 'Thank you. I don't know what I'd do without you every morning.'

He gives me a sad smile. 'I think you mean my coffee, but thanks.'

I watch him walk away until he rounds the corner out of sight. 'No, I mean you,' I whisper to the empty street.

That sad smile makes me realize how scarily wrong you can have someone. I thought I knew Leo. As well as you can know someone you chat to for two minutes a day, anyway. That's two minutes a day, six days a week, for the past two and a half years. If you add it up, that's quite a lot of time to spend talking to someone, and I still never knew. Leo would be the last person I would ever expect to be suffering with depression. It just goes to show that you never know what kind of battles people are fighting on the inside.

And I know I have to do something. Leo needs customers. He needs to feel important to the town – as important as he makes me feel every morning. Leo is kind. I've seen him knock the price of a coffee down for an old man who'd gone to pay and found he didn't have enough cash. I've seen him make a special batch of dairy-free muffins just so a vegan customer could have one. Every day I see him walking down the road towards the church-yard with a coffee and a bag of food for Bernard.

Doesn't he deserve some kindness in return?

Chapter 3

'All right, what's wrong with him?' Casey's standing with her hands on her hips when I close the door and turn around.

'What? Nothing!'

'Another waif or stray? Are you going to put Kitekat out for that one too?'

'I don't know what you mean,' I say, even though Casey's always moaning about me putting food out for the cats.

'At least he's handsomer than the old guy from the churchyard you insist on feeding and taking clothes to.'

'Looks don't really come into it when someone's homeless, do they?' I ask, mainly to distract her from asking me about Leo because she's going to want to know why I've just walked into the bank and pretended to work here, and I can't tell her the truth.

'I'm not having this conversation again, George.' She tucks a stray lock back into the bun that I know she hates having to hide her long hair in for work. 'So, the guy from the coffee shop ... homeless? Ill? Poor?'

'None of the above. Just a nice guy.'

'No such thing,' she says without missing a beat. 'What's wrong with him? Other than the teeth?'

'What's wrong with his teeth? He's got a lovely smile.'

'Yeah, for Dracula. He's got fangs!'

'He's got slightly sticky-out canines that do *not* look like fangs. They just make his smile wider. And he's self-conscious of them so don't go and offer to recommend a dentist in your usual abrasive way. He's too scared of the dentist to look into getting them fixed.'

'Isn't that a bit personal for a barista? How do you know so much about someone you buy coffee from?'

'Because he's friendly. He chats. And he's never *told* me he's self-conscious but you can tell from the way he smiles. And the dentist thing just came up, and let's face it, it's not like *anyone* actually likes the dentist, is it?'

She raises a disbelieving eyebrow.

'I talk to him, Case. Every day bar Sundays. He's a lovely –'

'Oh, spare me the "some men can be nice" spiel. Heartbreakers, the bloody lot of them. Led by, well, something bigger than their tiny brains.'

'Ah, yes. "He who shall not be named unless it's in an obituary for death by castration." Not all men are going to be like him,' I say. Casey hasn't always been so intolerant of men. She used to believe in love and wanted to find a happily ever after. Until her ex-fiancé found several happy endings with several other women.

'How can you still say that when the love of your life jumped on the first plane out of here when New York came calling?'

'Who wouldn't?'

'You, Georgia. *You* wouldn't. You chose to stay here instead of go off on an adventure with him.'

'He wasn't the love of my life, Case. And the only adventure would've been navigating around the airport for the first flight home.'

She rolls her eyes. 'Yeah, well, you've been single for *years* now, so let's get back to you and Mr Shining Knight in a fetching blue apron. If there was nothing wrong with him, he would've walked you to the door of the charity shop, about three steps further than this one, where you *actually* work. What's going on? Why have I just breached our security rules to let a non-staff member in before opening time?'

'It's complicated.'

'Things usually are with you.' Casey purses her lips. 'Well, at least he's young and nice looking. Single?'

'I have no idea. Not every man is a potential date, you know. It's actually possible to be friends with a guy.'

'Pah. Where's the fun in that? If everyone had that attitude, we'd all be as miserable as I was when I was engaged. Sometimes you don't need to get to the bottom of every teeny tiny feeling and fix a guy's every problem. Sometimes you just need a damn good shag.'

'Leo doesn't need a good shag, he needs ...'

'Ooh, Leo. Good name. Brings to mind all sorts of DiCaprio-related goodness. Coffee Apron Guy is way hotter than DiCaprio though, even back in the *Romeo and Juliet* days, and that's saying something. What does this Leo need and if you won't give it to him, do I have permission to?'

'No. And no. And if you want to help me *or* Leo, you can go and buy a coffee at lunchtime.'

'He *is* homeless. I knew it. I suppose I need to buy him a hot meal too?'

'No. Not everyone I know is "in need". Leo's just a friend. Without mentioning any part of this conversation, will you go and buy a coffee in It's A Wonderful Latte at lunchtime? Please? For me?'

She waggles an eyebrow. 'No part of this conversation but I can mention my *single* colleague Georgia, right?'

'No. No, no, no. Just a coffee. And no mention of me or where I work or *don't* work. This doesn't need to be bigger than it is. He makes really good coffees and they're way cheaper and less sweet than the overpriced cups of liquid sugar you usually get from the big coffee chains. And tell all your colleagues to do the same, please?'

'Here, you can tell them yourselves.' She opens the security-locked door behind the counter and beckons me through to the back. 'You're late, aren't you? When are you ever late, George? This Leo must be someone really special.'

I shake my head, knowing Casey will be like a dog with a bone on this. 'Just a guy I got chatting to. Makes good coffee. There's nothing else to it.'

'Well, it's nice to see you chatting to a man your own age and not old ladies and homeless men.'

'I work with old ladies. And I chat to one homeless guy because he's a nice, interesting guy; being homeless doesn't come into it.'

'Oh look, speaking of old ladies, two of yours are standing in the car park and they don't look happy about being out in this downpour.'

'Morning Georgia.' As we walk down the corridor connecting the back offices, Jerry, Casey's boss, comes downstairs with a mug of tea in his hand. I prepare myself for a bollocking but he doesn't even look surprised to see me. 'Locked yourself out, eh?'

'Er, something like that.'

'She's trying to impress a guy,' Casey says for me. 'He thinks she works here.'

'Oooh, tell me more.' Jerry clutches both hands around his mug and looks uncharacteristically excited. 'People can be funny about charity shops, can't they? Fancies a banker type, does he?'

'It's really not like that –'

'Feel free to use the bank as much as you want. I'll let everyone know to stick with the story.'

'You really don't have to. This is already getting way out of hand –'

'No trouble at all. My wife's favourite ever gift is still that Royal Doulton vase you kept for me. I *still* get rewarded handsomely for that every time she catches sight of it on the mantelpiece.

This is the least I can do. Come in whenever you want. Now, who are we looking out for?'

I think about it. On one hand, this is a huge lie, but on the other hand, what *else* am I going to tell Leo? I've already made the mistake of telling him I work here; I can't exactly go back on it now, can I? And the problem still stands. I cannot tell him I work for One Light because he'll realize who I am. The bank is really convenient because it's next door to One Light and we share a car park at the back with the other buildings in this part of the street. Our back doors are literally one step away from each other. It wouldn't be too difficult to come in here if he happens to be watching like this morning, and walk through and out the back into the charity shop. And I'm determined to help Leo in some way. I'm going to become his friend whether he likes it or not. This doesn't end at him walking me to work in a downpour …

'The bloke from It's A Wonderful Latte,' Casey says when she's decided I'm not answering fast enough.

'Oh, good going, Georgia!' He holds his hand up for a high five. 'Leo Summers. I know him. His father used to bank here. Lovely lad.'

I reluctantly slap his hand, feeling like this conversation has happened without me.

'Consider the bank at your disposal. Use us whenever you like. I'd love to be part of a good love story. It's like something you see in the movies, isn't it? Like your *It's a Wonderful Life*. My wife keeps saying it's on the telly but we never find time to sit down and watch it.'

'You definitely should. It's timeless and so heartwarming, especially at this time of year.'

'I know because she's made me watch it with her seventy thousand times over the years. Anyone would think she was named after the main character or something,' Casey says.

'It's a good film,' I say, glancing out the back window at Mary and one of the volunteers standing under their umbrellas, undoubtedly talking about how late I am, and I'm standing here discussing films.

'I don't like films that make me cry,' Casey says.

'My wife loves a good weepie. I'll make it a mission to watch it this Christmas.' Jerry leans over and unlocks the back door for me. 'Don't forget, come in any time you need to for your love story.'

'It's not a love story,' I protest.

'It's a coffee story,' Casey says. 'Apparently we're all having a coffee with lunch today. Georgia's paying.'

'Fine, but yours will be an apple pie latte,' I say, knowing full well that Casey thinks festive-flavoured coffees are an affront to humanity. 'It's not about money. It's about making Leo feel like his hard work is worth it.'

Even as I think it, I know it's pointless. Leo doesn't need to sell an extra coffee or two and another batch of muffins. He needs a massive increase in customers. Like every other business on this street has needed for years. Like One Light needs to sell more than a couple of Christmas party dresses and hideous old suits as Halloween costumes to stay afloat. A whole round of coffees for the bank might help for a day but it won't do anything in the long run.

I can't stop thinking about it as I go to rescue Mary and the volunteer from the sopping car park. My mind is elsewhere as I listen to Mary worriedly ignoring her own wet coat and soaking grey hair to make sure I'm not late for reasons of ill health, ask if everything's okay with my dad, and why I look so distracted.

I don't tell her I'm distracted because seeing Leo makes my day better every morning, and I've never realized how much truth there is in the saying that the saddest people always try the hardest to make others happy.

I know above all things that I want to help him. And not just because I fancy him, but because I've been handed a unique opportunity. He doesn't know that he's shared this with me. Or, at least, he doesn't know that I'm who he's shared this with. This is fate. He found a leaflet on the bridge that I put there. He owns a shop called It's A Wonderful Latte, named after my mum's favourite Christmas film. She didn't name me Georgia Bailey for nothing. This is fate telling me to be like Clarence, the guardian angel who stopped my namesake jumping off a bridge in the film. This doesn't just *happen*, does it? Leo needs help. And I'm going to help him.

I'm just not sure how yet.

* * *

It's while I'm in the window getting the mannequins dressed in our best evening wear and standing them around in groups like they're nattering at a Christmas party, setting up tables full of empty glasses and a sparkling tree in one corner of the display that an idea comes to me. I keep going outside to see how the window looks, and every time I do, I back up just a little bit more than needed so I can see around the corner and up towards It's A Wonderful Latte.

A woman is peering in the window, but her eyes fall on the gingerbread house and she turns away rather than going in. There are a couple of people around, but not one of them so much as glances at Leo's window.

'The windows look wonderful,' Mary says, having made no comment about them being left unfinished last night even though she must have noticed. 'Just as wonderful now as they did when you went out to check them the first sixty times.'

She knows something is going on. I can feel her eyes on me because I never go outside to see how the windows look from a customer's perspective this often.

Creating eye-catching displays that showcase the very best of our stock is probably the biggest part of my job. I know how hard it is to get anyone on this street to look at your window displays, and Leo hasn't even got a window display, he's just got a gingerbread house. It might be a good gingerbread house, but it's not going to make anyone stop in their tracks and rush into his shop. Windows on this street need to be special. This is no longer a street where people mosey about and leisurely wander into shops. These days, the only reason anyone walks down this street is because it's a shortcut to somewhere better. Window displays don't just need to be good, they need to be spectacular. They don't just need to be eye-catching, they need to grab people by the eyeballs and drag them through the door. Figuratively, not literally. That would just be weird. And probably painful and a bit messy.

It does get me thinking though. Window displays are kind of my thing. I got this job because of decorating a window. I'd gone for the interview at the flagship shop in Bristol, and one of the tasks was to decorate their window with only items in the shop. They loved what I did with it and offered me the job despite my lack of experience.

We're told again and again the importance of seasonal windows. It's December – everyone wants a bit of Christmas at this time of year, and Leo's gingerbread house isn't cutting it. It's doing nothing to attract customers, and customers are what he needs.

I go outside and look again, not even pretending to be looking at our windows this time. Normally Leo loves Christmas. It wouldn't hurt to remind him of that, and make his window a bit more attractive in the process, would it? I used to paint. Once upon a time, I wanted to be an artist, and my dad still has a shed full of my old paint. I could do something with that, couldn't I?

Chapter 4

It's dark when I go back to Oakbarrow High Street. The bag over my shoulder is heavy with spray paint and the tube that holds my stencils is battling for space in my hands with a torch, and my dad's old portable steps are swung over the other shoulder.

There are no streetlights as I walk down the main road through Oakbarrow, hoping not to run into anyone except Bernard, and telling myself I'm being stupid to worry about it. No mugger would bother with Oakbarrow anymore; there's nothing to mug.

I stop outside It's A Wonderful Latte and lower my bags carefully to the pavement. I don't know why I'm being quiet but everything seems quieter in the night, and, while I don't expect to see anyone, I think it's a good idea not to draw attention to myself.

Even so, I can't help looking up at the empty toy shop beside the coffee shop. I remember walking home on winter evenings and pulling on my mum's hand to get to it. It would often be closed, of course, but the window displays used to be spectacular. The old Hawthorne Toys building is four storeys high, towering above the other shops on the street, and on ground level there are two Edwardian-style bay windows on either side of the entrance. When I was young, the displays inside them would run all night, lit by spotlights and flameless candles. There used to be toy trains running around snow-covered model villages, nutcracker soldiers standing guard, dancing Santas, wind-up elves, and reindeers with flashing red noses. I often wonder if looking at those displays as a child helped my interest in window displays now. As an adult, it's an interesting concept to look back on. At One Light, our windows have to display as much as possible that we have to sell, whereas when Hawthorne's were still open, their displays were just to entertain anyone who walked by.

Maybe it's a sign that this is a good idea for Leo's window. I can't get inside to build a Christmas tree out of his pretty, festive cups or otherwise showcase his coffee, but I can make his window look attractive from the outside.

I wash the window down and remember a few days this summer of watching Leo out here, washing his windows in nothing but a vest and long shorts, soap suds clinging to his muscular forearms and water from the hosepipe dripping down his curved legs.

I shake myself. Now is not the time for thinking about Leo's forearms. Or legs. No matter how sexy they are.

I dry the window and crouch down, unrolling my tree stencils from their tube and spreading them across the pavement as I try to figure out the best design to do. I know I have to incorporate the gingerbread house as well as making the whole window look Christmassy.

I spray the bottom part of the glass solid white and start using my fingers to wipe off key parts to create the base of the scene. Just as I'm sticking my first stencil up, I hear footsteps coming. I listen to the telltale extra slap of a broken sole against concrete and sigh in relief – Bernard. I've been trying to find him a replacement for those shoes, but the man has got ridiculously large feet and One Light don't get that many pairs of size thirteens donated.

'Whatcha doing, Georgia?' Bernard asks, not sounding surprised to find me here.

'Just a little decorating.'

He stands back and folds his arms across his puffy coat and casts an appraising eye across what's done of the window so far. 'I know it's dark but you do realize One Light is on the opposite side of the road and around the corner, right?'

I smile at him. 'I know. I thought I'd try to spread a bit of Christmas cheer. Leo doesn't seem to have much this year.'

'Leo doesn't have much of anything this year,' Bernard says, seeming to hint at what I already know. 'Lovely guy though. Single too, you know?'

'Have you been talking to Casey?' I narrow my eyes at him, quite annoyed that Casey isn't the only one who seems to be obsessed with me spending time with a guy my own age. It's not that unusual. Really, it's not. 'Besides, I think Leo's got more on his mind than relationships at the moment.'

'I don't doubt it, but there's never a bad time to find love.'

'Love?' I snort. There's not much chance of that around here.

'Well, it makes life worth living, doesn't it?'

Did he say that with a hidden meaning? Or am I just imagining things?

Bernard is whispering for some reason, perhaps because it's so dark that it seems like whispering is the right thing to do, even though the street is completely deserted, but I follow his lead anyway. It never feels right to talk in normal voices in the dark. 'Where've you been at this time of night?'

'Just on one of my walks. Nightly patrol before I go back to my bench.' He points a gloved finger at the window. 'And you? Why the sudden interest in Leo's festive window?'

'I don't know.' Obviously I can't tell him the truth any more than I can tell anyone else. 'I get a coffee here every day. It just seems a bit unfestive lately.'

His look says he's expecting something more.

'And Leo seems sad,' I whisper. It seems okay to say this much to Bernard. I know he's a perceptive bloke, and I know he sees

Leo every day too – if anyone knows about Leo's current situation, it's him.

'I thought I was the only one who'd noticed,' Bernard says, surprising me. And making me feel a bit guilty because I *hadn't* noticed. 'He loves Christmas really. He's just struggling a bit this year.'

I watch Bernard try to shake off the sudden sense of sadness in the air. Bernard is not someone who ever looks on the gloomy side of life, despite the fact he lives on a bench in a churchyard. Nothing ever seems to get him down. 'Well, this'll help. Bring him in a few customers for those new festive flavours he's got. He brought me a cinnamon hot chocolate today and it was quite possibly the best thing I've tasted this year. He deserves more people to know that.'

I nod in agreement and tell myself that if I'm ever awake enough not to have caffeine one morning, I'll try the cinnamon hot chocolate instead.

'What if it rains? Shouldn't you be doing this on the inside? Won't it wash off in the rain?'

'Er, yeah, probably.' I glance up at the dark sky. Leo's blue and brown striped awning won't give it much protection if those clouds decide to open. 'But that's kind of the point. I didn't want to do anything lasting without Leo's permission. This is just snow spray, it'll wash off with a quick sponge-over or a heavy shower unless I give it a coat of lacquer, then it'll need a bit of scrubbing first. But he doesn't know I'm doing this and if he hates it when he sees it in the morning, at least he can get rid of it.'

'He won't do that. It's a work of art and it's not even finished yet. I'm going to be the first to come by tomorrow and see the finished scene.'

'Thanks, Bernard. It's really nothing. It's just stencils and lines.' I hesitate for a moment. 'But you won't tell Leo if you see him, will you? I don't want him to know it was me.'

'Of course not. Even if he questions me, which I'm sure he

will. He brings me a cuppa and a muffin twice a day, you know? He always stops for a chat, just like you do. You know me, I love to chat, and I enjoy that even more than I enjoy his coffee, and I enjoy *that* a lot. I won't breathe a word of this. I didn't see anything.'

I give him a nod of appreciation, turning back to run the side of my hand over my tree stencil to adhere it to the window.

'Thanks for these gloves, by the way,' Bernard says, wiggling his covered fingers towards me.

'You're welcome, they would only have gone for rags.'

'I don't believe that. There's nothing wrong with them and they still had the tags on. You could've sold them for a pretty penny. I bet you put your own money in the donation box and kept them for me.'

I shake my head because I'm a terrible liar and it's best if I don't say anything. 'There's a ham sandwich and a flask of tea in that bag, help yourself,' I say to distract him.

'Oh no, that's your supper, I'm not taking that.'

'I've already had mine, Bernard. Greedy thing that I am, I packed too much. You'd be doing me a favour by saving me having to carry it home later.'

I shine my torch towards the bag to give him enough light to see and watch as he takes the wrapped sandwich and flask of tea. 'I'll give this back to you tomorrow as usual, Georgia. Thank you.'

'You're welcome,' I say. 'Like I said, you're doing me a favour.'

He narrows his eyes at me in the torchlight. 'You say that so often that I don't believe you anymore.' He looks from me to the sandwich in his hand. 'I know you made this for me. And I wish I wasn't too hungry to turn you down.'

Guilt punches me in the stomach. It makes me feel stupidly privileged to have a soft bed and a warm house to go home to tonight. It's bitterly cold out here, my gloves are fingerless because I need my fingertips to create the pattern in the paint and I lost feeling in them before I even reached the end of my street. I know that when I get home, the central heating will still be on because my dad will have ignored my plea to go to bed and not wait up for me. Bernard feels guilty for taking a sandwich and a flask of tea on his way home to a sleeping bag and a wooden bench.

Like Leo takes him something to eat and drink every day, I save anything we get donated to One Light that I think will fit him or be useful to him. Anything from gloves, coats, and shoes to a heavy blanket and a rucksack. He's such a lovely guy who's stuck in a vicious circle of not being able to afford rent and not being able to get a job, especially when everyone in Oakbarrow knows him as the local homeless man.

'Can I do anything to help you?' Bernard whispers, his grey moustache scratching the edge of the cup as he takes a sip of tea, visible steam rising from it into the cold night air.

'No, you're good, thanks. I won't be here much longer. I only need to finish these trees and do some dots of falling snow. Just don't tell Leo you saw me.'

'Your secret's safe with me, Clarence.'

'Clarence?' I say in confusion. Clarence is the angel who stopped George Bailey jumping off a bridge in *It's a Wonderful Life* … does Bernard know more than I think he does?

He falters for just a moment too long. 'I'm sorry, it's been so long since I saw the film. I meant your namesake, of course, Georgia.'

I decide now is not the time to pursue it. If he did see something of Leo last night, then it's not town gossip for us to stand here and discuss. I'm not going to mention it, and I know Bernard well enough to know he wouldn't either.

'Stay warm, okay?' I say instead, even though I know it will be impossible in this weather. 'Goodnight.'

Bernard raises the flask of tea in an imaginary toast and I watch his back as he disappears into the darkness of the street. I'm glad Leo takes care of him too. I see how many people walk past him with a sneer and a look of disdain. I've always thought

Leo was lovely to look at and lovely to talk to, but now I know he's lovely on the inside too it makes me even more determined to make this window a good one. Leo is so important to this street. He deserves to know how different things would be without him. Maybe I am a bit like Clarence here. I've already stopped Leo jumping off a bridge. Maybe now I can show him how different life would be if he wasn't here.

Chapter 5

I'm glad it's December because my gloves hide the traces of white paint underneath my fingernails that won't come off despite the multiple scrubbings this morning. The pavements are slick with ice, unlike the days when the gritting lorry used to come through at six o'clock on an icy morning, shortly followed by a council man with a bucket of road salt to make the pavements safe for all the people hitting the shops early or walking to school with their kids.

The bricks and windowsills of empty shops are furry with thick frost, and my design on Leo's window is still intact. From the outside, his gingerbread house now looks like it's standing in a forest of white trees, surrounded by snowy ground and falling snow, and the frost has stuck to the white paint, giving my snow-flakes a sparkly, crystallized coating. I glance up at the clear blue sky, wondering if Mother Nature's addition to my artwork is the universe's way of telling me that I'm doing the right thing here, despite the fact that I shouldn't have taken that phone call in the first place. I definitely shouldn't be getting involved in Leo's life now, and Head Office would see it more as 'gross invasion of privacy' than any form of 'right thing'. Mother Nature's support will just have to be good enough for me. And hopefully the courts if I'm likely to be in serious trouble for this. You couldn't argue with Mother Nature as a defence witness, could you?

I take a deep breath as my hand closes around the icy door handle to It's A Wonderful Latte and I put on my best face for feigning innocence. Leo's setting out muffins in the display case behind the counter and he looks up as the bell tinkles.

'Wow, what a fantastic window,' I say with my innocent face firmly in place. 'And I thought you weren't doing Christmas this year.'

'Good morning, my favourite Georgia.' His face breaks into a smile but quickly turns serious again. 'And I'm not. I didn't do that.'

I glance between the window and him. 'No? Who did then? Fairies that come in the night? Elves?'

He narrows his eyes at me. 'I don't suppose you'd know anything about it?'

'Me?' My voice goes up several pitches. I now sound like a dolphin going through puberty. 'Of course not. What a completely absurd suggestion. I can't draw a stickman. Why on earth would you think I'd know anything about that?'

'Hmm.' He doesn't look convinced by my denial. 'I don't know. It's just that you were talking about the gingerbread house yesterday. I thought … I don't know. You were the first person I thought of when I saw it.'

I should probably be insulted, or maybe impressed by his powers of deduction, but honestly, being the first person Leo thinks of in any situation sends a little sizzle of excitement through me.

'Bloody vandals graffiti-ing my shop,' he continues. 'I'm going to have to waste half the morning washing it off now.'

I gasp in horror. 'Oh, don't do that! That's not graffiti, it's artwork. Look at the way it incorporates the gingerbread house. Someone's gone to a lot of effort to do that. Look at the snow-flakes and the way the actual frost outside has clung to the paint and made it sparkle. It looks fantastic in the daylight. Don't wash it off, please. It looks all festive and lovely.'

His blue eyes narrow again.

'I mean, do whatever you want, obviously. I don't care if you wash it off. If you don't like it, that's up to you.' I clear my throat and look away.

'So, what can I get you today, Georgia Bailey from the Oakbarrow branch of the Building and Loan?' There's such a fondness in his voice as he says it that it makes me smile involuntarily.

'I think I'll try your chestnut praline this morning, if –'

'Just one, right? Because I'm not accepting another coffee from you. It's not right.'

It's my turn to narrow my eyes at him. 'Fine. Just one.'

'So did you have a good night?' he asks as he turns to make my drink. 'You're early again this morning. Couldn't sleep?'

'Yeah, something like that,' I say, touched that he knows my work schedule so well.

'I thought so. No offence but you look like you were up half the night.'

'Oh, thanks,' I snort, knowing he doesn't mean it in a nasty way. He's just wheedling for more information about the window because he definitely suspects me.

'Sorry, my lovely.' He puts the coffee down on the counter and pushes it towards me. 'On the house to make up for the insult.'

I slap my £3.50 down on the counter and push it towards him in return. 'It's not to make up for the insult, it's to make up for me buying you one yesterday, and I'm not having that. It's just a coffee, Leo. Accept it.'

His eyes flick between me and the coins on the counter. 'Fine. But it's not happening again.'

'Okay.'

'Okay.' The bell rings as he opens the till and puts the money in.

'And now I'll have another one. Same again, please.'

He folds his arms and gives me a stern look. 'I've told you I'm not letting you buy me another coffee. What are you up to?'

'It's for me. To go. For later.' I take a sip of the coffee currently in my hand as if this somehow proves it.

He looks like he'd be more inclined to believe Pinocchio.

'I'm a paying customer. You can't turn me away.'

'No, I guess not.' He looks like he wants to argue but he knows I'm right.

'I bet Bernard will know something about that window,' he says over his shoulder as he turns around and fires up the coffee machine again. 'I'll have to ask him if he saw who did it.'

'I wouldn't bet on it,' I mumble under my breath.

'Pardon?'

'I said I'm sure he did. Bernard knows everything around here.'

The look in his eyes as he fits the white plastic lid onto the coffee cup says he knows that isn't what I said the first time, but he doesn't pursue it.

'To go. For later.' He puts the cup on the counter with a resolute thud and pushes it towards me.

'Exactly.' I give him the money, trying to ignore the little thrill as my gloved fingertips brush against his hand.

I wait until the till's dinged and he's torn the receipt off and handed it to me before I push the cup back across the counter towards him. 'For you.'

He bursts out laughing. 'I knew you were up to something.'

'I knew you wouldn't do it if I asked for two at once.' I grin at him and he looks like he's trying to be annoyed but he can't stop himself grinning back and it makes butterflies start zooming around inside me. 'And you have to take it. If you don't, I'm going to go to the soulless retail park and get a Starbucks and bring it back here for you, and I know you wouldn't be happy about that. By refusing it, you're actively giving your custom to the competition.'

There's a flash of recognition in his eyes. Soulless retail park is what we called it on the phone. I have to be more careful, although in all fairness, everyone around here who's lost business to the shiny new shopping centre calls it the same. It's not a reason for him to suspect anything. I'm just seeing things that aren't there because I know and he doesn't.

'What's this sudden obsession with making me drink coffee? I could be watching my caffeine intake for all you know.'

'You work in a coffee shop. I don't think caffeine intake really applies to you, does it?'

He laughs and then rolls his eyes. 'Well, maybe not, but ... why? Why this sudden desire to buy me a coffee?'

'Because I don't know what else you like. I nearly bought you an aubergine and put it in a sexy bra but I didn't know where to find one around here.'

'An aubergine or a sexy bra?'

'Either,' I say, thinking it's probably a bit early in the day to be talking about bras with Leo. Casey would tell me off for not making that into some kind of suggestive joke about my own collection of sexy bras, which is zero. It's been a while since I made any effort in the bra department.

'Why should you get me anything? You're a customer. I get you things and you give me money in exchange. That's how shops operate in general.'

'Ha ha,' I mutter at his sarcasm. I'm going to have to come up with a viable explanation and fast because he's looking at me expectantly, long dark eyelashes blinking over determined blue eyes.

'I just think people don't show others that they appreciate them enough. I walked home one night last week after you were closed, and it made me realize how much better you make this street.' *The twinkle in your eyes, the way I want to run my fingers through the curly mass of hair on your head.* 'The warm glow of light pouring out in the evenings, the gorgeous roasted coffee smell that filters right the way across the road, the festive window,' I wave at the display behind me, even though I probably shouldn't have drawn attention to it again. 'If you can't be nice to people at this time of year, when can you? I wanted you to know that you brighten my day and this street wouldn't be the same without you.'

It's a roundabout explanation, a bit rambly, and more forward than I'd usually be, but Leo needs to hear that he's important to people, no matter how much my cheeks have heated up. It's worth the embarrassment because his eyes have softened and his cheeks have gone pink.

'Yeah, well, business is not exactly booming so you'll probably be getting used to a street without It's A Wonderful Latte sooner rather than later.'

'All the more reason for you to let me buy an extra cup of coffee then, right?' I say, trying to ignore the pang in my chest at his words and how resigned he seems to it. Maybe I should act more shocked, but I already know how bad business is from the phone call, and even without that, I should have figured it out earlier. The coffee shop is empty, as it has been every other morning in recent months. When it first opened, I'd have to queue for a coffee even as early as half past eight, and at lunch-time you could just forget it. I'd be able to see the back of the queue from down the street and around the corner.

'Yeah, but you don't have to buy it for me,' Leo says before I have a chance to question him. 'I don't des –'

It reminds me of what he said on the phone and I want to reach over and squeeze his hand. Who am I kidding? I want to vault over the counter and give him a massive hug. Instead, I nudge my coffee cup against his on the counter, pushing it so his cup touches his hand. 'Whatever that was going to be, you're wrong.'

He drops his head onto his hands and exhales slowly, sounding and looking completely exhausted, and for another moment, the mask slips. The smile and the chitchat don't come as easily as he makes it seem. The flippant way he said he's going out of business is a much bigger deal than he's letting on, and as he presses his forehead into his hands on the counter, I can see the physical weight of that on his shoulders.

He looks up and blinks in the brightness. 'You know you're going to have to stay and drink it with me now, right?'

'Good, I was hoping you'd say that.' I give him a bright smile. Again, it's more forward than I'd usually be, but Leo needs to know that someone cares.

'Unless I'm going to make you late for work?'

I glance at my watch without actually looking at the time. 'Oh, I've got bags of time. It's fine. My manager's easygoing.'

'An easygoing bank manager, huh? Who'd have thought it? I thought you had to be uptight and serious to work in the financial industry.' He thinks for a moment. 'Although on this street, banking is a joke, isn't it? There's no money left to bank. You must've noticed the decrease in traders banking with you?'

'Er, yeah.' I stutter out a one word answer. I don't know the first thing about banking or the financial industry and it's absolutely ridiculous to let him think I work there, but at the same time, I'd only have to mention One Light and he'd put two and two together. Firstly, he'll wonder why I lied to him, and then he'll work out the rest about the phone call.

'Too early to talk about work, huh?'

'Er, yeah. I clearly haven't drunk enough of this coffee yet.' I take another slurp from my cup and go for a speedy subject change. 'Where's your mum today?'

'Early doctor's appointment.'

'Oh God, is she okay?'

'You worry too much,' he smiles. 'Yeah, just a routine blood pressure check and monitoring her thyroid medication. She's fine. Tough as old boots, she is. Nothing gets her down.'

'It must be nice to work with her?'

'It would be nicer if she could relax and enjoy her retirement,' he sighs. 'To be honest, even if I hired another baker, I think she'd still be here every day keeping watch, making sure they didn't put a quarter of a milligram too much baking powder in her famous gingerbread recipe. If I tried to sack her, she'd probably put *me* in the muffins.'

I laugh. 'She's a real character. Whenever I see her, she's whistling and humming around the kitchen. She seems to love it here.'

His eyes go distant for a moment as his gaze turns to the window. 'She's going to go crazy when she sees that window. She's going to want to track down who did it and get their autograph. They have window paintings in that charity shop next door to you and she always admires them and wants to go in and find out who they use.'

I freeze. Crikey, I'd remember if she'd ever actually done that, wouldn't I? What if she's been in and spoken to Mary when I've not been there? She's going to know it was me in a flash. I love doing a bit of seasonal window-stencilling on the inside of our windows. Nothing that obstructs the display, just a few flowers in the spring, eggs at Easter, falling leaves in the autumn. There are white snowflakes tumbling down now, although I did have the forethought to use a different stencil on Leo's window to avoid suspicion.

Leo's gaze is on the window but his eyes are still distant and he's not really seeing it. 'My dad would've loved it.'

'Did he like Christmas?'

'He *loved* it. He *was* Christmas personified. You were saying yesterday that you grew up here? Did you ever come into the café that was here before I bought this place?'

'Yeah, all the time.' I smile at the memory. 'My mum would come into town to do her shopping every Saturday morning and we'd always stop here for a hot chocolate and a toasted teacake on the way home. Especially at this time of year. She'd take me to visit Santa's grotto at Hawthorne Toys and then we'd come in here for a cuppa and something nice to eat, loaded down with bags of presents.'

Leo's eyes are suddenly intense; far from being distant, they're shining with amusement. 'Do you remember an old guy who used to sit at that table?' He points to a single table in the corner, next to the window, looking out. It's the only part of this shop that hasn't changed in thirty years. Leo redid everything when he took over, except that chair and table.

A memory stirs in my mind. 'Did he have a mop of white hair and a dark grey beard? Always had a newspaper or two spread across the table in front of him?'

He nods.

'Yeah. I remember him helping Mum with her bags one day when it was crowded. Another time, he overheard her wondering what the weather was going to do that afternoon and looked it up in his paper for us. He gave me 50p once. I must've been really young because it was, like, the most money I'd ever seen. Mum let me go into Woolworths on the way home and get pick 'n' mix with it.'

'He was my dad,' Leo says with a smile that's halfway between proud and sad.

'No way. Really?' I remember the man well, he was never without a kind smile and a friendly wave. 'He was like a permanent fixture here. He always seemed to be sitting there in that same seat, watching the world go by.'

'He loved it here. It was his second home. At this time of year, he was playing Santa at Hawthorne's next door so he'd be here between shifts. He was best mates with the owner of this place so he'd get changed in the staffroom here and sneak in through a door in the alley between us so kids would never see Santa until he was in the grotto.'

'No *way*,' I say again. 'Your dad was Hawthorne's Santa? The guy who always sat in that corner was Hawthorne's Santa?'

He nods.

'But he was the best Santa ever. He wasn't a man dressed up as Santa, he was the actual Santa.'

'I hate to break it to you, Georgia,' Leo says with a grin, 'but I feel it's my duty to inform you, as an adult, that Santa isn't real.'

I roll my eyes. 'You know what I mean. He was like Richard Attenborough in *Miracle on 34th Street*. He was the closest thing you could ever get to a real Santa. People used to travel for miles to see him. The queues were always ridiculous but no one ever complained because he was worth the wait. I never believed in Santa, I'd always known it was Mum and Dad who put the presents under the tree, but I still wanted to visit him because he seemed so real. Mum was a grown woman and she always said he even made her start to wonder …'

'That was my dad,' he says with that same half-proud, half-sad smile.

'I can't believe he was the same man who used to sit here in the café. Talk about breaking the illusion. I think you've just destroyed my childhood, Leo. He wasn't supposed to be someone who went next door and took a costume off, he was supposed to hop in his sleigh and go back to the North Pole with his reindeer and elves.'

Leo swallows hard. 'I like to think that's where he is now. If there's a heaven, that's what it would be for him.'

'How long ago did he die?' I ask gently. I can see he's holding onto his emotions by a fine thread, and I don't know if pushing the subject further is a good idea or not, but Leo needs a friend, someone he can talk to, and you don't get that by backing away from difficult topics.

'Three years ago last month,' he says, his voice sounding raw.

'I'm sorry.' I nudge the cup against his hand again, mainly because I'm scared that if I actually touch him, I won't be able to stop until I've climbed over the counter and wrapped him up in my arms. I know so much deep, private stuff about him that it's a struggle to remember that he doesn't know I know it. 'So you bought this place to honour him?'

'Not really. Kind of.' Leo smiles a sad smile, his eyes damp. 'He had always planned to buy it in his retirement. Like I said, he was best mates with the owner, they were due to retire at the same time, and they'd struck a deal years before that his friend wouldn't sell it to anyone else. I think Dad thought it'd be a nice, gentle job to keep him occupied. So they'd both retired and he'd just started the process of buying it, and then …' His voice cracks and he swallows again. 'He left the money, and my mum and sister agreed that we should carry on what he'd started and I should step into the shoes he'd always wanted to fill.'

'Wow,' I say, struck again by how you never know what people are going through behind a smile. Even with the phone call, I had no idea of the connection Leo had to this coffee shop or what had led to him buying it. I remember his smile as I peered in the window on the first day he opened. It must've been mere months after his dad passed. That day must've been so bittersweet for him, and yet his smile was bright enough to pull me in from the outside. 'That's a beautiful way to honour him. He'd be so proud if he could see it now.'

Leo pushes himself off the counter where he's been leaning and I focus on the line the edging has made where it's dug into his forearm. 'Yeah, well, pretty soon it's going up a creek with no paddle, so I doubt he'd be proud then.'

'Of course he would,' I say, but Leo doesn't look like he's listening.

'Flipping heck, it's quarter past nine,' he says, his attention on the clock on the wall. 'I've made you late for work. Your boss can't be so easygoing that he'd be happy about that.'

Bollocks. Never mind a boss, I've got a 73-year-old assistant manager who's sweet and innocent on the outside but has a backbone of steel and spikes of wrought iron when someone does something she doesn't approve of. Poor timekeeping is one thing of the many things she can't abide.

'It's easy to lose track of time talking to you,' I say, trying not to think about Mary and the two volunteers due in this morning, undoubtedly waiting in the car park out back at the moment. I've got the keys and I'm *always* there by 8.45 at the latest.

'I'm so sorry,' Leo says. 'I didn't mean to ramble at you like that. Talk about unprofessional.'

'Leo, don't. It was great. I love talking to you.'

It gives me a little thrill to see his cheeks turn red. 'I can close up for a couple of minutes and walk you in? I'll talk to your boss and take all the blame?'

'No, don't you dare. Your mum's not even here to mind the shop. You could miss a walking club of twenty customers in that time. Besides, I do *not* want you to bear witness to the terrible lies I'll have to come up with to satisfy my boss. I was thinking sheep in the road, does that sound realistic to you?'

'Hmm. Doesn't really work unless you live somewhere where there are actually sheep. Not a lot of sheep come shopping on the high street.'

'Yeah. Can't remember the last time I served one.'

It makes him laugh.

'See? I'm a terrible liar!'

'Ah, Georgia. If all else fails, tell him "women's problems". Always works for me.'

'Women's problems works for *you*?'

He grins. 'Genius, right? People are so confused by that excuse coming from a man that they don't even question it.'

'You're an evil mastermind under that sunny smile, aren't you?'

He does a gallant bow. 'I try my best.'

'I'll tell you what, before I run off, can I have three hot chocolates to go, please?'

'As a bribe or for use as a shield?'

'If you promise not to judge me – a bribe.'

'Good thinking.' He turns around and sets about making them. 'You're single-handedly keeping me in business today. Is this one bank manager who *really* likes hot chocolate or three managers to placate?'

I hate lying to him about this, it's so stupid, but how can I tell him anything different? 'One manager and two colleagues who'll have had to cover my desk for twenty minutes. They won't mind but one of your hot chocolates will certainly smooth the way,' I lie, thinking about the three old ladies freezing in the car park. A hot chocolate would give them something to dump over my head if they weren't all chocoholics.

'Yikes,' he says. 'I'd better put extra spray cream on top for good measure.'

I watch as Leo makes one cup after the other, obviously rushing to save me being even later than I already am, putting each one on the counter and filling them up with more squirty cream than should be legal at this time of day before fitting the lids on. Our fingers brush as I hand him the money and listen to the ding of the till again, a real old-fashioned bell ringing sound, and watch as he slots each cup into a cardboard cup holder and holds it out to me.

My hands close around the cardboard tray but he doesn't let go. Instead he pulls it back slightly, making me look up at him. 'Thank you, my lovely.'

His gaze is holding mine, his eyes so intense that I feel a delicious little shiver at the base of my spine, and I get the feeling he doesn't just mean for the multiple drinks I've bought this morning.

'Thank *you*,' I say, trying not to think about how easy it would be to use the tray to pull him across the counter and press my lips against his.

I reluctantly take the tray of hot chocolates in one hand and hoist my bag over my shoulder with the other. I don't want to go, but I've probably got another five minutes before Mary starts doing door-to-door enquiries and if she finds me in here, there's going to be no getting away with pretending to work in the bank.

'Sorry for making you late for work.'

'You haven't. It was ... nice,' I say, backing away but keeping my eyes on his, well aware that I'm likely to trip over my own feet and end up head over heels under three cups of hot chocolate in a minute, and I'm beginning to think there's already enough head-over-heels-ing when it comes to Leo.

'Let me get the door for you, your hands are full.' Leo dashes out from behind the counter and strides across the shop, pulling the door open for me with another jingle of the bell.

'Thanks,' I mumble, a bit too aware of the heat from his body as I squeeze past him in the doorway, and of how much I've heated up from his closeness. It's not normal to feel this hot on a cold December morning.

'Hey, Georgia?' he says as I go to say goodbye.

I stop and turn back, my shoulder millimetres away from his.

'Thank you. It was incredible to talk to someone who actually remembers my father. As Santa and as himself. That's what he would've wanted. To affect someone's life in some small way. He would've liked that.'

A lump forms in my throat as I go to reply, and Leo nudges his shoulder against mine gently. 'Sorry, I'm holding you up even more. See you tomorrow, right? Have a good day.'

I decide it's probably a good time to leave even if I don't want to. Crying in the middle of the street in front of Leo is not a good idea, and I'm sure I've just seen the flap of a lilac coat disappear around the corner, meaning that Mary's come out looking for me.

'It was the most interesting morning I've had in a long time.' I force my brightest grin and nudge his arm in return.

'Worth the bollocking from the boss?'

'Worth twenty bollockings from twenty bosses.'

'Aww.' He pushes his bottom lip out. 'Never have I felt more

72

valued in my entire life. Now I know why you'll always be my favourite Georgia.'

'Well, you'll always be my favourite Leo, even if you did destroy the Christmas illusions of my childhood.'

I hear him laughing behind me as I walk away and wave as I pass the window, and the grin he gives me is wide enough to break his face in two.

Now, never mind bollockings from bosses, I'm going to have a car park full of annoyed old ladies who are all skilled at beating people with walking sticks.

Chapter 6

I placate Mary and the volunteers' anger with hot chocolate and by telling them I was late because I was talking to a man and giving them free reign with questions. Yes, my own age. No, not homeless. Yes, single. Yes, handsome. No, I didn't get a date. Yes, I am going to see him again tomorrow but not for that reason. No, I'm not telling you his name so you can cyberstalk him on Facebook. I didn't know 73-year-olds knew what Facebook *or* cyberstalking was. The excitement of me talking to a single man my own age seems to obliterate any lingering annoyance at waiting around and being convinced I'd come a cropper and drowned in an icy puddle or met my demise in some other way. Mary must spend most of her time thinking up eccentric ways that people might've died.

I nearly do die just before lunchtime as I'm tidying a rail of children's clothes at the back of the shop after a customer has been rummaging. I catch a flash of purple and silver in hands and curly brown hair and turn around, almost as if the world is in slow motion, to see Leo at the door. I squeak in surprise and send a thank you up to any listening deities that his hands are full so he's using an elbow and his back to push the door open, giving me a chance to fly up the steps and into the back room, not missing Mary's look of interest on the way.

The initial flash of excitement that he's come to see me is instantaneously replaced with a shot of dread. He *hasn't* come to see me – he doesn't know I work here. So what's he doing?

I look around the back room in a panic. What if he's seen me and follows me out here? What if he asks Mary for the manager and she tells him who I am? What if she sends him through for a chat? I haven't told her anything about the whole bank debacle yet. I could go upstairs but then I'd lose any chance of eavesdropping on what he wants.

I spot a dressing gown on a rail next to the clothes steamer and duck underneath it, standing up so it covers my head. If anyone comes in, they'll just see a bulky dressing gown with a pair of legs, like a really weird ghost who's a bit late for Halloween and has run out of bedsheets.

Maybe I'm overthinking it. He had something in his hands … maybe a bag of donations? It's probably nothing to do with me. He's just got some old stuff to get rid of. That'll be it.

I hear the ding of the till as Mary finishes with the customer she was serving. It must be Leo's turn next. I shuffle further along the rail inside the dressing gown, the coat hanger doing its best to strangle me, but one of the Fisher Price toys at the back of the shop starts going off and all I can hear is a series of beeps as a child starts banging it.

Perfect.

I stand steadfastly still for a few tense moments, barely daring to breathe, my mind racing with questions. Leo's never come into the shop before and I never expected him to.

I hear the clatter of the door opening and closing. Was that him or just another customer? I strain my ears to listen to what might be going on out there, but now someone's talking on a mobile near the entrance to the back room. I'm destined to stay stuck here in the dark.

I hear Mary calling 'thanks' to someone and the sound of the shop door opening and closing again. Was that him leaving? How long do I wait before I dare to show my face again? If I pop my head round the corner and he's still in there, he'll see me.

It's a good thing I like working in retail because I'm clearly not cut out for a career in espionage.

Surely Mary will come through to tell me the coast is clear in a minute? But then again, she has no idea who I'm hiding from.

'George!' Casey yells, and our back door creaks open as she pokes her head round it.

'Oh good, there you are.' She doesn't even bat an eyelid when she clocks me hiding inside a dressing gown and I wonder if I should be offended. Is hiding inside dressing gowns really such unsurprising behaviour for me?

'A Leo situation has arisen in the bank. He wants to see you.'

'You're joking?'

'Nope. He caught Jerry and asked if he could speak to you. He told him you were on your break but Mr Coffee Apron said it was important.'

'Talk about all happening at once,' I mutter, casting a glance towards the shop floor. Leo must've left here and gone straight into the bank next door. Maybe that's good. It means he couldn't have talked to Mary for long or asked her too many awkward questions about window paintings.

'How do I look?' I ask Casey as I follow her out into the car park and through the back door of the bank, smoothing down my trousers and shirt, very aware that my clothes don't look like I work in a bank.

'Like you just got out of a dressing gown. What were you doing in there?'

'Leo came in … and I … it doesn't matter.'

'Hold still, you've got cotton in your hair. And I'll take this.' She reaches over to pluck a stray thread from my frizzy ponytail and yanks the tape measure from around my neck with a flourish as we walk down the corridor. 'The financial service industry

76

doesn't go around with tape measures on their person. Just FYI if you're going to continue this madness.'

I'd totally forgotten that. 'It's just because we get asked to measure stuff all the time in the shop. I drape one round my neck and forget it's there.'

'I know. I've removed many a tape measure from your neck when we used to go for a drink in The Bum after work on a Friday night.'

'When you used to hit it off with some local hottie and leave me to walk home on my own?'

'Been a long time since there were hotties around here ...' She sounds wistful as she rolls the tape measure back into a curl.

Speaking of hotties, I smile at the thought of Leo. Waiting to see me. *Wanting* to see me. And Casey thinks Oakbarrow is lacking in hotties. Since when do we call them hotties, anyway? What are we, eleven?

'Thanks for coming to get me, Case. You're a lifesaver.'

'You know, I'm all for going all out to get into a man's pants, but this is taking the biscuit, even for you.'

'I don't want to get into his pants.' I glance through the reinforced glass window in the heavy door that separates the staff area from the customers. Leo's leaning against the grey wall with his hands in the pockets of his blue apron, his hair looking windswept and like it needs fingers combed through it to set it back right. 'I want to get into his life.'

'But pants would be a nice bonus, right?' She shrugs her blazer off and hands it to me. 'Here, put this on so you don't look completely out of place as a bank employee.'

I take the dark blue jacket of her uniform and shove my arms into it quickly as she pulls the door open and pushes me through.

'Hi!' I squeak in surprise, mild hysteria making my voice so shrill that two customers queuing at the tills look over.

I stumble to a halt in front of Leo and try to maintain some shred of dignity by shaking my ponytail out and smoothing the blazer down. 'Casey said you wanted to see me? Everything okay?'

'Yeah.' He pushes himself off the wall he was leaning against. 'Can I talk to you? It'll only take a moment.'

He inclines his head towards an empty area of the bank, underneath a poster of a woman with an unnaturally white smile advertising mortgages. She wouldn't look out of place advertising tooth bleaching kits. Leo doesn't seem upset or agitated, but this is definitely not normal.

Instead of speaking, he holds his hand out, a clear invitation for me to put mine in his.

Casey could sense a man offering me a hand from five miles away and I don't miss her edging closer in my peripheral vision.

Unsure of what else to do, I slide my hand into his open palm. His hand is warm and his skin is rough against mine, and if I wasn't so worried about what he's up to, I'd enjoy the little shiver that goes down my spine.

His fingers close around mine, his thumb rubbing the top of them as he pulls my hand nearer and holds it up, sort of examining it.

'I know it was you.'

My heart leaps into my throat and my palms instantly start sweating so much that I'm sure he'll be able to feel it. So that's it. The game's up. He's obviously just been next door and confirmed it with Mary. He must've recognized my voice too. Or suspected because I went in the next day and bought him a coffee. I should've played it cool.

My heart is pounding so hard that I can barely hear myself think. I'm going to have to explain everything. The bridge. The call. Why I didn't tell him it was me the moment I realized it was him. Why I made it all ten times worse by pretending to work here.

Maybe it's a good thing. Keeping this ruse up is ridiculous. Other than losing my job, it will be better for both of us if the pretence ends. Maybe we can still be friends and it'll be better without the lie between us. But without my job, I won't be working here every day, I won't see him every morning, and I definitely won't be able to afford a £3.50 coffee every day.

I swallow hard and decide to feign innocence again. 'Know what was me?' I ask in an even squeakier voice that doesn't sound like my own.

'Oh, come on. You were talking about the gingerbread house yesterday.'

'Oh!' I'm not sure if I'm disappointed or relieved. 'You mean the window. Of course you do. I really don't know where you've got this idea from. I couldn't draw a dot-to-dot puzzle.'

'I'm sorry, but I don't believe you. See, something's been bothering me since this morning. You said the window looked good *in the daylight.* Now call me slow and stupid, but all morning I've been trying to figure out why the daylight would make a difference, and I realized that it only would if you'd seen it in the dark.' He waggles the hand that's still in his. 'That, and you have white paint under your fingernails.'

So *that's* what he was doing. Not holding my hand but assessing it for the traces of paint that my gloves hid this morning. 'Tippex! I was using Tippex on a, er, bank statement this morning. Wasn't I, Case?'

She looks up uninterestedly. 'Yeah. Loads of the stuff. Tippex everywhere. Customer's gonna *love* getting that in the mail.'

'You don't use Tippex on bank statements. I don't work in a bank and even I know that.'

At least he still thinks I work here. That's something. 'Well, aren't you lucky to have never had a bank statement that needed correcting then?'

'Georgia, you're a terrible liar.' He squeezes my hand gently, repeating what *I* said to him this morning. 'I know it was you who did the window. What I don't know is why you won't just admit it. You'll still be my favourite Georgia.'

I feel like I'm at a fork in the road trying to decide which direction to go in. I *could* just tell him. He knows it was me so what's the point in lying even more? But it feels like the thread of a jumper that you start to pull and before you know it, you've got an unravelled ball of wool at your feet. If I tell him it was me, he's going to want to know why, and then he's going to want to know why I care about getting more customers into his shop and reminding him of how much he loves Christmas, and no matter what answers I give, they're all going to lead back to the phone call. Contrary to my panic just now, he doesn't seem to suspect that the girl on the phone was me, and I need to keep it that way.

He's got a notepad and pen in the top pocket of his apron and I pull my hand out of his and pluck it out, trying not to think about the way my fingers accidentally touch his chest. I draw three lines with a triangle roof over them, add a window and a square for the chimney with some squiggly biro lines of smoke coming out. An aardvark could've drawn a better picture.

'There.' I hand it back to him. 'That's the extent of my artistry.'

'Anyone could've done that,' he says, raising an eyebrow at the drawing although he sounds a little less sure than he was before.

'Anyone could've done your window,' I fire back, hating the outright lying much more than the roundabout lying I've been doing up until now. 'Is your mum minding the shop? Did she get on okay at the doctor's?'

'Yes, and yes,' he says, narrowing his eyes. He knows I'm redirecting the conversation and he pauses as he decides whether to let me or not. 'And she absolutely loved the window. She's been out there taking photographs all morning. She got a customer to post them on Instagram and every two minutes, she's squealing some variation of, "ooh, we've got another like!"'

'She's adorable.'

'She'd love to know who painted it. She'd probably bake them a batch of mince pies to thank them. She's over the moon with it.'

'Well, if I hear anything, I'll let you know.' I give him a tight smile. This conversation is the most awkward one I've ever had with Leo because he knows it was me, I know he knows, and we both know I should just admit it.

Leo must sense the awkwardness too because he glances between me, Casey, and Jerry who's awkwardly tidying up some nearby leaflets that didn't need tidying in the first place. 'Sorry, I'm obviously keeping you from your work. I didn't mean to interrupt your break, but I had to come down this end of the street anyway so thought I'd pop in. See you tomorrow, right?'

'Right,' I say.

He nods slowly, and I can almost see him deciding he's not going to get any more information out of me today.

'Handsome chap,' Jerry says as the door closes behind Leo, finally looking up from his leaflets that until now have required the concentration of a life-changing exam accidentally translated into Ancient Egyptian hieroglyphs. 'He totally bought that you were on your break.'

'Yeah, thanks Jerry,' I say, feeling like we've all just ran a massive con on Leo. It's not a good feeling. 'And thanks for playing along and sending Casey to get me.'

'Ah, we're as quiet as every other business on this street these days,' he says. 'This was the most interesting thing I've seen for weeks. He really seems to like you.'

I snort. 'Oh, I doubt that, and even if he did, lying about where I work will soon put an end to it.'

'Key thing when it comes to getting into men's pants,' Casey says as I go back through the staff door. 'Choose a lie and commit to it. Don't start all this honesty rubbish that you usually bang on about. I often tell guys I'm an air hostess. They really get off on it. You should've gone for something like that, it's much more exotic than banker, but if finance is what turns him on … kinky.'

'Thanks for the sage advice, Case, I'll be sure to take it on board.' I slip out of her jacket and chuck it back to her, determined to keep my mind off turning Leo on.

'And FYI,' she calls after me, 'when it comes to seduction techniques, enquiring after his mum's recent doctor's appointment is not generally a turn-on for most men!'

* * *

When I get back into One Light, there's a tray of purple and silver It's A Wonderful Latte cups and two bags of muffins on the unit in the back room. The volunteers are upstairs in the kitchen, and Mary's watching the empty shop from the doorway between the back room and the shop floor with a muffin in one hand and a coffee cup in the other.

'Where did all these come from?' I ask in surprise.

'That chap from the coffee shop up the street,' Mary says as she swallows a mouthful of muffin. 'Never seen him in here before and suddenly he appears with all this.'

'Why? Did someone order it? What did he say?'

'No, it was a gift. He just put all this down on the counter and said, "You guys do good work here and I bet no one ever tells you that". I told him he was right – no one ever does – and he shrugged and said, "'tis the season" and left.'

'That was it?'

She nods.

'He didn't ask any other questions? Nothing about, like, who does the painting on our windows or anything like that?'

'Nope, nothing. He did look around a bit, like he was searching for someone, but he didn't linger. It's quite bizarre, isn't it?'

'Mm,' I say noncommittally.

So he doesn't know I did the window. And I was so sure he'd just been in here and asked, and that Mary would've said, 'Oh, our manager Georgia who, contrary to popular belief, *doesn't* work in the bank next door.' He just suspects because I'm a terrible liar and don't know when to keep my mouth shut.

'The volunteers attacked it like starving hyenas and have taken themselves off for a hot chocolate and muffin break upstairs. I've never tried one of his coffees before but this is really good.' She raises her cardboard cup in a toast.

'Oh, Leo, why'd you have to be so nice?' I murmur as I look over the array of goodies. He's brought us a huge takeout tray of coffee cups – four coffees, three teas, and three hot chocolates – and two huge bags of muffins, one pumpkin spice and one chocolate chip. And that's minus what the volunteers and Mary have already snaffled. I pick up a coffee and take a pumpkin spice muffin, and walk over to peer out at the empty shop with Mary.

'God knows how many people he thinks work here,' she says. 'He brought enough to feed the whole street.'

I smile at the thought – that's Leo to a tee. I doubt he's got a clue how many people work here, he was just making sure there was enough variety for everyone to have something they might like. 'Yeah, well, no wonder his business is failing if he keeps giving stuff away.'

I can almost see her ears prick up. 'His business is failing?'

'Er … well …' I stutter because I'm not supposed to know that. 'Every business on the high street is failing, isn't it? I'm sure he's no worse than any other business around here. But he probably will be if he keeps giving half his stock away to random shops.'

She looks like she can see right through me. 'Yes, it is a bit random, isn't it?'

I can't tell her that it's not random. I can't tell her that this is Leo's little way of thanking One Light for being there the other night. I don't know if he even realizes it was this branch he phoned, but I saw him look up at our sign when he walked me to the bank the other morning. 'Maybe he was feeling particularly charitable today.'

She gives me a knowing look and has another slurp of her coffee. 'And maybe it has something to do with that smile you can't get off your face and that mysterious man who kept you talking for so long this morning, and those hot chocolates you turned up with from *his* shop, hmm?'

'Of course not,' I say, feigning innocence again, but she's right – I can't get the smile off my face whenever I think about Leo. 'I just stopped in there as I rushed past on the way to work. After being held up by someone else. A different man.'

'Has anyone ever told you you're a terrible liar?'

I don't bother to try denying it. She's not the only person to tell me that today.

'By the way, if he comes in here again,' I take a deep breath because I know it's going to make her suspicion go from through the roof to through the earth's atmosphere, 'could you not tell him I work here? I mean, if he mentions my name or anything, I work in the bank. And if he asks anything about who does our windows, tell him Head Office hires a freelancer and it's nothing to do with us.'

She doesn't look as surprised by the request as I expected. 'Well, at least that answers why you ran off so quickly just now.'

'I know you don't like lying to anyone,' I start, ready to launch into my pre-prepared speech about certain omissions not exactly being lies as such, the speech that even I don't believe.

'George, in all our years of working together, I've never seen you get so het up over a bloke who was your own age and didn't sleep on a park bench. I'll tell him you're the Pope and you work on Jupiter if it'll get you a date. You can't spend every evening watching TV with your dad, you know.'

'I don't spend every –'

'I know. Some evenings, you work late to change the window displays so the shop doesn't look a mess when there are customers about. It doesn't get you any closer to finding a husband though. I was married with two children by the time I was your age …'

84

I tune out as Mary launches into her often repeated speech about marriage and babies, mainly to avoid the temptation to remind her, again, that I'm only 34 and it's not exactly as over-the-hill as it was forty years ago. I *do* want to find love and have a family, I just never imagined I'd be doing it in Oakbarrow, the same tiny town I was born in and haven't left in thirty-four years. Most of the men around here moved away as soon as they were old enough. Any that stayed, married their high school girlfriends and are settled with families. It's not an area that attracts new people, so when it comes to single men my own age, the pickings are not just slim, but they've probably snogged Casey at least twice. My focus for the past few years hasn't been on men – it's been on my dad and his failing health, and work. I was unpre-pared for the job of charity shop manager when I got it and I've spent years trying not to mess it up and make Head Office realize they hired a window decorator who's terrible at paperwork and saying no to people. Leo's the only man who's made butterflies flutter in my belly for many years.

* * *

'What are you doing out there for the umpteenth time this after-noon?' Mary demands from the shop doorway, hands on her hips. Even in the dark, I can see her foot tapping against the pavement.

'Pedestrian count,' I lie.

'We did that last month.'

'They're increasing them due to the dire amount of pedestrians left to count.' I make an excuse out of the completely inaccurate method Head Office insist we use to gauge how successful our window displays: by counting the number of people walking past against the number of people who come into the shop.

The truth is, I'm standing in the road at the corner by the bank trying to figure out if my window mural has brought Leo any extra customers today. Mary's a bit too observant in noticing that it's not the *first* time I've been out to see if anyone's stopping to look at it. When I look back again, she's disappeared and closed the door behind her, turning the sign from 'open' to 'closed' because it's five o'clock. It makes me realize how little work I've done today. If I haven't been out in the road staring at It's A Wonderful Latte, I've been eating the muffins Leo brought us.

'So, how many people have gone in?' Mary asks a few minutes later, making me jump as she appears next to me and nudges a cup of tea into my hand.

'Two. And a couple of others stopped to look but didn't go in.' I suddenly realize who I'm talking to and do a double take. 'I mean, er, into our shop. Obviously. For the pedestrian count.'

'Even though you're facing the wrong way and our shop's been closed for the last ten minutes?' She lets out a little giggle of laughter. 'You've been painting our windows for the past few years. Did you honestly think I wouldn't recognize your handi-work?'

I've been caught out and I know it. 'If you do, he could.'

'Why is it a problem if he does?'

'Well, he's not exactly happy about it. He was talking about washing it off this morning.'

'But he hasn't. Maybe he's got used to it now. Maybe he's been too busy with all the extra customers it's pulled in.'

'Wishful thinking,' I mumble.

'What were you trying to achieve?'

'I don't know.' I sigh and take a sip of my tea. 'I was just trying to do something nice. To cheer him up. To make his shop look as festive as it usually does. I wanted him to know that someone out there cares about him; I just didn't want him to know it was me.'

'How are you going to get a date with him if he doesn't know it's you?'

I raise an eyebrow at her. 'This is not about dating him. It's about … Leo needs … I just wanted to show him that someone would miss him … his shop … if he … it … was gone.'

'Are you going to do it again?'

'What, tonight? I could do …' I say as an idea sparks in my mind. I *could* do it again tonight, couldn't I? It would create a bit more interest. A few people stopped to look at it today, wouldn't they stop to look at it again tomorrow if it had mysteriously changed overnight? 'I only have access to the outside, not like in here where window paintings are safe unless a wayward child clambers into the display. Leo's is going to wash off as soon as we have a heavy shower. And I've already seen one kid trying to lick it. It's going to look pretty damaged soon. A quick refresh wouldn't be a bad idea, would it?'

'Oh, I don't think it's up to me to judge your ideas, George,' she says, leaving me with no doubt about how dreadful she thinks this one is. 'Are you going to tell me what you're not telling me? What was that all about with him bringing us muffins and coffee this morning? He's been there for years, he's never done that before.'

'Well, like he told you, 'tis the season.'

'It's been the season a few times since he took over that old café. Never once have we got muffins from him before, and today, you're running around in the night painting his windows, you're late for the first time in four years and you refuse to tell us who held you up, but you turn up with suspiciously purple and silver cups. The plot thickens like a donated book with half the pages missing.'

'Just trying to spread a bit of Christmas cheer.' I give her my brightest please-stop-questioning-me smile. I don't want to lie to her, but I'm doing enough damage to One Light's privacy rules as it is, I can't tell her the truth too. She's a good, honest, straight-down-the-line woman who tells it like it is. I can't share Leo's private turmoil with her, any more than I can expect her to know I took a phone call I shouldn't have taken and not tell Head Office about it.

'Okay,' she says in a tone that says she knows there's more to it. 'For what it's worth, I overheard a couple of customers talking about how clever it was this morning. If you're going to do another one tonight, you should use the gingerbread house again. It looks fantastic. You're wasted in retail.'

'It's just stencils and spray paint. A mouse could've done it,' I say, even though I'm blushing furiously. I love it when customers comment on how good our windows look in One Light. I've always dreamed of people seeing something I've painted and liking it. I just never imagined it would be on the window of a coffee shop on Oakbarrow High Street.

Chapter 7

That night, I tuck my dad into bed and put food out for the cats before I leave at midnight. I spent the rest of the evening sketching out designs at a perspective angle that will incorporate the ginger-bread house in Leo's window, and I've settled on painting a garden path up to the house with a fence made of sweets at the front and a garden full of holly at the back. The added colour pop of some red berries with everything else in white should be eye-catching.

The dark sky is cloudy instead of clear tonight so we probably won't get nature's added effect of frost making the design sparkle in the morning, but that's okay as long as it doesn't rain. The effort of lugging a bucket of water and a cloth with me to wash last night's design off and start again is keeping me warm enough that I don't even notice how cold the night air is.

The streets are as silent as they are every night. Yesterday's paint comes off easily with warm water and a gentle scrub and the glass squeaks as I rub it dry, ready for a new design. I stick up a row of circular stencils along the bottom and spray them, creating a fence made of doughnuts and a snow-covered garden behind. I'm just using my finger to draw a line through the snow to begin the path when I hear the telltale flap of Bernard's loose sole slapping against the pavement as he comes down the road.

'What a surprise to see you here again,' he whispers.

'Hi Bernard,' I whisper back, finding the whispering quite strange. We could talk in normal voices, it's not like there's anyone around to hear us.

'I overheard a few mentions of your window today,' he says with his usual beaming smile.

'It's Leo's window, I'm just … playing with it. I thought if I changed it again overnight, it might get a few more tongues wagging.'

'God knows there's nothing else to get excited about round here,' he mutters. 'Leo strongly suspects it was you, you know?'

'Yes, I know. Luckily, suspicion is just that. Did you see him today?'

'I'll have you know that I had nothing to do with his suspicions. He questioned me, of course, and I told him I hadn't seen anyone or heard anything. He was already asking about you, although he seemed to think you worked in the bank. I wondered if he'd got confused between you and your friend, but he'd moved on to something else before I could correct him.'

I breathe a sigh of relief. 'Yeah, about that …' I start, whispering the bank lie to Bernard, surprised when he just nods his agreement rather than questioning why I apparently now work in the bank. Is everyone I know so desperate for me to meet a man, that lying about my place of work is completely acceptable?

'Anything I can do to help?' Bernard asks, still whispering.

'Have a rummage in that bag – wait, did you hear that?' I say at the sound of a click in the tiny alleyway between the coffee shop and the old Hawthorne Toys building.

'I heard something. Shall I go and check it out?'

I shake my head. 'It's probably just rats having a scrape at the bins.'

'Can you not say the r-word too loudly? I'll get shut down by the Food Standards Agency for the mere mention of the word around here,' Leo says, stepping out of the alleyway.

Caught. Red. Handed.

'I bloody well *knew* it was you.' He looks between me and Bernard. 'And you, Bernard. Why am I not surprised? I knew you knew something when I saw you this morning.'

'It's not Bernard's fault. He was just passing by and stopped for a chat. I made him cover for me,' I say, distracted by how good Leo looks. He's wearing baggy plaid pyjama trousers, a plain white T-shirt with a navy dressing gown wrapped around him, and his feet are shoved into mid-calf work boots with the laces hanging open. It shouldn't be sexy, but it is. He looks like he's just got out of bed, and thinking of Leo and bed makes all sorts of naughty things pop into my head.

'You're my favourite customer – why are you vandalising my shop?' he snaps, a frown on his face.

'Vandalising?' I say, my voice going up several pitches in annoyance. 'I'm not vandalising, I'm trying to help!'

'By graffiti-ing my windows?'

'Graffiti?' I repeat again, surprised by his reaction. 'This isn't graffiti, it's a Christmas decoration.'

'A waste of everyone's time is what it is.' He sighs and pushes a hand through his hair, making his light brown curls even more askew than they were. 'And if it was that innocent, why are you hiding? Why are you doing it in the middle of the night? Why not come in one morning and ask?'

I fold my arms across my chest, well aware that my black coat will now have white paint on it from my hands. 'I didn't think you'd say yes.'

'I wouldn't have. That's exactly the point. You knew I'd tell you not to bother.'

I swallow hard. 'I think you're worth bothering with, even if you don't.'

He goes to reply but nothing comes out.

91

'She's not doing any harm,' Bernard says. 'You can't be angry about it. It looks very pretty and I did overhear a couple of people talking about it today.'

'I'm not angry,' Leo sighs and sinks back against the wall, shoving a hand through his hair again. 'I just don't know why you'd … bother.'

I watch him, the way his shoulders sag and his back hunches over as he leans against the wall. He looks exhausted, but I'm finding him hard to read. He doesn't look angry but his words are harsh and he seems annoyed with me, and I wonder what else I expected. I knew he wasn't happy about the window this morning. Did I expect him to do a dance of joy at finding me out here doing it again?

'Well, I'm going to leave you two to it,' Bernard says. 'It's late and my bench is calling me.'

'Do you want a coffee or something?' Leo asks him.

'No caffeine for me at this time of night or I won't get a wink of sleep. Thanks, though. You two enjoy yourselves.' He waggles his eyebrows at us like this is some clandestine midnight rendez-vous.

'Hey, have a rummage in that bag before you go,' I say, continuing the thought from before Leo came out. 'There's a flask of tea and a sandwich in there.'

'Oh no, Georgia, I really couldn't –'

'You'd be doing me a favour saving me having to lug it all the way home again. As usual, I overestimated how hungry I was.'

He pulls the sandwich and flask out of my bag and peers at it. 'Ooh, cheese and tomato, my favourite. Thank you, Clarence.' He brandishes the sandwich at Leo. 'And you, don't you be mad at my Clarence, she makes the best sandwiches in town. I'll be having words with you tomorrow if you don't behave yourself.'

I know it's only a joke but it still makes something go warm inside me.

'Clarence?' Leo asks with a raised eyebrow as we watch Bernard disappear down the street.

'I think he's got his *It's a Wonderful Life* characters muddled up.'

'Clarence was the guardian angel who stopped George jumping off the bridge, right?'

'Right.'

I can't think of anything else to say without giving myself away. The silence between us is thick and heavy and Leo's eyes are on the ground, concentrating intently on one of the cracks in the pavement. I look at the debris of my painting strewn around me, the bag of brushes and cans of spray paint, the stencils, the bucket of soapy water and wet patches on the concrete where I've splashed.

I should tell him right now that it was me the other night. This is the perfect opportunity, the best conversation opener I could've hoped for, but how do you begin to tell someone something like that? He's not going to greet me like an old friend, is he? He's going to be embarrassed, feel exposed, he'll probably think I took advantage of his vulnerability by not saying something the moment I realized who had been on the other end of that phone.

I look at Leo looking down and he doesn't look mad – he looks like someone who needs a damn good hug.

'I see you've mastered the "telling Bernard he's doing you a favour" trick to get him to accept help.' Leo looks up and meets my eyes in the darkness.

'Yes,' I say, my voice sounding rough in the cold air. 'You too?'

'It's the only way he'll take anything. If I give him money, I have to tell him I found it in the road and it wouldn't be right to keep it, and my mum bakes him something fresh every day and I have to tell him it's the leftovers of what we didn't sell otherwise he'll refuse it or try to pay for it.'

I laugh despite myself. 'He's a great guy. I hate him sleeping outside in the winter like this, it's freezing.'

'I know. I'd give him a job in a heartbeat if I had the work

93

for him, but …' he makes an empty-handed gesture. 'At least his roommates are quiet. Dead quiet.'

The laugh takes me by surprise even though it doesn't seem like the time for cracking jokes, and we look at each other for a long moment until he shivers. 'It *is* freezing. How about you? You want to come in for a cuppa?'

'I thought you were mad at me?'

'I am. But I can't tell you how mad I am because my teeth are chattering and I can't feel my fingers.' He yawns and I can see him shivering. 'Please. Leave your stuff and come in for a hot drink?'

'Well, you know how much I like your hot drinks,' I say, trying to ease the awkwardness of the situation.

He smiles at me as he pushes himself off the wall and stumbles upright, looking like each movement takes more energy than he has.

I follow him down the narrow alleyway beside the coffee shop and he lets us into the kitchen through the door he came out of. He toes off his boots and pads across the tiled floor in plain white socks to flip the light switch on.

'So are you on some kind of stakeout?' I ask, looking at his dressing gown. 'Were you spending the night here to catch me?'

'Something like that.'

'How did you know I'd be back again? That window really bothered you so much that you'd camp out here overnight on the random off-chance that I'd come back?'

'Sure,' he says with a shrug. There's a tone of finality in his voice that gives me the feeling he doesn't want to be asked any more questions. 'And I'm not mad about the window, I'm disappointed that you lied to me.'

I bite my lip to stop myself smiling. 'Did you really just pull the "I'm not mad, I'm disappointed" line on me? A favourite of parents everywhere?'

His mouth tries to twitch into a smile. 'You're my favourite customer. I *love* talking to you every morning. I asked you outright today if you did the window and you lied to me point blank. I thought you were trustworthy.'

'I'm sorry,' I say quietly. 'It wasn't for malicious reasons. I thought you were really angry and were going to tell me never to set foot in your shop again.'

'I couldn't do that. My days would be a lot darker without you.'

I think my whole body flares as red as his cheeks do.

'Sorry,' he mumbles. 'I didn't … I don't … I mean … kettle! I can't be bothered to fire up the coffee machines at this time of night, and Bernard's probably got a point about caffeine at 1 a.m. anyway. There's a kettle upstairs; stay here and I'll go and put it on and you can tell me why you've decided to use my window as a blank canvas.'

'It's not …' I trail off as he continues his adorable rambling.

'Stay here. The shop's through there, you know your way around, don't you? There might still be some residual heat from the fire. Why don't you go and get comfy and I'll get that cup of tea? Stay here, I'll be back in a tick.'

I wonder if he realizes he told me to stay here three times? I listen to his footsteps go up the stairs at the back and the creak of the floorboards above me as he walks across them. I start wandering towards the main part of the shop but something doesn't add up. He looks for all the world like he's just got out of bed. He had no reason to think his mysterious window painting was more than a one-off and certainly no reason for it to be worth staying the night on the chance he might catch me out. I have a horrible feeling that I know exactly why he's here in the middle of the night in his pyjamas and why he's so keen for me to stay downstairs, and if I'm going to push myself into Leo's life and make sure he knows he's got a friend he can talk to, I have to get him to talk to me first. I give him a couple of minutes and then I follow him.

I go back through the kitchen and out a side door, into a hallway that's lined with boxes that have wholesalers' labels on them. 100x candy canes. 100x mint hot choc pods. 100x creamer. At least he's well stocked for the season.

'Leo?' I call as I start up the staircase at the end of the hallway, knowing he's not going to be pleased to see me. 'Sorry to be a pain, but can I use your bathroom really quick?'

He appears at the top of the stairs almost instantly, his arm holding his dressing gown open across the doorway into the staffroom, clearly trying to block it. 'There's a customer bathroom in the shop. You can use that.'

'Oh, I'm up here now and that's a *really* long way to go back down when you need the bathroom,' I lie, cringing at how crap my excuse sounds. I sound like a toddler still struggling with potty training.

He stares at me for a long moment and I see the moment he gives up cross his face. He drops his arm in defeat and steps back, his head bowed as he disappears back into the tiny kitchen like he can't get away fast enough.

'There.' He waves a hand vaguely towards the door next to the kitchen without looking up.

I hate being right. Maybe that's an odd thing to hate, but in this case, I would've loved to be wrong. I lean against the doorframe to the staffroom and take in the sleeping bag and pillow on the floor, the open novel on the carpet and the reading lamp glowing even though the bare bulb hanging from the ceiling is off. 'Are you sleeping here?'

He comes to the kitchen doorway, backlit by the light in there and the semi-darkness in the larger room. 'No, I'm kite surfing.'

The deadpan tone in his voice makes me laugh, and he looks between the sleeping bag and me and down at his pyjamas. 'Can't really deny it, can I?'

'Why?' I ask softly.

He goes to answer but stops himself and thinks for a moment

before speaking again. 'You know what, I don't mean to be rude, but you're a customer and I'm not going to burden you with my business woes. That would be unprofessional.'

'But I'm asking. Not as a customer. Just as a … vandal you've caught graffiti-ing your windows?' I say, trying to do an encouraging shrug.

'I thought you needed the bathroom?'

'Oh. The urge has faded.' I shake myself. 'I mean, yeah. Thanks.'

I let myself into the bathroom and look around. There's one of those rubber shower hoses that fit over the taps coiled up beside the sink with a bottle of tangerine shower gel. Both are covered in water droplets and have obviously been used recently.

He's living here. I know he is. He's sleeping on the floor in that freezing cold staffroom and showering in this bathroom the size of a matchbox. I poke around but there's not much to see. A cracked mirror on the wall above the sink, a bin, a loo, a pack of toilet rolls. On a scale of enough space to swing a cat, this bathroom isn't big enough to swing one of the cat's fleas.

When I think I've been in there long enough to convince him I actually needed the bathroom, I flush the chain and wash my hands.

Leo's waiting in the staffroom doorway with two cups of tea in his hands. 'Come on, it's warmer downstairs.'

I shiver as he turns away, tempted to say it's probably warmer outside. This is a million miles away from the bright, warm, gorgeous-smelling coffee shop I know and love. This is cold and dank with a vague smell of dampness permeating the whole room. I can't help peering into the kitchen as I pass. It looks like a tiny office that someone's put a microwave and kettle in. The cold shiver this time has nothing to do with the temperature and everything to do with how unfit this is for human habitation. This is a staffroom. It's somewhere people walk through on their way to the bathroom. Somewhere for staff to dump their coats when they come to work. Somewhere someone would sit at the desk in the corner, next to the filing cabinets along one wall, and do a bit of paperwork. It's not where someone should be living.

'So this is why Bernard was whispering,' I say as I follow Leo down the narrow staircase. 'He knew you were here?'

'I guess so.'

'He was whispering last night as well. He knew you were here then too. He knows you're always here, doesn't he?'

This time he grunts in response, which comes out more affirmative than he probably meant it to be.

In the hallway, Leo uses his elbow to press the door handle down and pushes the door open with his back because he's got a drink in both hands.

'You're good at that,' I say, because it's the same way I watched him walk into the shop today.

'I serve coffee for a living. You get used to opening doors with spillable drinks in your hands.' He holds the door open with his foot to let me go through into the kitchen, looking and sounding like his usual self for the first time tonight. 'You don't want to imagine the kind of messes I made in the first few weeks of opening.'

I grin as he uses his foot to slide the kitchen door open and lets us into the main part of the coffee shop, heading for the cosy sofas near the open fire in the corner. It's usually roaring away in the daytime but there's barely an ember left glowing now and I wrap my coat tighter around me.

Leo puts the cups down on one of the tables in front of a sofa and switches on a couple of wall lamps near the fire to give us low light. 'Sorry, it's too late to put the main light on. I don't want anyone from the council getting wind that I'm still here, they'll probably hit me with residential property restrictions on top of everything else.'

'It's fine. It's nice and cosy,' I say, despite the fact I wouldn't be surprised to see a polar bear pop out from behind a table having genuinely mistaken it for the Arctic Circle.

I sit down and pick up my mug of tea, wrapping my hands around it gratefully as Leo leans over the fire guard and prods at the dying embers with a poker. For a moment, it looks like they might come to life again, but they turn black and disappear into the ash instead. He sighs, groaning under his breath as he gets up and comes over to sit on the opposite end of the sofa.

'Going to tell me why my favourite customer has decided to graffiti my shop?'

'I was trying to help,' I say, watching the way his hands curl around his cup as he picks it up. 'You're acting like I'm out there tagging swear words all over your building. It's Christmas and I wanted to make it a bit more festive. I knew you'd say no if I asked because you won't even let me buy you a coffee in the mornings and I didn't want you to think you owed me anything in return.'

'Yeah, but why? I don't get why you care about my Christmas window. What do you get out of it?'

I bite my lip as I look at him. I wish he could just accept a little kindness, even if he thinks he doesn't deserve it. 'I'm not trying to get anything out of it. You said something about being up a creek without a paddle and I thought it might bring in some extra customers. I love this place. I love coming in here and talking to you every morning and I'd really miss it if it was gone.'

He thinks before he speaks. 'I only said that to you this morning. You'd already painted it by then.'

Bugger. 'Er, it was obvious from the day before, when we talked about the gingerbread house.' I wave my hand in the general direction of the window where the gingerbread house is still sitting, surrounded by a half-finished painting on the opposite side of the glass. 'We're always told to make a huge thing of our Christmas windows, they're the biggest window of the year and the best time to draw in new customers while people are Christmas shopping.'

'At the bank?' His forehead furrows in confusion. 'There's

nothing in your windows except mortgage posters and something about ISA accounts advertised by women who belong on dentists' walls.'

Well, this is going swimmingly. 'And I'm going to make sure my boss puts tinsel round the windows first thing tomorrow morning. And fairy lights.'

Oh, Jerry's going to love me for this, isn't he? There's a miniature Christmas tree on a side table in the bank and that's the extent of their festive decorations. There's *never* been tinsel around the windows of that building, and now Leo's going to be a bit suspicious if none goes up in the next couple of days after I've said all that.

'And you *did* get a few extra customers today,' I say, barrelling on without letting him get a word in. 'A few people walked past and stopped to look at it. A couple of them came in, and –'

'And you just happen to know that, do you?' he says, but instead of sounding annoyed, he looks like he's trying to contain a smile.

'Lucky guess?' I offer, cringing internally. I am *terrible* at this. 'Bernard said he'd heard people talking about it, and you said yourself that your mum got a few likes on Instagram.'

'So what are you doing back here tonight? Why have you washed it off and started again?'

'I thought if a couple of people were talking about it today then a few more people would talk about it tomorrow if it mysteriously changed overnight, and maybe a couple more would come in and buy a coffee, and –'

'But why? *Why* are you trying to help me?'

Because I like you. Because I know what your beautiful smile hides. 'Because you make a wonderful latte?' I say, cringing again at my terrible attempt to lighten the mood.

He bursts out laughing and it makes me smile just to see him not looking like he's got the weight of the world on his shoulders for a moment. Pun coffee shop names will always have their uses.

'I think we all need a bit of help sometimes,' I say carefully. 'And it's okay to admit if we're feeling a little out of our depth.'

I almost squirm under the intensity of his gaze. Even in the low light of the coffee shop, it feels like he's studying me, trying to work me out, and I wonder if I've finally said too much, if that was too close to what I said on the phone, and this time he's going to know.

'George ...' he says eventually, 'I'm assuming it's okay to call you George given the *It's a Wonderful Life* connection. I appreciate that you're trying to help but you're wasting your time. It's the middle of the night and I know how early you have to get up for work and you should be in bed right now, not outside freezing to paint me a window that's not going to help.'

'How do you know it's not going to help? Just because your business rates have gone up?'

'How'd you know that? I know I rambled too much about my father this morning but I didn't start going on about my business worries too, did I?'

'Well, everyone's have gone up, haven't they?' I say smoothly, quite pleased with myself for covering that so quickly.

'You work for a national corporation and you don't own your building. You're telling me that you have any involvement in the bank's business rates?'

'Er, no, I just ... um ... it's a bank. You hear people talking in there. About money. Obviously.'

He doesn't look convinced.

'My boss mentioned it,' I try again and then growl in frustration to try to distract him. 'Look, it doesn't matter about that, but what it boils down to is that you need more customers and your windows aren't exactly reaching out and dragging people in.'

'I know.' I expect him to elaborate but he doesn't say anything else. Both his hands are still wrapped around his mug and he holds it up against his chin as if he's trying to absorb warmth from the tea. He leans back and snuggles into the sofa and turns towards me, letting his head drop against the backrest. He lets out a long sigh like he's trying to relax, but none of the tension drains from his body.

'You look tired,' I say, fighting the urge to reach up and tuck his curls back from where they've flopped over. 'Were you asleep when you heard us outside?'

He snorts. 'Asleep would be too kind a word for it. I was staring at the ceiling wondering if a swift hammer to the forehead might help.'

I put my hand on his arm without thinking. 'No. No hurting yourself.'

'I was joking.' He gives me a tired smile. 'I'm too much of a wuss to actually do it.'

Is that what he thinks about the other night too? That he was being a wuss by not going through with it? I should let go of his arm but I give it a squeeze, the soft dressing gown creasing between my palm and his skin, and I suddenly don't care about saying the same thing. Leo being okay is more important than him not figuring out who I am. 'It's okay not to be okay, Leo,' I whisper. 'You don't have to be the bubbly, happy, smiley guy all the time. It's okay to struggle sometimes. No one has it completely together all the time. We all have days when it seems nothing will ever be right again, but it will, just as long as you don't give up.'

'You're the second person to say that to me this week,' he murmurs, not giving any outward sign that he recognizes the person saying those words.

'Well, she was right too.'

'How do –'

'Your mum, right?' I cover quickly. I've got to start thinking before I speak.

'Er, yeah,' he mutters, closing his eyes.

I still haven't taken my hand off his arm so I give it another gentle squeeze. The urge to shift nearer and hug him is so strong that my other hand tightens around my empty tea mug hard enough that the ceramic might break. I want to sit here and stroke his hair until he falls asleep, to rub his shoulders, to hold his hand, to do anything just to make him know he's loved. I can't just sit here and pretend I don't know what's happening.

I let my fingers rub his arm gently, wishing the dressing gown would disappear and I could touch his skin. 'Are you going to tell me why you're sleeping here?'

'I told you, I'm not going to unburden my private life onto a customer.'

'You've made me this tea for free. Technically, I don't count as a customer tonight.'

'Nice try.'

I sigh and sit forward, reluctantly taking my hand off his arm and putting my empty mug down on the table in front of us. 'Let me guess then. Not as a customer, as someone else who works on this street.'

'Be my guest,' he says, nonchalantly gesturing towards the empty shop without opening his eyes.

I get up and walk to the window and peer out into the blackness of the street. 'We're dying on our arses.'

He lets out a burst of laughter. 'That's a very blunt way of putting it.'

'It's true though, isn't it?' I gesture through the glass. 'Look at this street. The only thing for sale on it are the shops, and even the bookies and e-cigarette places don't want them. Every other high street in the country is overrun with bookies and e-cigarette shops, so that goes some way to showing how bad it is out there. I work here too, Leo. I know how hard it is to get customers.'

'It's not the same for you though. You're not selling a product. You will always have people coming through your doors because people will always need somewhere to keep their money. A high street could close down shop by shop and the bank would still be there because locals will still need it. Coffee is a luxury that people don't need anymore.'

I keep forgetting I'm supposed to work in the bank. I'm talking like the manager of a charity shop that's likely to have our branch shut too. 'If that was true, Starbucks would be out of business, and they're not, they're thriving.'

He grunts.

I take a deep breath, hoping that I'm right on this one because it isn't something he revealed on the phone, and also hoping that if I am right, he might start to open up to me. 'I don't know where you were living before but I think you've given up everything to plunge every bit of money into keeping the shop afloat, and you've done everything right, and this place is amazing, but you're still not winning, and it's not because of your amazing coffee, it's because of Oakbarrow High Street.'

His gaze is holding mine across the shop when I turn back to face him, and again, I can't read him. I'm not sure if he's going to cry or throw me out. Eventually, he lets out a long breath and leans forward, dropping his head into his hands and pushing his fingers through his hair. 'Why do I feel like you'd see right through me if I lied to you?'

I turn around and sit on the window ledge next to the gingerbread house, facing him.

'I sold my house, okay?' He says it so quietly that I can barely hear him, his voice muffled behind his hands. 'I sold my house so I'd have some money to invest in the business. It was a last-ditch attempt. I bought a bigger, better coffee machine, I bought a load of new varieties and flavours, I got the outside repaired and painted. I thought if I made it look nice, people would come, and I'd earn enough to rent a flat, and I just … haven't. So yeah, you got me. I live here. I sleep on the floor in the staffroom, I shower in the bathroom, I eat my supermarket value range instant noodles in the kitchen and I have a lot of boxes of coffee that no one wants.'

'How long?'

'Few months. Give or take.'

I remember him getting the outside revamped. I remember builders up on scaffolding. I remember him saying they'd been rained off a few times and wondering if he should've waited until the weather improved in the spring. That's more than a few months. That's nearly a year.

'What about your mum?'

'Yeah. If you see her, could you not mention it? She doesn't need the worry.'

'I mean, couldn't you stay with her?'

He's quiet for a while. 'I don't want her to know how bad this is. If I tell her I need a place to stay, she'll know. I mean, she knows I left my house, but I told her a friend needed some extra rent and I was staying with him as a lodger to help him out. I don't want her to know how badly I've failed at this shop that was so important to my father.'

'What about heating? It's freezing in here.'

'Heating costs money. More money than I can afford.'

'But you have to look after yourself. You have to be well. This can't be healthy.'

'I have to heat it during the day for the customers, but at night... Even the wood for the fire costs money, and I'd rather not attract attention with smoke pouring out the chimney at all hours and let everyone know I'm living here.'

I think about him coming back here the other night. Wet and cold. I thought he was going home to a warm house, making something warm to eat, and snuggling down in a nice warm bed. Instead, he must've come back here, to a dark and freezing shop. I made him promise he'd have a hot shower, but the only place he could possibly shower in that miniscule bathroom is leaning over the toilet with a hosepipe from the sink. When I pictured him going home and cuddling into bed, he was actually getting into a sleeping bag on the floor. No wonder he groans every time he moves. It's wrong on so many levels, and what's worse is that he's been living like this for nearly a year and I've never noticed. I've always thought he must get here by eight o'clock in the mornings to be open for people on their way to work, and the shop's shut by the time I walk home in the early evening, but he's usually still in there, scrubbing the counters and sweeping the floors, because I wave as I go past. Even the nights I work late to do the windows, I had no clue he was still here. All the lights would be out, the fire dead, and no hint whatsoever that someone was inside.

'I'd really appreciate it if you didn't tell anyone,' Leo says, bringing me out of my thoughts. 'Bernard's the only person who knows and I'd like it to stay that way.'

'I promise.'

He looks up at me, curls flopping forward with the movement. 'And I'm sorry I overreacted a bit earlier. I get that you're trying to help, I just don't like being lied to.'

I gulp. I've done nothing but lie to him since the day after the phone call. He's going to hate me if he ever finds out.

I sigh and slouch against the window, feeling lost and defeated. Things are much worse than I thought for Leo, even worse than he shared on the phone, and a festive scene on the glass isn't going to make much difference.

'What's your outlook?' I ask, wondering if he's going to clam up again.

'My business rates go up in January and I'm already over six months behind. I'm going to have a few weeks after Christmas to clear the arrears, or I've got no option but to declare bankruptcy and let this place be repossessed. And it feels a bit pointless to carry on trying. Even if I somehow manage to pay what I owe, I can't begin to afford the new rates, they're astronomical.'

I sigh again. Just like every other shop that's closed down one by one. Hardly any customers, so hardly any income, so no chance whatsoever of paying the fee the council impose for the privilege

106

of trading here. Charity shops are exempt which makes me feel ridiculously guilty and even more guilty for not telling him.

And I'm once again struck by how much of a front he puts on. It's A Wonderful Latte has obviously been in trouble for many months, and never once has Leo's smile faltered when I see him. He should be selling everything he can, and yet he still takes Bernard something to eat and drink twice a day, he still brought us a huge amount of coffee and muffins yesterday. He's just as lovely as I always thought, kind, and generous to a fault, and I *hate* the idea of him losing this place that obviously means so much to him and his family.

'Half the time, I think they're trying to drive this whole street out of business so they can demolish it and build a fancy new companion mall to the soulless retail park,' he says.

'Who? The council?'

He nods. 'Ignore me, I probably sound like a paranoid lunatic trying to blame someone else for my own failure. I'll be ranting about conspiracy theories next. Did you know people reckon that Paul McCartney died in 1966 and was replaced by a lookalike? Apparently you can hear it if you listen to certain Beatles songs backwards.'

'And the moon landing?'

'Oh, fake, obviously. A cover up to hide the gazillions of little green men zipping around up there.'

'Who all popped down to kill Paul McCartney in 1966?'

'Of course! We should post this one online, it doesn't get more nonsensical than Paul McCartney and aliens. And ol' Macca's always relevant at Christmastime, isn't he?' He hums the chorus of 'Mull of Kintyre' under his breath and we both start giggling.

'I know what it's like to work here too.' I say when I can breathe again, refusing to be deterred, no matter how nice it is to see him smile. 'Another shop shuts every week. It's not you that's failing, Leo, it's the street itself.'

'It's nice of you to say, but –'

'When this was the thriving café that your dad loved so much, the world outside was different. There was no internet shopping. There was no retail park ten minutes' drive away with everything you could possibly dream of under one roof and free parking. The high street was all we had. It was a bustling hub for the whole of Oakbarrow.'

'Exactly,' he says. 'You hear about high street restoration projects all the time, but our local council have left us to rot. There's so much they could be doing to improve things. Instead we've got dead streetlights, parking restrictions with ridiculous fines, and business rates that are beyond unreasonable. It feels like the sooner they get rid of the few of us who are still here, the better.'

I wonder why I'd never thought about it before. He's right, there are plenty of things the council should be doing, but they probably don't have the budget to waste on places that aren't worthwhile. No one cares about Oakbarrow High Street anymore. Not anyone who doesn't work here, anyway.

I turn around again and peer out into the darkness of the street. 'Do you remember what Oakbarrow used to look like at this time of year?'

He groans under his breath as he hauls himself off the sofa and comes over to stand next to me, leaning on the low shelf and looking out, pressing his forehead against the window.

'It used to be amazing, didn't it?' he whispers, his breath fogging up the glass. 'A real winter wonderland. I remember walking along this street with my dad and feeling like magic could happen.'

'It always felt like everything happened here. Do you remember the carol services in front of the churchyard?'

'They were amazing, weren't they? My family have voices that make braying donkeys sound like Pavarotti, but somehow we all sounded like angels singing there. And the tree. It was the biggest one I'd ever seen in my life.'

'I was thinking about that the other day. My dad used to be in charge of decorating it.'

'Wow, really?' he glances at me. 'I loved that tree. I remember going to school on the days it was put up and by the time we got out of school and walked home, it was beautifully decorated. Dad always told me that elves came down from the North Pole to do it.'

I smile at the thought. 'I'll tell my dad that when I get home. He'll love it. It's been a long time since we had a tree like that on this street.'

'It's been a long time since we had anything on this street,' he says, turning around and sitting on the little ledge.

He smells good, clean and citrussy, like the shower gel I saw in the bathroom, and he's too near. Near enough that if I leant my head just a little bit to the side, it would rest on his shoulder, and the temptation is almost too much. 'It always used to snow then,' I say to distract myself. 'It never snows anymore.'

'Want me to ruin some more of your childhood?' He looks at me and waggles his eyebrows.

'You're not going to tell me the Mickey Mouse you meet at Disneyland is just a man in a costume, are you?'

He lets out a burst of laughter. 'Of course not. Obviously the Mickey Mouse you meet at Disneyland is a completely real giant talking mouse. No, I was just going to tell you that Hawthorne Toys had a couple of snow machines. They used to turn them on in Santa's grotto so it was always snowing in there, but some days, after the schools had broken up for Christmas, they'd stick them in an upstairs window and make it snow onto the street below. I mean, it was only foam and it didn't reach far past the shop, but as you walked in the front door, you'd often get fake snow on your head.'

'You know all the secrets of this street, don't you?'

He shrugs. 'Well, none of their fancy machines did Hawthorne's any good in the end, did they? Even though they were the biggest toy shop in this part of the country and people used to travel from miles away to get their Christmas presents there. We're remembering them as children, and to me stepping into that shop was like stepping into a magical Aladdin's cave, a treasure trove of everything I never knew I'd dreamed about, but with the cynicism of an adult, I can look back and see that they were overpriced and old fashioned.'

'But that was part of their charm. The wooden trains and bears with moveable limbs and rag dolls. They were toys that would never go out of fashion. The atmosphere in that place was something I've never felt anywhere else. It was magical.'

'Until Woolworths came along selling Barbie dolls for three quid. And then Amazon, and that was like the death knell. The street hasn't been the same since they went out of business.'

'Them and the Christmas craft market,' I say. 'Since that didn't come back a couple of years ago.'

'That market was amazing,' he says. 'Literally thousands of people came to Oakbarrow on Saturday and Sunday mornings. They kept me in business for the first year. Even if trade was slow in the week, I'd more than make up for it on the weekends.'

'Yeah, us too. It was like those tiny little harbour towns that are quiet, and then once a fortnight, a cruise liner pulls into the docks and lets three thousand people off to go shopping.' I realize I've slipped up again and have to cover quickly. 'I mean, they all used to come into the bank to check their balances and pay their bills. Do you know why they left?'

'Priced out, I think. Same as every other business around here – fewer customers and higher fees.'

'People used to talk about that market all year. I know the regular market was there every week but that one craft weekend in early December was on the calendar from July. People waited to start present shopping because they knew they'd get pretty little handmade gifts there. There were free bus trips to it and everything. Everyone wrote their Christmas cards by that date because they knew they'd see all their friends there.'

'And then they used to wander down the street and stop in a

coffee shop for lunch,' he says. 'But those days are gone. The only people still here are the ones like you and me, still trying to resuscitate a dying duck that should've been put out of its misery long ago.'

His fingers curl around the windowsill in frustration, so close to where mine are resting that I can feel the tiny hairs on his hands. I fight the urge to move my pinky just a millimetre so it would be touching his. I look down at our hands; his big and chaffed and mine small with unshaped nails and hints of white paint, and tell myself all the reasons it would be a bad idea.

I needn't have worried because his hand shifts minutely and his little finger accidentally touches mine anyway, and it makes me jump because of how cold his skin is.

'God, you're freezing.' Without even thinking, I lift his hand and wrap both of mine around it, trying to warm him up.

'Sorry, I hadn't noticed.'

I press his fingers into his palm and rub my hands over the fist he makes, and when I hold a hand out, wordlessly asking for his other hand, he surprises me by slipping it into mine without hesitation. I rub them until they start to feel a bit warmer from the friction, and even then, I don't let go, because I'm quite happy to sit here holding Leo's hands. Warming him up is just a handy excuse.

'We're not the only ones who still care.' I shake myself and look out the window again. Instead of focusing on the warmth coming from our joined hands, I think about my regular customers in the shop. People who come down once or twice a week just to have a browse and see what new things we've put out. People who remember how incredible this street was twenty years ago. People who *still* come here and wander along the high street even though there's very little left to look at.

'The only reason anyone walks down this street is because it's a shortcut to somewhere better,' he mutters. 'Believe me, no one cares.'

111

'Believe *me*, they *do*,' I say with conviction. 'People looked at your window today.'

'Yeah, about three people.'

'Three people today. It'll be more tomorrow.'

'Do you wake up this full of positivity or is there some kind of potion you take?'

'Says the guy with the brightest, sunniest smile in all of Oakbarrow.'

The smile he gives me this time is muted and sad. 'Not tonight.'

'I know, I caught you without your mask on.' I nudge my shoulder into his gently. 'But you're giving up on people too easily. We were doing pedestrian counts last month and there are still people here … they just have no reason to stay.'

'Footfall surveys?' His forehead screws up in confusion. 'In the bank? What difference could a pedestrian count possibly make to a bank? It's not like you're selling products that need to catch people's eyes …'

'We're selling financial products,' I say swiftly, glad of all the times I've listened to Casey complaining about her day. 'You want people to see your adverts and decide that you're the bank for them. Our windows have to work just as hard as any retail establishment.'

He looks sceptical.

'Never mind that. People need an incentive to stay on Oakbarrow High Street, not just hurry past and glance at a pretty window. You have to give them a reason to actually come into the shop.'

'It smells nice and it sells coffee and cake?' he offers, sounding like he's politely trying to figure out how to tell me I've lost the plot. 'Coffee and cake are generally good incentives to do anything in my opinion.'

'Agreed.' I grin as an idea forms in my head. 'People talked about your window today. People were interested. What if it's not just *your* window?'

He starts disentangling our hands and gives me a look that says he wants to edge away slowly.

'I could go and paint something on other shop windows every night and you could offer a free candy cane to anyone who spots it.'

'What?'

'Yes!' I punch the air in victory. 'This is it, Leo! I can go and paint something, some little festive picture on the other shop windows every night, and you put up a sign saying there's a free candy cane for anyone who spots it. I saw your wholesaler's box of candy canes in the hallway. It's cheap, it's festive, it'll use up some of your stock, and quite a few parents still walk their kids to school this way, so kids could get involved.'

'Yeah. That's really going to endear me to parents, isn't it? Let's get their kids all hopped up on sugar and encourage their addiction to rotting their teeth.'

'You serve caffeine for a living. We all know it's bad for us but we drink it anyway. You have no leg to stand on when it comes to pushing unhealthy things. Going out and painting a picture on a shop window at night means nothing. It's just more graffiti. If people, particularly kids but maybe adults too – who doesn't love a candy cane after all – have an incentive, then it'll be worth looking for. If kids get involved and drag their parents in here for their free candy cane, maybe Mum or Dad'll be tired, over-worked, stressed out, and maybe they'll see your specials on the wall and think "ooh, a caramel pecan latte sounds like just the ticket."'

'That's exploitation.'

'All selling is exploitation. All sellers exploit what people think they need. We need to get people through the door. I'm not talking about the hard sell. I'm not saying that if someone pokes their head in, you grab them by the ear and don't let go until they buy three coffees. You offer a free thing that people choose to come in and get. You make sure that box of candy canes is out the back so they have a few precious seconds to stare at the cakes while they wait for you to go and get one, and if they don't want to buy anything then they don't have to.'

'You are *wasted* working in a bank. You're a cutthroat marketing genius.'

'Oh, come on. It's basic business. You have coffee to sell and no one's buying it. Give people a fun, free, seasonal incentive to come in and you improve the chances of selling at least some of it.'

'A free candy cane isn't very exciting, is it? You can buy a box of twelve for a quid in the supermarket. We need something more.'

I smile at him getting involved, at his use of 'we', at the brightness that suddenly lights up his eyes. 'How about a raffle?'

'A raffle?' he snorts. 'That's a word I haven't heard in a few years.'

'People love a good raffle. Everywhere seemed to have raffles when I was young but no one does them anymore. It's perfect, Leo. A candy cane and a raffle ticket – something for kids, something for adults.'

'For what though?'

'I don't know.' I shrug. 'A hamper? Hampers are big at this time of year because they're a bit of something for everyone. We could get a hamper online and use it as a raffle prize. It'll cost something upfront but hopefully you'll sell enough coffees to cover it.'

'Don't worry about that. As far as I'm concerned, the business is going under in January. I have nothing to lose by investing in a decent raffle prize. A couple of hundred quid for a hamper will make no difference to how much trouble I'm in.'

'Okay, well, not exactly the most positive outlook but as long as you're with me. What do you think?'

He's quiet for a long while, lost in thought, and I'm almost bouncing on the spot with excitement. Now I really do look like a toddler who needs the loo. I think we're onto something here. It's why One Light hasn't shut our branch yet. Why our windows have to be absolutely cracking. Why they insist on them being done overnight so they magically appear to passersby the next morning, rather than customers seeing us clambering around trying to preserve the dignity of naked mannequins. We rely on the donations we display in the window to pull people in; those are our selling points. You can't really make coffee more attractive than it already is so Leo needs something else to draw people in to It's A Wonderful Latte.

'I'm not as bouncy as you, but I see where you're coming from,' he says eventually, pressing his toe and heel alternately against the skirting board behind us. 'But George ... all this rests on you.' He inclines his head towards the window. 'I can't paint like that. Are you really telling me that you're going to come out and paint something like this on shop windows every night?'

'Sure, why not? It has to be at night to maintain the magic. These windows have to just appear as far as anyone else is concerned. It loses the magic if kids see me on a ladder painting as they walk home from school. Remember what you just said about the tree being decorated? All the kids in my class knew that my dad decorated it while we were in school, but there was still a part of everyone that wanted to believe Santa's elves had done it while our backs were turned.'

He lets out a breath and closes his eyes, letting his head drop.

'I'd miss you if you were gone, Leo,' I whisper, nudging my knee against his, hoping he knows I mean him and not just the shop.

He looks up and gives me a smile. 'I'd miss you if I was gone too.'

My chest flutters at his smile because it feels completely real for once. It doesn't feel like the masked bright smiles he gives me each morning, and it's unlike the tight, sarcastic ones I've seen tonight. It feels like Leo's real smile, the one you only see if you know him well enough.

'So do I have permission to carry on graffiti-ing your window?' I ask after a long silence. 'Because I know exactly how to kick this off and it starts here...'

Chapter 8

A quarter of an hour later, Leo's disappeared upstairs and I'm in the street, trying to envision the picture from outside and setting up lines of masking tape as markers for when I paint it inside.

'Hey,' I say when Leo comes back out with a cup of tea in each hand. 'What are you doing? Why are you dressed?'

The dressing gown and plaid pyjamas are gone and he's wearing light jeans and a black parka jacket over a dark top. He shouldn't look this sexy. I'm used to seeing him in his work uniform of a blue coffee apron and black T-shirt, which, although it has a certain charm, doesn't exactly ooze sexiness. It hadn't occurred to me that he might look even better in normal clothes.

He still has that unguarded softness he had earlier as he leans against the wall and holds one of the teas out to me. 'Just wanted to see if I could help.'

'You got any raffle tickets?' I ask as I gratefully take the mug from him. It really is freezing tonight.

'What do you think?' He gives me a look so incredulous that it nearly makes me burst out laughing. 'Doesn't everyone keep a book of raffle tickets on their person at all times in case of raffle emergencies? Of which, there are many?'

'That old stationery shop down one of the side streets will be open tomorrow morning,' I say, ignoring his sarcasm. 'They'll do books of raffle tickets. I'll pick a couple up on my way in.'

'A couple? You're really optimistic about this, huh?'

'People *looked* at your window today, so tomorrow, we give them something to *do*. Picture this …'

I put my mug down on the narrow ledge and spread my hands out, indicating some of the masking tape guidelines I've already put up. 'You know that scene at the end of *It's a Wonderful Life*, where George is running through the street shouting "Merry Christmas" to all the buildings?'

He gets up and comes to stand next to me, obviously trying to imagine it, and I'm still not sure if he thinks this is a good idea or that I'm a bit barmy and he's biding his time until he can get rid of me. 'You want to paint that on the window?'

I nod.

'Well, I can't think of a more fitting scene given your name and the name of the shop.'

'Right?' I say with a grin. 'Picture this scene. There's loads of snow on the ground and it's still falling. There are a couple of big trees in the middle of the road, here.' I use my finger to indicate where they will be. 'There's this figure running through the snow, buildings on either side …'

'Like the Building and Loan and the bank,' he says, stepping forward and tracing his finger along the window. 'The movie house, the emporium …'

'Yes! And the sign that says "You are now in Bedford Falls", right? Except we leave out the Bedford Falls bit, and you offer a candy cane and a raffle ticket to anyone who comes in and tells you where it is.'

'And we could add a couple of extra clues too, like a bell and some angel wings?'

'Yes! Brilliant!'

'It's one of the most famous movie scenes in existence. It's not exactly the puzzle of the century, is it? I doubt Mensa will start getting worried about their members failing it.'

'It doesn't need to be. This is just a start. As it'll be on the inside of your window, it can stay and you can put one of your pretty chalkboards up with the instructions and the prize, and tomorrow night, we'll do something else. We can make it like the Elf on the Shelf thing, a scavenger hunt for kids to find each day's picture and drag their parents in for a free candy cane. What do you think?'

'I think it must be fate that my shop is called It's A Wonderful Latte and Georgia Bailey has come to save the day with Bedford Falls.' He cocks his head to the side as he looks at me. 'If I say I love it, will you stop bouncing like that? I'm not sure if you're excited or if you're about to wet yourself.'

I grin at him, loving the ease in his humour compared to how downtrodden he sounded earlier.

'I love it,' he adds before I get a chance to respond. 'If anything can make it feel like Christmas around here, it's *It's a Wonderful Life*. It really makes you realize how precious life is … and how important friends are.' His cheeks turn red and he rushes off like he's said something wrong. 'I'll just go and grab that chalk-board.'

'Did you know *It's a Wonderful Life* was the film that invented fake snow?' Leo asks when he comes back with a square chalk-board and a box of chalk. 'Before that, they just used cornflakes painted white.'

'I did not.' I watch him as he perches on the windowsill and starts drawing green holly leaves at the corners of his board. 'I'm going inside to start painting in a minute. You don't have to stay, you can go back to bed.'

He looks over with one eyebrow up and one down. 'Are you kidding? You're doing this for me. I'm not going to abandon you halfway through. Going to walk you home afterwards too.'

'You don't have to do that. I work late all the time, I always manage to get home safely. I dragged you out of bed earlier, you should go back and try to get some sleep. I can manage.'

'I know, but it's nearly 2 a.m. and if you think I'm going to let a lady wander the streets on her own at this time of night, you're mistaken.'

'Leo …' I say, feeling myself melting. I feel guilty because he's obviously knackered, but I love that he's such a gentleman. From the way he opens doors to the fact he walked me to work in the rain the other day. Casey is always regaling me with tales of men she's met, and they're usually a far cry from the chivalrous type. She thinks the most gentlemanly thing a guy can do is ask permission *before* he shoves his hand up your top.

'How often do you work late?' he says, having a sip of tea. 'I've been here for a while now, I've never seen the lights on in the bank after hours. I would've thought it was a security risk.'

I gulp. 'Oh, they're fine about it. It's not like a big city bank with vaults of gold bars and safes full of valuables, is it? It's just a local bank. No one would bother robbing it.'

'There's still money in it though. I would've thought allowing someone back after closing was an invitation to robbers. I thought banks were majorly strict with security.'

Blinking heck, I'm sure he's got a point. Casey works nine to five-thirty and that's it. She can never understand why I often stay late at the shop, or go home to sort out Dad's tea and then go back. 'They're easygoing,' I lie, hating myself for lying to him. He's so sincere, like he's genuinely concerned about the bank's security, and I'm an idiot for trying to convince him I work there. 'And you don't have to walk me home. I don't usually work this late and I'm much more likely to run into muggers earlier in the night. It'll be safe now.'

'I don't think criminals have a bedtime, you know,' he says, making me laugh. 'I'm not going to let you walk the streets on your own at this time of night and that's all there is to it. The least I can do is make sure you get home safely.'

'Well, who's going to make sure you get home safely? If you're going to be like that, *I'm* going to have to walk *you* back here afterwards. I can't let you wander around the streets of Oakbarrow alone at night, Leo, you might run into a mugger.'

He smiles even though he looks like he's trying not to. 'At which point, I would have to walk you home *again*, and we're basically just going to be walking back and forth together until opening time.'

Which, admittedly, is not the worst way I could imagine spending a night. I give up on arguing with him. The idea of spending more time with Leo, even the fifteen-minute walk back home, is absolutely fine by me.

* * *

'So how does an artist end up working in a bank?' he asks as we walk side by side through the empty town. 'It doesn't strike me as the most creative of places to work.'

'I'm not an artist.' I feel my cheeks flush. I wanted to be once and it's been a long time since anyone thought I was. 'I mainly use stencils and masking tape. Anyone could do it.'

'You freehanded that whole window tonight,' he says. 'Don't try to make me believe you're any less talented than you are. I had no idea you could paint.'

'It's really just slapping a brush around or spraying a big area and then using a finger to remove paint from key places to make the image. It's easier than proper painting.'

'It looked insanely difficult to me.'

'It's really nothing. Just another element of visual merchandising. In this day and age, you have to use every possible thing you can to make your windows stand out.'

He glances behind us as we get further away from the shop and I know what he's getting at – the bank windows don't stand out at all.

'Well, mine looks amazing. Thank you,' he says instead of mentioning the bank again.

'Hopefully you won't be the only one who thinks so,' I say, trying and failing to stifle a yawn. It's well past 3 a.m. and I was out late last night too. Now I've stopped painting, a wave of tiredness is threatening to pull me under and it only gets heavier as I think about having to get up in four hours and we're not even home yet.

'You're knackered.'

'Nah, I'm fine,' I say around another yawn. 'What's the highest number of espresso shots you've ever put in a coffee before? Because I think we're going to beat that record in the morning.'

'Five,' he says with a laugh. 'There's a point where it goes from coffee to fuel for a jumbo jet, and that's not a line you want to cross. I did once and I was jittery for a week.'

I look up at him with a smile and he smiles back. His gloved hands are so near as we walk, our sleeves brushing against each other, making me feel warm and tingly with every step, and if I reached my little finger out just a titch, I could curl it around his. It's so tempting, to take his hand and give it a squeeze, and he's walking so close, and I don't get the impression that he'd pull away ... but I feel like I'd be taking advantage. I know he's struggling at the moment, I know he's vulnerable, and the worst part is that he doesn't know how much I know. He needs a supportive friend, not a lovesick puppy with a crush on him. Taking his hand and clinging onto it, telling him I don't know what I'd do without him ... it wouldn't help.

'Don't you get lonely living in the shop?' I blurt out instead.

'Lonely?' He thinks for a moment. 'That's an odd choice of words. Why lonely?'

'It just seems like a very lonely place to live. It's so quiet at night. I know it's quiet during the day too, but there's just ...'

'A blanket of silence so loud it's deafening?'

'Exactly.' I smile at his way with words, and look up and meet his eyes, trying to convey that I understand.

He smiles back. 'Yeah, I get lonely, but no lonelier than I'd get in a house. It's funny how things turn out, isn't it? When I was little, I always thought it would be the coolest thing in the world to stay in a shop overnight.'

'In Hawthorne's, right?'

'Oh, of course.'

'Me too. My mum and I were sometimes there at closing time and I always used to wonder if I could sneak back in and hide somewhere. It wasn't worth the certain death from my mum for worrying her though. Even recently, I tried to persuade my best friend to do that bookshop sleepover experience but she was having none of it.'

'A coffee shop might not be quite the same, but I can tell you it's not nearly as much fun as an adult.'

'Do you go back to your mum's often?'

'Sometimes.' He glances at me. 'Not as often as I used to. Things have been a bit awkward with my sister lately so I tend to stay away if she's going to be there. My mum's great though. She brings me in Tupperware containers of everything she cooks. I'll never go hungry with her around.'

'What happened with your sister?' I ask. I'm being too forward and I fully expect him to tell me to mind my own business, but I give him what I hope is an encouraging nod. 'She didn't try one of your mince pie coffees, did she?'

'Hah.' He laughs and seems to relax a bit. 'Very funny. Nah. Becky's just … although she completely agreed that we should use the money Dad left to buy the coffee shop, she's never set foot in the place. I think it's a memories thing, you know? Whereas I like being there because of how much he loved it, I like remembering him there, I don't think she can cope with it. My niece was doing a Saturday job at the shop for the experience and a bit of extra cash, and in recent months, I've had to end it. I've got no work for her to do and no money to pay her with, and my sister doesn't believe that trade is as bad as it is and she thinks I've done it out of spite or something.' He sighs. 'It's really just a big mess.'

'Have you tried talking to her?'

''Til I was blue in the face. Didn't help. The best thing I can do is stay out of the way. They're better off without me.'

'No one's better off without you,' I say forcefully. 'Don't say that. And cut yourself some slack. Things aren't easy at the moment. It'll come right in the end.'

I hate that he honestly thinks anyone might be better off without him. This is another thing he didn't tell me on the phone the other night and I'm suddenly desperate to know what else he's keeping bottled up, because I'm still certain that keeping everything inside is what led him to that bridge.

'I'm sorry, I'm sure you didn't want to know any of that.'

I nudge his arm, ostensibly to steer him around a corner and onto my road, but really just to have an excuse to touch him. 'Of course I did. We're friends, right? Friends share their problems.'

'After today, I think you're the best friend I've got.'

I grin. 'I am absolutely okay with that.'

'Do you know what that entitles you to?'

Oh, I could think of a few privileges. Most of them involve running my fingers through your hair.

'Free coffee for the rest of ever,' he finishes before my mind can run off in all sorts of directions.

I laugh. 'I'm not taking free anything from you. You need to sell every coffee you can at the moment. If you're going to stop me paying for coffee, then I'm going to stop coming in.'

'You wouldn't,' he says with a grin. 'I know you better than that. You have a caffeine addiction to feed. I give it until lunchtime before you're banging on the door begging for a fix.'

I poke my tongue out at him because we both know he's right.

Nothing could stop me going into It's A Wonderful Latte every morning and it has very little to do with the coffee.

'Well, unfortunately this is me,' I say as we reach my house. I'm in half a mind to keep going, walk around the block and say I got lost in the dark just for an extra few minutes with him, but it's not worth being caught out when he inevitably sees right through me.

The little tabby cat that hides in the hedgerow slinks out and wraps herself around our legs in turn, meowing all the while.

'Aww, puddy tats.' Leo crouches down to stroke her, being insanely adorable in a way that someone who uses the word 'puddy tats' has no right to be.

A black cat jumps up on the fence and I reach up and give him a head rub. If they're expecting Kitekat at this time of night, they've got another thing coming.

'I see you've got a dead mouse.'

My dad's left the outside light on and it's lighting up the corpse of a mouse on the doormat in front of the door. 'Oh, joy. Just what you want at four in the morning.'

He laughs and then slaps a hand over his mouth for being too loud. 'Sorry,' he says in a whisper this time. 'It's a mark of affection. They only do it because they like you and don't want you to starve to death and they think you're too pathetic to hunt for yourself.'

'"Don't want you to starve to death" is about the highest endorsement you can get from a cat, isn't it?' I mutter, wondering where I left the dustpan to clear up the mouse.

Another cat jumps down from the roof of our neighbour's house and sits on the fence, flipping his sleek tail and waiting for food.

'Crikey, you've got loads,' Leo says.

'I haven't got any. They're all strays.'

'Strays?' He looks up and down the road with a doubtful look on his face. 'This doesn't look like a typical stray cat area.'

'All right, they're probably greedy overfed house cats like my best friend keeps saying and I'm being taken for a mug, but look at their little faces. If they meowed at you for food, you'd give in too.'

He bends over to stroke the tabby who's still rubbing herself around his ankles and she doesn't dart away like she does usually. 'That I would.'

'So ...' he says as he stands back up. 'God, George, I don't know where to start ...'

'We've got a sofa,' I blurt out.

He looks at me quizzically.

'If you wanted to stay. It's comfortable and warm, my dad wouldn't mind at all, and there's plenty of food in the fridge and hot water if you want a shower, and –'

'No, thank you,' he says, so abruptly that I wonder if I've offended him by offering.

Instead, his breath hitches and when he speaks, his voice is wobbly. 'But I can't believe you'd offer. You don't even know me.'

'Ah, we've talked every day for, what, two years? I think we know each other pretty well by now,' I say, even though the exact opposite is true. Anything I think I know about him is just the superficial meaningless stuff he shares with customers. Until tonight, all I knew about the real Leo is what he shared with a stranger that he doesn't know is me. 'I hate the idea of you sleeping there. It's cold and you're obviously aching from the floor.'

'You don't know that. I could've gone mountaineering up Kilimanjaro at the weekend and be aching from that.'

'You could have,' I say with a tone that implies he's more likely to have wrestled a shark while wearing Lady Gaga's meat dress. Him or the shark.

He raises both eyebrows with a smirk and I sigh. 'The offer's there, always. I'd sleep better knowing you were warm and comfortable.'

'Thank you,' he whispers, and I try not to watch the way his

Adam's apple bobs down his throat as he swallows. 'But you're not going to sleep at all if I hold you up for much longer. I should …' he waves a hand vaguely over his shoulder.

I'm enjoying his company and I don't want him to go yet, even though it's nearly four and sleep is going to be a thing of myth tonight at this rate. 'I don't know how I'd have fought off all those muggers without you.'

He pushes a hand through his hair and gives me a shy smile, and I get the feeling that muggers were just an excuse to walk me home, and I feel a little bubble of excitement that he wanted to *and* that he thought he needed an excuse. 'I'm sorry I've talked so much tonight, you must be sick of the sound of my voice.'

'Not at all.' What I really want to say is that I love his voice; he's got a typical Gloucestershire accent and a warm tone that makes you feel comfortable when he talks.

'There's something about you that makes it impossible for me to shut up. I feel, like, a familiarity, like we're old friends or something.'

'Thank you for letting me see behind the mask,' I say. 'I knew you couldn't be that smiley all the time.'

'Just 99.99 percent of the time?'

I smile even though it's not particularly funny.

'I used to be,' he says quietly. 'But … well …'

'Life?' I offer.

'Yeah.' His lips quirk up at one side. 'Damn life, always getting in the way.'

'It has some good points too.'

'I know.' He looks at me so unwaveringly that my breath catches for a long moment.

You can almost feel the snap in the atmosphere as he suddenly looks down, shuffling in place and sending the timid cat running back into the hedge. 'Thank you for everything you've done tonight. Honestly, George, the words sound so insignificant for how much it means that you want to help, that you'd go to so much trouble for … me.'

I don't get a chance to worry about how sad it makes me feel that he genuinely thinks he's not worth helping because he suddenly wraps his arms around me. I'm too surprised to move for a moment, and then I realize what he's doing and snuggle into his embrace. I slide my arms around his waist and squeeze him tighter, trying not to think about the citrusy spice of his shampoo that takes over my senses, or the strength in the arms around my waist, or the tingle of my skin as his stubble brushes my neck.

'Thank you for a wonderful night,' he whispers, the low vibration of his voice so close to my skin making me shiver.

'You're freezing,' I say as the shell of his ear presses against the side of my face and it would feel warmer if someone had put an ice cube there. 'Your ears must be numb.'

'What ears?'

'Ha ha,' I mutter.

Neither of us makes any attempt to end the hug, and it's gone on a bit longer than normal now, but I'm warm where my body is pressed against his, and I let my fingers trail up the back of his coat and, as much as I want to run them through his hair, I end up awkwardly stroking his shoulder instead. My mind whirrs as I stand there. Am I holding him too tight? Is he desperate to pull away but doesn't want to hurt my feelings? Does he actually want to hug me? Or is he just embarrassed that he's opened up so much tonight?

The problem is solved when there's a loud meow behind us, and we jump apart in surprise to see the black cat sitting on the gatepost, looking as annoyed as only a cat can.

'I think that was a distinctive "Goodnight, Leo" in cat language,' he says with a nervous giggle.

'You don't have to go.'

'Yeah, I do.' He glances at his watch. 'I've seen you just after eight for the past few mornings, so you must have to get up at seven or earlier. That's three hours away.'

I sigh. I have an overwhelming urge to bundle him into the house, wrap a blanket around him, make him something warm to eat, sit him on the sofa and stroke his hair until he falls asleep. 'Thanks for all the cups of tea and coming out to help. It was fun talking to someone who gets my love of *It's a Wonderful Life*.'

'Same. So many people don't get the connection. I always get customers coming in and saying the name is too presumptuous and shouldn't they be the judge of whether it's a wonderful latte or not.'

I roll my eyes. 'There's no helping some people.'

'Maybe more will get it once they see your depiction of Bedford Falls in the window. It's got me thinking that I should get some more memorabilia made up. I could get a framed film poster and an "every time a bell rings" wall quote, couldn't I?'

'You haven't lost all hope then? Earlier on, I thought you'd completely given up?'

'It's hard to be anything but positive with you around.' He blushes as he says it. Even in the low light from the streetlamps, I can see his face reddening.

He still doesn't make any attempt to leave and I get the feeling he's delaying it as much as I am. I don't want him to go but it's 4 a.m. and it seems a bit stupid to just stand in the street looking at him until daylight.

I stay by the front gate and watch as he walks away. I can't ignore the little thrill when he stops at the end of my street and turns back. He smiles and waves before he disappears around the corner and out of sight. If my heart is beating faster as I creep indoors and pad up the stairs, it's because he opened up a bit tonight. He actually became my friend. I became someone he can trust, someone he can talk to, and that makes all the lies worth it. As long as he never finds out.

Chapter 9

'People are admiring your window,' Mary says, shaking her umbrella in the doorway. 'It's a good job you painted it inside or it would've washed off with all this rain.'

'I don't suppose you saw anyone going in?' I ask her from the till. Mary volunteered to do the milk run to the nearest supermarket on the outskirts of town and also popped up to peer around the corner and spy on Leo's window for me. I'm manning the till on the shop floor, but it's so wet outside that customers have been few and far between.

'Well, no, but I was only out there for two minutes and it's a horrible day. I'm sure people have gone in too.'

I sigh. I want this to work so badly for Leo's sake. Not that I expected hordes of people to suddenly appear overnight, but even a slightly promising upswing in coffee buyers would've been nice.

'That's one heck of a trek,' she says, shrugging her coat off and going into the back room to dump her supermarket carrier bag before coming back out and smoothing down her wiry grey hair. 'I remember when that lovely greengrocer was only three shops down. And then that silly supermarket opened up and put him out of business.'

'And then the street died and put the supermarket out of

business itself. You can't say fairer than karma.' I give her a wink. 'And you only remember the greengrocer because you were head over heels for him and he used to flirt with you when you went in to get our milk and teabags.'

'I'm 73, Georgia. I don't flirt.'

I laugh to let her know I'm only teasing.

'He was much too young for me, anyway. I was old enough to be his mother!'

'He was 65 if he was a day! Maybe a bit of a toyboy but no more than a couple of years younger than you. I think the only reason you're still working here is because you live in the hope he'll come back one day.'

'I don't think there's any chance of that. Oakbarrow is no longer a street that anyone would come back to.' She suddenly realizes that she didn't deny it and shakes herself. 'I mean, that is absolutely untrue. He was a friendly gentleman and nothing more, and I'm still working here because I live in the hope that things'll pick up one day and Oakbarrow will go back to how it used to be. If you carry on like that, you're not going to get the cup of tea I was just about to make us.'

I grin and put my head down on my arms and let out a long breath. The late night is definitely catching up with me, despite the extra strong coffee this morning. Some days I'm grateful for the lack of customers because there's no one to see me leaning on the counter and considering a nap at the till.

Instead of going to make the promised tea, Mary comes to stand next to me, her pink chenille jumper brushing my arm. 'Speaking of flirting, why are you so worried about how many people are going into the coffee shop?'

'Oh, I'm not, really. It's doesn't matter –'

The look she gives me is enough to stop me in my tracks. It's that motherly, concerned look with a hint of fierceness that lets me know she will see right through me if I make something up.

'It's just supposed to get people into the Christmas spirit. It's such a well-loved film, I thought it might inspire a bit of festive nostalgia in people, preferably over a coffee. Leo deserves better than this. I wanted the window to give people a reason to stop, rather than just rushing by without looking at anything but their phones in their hands.'

'You know how quiet we are on rainy days ....' Mary starts but she's cut off by Casey.

'George!' Casey comes in from the back carrying two It's A Wonderful Latte cups, which she plonks on the counter in front of me and Mary. 'There's been another Leo situation in the bank. He just came in looking for you. He brought us a tray of hot chocolates, two of which were definitely intended for you two.'

'Oh God, what did he say? What did you tell him?' I say, feeling my heart jump into my throat.

'Relax. I told him you were on your break and offered to get you, but he said he couldn't stop as they're quite busy, and to tell you he's looking forward to seeing you tonight. At which point, I nearly keeled over and died of shock because you've got a date. A date, George! Why didn't you tell me first thing this morning? This is monumental news! This is "phone me in the middle of the night" kind of news! This is –'

'It's not a date.'

'He's single, you're single, and you're seeing him at night. Of course it's a date.'

'How do you happen to know he's single, Case?' I narrow my eyes at her.

'I asked him, dumbcluck.'

'Casey! You can't just –'

'Of course you can. Men need directness. They don't understand subtlety. You need to walk up to a guy in a bar and say, "You're hot, I want to sleep with you," otherwise you'll be arsing around all night with buying drinks and trying to spot wedding rings and that sort of nonsense. Straight up and to the point, that's what works.'

'Yeah, but firstly you're a bombshell and you can get away with that sort of thing. I cannot. And secondly, Leo's quiet and shy, he'd run a mile at that sort of approach, and thirdly, I don't want to sleep with him.'

'You painted that Bedford Falls scene in his window because you *don't* fancy the pants off him and want to get into his bed?'

'It's nothing to do with that. He's a lovely guy and he needs customers. I'm just trying to help.'

'The man thinks you work in a bank,' she says. 'How does that *help* him?'

'It's complicated,' I say for the millionth time. I'd probably be better off just telling her it's all a ploy to seduce him. She'd be over the moon. 'And you can't just ask him about his relationship status, it's –'

'Oh, relax. It was last week when you made me go in and get a coffee at lunchtime. I also made sure he wasn't gay, just to put your mind at ease. Also not divorced, no kids, no mother issues, no crazy exes, and no unhealthy fascinations with alien porn or otherwise. You're welcome.'

Mary chokes on her hot chocolate. 'I'm not sure that's something he'd admit to a complete stranger in a public place.'

'Desperate times, desperate measures. It's been so long since Georgia's had a date that even alien porn is no longer a deal breaker.'

'Oi! It's not been *that* long!'

'Oh, please. Last time you had a date, there were still dinosaurs roaming the earth and people went around shouting "yabba dabba doo" a lot.'

In all fairness to her, she's not exaggerating that much. It has been a while. 'I'm not interested in one-night stands. I want to fall in love. The guys that you try to introduce me to only want to fall as far as the nearest bed.'

'Actually most of them are complete exhibitionists and would happily do it in the car park,' Casey says with a wink.

'Oh my goodness, you young people,' Mary fans a hand in front of her face, blushing. 'I'm glad there are no customers to overhear this.'

'It's all beside the point anyway because I'm not going on a date. I'm only seeing him to paint the next window.'

Casey's forehead screws up in concentration. 'What's that a euphemism for?'

'You have a one-track mind when it comes to men,' I tell her fondly.

'Ah, you're no fun.' She taps her hands on the counter like I'm a lost cause. 'Why does Mr Coffee Apron think we all like hot chocolate, anyway?'

'Because he's the most kind and thoughtful guy anywhere.' I smile involuntarily as I explain about getting hot chocolates for Mary and the volunteers the other morning and Leo being attentive enough to remember and think I meant my bank colleagues.

'Yeah, well, on your date tonight, tell him I don't like hot chocolate and next time he can bring coffee. Just plain strong coffee, none of that festive rubbish.'

'How about I tell him to stop being so generous and bringing free hot drinks to people who don't appreciate them? And that "festive rubbish" is the best thing you'll taste all week if you'd give it a try.'

'Snog him and I'll buy one every day for a month.'

'I don't want to snog him.'

'George, we've been friends since school. I know when you're lying.'

I roll my eyes because I actually wouldn't be opposed to snogging him but she'll never let it drop if I admit it.

'He wants to snog you anyway. Didn't he ask you out once?'

'What?' I say in confusion. 'Leo has *never* asked me out. Trust me, I'd remember.'

'Yes, he did. You dragged me in for a coffee one Friday morning and he was talking about some play that was on in Gloucester and then he asked you what you were doing at the weekend.'

'I remember, Case, but the two things were not connected.'

'Of course they bloody were. You said you were working and he looked heartbroken. If you'd given him a more open-ended answer, his next sentence would've been to ask if you wanted to go and see it with him. I just thought you didn't like him so I didn't prod you about it.'

'All the blokes you snog have stuck their tongues in the wrong hole and scrambled your brains. He was just being his usual friendly, conversational self. Believe me, if Leo had asked me on a date to the surface of the sun, I would've jumped at the chance.'

She shrugs. 'You've been single for so long that your dating handbooks are probably written on cave walls. You don't understand modern men.'

'He knows I work Saturdays, so he always asks me what I'm doing on Sundays. Whenever I say "nothing", he doesn't ask me out.'

'Well, no, obviously he doesn't *now*. He thinks you're not interested, you rejected him.'

I shake my head, losing patience because of how much I wish she was right, but she absolutely isn't. Leo is the last person I'd reject.

She rolls her eyes at me. 'I'd best get back before Jerry comes looking for me. He was super impressed with the hot chocolate. He's still not keen on those tinsel and holly garlands you put up in our window though. Says they're a fire hazard and if anyone from Senior Management comes down, they'll have to go.'

'What is it with people being grinches around here?'

'I know, I know.' She holds her hands up. 'I told him it was to "*lubricate the path of true love running smoothly*". He said that sounded like one of his wife's saucy novels and good luck to you.'

'Thank him for me again, will you? He's being amazing to let me wander through the staff-only areas every morning. It's really good of him.'

'He's a sappy old sod, really. Still believes in *twue wuv* after being married for some godawful number of years.' She taps the counter as she walks away. 'Enjoy your date tonight. Wear something slutty! And do your make up!'

'It's not a date!' I call after her just as a customer comes in and stands dripping on the mat inside the door.

'Date or not, your fancy man makes a fine hot chocolate,' Mary says. 'But don't wear anything slutty, it's too cold, you'll catch your death.'

'Although if you wear a thin top, you've got an excuse to borrow his coat,' the customer says as she wanders past the counter. 'Men like being made to feel all macho and protective.'

'Thanks,' I say, wondering if there's anyone in the entire universe who *hasn't* got the last time I went on a date marked on their calendar.

* * *

'Hello, lovely.' Leo's smile lights up the darkness as he opens the side door of the coffee shop that night. 'I was going to call you my favourite Georgia again but after last night I think you're my favourite human in general. Kettle's on. Have you had a good day?'

It's infinitely better since he called me that. My heart is suddenly hammering and my palms have gone sweaty. I've never been anyone's favourite human before. 'Er, yes, thanks,' I stutter. 'Busy with, er, money. As expected in a bank. Lots of money and financey things.'

I want to stab myself in the eye. Why couldn't I just have said 'yes, thanks,' instead of getting into the technical world of 'financey things'. One day he's going to ask me for financial advice and the limit of my knowledge is putting your card into a machine, entering four numbers, and abracadabra, things get paid for. 'More importantly, how was your day?'

'It was good. Better than expected.'

'Thanks for the hot chocolate earlier,' I say. 'Sorry I missed you.'

'I seem to have a knack for turning up when it's your break time.'

'That you do,' I say with a nervous giggle. Trust him to blame himself and not realize I have an abnormal amount of break times because I don't flipping work there. 'Casey said you were busy?'

'Compared to recently, yeah. I'm not exactly turning customers away due to overcrowding, but I gave away ten candy canes and raffle tickets, and that's not bad for the biblical rain we had. There was a bloke going around earlier looking for two of each animal he could find, if that's any indication of how bad it's been.'

I try to stop myself laughing as he meets my eyes and his expression changes from a wide grin to a secret smile that feels like it's just for me. 'And yet, as if by magic, tonight the skies are clear and there's no rain in the forecast. Mother Nature's way of supporting the spreading of Christmas cheer?'

'That sounds quite saucy. Spread your legs and let me sprinkle my Christmas cheer around …'

I dissolve into a fit of giggles. 'Oh my God, Leo, that's terri –'

He holds up a hand. 'It's okay, I'm embarrassed for myself.' His cheeks are red but every time he meets my eyes, his grin gets wider. 'Getting away from the spread of Christmas cheer before I embarrass myself beyond recovery … how tired are you on a scale of one to ten?'

'Not a big enough scale,' I mutter. 'How about you? You were up just as late as I was.'

At least he doesn't look like he's just got out of bed today. He looks insanely good actually, in faded jeans and a loose black turtleneck jumper with lines of grey ribbing running through it. It's not quite as endearing as the plaid pyjamas and dressing gown but there are definitely some benefits to the way the soft knitted material curves over his biceps.

137

'I actually got some sleep once I got back. I was knackered but ... I don't know ... kind of less worried than I have been lately. Usually I lie down and my mind starts whirring about all the "what ifs" and things that might happen when I lose this place, but last night, I closed my eyes and didn't wake up until Mum knocked on the door to start her shift. The adrenaline rush of having to get my sleeping bag and stuff put away before I let her in was enough to make me forget about tiredness for the rest of the day.'

'That's good.' I want to hug him so badly. It shouldn't be like this. 'She really doesn't know you're sleeping here?'

'Nope. I stuff my essentials in one of the staff lockers every morning. She just thinks I start early and work late. It's fine. I don't usually sleep as late as I did this morning.' He awkwardly rubs the back of his neck. 'Thanks for listening to me last night. I haven't been sleeping much and I think just getting it all off my chest, finally saying aloud what the situation is ... it really helped.'

'You don't have to thank me for that. I'm always here to listen. I love talking to you, Leo.'

His cheeks go red but his smile looks brighter than it has for a while. 'I ordered a massive hamper and put a picture of it on the chalkboard in the window so people know what the prize is, and there's another chalkboard ready to write something about finding the new picture of the day. What's the plan for tonight?'

'Nothing more than I was saying last night, really. We leave Bedford Falls up and let people carry on identifying it, and I'll go and paint something festive on a different shop window, and you do the whole "raffle ticket and candy cane" thing for anyone who finds it and tells you where it is.'

He nods slowly. 'I had an idea ...'

'Go on,' I say, feeling myself light up at him getting involved. I like seeing him smiling and enthusiastic instead of as despondent he was the other night.

'Why don't we do something fun and cheeky? Something like Santa trying on a dress on the clothing shop window, Santa picking out a nightie for Mrs Claus on Aubergine's window ...'

I couldn't stop myself from giggling if I tried. 'There's cheeky and there's cheeky, but I love where you're coming from. Something that ties in with the theme of the shops.'

'Exactly. Let's remind people of what these shops used to be. And if you want to keep it strictly non-X-rated, we could go for, like, Santa reading a book on the old library building, Santa building a bear on Hawthorne's, Santa writing his Christmas cards on the old card shop window. You know what I mean?'

'Yep,' I say, grinning. 'But mainly I love the way your mind works. And the first thing you think of is Santa crossdressing and buying sexy lingerie.'

'You don't want to know what my first thought for the old Blockbuster's was.' He winks at me and I know my face has gone red from laughing so hard.

He's laughing too and I find myself watching him. He seems different tonight, lighter somehow, not as weighed down as he has been. The laughter reaches his eyes in a way his smiles haven't lately.

'This is brilliant, Leo.' I can't resist the pull of seeing if that jumper is as soft as it looks so I reach out and put my hand on his arm.

He smiles and rests his hand on top of mine and my fingers tingle as his rub across them softly.

It would be so easy to kiss him. We're close enough and he's just the right height that if I pushed myself up on my tiptoes, our lips would perfectly align. There's something intense in his eyes too, and the thought that he wouldn't be opposed flickers across my mind, but it's closely followed by remembering why I'm here.

Kissing Leo would be taking advantage when I know he's vulnerable. I know he's got more important things than relationships on his mind at the moment. Trying to get him to open up and helping him to save the coffee shop is one thing, but kissing him now, with what I know and he doesn't know, would feel too much like some underhanded way of tricking him into a relationship. It's bad enough that I'm doing this, but if One Light ever found out that I'd not only taken a phone call that wasn't meant for me, but used it to get myself into a relationship with the caller … I could definitely be arrested for that.

I slide my hand out from under his and step away, but not quick enough to miss the look of disappointment on his face. 'What other ideas have you got then?'

'Plenty. Santa feeling some melons in the old greengrocer's. Getting a round in for the reindeer up The Bum. Buying flowers for Mrs Claus on the ex-florist's window with a note that reads, "Sorry, I cheated on you with a randy snowman."'

'You do realize our primary audience are kids walking to school, right?'

'An overly friendly snowman?' he offers, and I try to give him a stern look between bouts of laughter.

'Sorry, I appear to have the brain of a teenage boy when it comes to Santa pictures. I'll behave, although I should warn you that things tend to go wrong when I try to behave. It's such a rare occurrence that it tips the world off its axis or something.' He waggles his eyebrows and his gaze locks on mine and something inside me flutters.

He's always been a little bit flirty in the coffee shop but it feels like it's gone up a level lately.

'You can misbehave all you want,' I grin at him, 'but we're not painting naughty pictures on these windows. We're trying to spread Christmas cheer – something that stands out from the rest of the ugly graffiti around here. One picture per day, fun not naughty, like Santa reading his newspaper on what was once the newsagents.'

'Santa getting pick 'n' mix at the old Woolworths?'

'Yes!' The image appears instantly in my head. 'That's brilliant, Leo! We'll start there tonight. It's a huge window with blackout shutters inside so the paint will show up well, it's in a great position right at the top of the high street so anyone coming down towards the school will have already seen it before they reach here, and it was a popular shop that everyone loved. It's the epitome of everything that's gone wrong with this town, from loud, bright, busy Woolworths to a manky old building with graffiti up the sides warring for space with pigeon poo. It's perfect!'

'I only usually see you this excited when I get my new coffee flavours in, but now I see that you get equally excited about pigeon poo.' He grins. 'I'll get my coat before you hit me with that paintbrush.'

* * *

'You didn't have to do that,' I say as we step out from the alleyway and onto the main street. It's earlier than it was last night, only 10 p.m. because it had to be dark and relatively safe from being caught, but I can't manage another 4 a.m. finish. He's made us a cup of tea each in takeout cups to retain the heat, and now he's insisting on carrying my bag of paints.

'You don't have to do all this for my sake. The least I can do is make a hot cuppa. Don't forget, I know what time you went to bed last night.' There's a cheeky glint in his eyes as he waggles his eyebrows, leaving me in no doubt that the innuendo was intended.

'My best friend would die on the spot if she heard you saying things like that out of context.'

'Desperate for you to "find someone nice, settle down and get married?"' he asks, putting on a high voice.

'Something like that,' I mutter, trying not to laugh at the thought of Casey using quite that turn of phrase. She prefers things like shag and snog, and she'd probably disown me if I got married. 'Your mum?'

'Yeah. Barely a day goes by when I don't get some variation of, "I ran into so-and-so at the bingo, and do you know, her daughter's just got divorced. I told her to stop by for a coffee sometime."'

'Well, that's nice,' I say, feeling irrationally jealous. It's been so long since I was interested in a man, I've forgotten the more unwelcome feelings that come with it.

'Not really. My life is too much of a mess at the moment. I couldn't drag all this baggage into a relationship. Who would want me anyway? I'm not far off 40 and I'm going to be declaring bankruptcy in a month.'

How is it possible to want to hug someone this much? He's one of the loveliest people I've ever met, how can he have such low self-esteem? 'There are women out there who would think you're the perfect age for them and that your bank details are completely irrelevant.'

'I don't think those women are in Oakbarrow,' he says with a shrug. 'What's the point anyway? I've never had a relationship work out. On the rare occasions I've tried one, they always get to the point where I've *just* started to give my heart away and then … bam. She realizes she wants something different, or someone different, or someplace different. I'm in Oakbarrow for the foreseeable future and it's not really somewhere you meet a lot of people, is it?'

'Tell me about it,' I say. 'I was with someone for five years in my twenties; thought it was the real thing until he got a job in New York and couldn't get away from Oakbarrow quick enough.'

'You didn't want to go?'

'It was tempting, but I couldn't leave my father, and something had always stopped me from taking any sort of plunge with him even though I told myself he was *the one*. He left with lots of promises of going long distance and coming back to visit, and about three days later, he was tagged in a Facebook photo of him in a New York nightclub with his hand down a New York woman's bra and his tongue down a different New York woman's throat.'

'Yikes.' He winces. 'At the same time? Was he a contortionist?'

I burst out laughing. 'Thank you. I don't think I've ever laughed about that before.'

'No one since?'

'Despite Casey's best efforts, no. Like you said, you don't exactly meet a lot of people around here, and I'd rather be alone than with someone who couldn't wait to get out of Oakbarrow and would expect me to leave my family or my job.'

'Same. I've stopped even thinking about relationships in recent years. My father dying changed a lot for me because it was so unexpected. You'd think it would make me want to grab life by the horns but it was kind of the opposite?' He asks it as a question and I nod to show my understanding. 'It made me ... I don't know ... afraid, I guess. Afraid of taking any risks. Afraid of *everything*. I'm already too old to be waiting for my life to start ...'

'And too young to be so jaded?' I offer. I want to slap my hand over my mouth as soon as I've said it. It's *exactly* what we said on the phone the other night.

He looks at me and I'm sure he knows.

I swallow and imagine all the ways this might play out. Will he be angry? Will he wrap me up in his arms like a long-lost friend?

But all he does is give me a soft smile and shake his head. 'Exactly. I love that you understand that. I've always thought it was just me. It's like I've been in freefall since he died, watching life move on around me and waiting for *something* to happen to make me move on with it, but too afraid to actually do anything about it. I'm definitely not in a place for a relationship at the moment.'

'Anyone would be lucky to have you,' I say, glad the darkness covers my blush.

'You too. There are no words to describe how much of an idiot your ex was.'

I laugh. 'Casey's found *many* ways to describe him, none of them repeatable in polite company.'

'Oh, go on, tell me. I'm most definitely *not* polite company.'

I giggle. 'Well, most of them involve testicles and the removal of them with an increasingly painful array of objects. She also Googled testicle recipes and considered adopting some piranhas.'

He laughs too. 'I'd best be careful not to get on the wrong side of her then. Can she be bribed with coffee?'

'No, and if she asks you to put your hand in a tank of water, don't do it.'

'Believe me, it's not my hand I'm worried about!'

Our footsteps echoing against the damp pavement is the only sound as we walk through the quiet street, up past Hawthorne Toys, the florist with a battered old sign that says 'established in 1902' but has been shut for a year now, various clothing boutiques that have come and gone, and what was once a busy card shop. We pass a bakery with green awning ripped and hanging off in places, and a hairdresser's that used to be open all the time and now only operates one afternoon a week.

It's easy to walk past these places and ignore them. They're part of the furniture on Oakbarrow High Street now, and after an initial jolt of sadness when you first hear that yet another shop has closed its doors, they just sink into the background, and I pass their empty fronts every day without noticing them.

We get to the old Woolworths; a beacon at the northern end of the high street. It's set back from the road, with trees planted in diamond-shaped flowerbeds outside. The trees are just dead twigs now, but even in the summer, they're not exactly bursting with life, and the only flowers that surround them are empty lager cans and cigarette butts. There used to be a couple of benches popular with men waiting for their wives, but they've long since been stolen – just splintery chunks of wood left on their concrete bases where thieves have chopped them off with an axe.

'God, I loved this place when I was little.' Leo puts my bag down on the pavement and steps back, looking up at the empty building in the darkness. 'Woolworths had everything, didn't they? Toys, sweets, clothes, stationery, tools, bits and bobs for the house. My mum bought an umbrella for a quid there and it lasted for about fifteen years. It's just one of the many amazing shops that Oakbarrow used to have. Now it's just a hell hole but even hell holes have more good points than this.'

'Hell holes don't have It's A Wonderful Latte. That's one thing going for Oakbarrow.'

'I love your positivity, George, but It's A Wonderful Latte is going *from* Oakbarrow in a few weeks unless magic happens.'

'Christmas is a time for magic.' I crouch down and unzip my holdall and start pondering what I need and how best to do it. I put up a couple of masking tape markers and Leo goes across the road to get an idea of how it will look from a distance. I've barely got the outline of a pick 'n' mix stand painted before we hear the familiar flap of a loose sole against concrete.

'I was hoping I'd find you both tonight,' Bernard says, coming down the road towards us. 'And together too. What a treat.'

I can't help smiling as we both say hello to him. He never fails to appear.

'So you've left your own windows and started on others?'

'It's like a little festive scavenger hunt.' Leo explains the whole plan to him. 'It's all George's idea.'

'And Leo's disturbing cross-dressing Santa fantasies that make it all come together,' I add.

He catches my eyes and raises both eyebrows and I grin at him, holding his gaze for a bit too long.

'Maybe he's onto something, you know. Maybe Mrs Claus doesn't exist. Maybe Mrs Claus has been Santa in disguise all along,' Bernard says, making us both laugh. 'And people are all for gender neutrality these days, aren't they? Why can't Santa wear a nice dress if he fancies? Well, other than being a bit draughty for all that nipping up and down chimneys.'

Bernard stays for a while, reminiscing about penny mix sweets while I paint their names into little signs in the pick 'n' mix counter with a tiny brush and some dark paint.

Leo gives him a tenner and tells him we found it in the road and I tell him I've overestimated a midnight snack again and Leo making us both a drink meant I didn't need my flask. He doesn't buy either lie, but he's smiling as he walks back towards the churchyard. 'Thanks, Leo! Thanks, Clarence!'

'Does he ever sleep?' I glance at Leo, who's sipping his tea as he watches Bernard disappear down the street. 'I've seen him every night I've been out to do this, and he's around every night I work late too. I always pack a sandwich and a flask for him because he's always there.'

'If he knows you're working late, he's probably protecting you.'

'What?'

'He's been attacked a few times. And you can't tell him I told you that because he doesn't want any sympathy. I think that's why he generally wanders all night and you can always find him asleep on his bench during the day. He feels safer sleeping in daylight hours.'

'Attacked how? Why would anyone attack Bernard? He's the friendliest, most harmless bloke there is.'

'Attacked for being homeless. I think people mostly just kick him or spit at him as they walk past, but there was one time that he was really hurt. He was asleep and three drunken teenagers jumped on him and kicked his head in. It's how I met him. I was here late and he somehow managed to stagger up the road, saw my light on and knocked for help.'

'I had no idea.' I shake my head sadly.

'He was in such a state, bless him. Bruised and battered, with a massive head wound. I was never sure if he had concussion or was just in shock because he wasn't quite "there", you know what I mean? He wouldn't let me call an ambulance but he let me clean him up and make him a cup of tea. I tried to get him to stay but he wouldn't. The next morning I took him a coffee and a pastry and went to see how he was …'

'And you've been doing the same thing every day since,' I finish for him.

Leo shrugs and looks at the pavement, and I smile at his bashfulness as he continues. 'He's become a bit of a father figure to me now. I go down and see him every morning and just after closing time at night. I beg him to come in for a coffee and to keep warm but he won't. He's worried that he smells and sitting near a homeless man would put other customers off.'

'That's ridiculous.'

'I know. I feel like I'm failing him too. I couldn't save my father but I swore I would make Bernard's life better and I haven't even got that right. If the shop was busier …'

'What happened to –'

'Why does he call you Clarence though?' Leo says hurriedly, clearly not going to let me ask about his father. 'It's weird. Have you corrected him?'

'Of course. I think he just forgets,' I say, hoping Bernard won't be offended that I'm implying he's going senile.

'But he knows your real name, and I know he knows the plot of *It's a Wonderful Life* because we've talked about it before.'

'He lives in a churchyard. I doubt Christmas films are top of his priority list.'

'*It's a Wonderful Life* is so much more than just a Christmas film. It's life affirming.'

I remember saying the same thing to him on the phone. 'You really have a wonderful life. You can't throw it away because things have gone wrong. Nothing is so big that it can't be overcome with a bit of support and a good friend or two.' I cough. 'I mean, that's the plot of the film. Nothing else, obviously.'

147

I focus so hard on painting that the window glass squeaks under the pressure from the brush. I'm sure Leo's eyes are boring into the back of my head and I can't bring myself to turn around and check. I'm going to give myself away if I don't start keeping my trap shut.

'You have made Bernard's life better,' I say to the window instead. 'He talks about you like a proud father. You care about him. That's what really makes a difference.'

'I could say the same about you. You care about saving my shop when even I've given up.'

'I don't think you've given up,' I say, thinking about his enthusiasm tonight and constant stream of ideas for pictures fitting each shop on the street. 'I think you just needed a reminder that no one is a failure if they have people who care about them.'

'You really love that film, don't you? I thought I loved it but you know it even better than me.'

'It was my mum's favourite,' I say as I fill in Santa's beard with white paint. 'She used to make a point of watching it every time it was on TV at Christmas. I despised it growing up; I thought it was long and boring and I hated being named after it, but after she died I watched it and it reminded me of her, and I grew to understand why she loved it so much.'

'When did she die?' he asks with a soft tone in his voice that lets me know I could ignore the question and he wouldn't push it.

'A long while ago. Fourteen years ago, when I was twenty. Cancer.'

'Does it ever get any easier?'

I look over my shoulder at him. He's resting his nose on the plastic lid of his cup but he looks like he's hiding his face rather than drinking. I could lie and give him the usual 'time heals' spiel, it'd probably make him feel better, but I've already told Leo enough lies. 'No.'

'So I gathered,' he murmurs.

It would be so easy to put my brush down and hug him. From up here on the second step of my portable stepladder, he looks small and cold with both hands wrapped around his cardboard cup that can't be giving out much residual heat now. There's a vulnerability about Leo when we're alone that he's never showed in the shop, and now I know there's obviously more to his father's death than I'd thought, it goes some way towards explaining why he's struggling so much.

I'm so focused on him that I'm not paying attention to where my feet are and I wobble on the ladder. He instantly puts his cup down and comes over, one hand stabilising the ladder and one hand on my lower back to steady me. The heat that rises up my spine has nothing to do with the wobbly ladder, and I wonder if he realizes that his sudden closeness is making me even wobblier, in a not altogether bad way.

Chapter 10

It's earlier when he walks me home tonight and we're walking slowly to admire some of the Christmas lights still on in people's houses. The smell of woodsmoke puffing out of chimneys and fairy lights twinkling in windows and along garden hedges makes the world feel magical in a way that it doesn't for the rest of the year. On Oakbarrow High Street, it's easy to forget that it's Christmas when the most festive thing we've got is the Santa-red lace with white fur trim basque in Aubergine's window. It's nice to walk through the residential streets and realize that the residents still know it's Christmas.

'Don't forget to put that picture on your social media in the morning. Facebook, Twitter, Instagram. And if you can get your mum to pose with it and run the accounts, even better. People would probably love the story of your little old mum getting into Facebook for the first time.'

'She'll be thrilled. She's loving it. I'm a bit scared she's going to get into Tinder next.'

I giggle at the thought and try not to be entranced as Leo pushes his curls up underneath the thick-knit red bobble hat he's put on and pulls it down over his ears. 'You really think social media will make any difference? People "liking" us from miles away doesn't mean that anyone's actually going to come and buy a coffee. It's easy to click a thumbs up button as you scroll through a timeline, it doesn't translate into actual visitors.'

'Maybe not, but it can't hurt. You have nothing to lose by posting the pictures online, and if your mum's enjoying it, then even better.'

'So, leaf of dandelion, a frog's toenail, actual rays of sunshine, and fragments of stars?'

'What?' I ask in confusion.

'Your positivity potion. What was the recipe again?'

'Oh, ha ha. Excuse me while I collapse from amusement.' I whack his arm even though it does make me want to laugh, and he laughs too, his shoulder bumping against mine with the movement.

There's the wintery skeleton of a magnolia tree in someone's front yard that's been strung with twinkling white fairy lights and we stop on the pavement underneath it and look up. When I walk past in the spring, the owner is always out here sweeping up fallen magnolia blossoms that are spreading across the road and dropping into his neighbours' gardens. My dad always says the tree is more trouble than it's worth, but it looks incredible tonight.

'You ever want to just keep walking?' Leo says as we set off again.

'Walking's a form of exercise so I generally like to stop doing it as soon as possible.' I was hoping he'd laugh but he doesn't. 'Walking where?'

'I don't know. Anywhere away from here. Sometimes I dream about following one of these roads and just keeping on until I'm somewhere else and Oakbarrow and everything in it is a distant memory.' He glances at me and something in his eyes makes warmth pool in my belly. 'Apart from you.'

I blush, even though I get the feeling it's more of a metaphor than an actual possibility. 'I quite like Oakbarrow. I'd love to travel but I can't imagine anywhere else ever being *home*.' I nudge his arm with my elbow. 'There are good people here.'

He glances over at me and smiles, igniting that familiar flutter in my stomach along with the warmth.

'Are you really that unhappy here?' I ask, wishing I had the right to link my arm through his and pull him closer.

'I don't know.' He tugs his hat down further even though it didn't need the adjustment. 'This wasn't what I had planned for my life. I left for uni and I was never going to come back, but I was out of my depth there and couldn't hack it so I ended up back on my parents' doorstep before the first term was over. I wanted to travel but didn't have the money, so Dad got one of his friends to give me a job, which I hated, but couldn't afford to throw back in his face. I saved up and I was about to go off for a few months to eastern Europe, Poland, Hungary, places like that because they're cheaper than other parts of Europe, but then my mum had a car accident. She recovered well and you'd never know it now, but at the time, it knocked the family for six. I couldn't go off and leave everyone in the middle of that. Couple of years after that, my sister got pregnant and the father wasn't interested. She was terrified and had loads of health problems during the pregnancy, and Mum and Dad were big on supporting her as a family. I couldn't leave, and then there was a baby that she didn't cope well with, and Uncle Leo couldn't leave then either. And then Mum and Dad were desperate for me to put down roots here and offered to match what I had in savings and buy a house, and I … didn't know how to say no. It was immature and ridiculous to blow so much money on a trip abroad that would ultimately be nothing but a good experience, when the alternative was to do something sensible and get on the property ladder. So I did. And now I'm not, and you know the rest.'

'Just like George,' I say. 'He always wanted to leave Bedford Falls but kept putting aside his own dreams for the sake of the family.'

'Oh, I wouldn't put it quite like that. I wanted to see a bit of the world, but it was my decision to stay here. I could've told everyone else to go stuff themselves and gone anyway.'

I think about the Leo I know, how much he cares about people and looks after them. Bernard, his mum, the effort he puts into something as simple as a hot drink, the care he takes to put my name in fancy writing on each coffee cup, and to remember *exactly* how I like my coffee. No matter how much he wanted it, leaving would never have been an option.

'Sorry, I'm rambling again,' he says. 'Ignore me, I didn't mean to tell you my life story.'

'I like hearing it,' I say, loving the pink flush to his cheeks as he ducks his head and shoves his hands deeper into his pockets. I get the feeling he's not going to say any more unless I do a bit of wheedling. 'What did you do before the coffee shop?'

'Everything. My father always told me my problem was that I had no idea what I wanted to do with my life. When I was young, I always thought there'd be this magical click and you'd suddenly know the job that was meant for you, but it just doesn't happen in real life. I was never good at anything in school. I never particularly liked any one thing more than any other. I chose college courses based on exam results, uni courses because it was what you were supposed to do. I've floated between different jobs, everything from packing in a factory, answering phones in a call centre, loading goods into cars at a DIY store, supermarket checkouts, you name it. My one chance to do something meaningful with my life was to use Dad's legacy and make It's A Wonderful Latte something he would've been proud of, and you know how well that's going.' He groans and tugs his hat down even further like he's trying to hide inside it. 'God, you must want to throttle me for prattling on. Why aren't you telling me to put a sock in it? You don't want to know all this stuff.'

'Sure I do. We're friends, aren't we? Friends talk to each other.

Besides, it's far too cold to take your socks off and put them anywhere so keep talking.'

He laughs. 'You're a good listener. Has anyone ever told you that?'

'Not really,' I say with a shrug, wondering how he'd feel if he knew the girl who listened to him the other night has spent the following week getting herself entwined in his life. He wouldn't think I was such a good listener then.

'Well, I'm going to force myself to shut up before you hack your own ears off with this holly leaf.' He plucks one from someone's hedge as we pass their garden and starts tearing it into shreds, heedless of the thorns. 'How about you? Oakbarrow born and raised?'

'Yeah. Lived in the same house all my life. I always thought I'd get married and come back to settle down here one day, but I *had* planned on leaving first. It's not something that's on the cards anytime soon though.'

'Why not?'

I do a slow shrug. 'My dad is old and frail. I couldn't leave him on his own. And I love my job, it would be stupid to give up that security. And I'd miss my best friend, and all those cats rely on me for food, and –'

'Where would you go,' he looks over at me, 'if you didn't have that long list of excuses?'

'They're not…' I sigh, giving up on bothering to protest.

'Justifications then. Believe me, I have a long list of them too. They seemed like reasons at first but the older I get, the more they feel like excuses. Sound familiar?'

'No,' I mutter, looking away. He's hit a nail that I don't want to deal with on its ugly bulging head. It's easier to just get on with the life you have than to dream about something you'll never have the courage to do.

'Mine would be Scandinavia,' he says. 'I love that area of the world. My dream trip would be to tour Norway, Denmark,

Sweden, and Finland. They're said to be the happiest places in the world. I'd love to spend some time there and find out what they know that we don't.'

'Paris,' I say before I realize I'm going to answer him. My voice catches and comes out in a hoarse rumble.

'The City of Light built over one of the largest mass graves in history. That would be my next choice of places to visit. Notre Dame, the Eiffel Tower, Sacré-Cœur, the Louvre. Do you know there's a bookshop there where you can live in exchange for working in the shop?'

'I know. I always wanted to do that.' I look up at him and he looks so interested, and like he'd understand, that I want to tell him something no one but my mum and dad have ever known. 'I got into a school there once. An art college when I was seventeen.'

'In Paris? Wow.' He nods approvingly but the expression on his face changes as he considers it. 'But?'

I think for a long moment. 'But the world seemed too big.'

'What does that mean?'

'My parents didn't want me to go. They thought I was too young and it was too big a move. I'd never lived away from home before and they were worried sick about me suddenly moving to a different country where I didn't speak the language. I'd applied thinking I'd never get in, gone for an interview thinking I didn't have a hope in hell; it was such a surprise to get accepted that I just kind of went along with it in shock. I didn't really think about the practicalities.'

'Did you want to go?'

'Yeah, at first, but the more my mum and dad worried, the more worried I got, and suddenly it seemed terrifying rather than exciting.'

'So you dropped out?'

'Right before the first term began.'

'Regret it?'

155

'Well, I found a job here and started earning money and gained some independence, and –'

'That means yes.'

I frown at him. 'What would I have got out of it? Painting's just a hobby. It's not a viable career. You have to do something else as well and if you're really lucky, you might sell a canvas or two for a tiny price that's got nothing on the amount of hours you put in, but if you try to charge a decent price then no one buys. I did the sensible thing and got a job at a clothes shop in Gloucester and that was far enough.'

He knocks his arm against mine again. 'As one person who's never escaped Oakbarrow to another, I get it.'

I nod, feeling abnormally tearful. I want to grab his arm, slot mine through it, pull him close and rest my head on his shoulder as we walk. I've never talked about this with anyone before. It's impossible to tell people you live with, work with, and see every day that you'd rather be somewhere else. It would make them feel like a burden, and I'd never want that. The only time I've ever mentioned it is after a glass of wine too many with Casey and her equally tipsy response was, 'do you want a lift to the train station?' like it's that simple. Leo understands that it isn't.

'It didn't matter anyway. Within a couple of months, my mum had been diagnosed with cancer. I would never have stayed there while she was ill, so looking back, it was probably better that I never started at all.'

He suddenly steps nearer and swings an arm around my shoulders, pulling me closer and tucking me into his side, his head dropping to rest against mine for a moment. 'I'm sorry,' he murmurs. 'Sometimes life is crap and there's nothing you can do about it but that doesn't make it any less crap.'

The simple truth of the statement makes me smile. He says I'm full of positivity, but hearing someone say such an unflinchingly honest, simple fact does actually make it seem better. 'Talking to someone who understands is nice though.'

'Oh God, don't I know that? You're so easy to talk to, George. You remind me of someone I spoke to the other night –'

'Oh look, here's my street!' I say a bit too enthusiastically. He might not even mean me but I'm not sure I want to find out. 'I wonder what cats are around tonight? They really took a liking to you last night, you'll have to come and say hello and see who's meowing for food.'

If he notices my whiplash-inducing subject change, he's too polite to mention it.

Pussycats are few and far between tonight; even the tabby who doesn't usually venture outside the hedge has gone mousing – or back to her own warm home with her own family of generous foodgivers, as Casey would say – and Leo looks disappointed as he pulls his arm away from my shoulders.

'Well, thank you for another wonderful night, Miss Bailey.' He steps away and the cold night air seeps through my coat like his arm has been around me for ages, not mere minutes.

'Thank you,' I say, forcing a smile. 'And thank you for listening. I've never …' I watch like an out of body experience as my nose burns and my eyes fill up, unaware until that moment of how much it meant to share the feelings I bury inside with someone who understands them.

In the blink of an eye, Leo's wrapped me up in his arms and pulled me into a bear hug, his warmth enveloping me, the familiar sweet but sharp scent of his tangerine shower gel surrounding me.

'Believe me, I know,' he whispers against my hair. 'Didn't you notice how choked up I was in the shop the other day? Talking to someone who understands is…' he pauses for a moment and moves his head around like he's looking for the right word, 'a lifesaver.'

I reach up and pinch the bridge of my nose, trying to think of something happy, like puppies and rainbows. Maybe that only works when you've got a long journey ahead and you need a wee before you leave the house so you force yourself to sit on the loo and think of waterfalls. I wasn't supposed to unload onto Leo. I was supposed to be trying to get him to unload onto me.

Although the hug is a nice side effect. I sniffle and wrap my arms around him too, holding him tight, wondering if he'd mind if we stood here until 4 a.m. again just hugging. It would be worth another day of utter exhaustion to not have him pull away yet.

When he does pull away, the atmosphere between us is suddenly different. The campfire that's been ticking over in my belly is suddenly a roaring blaze and Leo's eyes have gone from sympathetic to lustful. Instead of moving away, he rests his forehead against mine and tucks a frizzy bit of brown hair that's escaped my ponytail back behind my ear. 'God, George, you make me want to live again,' he whispers, his breath warm against my cheek. 'It's been so long since I felt anything …'

His mouth lowers and I push myself up on my tiptoes, working on autopilot. My brain has turned to mush and is probably filled with little people rushing around screeching 'Eeeeeeeeeeeeeeeeeeee' at the thought of kissing Leo, if they haven't all died of embarrassment at the amount of times I've fantasized about this very moment. He's so close that everything else has faded away; there's nothing but him, the scent of citrus, and the leftover spicy tang of the loose tea he was making earlier. My knees threaten to buckle as his warm upper lip brushes against mine, barely a touch, but it's enough to give us both a shock and Leo jumps back, leaving me floundering towards the hedge for support.

'God, I'm so sorry, I don't know what happened there.'

I touch a finger to my lips at the spot where his touched mine, a burning mark that I'm sure must be visibly on fire. 'It's fine, Leo. I wanted …'

This time he pulls the hat off his head, stretches it out and pulls it back on so hard that it nearly covers his eyes. 'I'm sorry,

George. I wanted … I mean, I've been feeling … for you … and you obviously don't … the same …'

He turns around and looks up the street, clearly annoyed with himself. I'm desperate to go over there, slide my hand onto his shoulder, turn him back around to look at me and tell him I think I might be head-over-flipping-heels in love with him.

But it's so, so wrong. I've wheedled my way into his life on a lie, and if he knew the truth, he wouldn't want to kiss me. And letting it happen now would be … a million words fill my mind. False pretences. Entrapment. Taking advantage. Even though I want to tell him that I'd rather kiss him than win the lottery.

'I'm sorry, George, I shouldn't have done that,' he says, not looking me in the eye. 'There's someone else. No. Wait. There's not someone else. I was talking to someone the other night and I thought … I mean, she saved my life, and I … I don't know what I thought. I met someone. No. I didn't meet her. I thought I felt something. There's just …' he sighs, looking completely at a loss for what to say.

I've never been very good at hiding my feelings and it's a hard-fought battle to stop the sting of disappointment showing on my face. I had no idea he was involved with someone.

'I keep looking for her but I think I've got the wrong place. You don't know anyone working next door to you, do you?'

I shake my head … Wait. She saved my life. I didn't meet her. *Next door to me because he thinks I work in the bank.* He couldn't mean *me*, could he?

'I don't know the first thing about her. I only spoke to her on the phone once. She could be married. She could be a very young-sounding 90-year-old. I don't even know her name. I just thought I felt something and I can't kiss someone else while I'm still this messed up.'

This time, never mind showing disappointment, I struggle not to do star jumps on the spot. I *did* feel something during that phone call, and more importantly, he felt it too. It's not just the gargantuan crush I've had on him for the past two years. He felt that connection between us on that one wonderful night too. He just doesn't know that I'm me.

'I need to find her and prove myself right or wrong, either way.'

Oh, Leo. She's standing right in front of you.

'Find her?' I gulp as the sudden realization of what he said hits home.

'I don't know how yet. It seems impossible.'

'Probably is. Best to leave well alone.'

He looks surprised at the abruptness of my answer. 'I don't think I can do that.'

'Well, good luck,' I say in the falsest cheery voice I've ever used, sounding like a hyperactive howler monkey who's snaffled six Terry's Chocolate Oranges and got into the hidden bottle of Christmas sherry.

'Thanks.' He rubs the back of his neck awkwardly. 'I'd best go before I make an even bigger fool of myself. Sorry, George. I'll understand if you don't want to do this anymore. I didn't mean to do that. It won't happen again, I promise.'

That's a shame. 'Don't be daft. Nothing happened. See you tomorrow. And good luck finding your mystery woman,' I call after him as he walks away.

He glances back at me with a strange look, like he's trying to figure something out, before he gives me a wave and pulls his coat higher up around his neck and walks away with his hands in his pockets.

Maybe it's not too bad, I think as I stand at my gate and watch Leo's back until he turns the corner. He's been in the charity shop a couple of times and he hasn't found me yet. I'm sure he'll forget all about it soon enough. Our leaflet doesn't specify that the charity shop is in Oakbarrow, he'll probably think he phoned a different branch and it'll all be fine.

There's nothing to worry about.

Chapter 11

A few days later, Leo and I have been going out every night. We've had Santa admiring a bunch of grapes on the old greengrocer's window, Santa sniffing a bunch of roses on the florist, Santa trying out a new belt for his robe on what was once an independent clothing boutique, and Santa getting his hair trimmed at the hairdresser's. It's not exactly filling the streets, but Leo's given away nearly a hundred candy canes and sold a few extra coffees, Maggie had to make an extra batch of gingerbread reindeers by midday on Monday, and at least one person a day has been stopping to take a selfie in front of the Bedford Falls window.

Neither of us have mentioned the almost-kiss again, and Leo hasn't said another word about his mystery woman. I'm hoping he's given up on finding her and that's the end of it.

Until he walks into the shop on Wednesday morning.

'Oh, Leo!' Mary says suspiciously loudly.

I'm taking off the clothes that haven't sold in the children's section, nowhere near the back room doorway, and I let out a squeak of surprise, looking around desperately for somewhere to hide.

I do the only thing I can think of. I dive into the household rack and drape a curtain over my head. There are a few customers in and a lady examining a bedsheet nearby gives me an odd look.

'Checking the rails for rust,' I whisper.

The rail is a wide circular stand with a rotating chrome wheel where we hang household goods like curtains and duvet covers. It's just about wide enough in the middle to hide behind with a bit of strategic draping. It'll take me hours to fold these sheets up again when Leo leaves.

'Oh, you lovely man,' Mary says as Leo puts a tray of coffees down on the counter in front of her. 'You didn't have to do that again.'

'Ah, I have an ulterior motive this time.' Leo gives her a cheeky smile, the kind that would charm her out of her last Rolo. And Mary *really* loves Rolos. 'I'm wondering if I can wheedle some information out of you.'

'Wheedle away,' Mary says, giving him the kind of bashful smile she used to give the greengrocer.

'Unwanted stalker, is it, love?' the lady asks me. She's obviously noticed that my attention is on something a lot more interesting than rust.

'Something like that,' I mumble. If Leo looks round, he's going to wonder why this poor woman is talking to a curtain.

'Ooh, if you don't want him, point him in my direction. He can come and hide in my bushes any day.'

I stifle a laugh to avoid detection and give her a grateful smile for acting like seeing the staff hiding in a rack of curtains is something you see every day.

Thankfully, she wanders away to browse the bric-a-brac. I love talking to customers but in the middle of the household rack, while the guy you're hiding from is standing a few feet away, is not quite the *ideal* place for it.

'Are you the manager?' Leo asks Mary.

'I might be,' she says slowly, casting her eyes towards the household rack.

I risk a thumbs up. The last thing I need is Leo thinking there's some mysterious manager missing from the shop. Him coming in here is doing nothing for my cardiac health.

'Oh good.' Leo obviously accepts her uncertain answer as an affirmative. 'This is going to sound really strange but do you have a young woman working here, English accent, probably around my age, likes chocolate?'

Mary looks at a loss for what to say.

'She works nights and does something with the mannequins,' he adds, gesturing towards the ones in the window. 'I don't know what but she was getting one out of a cupboard under the stairs.'

'I don't know what you're talking about,' Mary says slowly, her eyes flicking towards me again. 'I'm the manager, there's just me here and some elderly volunteers who sort donations in the back. We're a right gang of old fogies. No one young, and definitely no one who works at night. You must've got your wires crossed.'

'Really?' Leo's shoulders slump and he looks deflated. The smile he had when he went up to the counter is gone. 'I was so sure I was going to find her here. Are there any other branches in the area?'

'It's just us, I'm afraid. The flagship shop and headquarters in Bristol is our nearest branch. Other than that, there's one all the way up in Nottingham, if that helps?'

There we go, that'll solve the problem. He'll think he phoned Nottingham and be done with it. Thanks, Mary.

'How about visiting staff? Anyone who might've been here after hours one night about a week and a half ago?'

I can tell Mary's dying to blurt it all out. Lying is one thing she really disapproves of and if she didn't already have a soft spot for Leo, that cheeky smile when he came in would've cemented one. I just have to hope she hasn't been talking to Casey and cooked up some plan that revealing the truth would result in me getting a date or something. That would be Casey's unceremonious approach.

'There's really no one. We aren't open at night. We're all over seventy and like to be tucked up in bed by nine with our cosy slippers and Horlicks.' She smiles at him. 'Are you *sure* you've got the right place?'

'I thought I had …' He thinks for a moment. 'What if I've got her age wrong? She could've been older than she sounded, or younger maybe?'

He sounds so hopeful and the look on Mary's face speaks volumes about how annoyed she is to have been dragged into my lies. 'I'm sorry, there's no one like that working here. I wish I could help you more than that.'

He nods, looking so heartbroken that I want to leap out of my curtain and into his arms. 'Sorry to have bothered you. Thanks for your time.'

'Thanks for the coffees,' Mary says. 'Sorry I couldn't help you.'

He lingers as he goes to walk away, looking around like the answer is suddenly going to jump out at him from the clothing rails. I shuffle a bit closer to the rail giving me cover. There's a grandpa nearby looking through the children's dressing up clothes and he always wants to chat about his grandkids, and if he spots me in here, my cover will be blown.

Finally, Leo gives Mary a wave and heads for the door. I breathe a sigh of relief and go to start extracting myself, but Mary's got a purposeful look on her face that doesn't bode well.

'Leo, why?' she calls after him.

Bollocks. I wish I could bang my head against the rail. Just let him go. This isn't something he needs to investigate any further.

Sure enough, he does a U-turn and comes back to the counter. 'I spoke to someone the other night. I meant to phone the main One Light helpline but I called the wrong number by mistake.' He picks up a leaflet from the stack on the counter and points to the phone numbers. 'They're close together and it was dark and bucketing down. The leaflet got wet and I was clutching it so hard that I must've rubbed the ink off. I've still got the leaflet but both numbers are unreadable now, so I couldn't try ringing again, but I got my phone bill this morning and it's showing as a local number on there. I Googled it and it's this shop.'

Double bollocks. Many, many bollocks. I hadn't even thought of that. We don't have the privacy servers the helpline has. Of *course* our number would be on his phone bill.

'If this is about your phone bill, you can get in touch with our Head Office, I'm sure they'd be happy to reimburse you.'

He shakes his head and puts the leaflet back neatly on the pile. 'It's nothing to do with money. I don't care about that. I'd pay anything to have that conversation again. It was worth more than money. I just wanted to meet the person I spoke to. To tell her how much it mattered. And I'm never going to find her, am I?'

He's really looking for me. I feel a little shiver of excitement. He *did* feel something too. It really did mean as much to him as it did to me. I wasn't imagining it. It wasn't just wishful thinking. He thinks I'm worth looking for. And then the dread hits me because I've ruined it, haven't I? I can never tell him that I'm the girl on the phone. Even if he accepts that he won't find her and gives up, even if we feel whatever it was we felt when he walked me home the other night again, he'll always wonder who she was, and if he ever finds out the truth then kissing will be the last thing he's interested in with me.

He sounds so dejected and I can tell from Mary's face that she's desperate to make him feel better. 'I honestly think someone's got their wires crossed here. Even if one of our staff had been here at night and answered your call ...' I see the shock appear on her face as she suddenly registers what he's saying. She looks like even her knee replacement wouldn't stop her climbing over the counter and giving him a hug. She swallows and composes herself. 'They would have given you the correct number for the helpline. No one here has the kind of training to answer a call like that. I'm sorry, I don't know what else to tell you. None of us would've taken that phone call.'

I gulp. Mary spends so much time imagining all the ways

people might've died, she's probably got some really inventive ways to kill me up her sleeve.

He looks beyond dejected as he stares over the counter. 'Is that your only phone?'

'Yes,' Mary says, her face not hiding her confusion.

'She told me about it,' he says wistfully.

'She told you about our *phone*?' Mary says in disbelief, glancing at the household rack again.

Bugger. I knew the phone comment would come back to bite me in the backside. Mary's still looking in my direction so I stick a hand out from under a curtain and make an empty-handed gesture. I have no idea why I mentioned the phone either.

'Well, I'm sure there are loads of old phones like this still in use,' she says smoothly. 'Your mystery woman could have been anywhere.'

'I guess so.' He nods, his whole face looking like he's just found out his winning lottery ticket is a forgery. 'Thanks for talking to me, sorry to have wasted your time.'

Mary looks like she might cry. 'Leo?' she says as he walks away. 'If you ever need anything, we're always here.'

'Thanks.' He nods and waves as he goes out the door.

'Bank! Ouch!' I stand up and clonk my head on a coathanger. 'I'll tidy this in a minute!'

Leo's going to expect me to be in the bank when he walks past in approximately three seconds, and after that interrogation, I cannot risk him suspecting anything. I rush out the back, skid into the car park and hammer on the back door of the bank.

'Thanks, Jerry!' I yell as he lets me in and I nearly knock him over in my rush to get to the counters. I punch in the code to the security door between the back offices and cashiers, feeling ridiculously grateful that Jerry trusts me enough to share it with me, and nearly fall over myself as I slam into the counter next to Casey and come to a halt.

Leo walks past at that exact second, peering through the

window. He stops and waves when he sees me, grinning a huge grin that I know he wasn't grinning two seconds ago in One Light. I wave back through the glass screen that separates cashiers from customers, and his smile gets wider as he carries on walking, not seeming to notice that I'm not at a counter of my own or that Casey is staring at me like I've sprouted a second head from my armpit.

'Are you all right, dear?' the customer she's serving asks.

'Fine, thanks,' I pant, bending over to try to get my breath back. It's not far but I don't think I've run that fast since Tesco had Maltesers on offer.

Oh well. At least he's seen me in here. That's the first time someone hasn't had to go and collect me from a 'break'. He won't doubt that I work here now.

'You know, the gym is a lot easier,' Casey says when the customer has gone. 'And you get the added bonus of meeting fit guys there.'

'Did he see you where he was meant to?' Jerry asks, bustling out from the staff area.

'He did, thanks.'

'It's working!' He claps his hands together. 'What a bit of fun. You will invite me to the wedding, won't you?'

I force a smile. 'Of course. And I'll hang onto any hats we get donated in case your wife wants one.'

'Ooh, lovely,' he says, like this is some kind of soap opera.

It doesn't seem as harmless as it seemed at first. It doesn't just feel like I'm telling a little white lie now, it feels like I'm running a full-on con on Leo, and it's only getting worse. The more nights I spend outside in the cold on Oakbarrow High Street with him, the more we talk, the more I like him. The more things feel special with him. But how can anything feel special when he thinks I work somewhere I don't, and I've got everybody I know lying for me? I wish I'd been honest from the start. I should have told him it was me the moment I realized it was him in the coffee shop the next morning. Because this – this lying, pretending, hiding in clothes rails and letting Leo think the person he spoke to is a figment of his imagination – this isn't helping anyone.

When I get back into One Light, the shop floor is empty of customers and Mary's started tidying up the household rail.

'I'll do that.' I shoo her away, surprised when she actually leaves me to it and goes back to the counter.

I pull a pair of curtains off the hanger and throw one over the rail, starting to fold them again one at a time. I'm waiting for the onslaught from Mary, I can feel her eyes burning into the side of my head, but she doesn't say anything. Maybe she didn't figure it out after all …

'Suddenly the missing pages of that book magically glue themselves back into place.' She crosses her arms and when I risk a glance at her, she looks as stern as a headmistress about to suspend me from school. 'Let me guess, he phoned while you were working late thinking he'd got the helpline, and you *didn't* think it might be an idea to enlighten him?'

'I told him it was the wrong number, but he was … not in a good place, Mary. We'd been talking for a while before he realized his mistake, and he felt so bad about it that I didn't want to make it into a big deal and make him feel worse. I tried to give him the right number but I didn't know how to. I didn't want to reinforce how awful he was feeling and risk him doing something stupid.' I yank the folded curtain onto the hanger and start on the other one.

'Why had you been talking for a while? What happened to the standard greeting when we answer the phone? We *have* to say 'One Light charity shop' to avoid any confusion in case this exact thing ever happens.'

'It was eleven o'clock at night and I thought it was a telemarketer. I'd just stubbed my toe and was mid-choke on a fun-size Crunchie, I didn't want to talk about qualifying for a government grant for a new sodding boiler.'

'George, the people who work on the helpline have had months of training to deal with calls like that. You've had none. The extent of your training is a tour of the premises that we all had during our two-week induction. That was four years ago in your case, more than I care to remember in mine. We're not qualified in any way, shape, or form to …'

'We're not qualified to talk?' I snap, regretting it instantly. Mary doesn't deserve snapping at. 'Leo needed someone to listen to him. He's putting on a brave face and being strong for *everyone* in his life, and he fell apart. He didn't need someone with four psychology degrees and months of practice in saying the right thing, he just needed to unload how he was feeling to someone neutral.'

'Someone neutral who has a massive crush on him?'

'I don't –' I stop myself before I deny something that's unequiv-ocally true and yank the second curtain of the pair back onto the hanger, and start on the smooth plastic shower curtain that slid onto the floor while I was hiding. 'I didn't know it was him until the next day. His voice was thick from crying and there was rain pounding and the wind was howling. It was only the next morning when I went to get my latte that I realized.'

'When you first started here, the volunteers always laughed at how much you hated coffee. Now, there hasn't been a day in approximately two and a half years since It's A Wonderful Latte opened that you haven't come down the road with a cup of the stuff …' She sighs and picks up one of the cups Leo delivered. She's left the tray in the back for the volunteers and brought us a cup each out here. 'Admittedly he does make a good coffee.'

I put the shower curtain back onto the hanger and clip the slippery material in place, then pick up a fitted bedsheet that needs refolding about a thousand times a day.

'At least I now understand the constant running next door. If he sees you in here, he'll know who he spoke to, won't he?'

I nod, feeling ashamed that I didn't have the forethought to realize how wrong this would go.

'And you've been helping him ever since because you know what he told you on the phone and he doesn't know you know.'

'If that wasn't the most confusing sentence ever it would be about right.'

'Georgia, if Head Office find out …'

'You're not going to tell them, are you?' My heart suddenly starts pumping harder.

'Of course I'm not. You're like the daughter I never had, George, I'm not going to tell anyone something that's going to get you fired from a job you love and you're brilliant at. But you do know that they'd fire you instantly, don't you?'

'Of course I do.'

'And if your subsequent involvement with him gets out … it doesn't look good. In terms of the actual law, I think that's at least one privacy law you've broken and can be prosecuted for –'

'What if it was your son?' I say quietly. 'What if your son was having a breakdown on a bridge because he'd gone to jump from it and couldn't go through with it? What if he was at absolutely rock bottom and he reached out to someone for help, and that person told him, "Nope, sorry, can't help you, go away"?'

Mary shakes her head sadly. 'You don't have to defend yourself to me. I would've done the same thing. But now all the stuff with the windows … You've worked your way into his life with information that he doesn't know he told you. That's invasion of privacy, George.'

'Then I just have to make sure no one ever finds out.' I slap at the fitted sheet in frustration because the rounded corners make it impossible to fold neatly, grunting as it unfurls into a tangled mess rather than lying flat.

Mary puts her coffee cup down and comes over to take one side from me. 'They won't find out from me.'

I take it for what it is – Mary's own particular brand of acceptance, shown through helping me fold household goods. I know she doesn't approve of what I've done, but she's going to stick by me anyway.

'I can't believe he's suicidal.' Mary says when the household rail is back in order and the shop floor is still empty. 'He always seems so happy. It took me ages to work out what he was talking about when he was in earlier.'

'I don't think he is now,' I say, already worried that I've revealed too much of Leo's private business to Mary. I trust her infinitely, but it still feels like something that was meant to remain confidential. 'But something like that doesn't just go away. He needs support and he's still the guy supporting the rest of his family. He won't open up to them. I want him to know he's got someone to support him too. I know I haven't handled it in the best way, but I would rather break the law and lose my job than see him end up on that bridge again.'

'You're a good girl, George, and he's a lovely man. He's always so friendly and he never stops smiling. It just goes to show that none of us know what people are going through on the inside.'

I give her a sad smile. 'Sometimes the people who smile the widest are the ones who are suffering the most.'

Chapter 12

The bell jingles as I walk into It's A Wonderful Latte a couple of mornings later and stop in surprise. Leo grins at me from behind the counter and I can't help smiling as I covertly point towards a woman sitting at a table. 'A customer,' I mouth to him.

He holds up three fingers. 'My third today,' he whispers, leaning across the counter so I can hear him.

'And Christmas decorations.' I take in the bare tree by the fire that he hasn't got around to decorating yet, coiled garlands beneath the window ledge waiting to go up, hanging icicles around the outside of the cake display, and tangled balls of lights on the floor behind the counter.

He smiles. 'Yeah. Christmas inspiration finally struck and I dragged the boxes up from the basement this morning. I think it was that Santa buying cupcakes I watched you paint on the old bakery last night. Our nights out are inspirational, even though all I do is drink tea and watch you work.'

'That's not true, you do all the carrying and washing off the picture from the night before, and your inventiveness when it comes to Santa doing naughty things is unrivalled. I don't know what I'd do without you.'

He blushes at that and I love how easy it is to make him blush.

'And look.' He pulls his phone from his pocket and holds it out, and I feel a little spark as our fingers touch when I go to pull it closer. 'We've got two hundred likes on last night's photo and I only put it up an hour ago. Not bad considering only seventeen people like our page, and even that's gone up, it was thirteen last week.'

'Onwards and upwards,' I say with a smile. I hadn't realized until now that even I didn't expect the windows to help much. I'd hoped that it might pique the interest of people who walk past every day and maybe attract a few extra customers, but it was mainly a way of staying a part of Leo's life.

'There have been people outside taking pictures and Googling on their phones to find out where the picture is. I nearly didn't serve them on principle because it should be a crime not to recognize one of the most recognizable scenes in cinematic history.' He winks at me. 'But seriously, it's a candy cane and a raffle ticket. It's not worth the trouble.'

'I think it's more about having something to get involved in. Don't forget, everyone who walks down this street regularly has watched it gradually die. This is the most interesting thing that's happened on Oakbarrow High Street for years. It's not about getting a candy cane, it's about getting involved in something.'

'And it's all down to you.'

'No, it's not. It's down to you not giving up.'

'George …' He slides his hand across mine where it's resting on the counter and both our gazes are drawn there as he squeezes my fingers. He goes to say something else but Maggie pops her head round the kitchen door.

'Is that Georgia? I told you to send her in as soon as you saw her.'

I don't miss the curious look she gives our joined hands and Leo pulls his away and fiddles with the ties of his apron instead.

'Mum's made you some of her finest mince pies and you've run out of other flavours to try so I'm making you a mince pie

173

flavour coffee whether you like it or not.' He slides the kitchen door open and gestures for me to come through.

'I knew you were going to get me eventually.'

He lowers his mouth to whisper in my ear as I squeeze past him, and I get the feeling he could move if he wanted, he's just choosing not to. 'If it's that bad, I give you permission to pour it down my neck.'

I raise an eyebrow, staying pressed against him in the doorway for just a bit longer than necessary, enjoying the closeness and the heat from his body, and the cheeky smile on his face that says he knows exactly what he's doing and he's enjoying it too. 'That's an impressive confidence in your products.'

'Yes, it is.' He looks me in the eyes and a grin spreads across his face. 'I also have a change of clothes upstairs, just in case.'

I'm still smiling at him when Maggie pulls me into a bear hug. 'Thanks for all you're doing for the shop. Has Leo told you how many people are "liking" your work online?'

'He was just saying …' I start, because I hadn't even thought of it like that. Other than a few stencilled snowflakes on One Light's window, this is the first time I've handpainted something that's being seen by anyone apart from the times my dad ventures down to the shed where I keep some old canvases. Painting is something I gave up on years ago, after the Paris school palaver and Mum's death, and now I haven't done any for years. Painting Bedford Falls and drawing Santas on shop windows with Leo feels so different to how I used to feel when I sat in front of a canvas that I hadn't even connected the two things. He's so excited about it that he makes me feel excited about painting again, the way he scrolls through the photos he's taken each night as we walk home and shows me the best ones, the way he genuinely seems to love it. I never thought I was much good but he makes me feel like Van Gogh. With both ears.

'Do you do any other painting? I'd love to commission a proper canvas for the shop after Christmas. Bedford Falls again to remind customers of our Christmas window and fit in with our *It's a Wonderful Life* theme?'

'Er, maybe,' I stutter, surprised that she'd want one.

Leo reappears before I can process the idea of painting again or give a proper answer. He sets a purple and silver cup down on the table in front of me and steps back, his hand on the collar of his shirt, pulling it away from his neck and showing a bewitching hint of skin that makes me consider pouring the drink down his neck solely in the hopes that he'd have to take his shirt off in front of me.

Instead, I pick it up and take a careful sip and am immediately hit with the familiar tang of coffee combined with the rounded, buttery flavour of sweet pastry and just a hint of winter fruit. It's the closest thing you can get to Christmas in a cup and the flavours complement each other surprisingly well. It makes me want to go and buy a box of mince pies just to remind myself of why I dislike them, because this is gorgeous.

Leo and Maggie are both watching me expectantly.

'Bleurgh, disgusting,' I say, struggling to keep a straight face, and Leo's smile gradually getting wider is doing nothing to help matters.

'You're a terrible liar,' he says, his eyes twinkling. 'I know it and you know it.'

I really hope there's no hidden meaning to that.

'Go on, there's a sentence in the English language that goes like this, "Thank you, Leo. You were right and I was wrong." You can try it if you like.'

My face is aching from how much he's making me smile. 'All right, I'll give you this one. It's the best of your winter flavours by a long shot.'

'Boom.' Leo mimes his head expanding. 'And you won't doubt me again, and when I get my spring syrups in, you'll trust me on which is the best? Because I've heard rumours of a hot cross bun flavour for Easter …'

'Anything you say, Coffee Master,' I say, not sure if I'm grinning because of how sexily smug he looks or because this is one of the first times Leo's said anything positive about It's A Wonderful Latte still being here after January.

The bell above the door jingles and Leo backs out of the kitchen doorway to serve whoever's come in, leaving me alone with Maggie.

'And these are for you.' She hands me a white cardboard cake box with a red ribbon on top. 'I made them this morning. I promised I'd make you a batch, didn't I? I can't let you go around saying you don't like mince pies without at least trying one of mine.'

I put the box down on the kitchen unit and start undoing the twine tying it, but she stops me. 'I won't embarrass you by making you eat one now and having to pretend to enjoy it if you don't. Take them with you and tell me you enjoyed them tomorrow. I'll never know if you pop them in the nearest bin.'

'I'd love one actually. I missed breakfast and Leo's coffee has convinced me to give mince pies a chance,' I say, both of which are true. The late nights have meant quite a few mornings when I've overslept and had to skip breakfast to get out of the house on time, and this coffee *is* delicious.

The pie I get out of the box is sprinkled with crystallized sugar and has a cutout of a holly leaf on the top. The pastry is flaky and buttery, and the foil case is still warm in my hand.

She watches me as I bite into it carefully, the top cracking and sending pastry flakes fluttering into the empty case.

'Mmm,' I say before I've even tasted it, trying to do a thumbs up with both hands full.

God, this is gorgeous. The fruity, spicy filling with just a hint of cognac, the creamy all-butter pastry and sweetness of the sugar. It's different to the mince pies you buy in the supermarket, and she's right – even if you hated those, you'd enjoy this.

I swallow a mouthful and have a sip of coffee. 'This is amazing,'

I say, trying to paw stray pastry flakes away from my face, convinced I've managed to spread crystallized sugar round to my ears. 'This is the first mince pie I've ever enjoyed. *Now* I see why they're a British tradition.'

'Well, we actually sold some in the shop yesterday so hopefully you won't be the only person to think so.'

'I won't. You and Leo do such beautiful things here, you both deserve more people to find out about them.' I take another mouthful and look away, aware of her watching me.

'You're the first girl he's liked in a really *really* long time,' she says eventually, putting such an emphasis on the 'really' that I wonder if she's been getting tips from Casey on how to describe love lives. 'He talks about you all the time.'

'We've been doing the window stuff together. It's taken over my life too, I spend all day coming up with ideas and other ways we can promote the shop. It's pretty much all I think about too.'

'Not in that way.'

I wish I could believe her, but whatever Leo thinks about me is based on a lie. I look at the kitchen door, willing him to come back just to end this awkward conversation. I wish I could tell her how much I talk about him too, how much of my time is spent thinking about him, wondering where he is, what he's doing, if he's okay. I wish I could tell her how much I wish I hadn't put this thing between us, this lie that will never be overcome.

I swallow hard. 'He's a lovely man. You must be very proud.'

'Evasion by compliment. Very good.'

I go to protest but she holds a wrinkled hand up. 'Georgia, I'm 77. I've seen it all. Trust me when I say he likes you. In *that* way. What you do with that information is up to you, but –'

'So, is my confidence in my mum's baked goods as misplaced as my confidence in my coffee was?' Leo asks, sliding the kitchen door open and leaning in.

'If I answer that, your head's going to be so big that it won't fit through the door.'

He grins. 'I'll take it you're now a mince pie fan then?'

'Oh my God, these are like mince pies with superpowers. And that coffee is just too good. I was saying that you both deserve so many more people to know about this place.'

'You're very sweet, George, and I'm sure your bank colleagues will appreciate them if you're just being kind.'

'Oh, do you work at the bank?' Maggie asks me before I can tell Leo I meant it.

'Er… yes?' I say, wondering what other possible answer there could be. What if she knows I don't? I look around for the nearest exit, wondering if it's quicker to run for the side door or vault onto the unit and make a break for the window.

'Oh, good. What do you think about the forecast from the Bank of England? I've got some savings and my friends are always telling me to invest money in stocks and shares rather than just leave it sitting in an account. Do you think the interest rates will go up like they say?'

I breathe a sigh of relief. Oh good, it's just financial advice.

'Hmm.' I pretend to mull it over like it's a complicated question. Can I get away with asking her to repeat it in English because I didn't understand a word?

Leo and Maggie are both watching me expectantly and I wonder if I've got time to stall them with a quick bathroom trip to text Casey for help.

'Judging by the FTSE index,' I say, using a term I've heard on the news. It's something financial even if I haven't got a clue what it is. 'And the, er, Wall Street wolves…' That was a film, right? 'The deflation isn't going into administration so there won't be any negative equity by the end of the tax year …' There. I must know more financial terms than I think I do. That made perfect sense, right? 'So, er, probably?'

Leo's forehead is screwed up in confusion by the time I've finished and Maggie is looking like she wishes she'd asked a walrus instead – it would probably have given her a more coherent answer.

'Oh, look at the time.' I glance at an imaginary watch. 'I'm going to be late again.'

I gather up the box of mince pies and the coffee, nearly dropping both in my rush to get out of there before someone asks me to explain anything I just said. 'Thanks again for these. They're both gorgeous!' I say as cheerily as a budgerigar on a sugar rush.

'See you tonight,' I chirp as I squash past Leo in the doorway again. It's probably best not to linger this time.

'How about Santa writing a letter on the stationery shop tonight? Can it be –'

'No, it can't be to Mrs Claus telling her he's leaving her for a penguin. Not the animal or the biscuit,' I say, pre-empting Leo's next thought.

He pushes his bottom lip out, grinning. 'Aw, you're no –'

We're cut off by the sound of the bell jingling as someone else comes in. Even though I'm rushing, I can't help nudging Leo in excitement. Another one. That's five customers and it's not even … oh, bugger, it is 9 a.m. now. I'm late *again*.

'Have you seen this?' The man who's just walked in flaps a newspaper towards us as he comes up to the counter.

'No,' Leo says, squishing his way out of the doorway as the man lays the paper open on the counter.

I know I should go because Mary will be waiting in the car park again, but I can't resist the urge to go over and have a peek. Maybe a mince pie will appease Mary?

'The weirdness of Oakbarrow's festive pictures that are bringing its high street back to life.' Leo reads the headline, and I peer over his shoulder to see a huge picture of the front of It's A Wonderful Latte displaying my Bedford Falls picture in all its glory.

'Wow,' I say, looking at the full-page article that's all about us.

'Oh my God, we've made the local paper,' Leo says, smiling so wide I'm sure his jaw must be aching.

'Random pictures are popping up every night and only the local coffee shop seems to know anything about them,' he continues reading, 'although owner Leo Summers remains silent on their origin. When asked, he simply replied, "A little bit of Christmas magic."'

'You didn't tell me you'd had a reporter in,' I say.

'I didn't realize he was. There was a bloke who asked me about the pictures a couple of days ago, but he just ordered a latte and left. I didn't think he was a reporter.' He shakes his head, unable to stop smiling. 'This is fantastic.'

'The best part about these pictures is the sense of nostalgia they bring in their nod to what the now-abandoned shops used to be,' I read out loud from the next part of the article. 'Surely anyone who grew up around these parts remembers popping into the greengrocer's for their bread and milk and whatever bruised fruit was going for 10p a bag. We all remember the pick 'n' mix stand in Woolworths. We remember wandering around Hawthorne's at Christmas with a sense of wonder in our hearts. These pictures remind us of what Oakbarrow once was, and for the first time in many years, walking down Oakbarrow High Street has been a pleasant experience.'

'Wow,' Leo says, still shaking his head in amazement.

'It's very true,' the man who brought the paper says. 'Whoever's doing your artwork has got exactly the right idea about reminding people how great this street used to be.'

Leo's eyes meet mine and his smile somehow manages to get even wider, and I've been smiling for so long that I might need a dentist's help to readjust my jaw. We're just stood here smiling at each other because it's been a fair fifty-fifty project. The artwork might be me but the ideas are mainly Leo's. The inventiveness and fun factor are all him, which is exactly what made It's A Wonderful Latte stand out when it first opened.

'They think it's one of Santa's elves,' the man says. 'My granddaughter said that's what the teachers are saying in school.'

It's not like I could stop smiling anyway, but that makes me smile even wider.

'Which means they're talking about it in schools,' Leo says. 'That's exactly what we were hoping for and more.'

'A lot of people are talking about it,' he says. 'My wife came in from the hairdresser's yesterday and said it was all anyone had talked about. It's made everyone remember what this street used to be like.'

Leo continues reading the article. 'Regardless of who's behind these mysterious paintings, whether it's one of Santa's elves, the ghost of Christmases past, or the Christmas Banksy of Oakbarrow, if you're on the high street this December, look out for one of these fun pictures and be sure to pop into the coffee shop next to the old Hawthorne Toys building for your chance to win a luxury hamper. Even if you don't win, you're at least guaranteed A Wonderful Latte and a timely reminder of one of our best-loved Christmas films.' He lets out a very unmanly squeal that's almost loud enough to rival my seen-a-spider squeal and turns to face me, looking so excited he might burst. 'Oh my God, George!'

Before I know what's happening, he throws his arms around my waist, picking me up and swinging me around as I try not to drop the box of mince pies in my hands or spill my coffee down his neck, despite the possibility of it leading to shirtlessness.

His stubble burns my skin in the best possible way as his lips find my neck and he presses kiss after kiss there. It doesn't mean anything, I tell myself. Just an overexcited display of emotion that he can't fully let out with customers in the shop. His arms squeeze tighter and he swings me around again before setting me back on the floor and pulling away, his eyes on my neck at the spot where he just kissed me, refusing to look any higher and make eye contact.

He shakes himself and turns back to the man at the counter. 'You're the newsagent, aren't you?'

'Yeah. Someone painted a picture of Santa reading a paper on my window last week and people kept phoning and asking if it meant I was coming back to work. I came for a wander down

181

the high street at the weekend and it's so much busier than I remember, and I miss my old shop so much. I thought it couldn't hurt to try opening again.'

'That's fantastic,' Leo says. 'If only we could get a few more like you to come back, this street could be somewhere worth saving again.'

'You can keep that.' The newsagent pats the paper. 'I thought you might like a copy if you hadn't seen it. I'll have a black coffee to go as I'm here. May as well get my first day back at work off to a good start, eh?'

He chortles to himself as Leo starts making his drink. I want to stay and talk about how fantastic this is, maybe find an excuse for another hug, but another customer comes in who will need serving too, and it's now late enough that no amount of mince pies will save me from Mary's wrath.

Leo's facing the coffee machine so I touch his shoulder as I slip past. 'See you later.'

'Hey,' he reaches out and catches my hand, giving it a quick squeeze, 'thanks, George. I'll fetch some apologetic hot chocolates down later for making you late again.'

'You really don't have to,' I say, but the coffee machine finishes off the newsagent's drink with such a loud puff of steam that it drowns me out. Casey, Jerry, and everyone else at the bank deserve much more than a hot chocolate for the nonsense they're letting me get away with, and Leo really doesn't need any more reasons this morning to wonder if I'm not quite as financially astute as someone who works in a bank should be.

Chapter 13

'I can't believe we got in the paper,' Leo says when I go in through the side door that night. 'Mum's bought six copies, she's getting at least four of them framed as Christmas gifts.'

'I took a copy home for my dad and he wants your autograph. I think he was relieved to find out that when I go out in the nights to paint pictures on shop windows that I am actually painting pictures on shop windows. God knows what he thought it was a cover for.'

He laughs. 'I was stalking the newspaper website earlier and the article has been shared a few hundred times. And our post of last night's picture that I showed you this morning has got over a thousand likes now.' His smile is so wide that it makes the room seem lighter than it is.

'Thanks for the hot chocolates you dropped off at the bank earlier,' I say. 'Sorry I managed to miss you again. I particularly liked the "Christmas Banksy of Oakbarrow" you'd written on my cup.'

He grins. 'Well, I was hoping to hand it to you in person, but you were on a break *again*. At least I know why you're okay with late nights now – it's clearly because you do absolutely no work during the day.'

'I do! You just have terrible timing. You must wait for me to disappear and then come in. I'm starting to think you're actively trying to avoid me.' Deflection. That'll throw him off the scent.

He's grinning as he answers. 'Actually, I was really hoping to catch you just so I could squeal about the article some more, but I couldn't stay because we were so busy. Mum had a queue to the door by the time I got back.'

'That's fantastic. I thought it looked busier outside today.'

'Yeah. It's brilliant that the newsagent has reopened, and the light was on in the florist's shop today and someone was inside cleaning. I reckon they're thinking about coming back too. It's been there since 1902, it can't have been an easy decision to close up.'

'This is exactly what we need. More shops so people have got a reason to come here. If enough shops reopened and customers came with them, we could get enough people together to fight the hike in business rates. The council aren't going to listen if there are only four businesses on the street, but if there are twenty-four who are making a profit and bringing people to the area then they can't ignore us.'

'In that case, we'd better go and do another picture for our adoring fans.' He winks at me. 'You fill the bucket, I'll make the tea.'

Leo disappears upstairs and I run hot water into my empty bucket in the kitchen sink to wash off last night's picture of Santa getting a spray tan on the tanning shop, complete with orange skin and tiny white boxer shorts. I wander over to the kitchen table where the newspaper is open on the page of our article and read through it again, even though I've already read it approximately forty times today. People are raving about my artwork, something I never thought would ever happen, and it's all because of Leo and his belief in me. It all feels a bit unreal, and for the first time, like we're actually making a difference here. We really have a chance of making Oakbarrow High Street better.

When Leo comes back, he's got the usual two teas in biode-gradable takeaway cups which he somehow manages to carry in one hand. I go to lift the bucket out of the sink but his fingers close around the handle, the side of his hand pressing against mine, and I feel that familiar spark, the one that makes me want to keep touching him, no matter how miniscule the touch is.

'I'll carry this. You lock up.' He tosses me his keys and I catch the huge, jangly bundle. 'It's the one with the blue cap.'

'Do you have enough?' I shake the heavy mangle of metal, trying to locate one blue-capped key in the muddle of keys. 'You own one coffee shop. Starbucks' bosses wouldn't have this many keys if they had one for all their branches.'

'They were Dad's. He always had them on him. I don't know what they're all for, I just always remember him with this clink-clank of keys in his pocket so I like to keep them on me.' I feel his eyes on me as he speaks. 'Sorry, I know it's stupid, it's just something of his that I like to feel in my pocket. Kind of a reminder that I'm doing the right thing.'

'It's not stupid.' I part the keys in my hand, trying to work out which shade of blue, in the many shades of blue key caps, painted tops, and keyrings, actually locks the coffee shop side door.

'What's *Santa's secret entrance*?' I ask as my fingers fall on a smooth metal key with a handwritten tag attached and a red and green enamel 'H' dangling from it.

'Dunno.' He shrugs. 'Something to do with Hawthorne's?'

'Your dad had a key to Hawthorne's?'

'Makes sense. Like I said, his mate used to let him change into his Santa gear and leave his stuff here, then he'd go out through this alley and into Hawthorne's basement door round the back there.' He points to the end of the alleyway past the bins. 'They always called it Santa's secret entrance. I assume it's the key to that.'

'Do you think it still works?'

He raises an eyebrow. 'Are you saying you want to give it a try?'

I look up at the side of the building towering above us. It's always been a pinnacle of this street. Two storeys taller than any other building and with roof tiles patterned to spell out 'H Toys' at the back, meaning you could always see it from the motorway whenever you drove towards Oakbarrow. When I was little, Mum and Dad would always tell me to look out for Hawthorne's so we'd know we were almost home. It was such an impressive building back then and people used to travel for miles to visit it, and even now, after a decade of disrepair, it's still instantly recognizable.

'You haven't answered but I feel we might need a quick revision on what constitutes breaking and entering,' Leo says.

'But we've got a key,' I say. 'Do you think they'd still have a burglar alarm?'

'Well, the security company they used went out of business years ago, the original owner is dead, and the shop's been abandoned for at least a decade, so I doubt it.' He looks at me with one eyebrow quirked up and one lowered. 'You're serious, aren't you?'

'Wouldn't you love to see what it looks like now?' I say excitedly. 'You're always talking about how much you loved Hawthorne's. It's like the wreck of the Titanic on the ocean floor but with hopefully less barnacles. I can't believe you've had a key all this time and you've never broken in!'

'Some of us like to obey the law. Besides, I didn't know I had a key. I've never paid much attention to what's on there other than the ones I use.' He looks between my face and the keyring in my hands. 'And now you've said it, I've suddenly never wanted anything more in my life.' His face breaks into a huge grin. 'Quick, dump everything in the kitchen and I'll grab a torch.'

* * *

186

'And I thought you were such a good, law-abiding girl, George,' Leo says as he brushes cobwebs away from Hawthorne's basement door and inserts the key into the rusty lock. 'You're a bad influence on me. My mum'll never make you mince pies again if we get arrested for this.'

'Almost persuasive enough to turn back but not quite.'

He glances up and smiles and for one weird moment, his eyes linger on my lips and I think he's going to kiss me, but he quickly looks back down at what he's doing. I must've been imagining it. Those overexcited neck kisses this morning did something to me and now I'm just fantasizing about Leo's mouth at odd times. That must be it.

The door creaks in the silence of the night as he pushes it open inch by inch, like he expects an alarm to start shrieking and laser beams shining across the room. All that happens is we obviously disturb a moth's nest because a series of irate moths come flapping out into the night.

'Not quite the large, angry guard dog you were expecting?'

'Ha ha,' he mutters, pushing the door open fully and peering in.

'Go on.' I give him a gentle shove. 'Stop being frightened of living.'

'What?' He turns to face me and my cheeks heat up instantly. It's too close to what we said on the phone and I should've realized it before the words were out of my mouth.

'I mean, stop being frightened of *anything* living, they're just moths,' I amend, quite pleased with my quick thinking. It's a shame it's not quick enough to make me shut up before I get into these messes in the first place.

He narrows his eyes at me and I'm just about to create a diversion when he speaks. 'Says the girl whose biggest concern about me sleeping on the floor is that spiders could come and get me in the middle of the night.'

'It's not my *main* concern.'

He makes a noncommittal noise as he leans past me to shut the door behind us, leaving us in complete darkness on a small landing area with far too many cobwebs. He flips the torch on and shines it around to get our bearings. We're in a stairwell at the back of the shop, with steps below us heading down to the basement area, and steps above leading up to what I guess is the shop floor.

Leo shines the torch upwards, revealing cobweb bunting strewn between every stair rail and crisscrossing to the wall, and I'm not sure if the cobwebs have collected dust or if we've found several *really* worrying new species of spider.

'Sorry, I've only got one torch.' Leo offers me his arm and I slip my hand through it automatically. 'Stay close so you don't trip over anything.'

I could easily use the torch on my phone, but the heat from his body and the softness of his jumper under my fingertips make me realize that it'll be more enjoyable if I 'forget' my phone light.

'You've been here before,' I say, holding his arm close as he navigates expertly up the stairs.

'Not since my dad was working here. Didn't think I'd ever be here again either. Thanks, law-breaking friend.'

'Oh, come on. It's not exactly the start of an illegal drug smuggling and money laundering ring, is it? It's testing a key we found to see if it works. I'm not about to open my jacket and offer you six kilos of cocaine and a few bottles of poison.'

The smell in the stairwell is cloying with musty dampness and dust that hasn't been disturbed for years, and we leave footprints behind us in whatever the muck on the steps is. The stairs keep going, and I realize this is a secret stairwell hidden away from customers' eyes. It was probably a fire escape once, but stairs zigzag above our heads, joining each floor of the shop to a multitude of storage rooms. No wonder I used to watch staff disappearing out the back to collect orders and think they'd gone to Narnia.

The first sets of wooden and glass double doors that we come to are instantly recognizable as the ones that stretched out behind the checkouts on the first floor. Leo puts his hand on one and pushes, a cloud of dust flying around us as the door creaks, the hinges groaning after so many years of rusty stillness. He steps through and holds it open for me.

'Wow,' he says under his breath, shining the torch around.

We've come out behind the checkout area, one long counter built from brightly-painted giant Tetris blocks with four separate tills stood along it, frozen in time. I can't imagine anywhere in Oakbarrow needing four tills running now, and it's hard to believe that anywhere ever did, and yet I can remember how long the queues here would get, especially at this time of year.

Leo uses his hand to cover the torch beam as we venture further into the shop because we're near the ground floor window and could be seen if anyone happened to walk past.

'It's like a time capsule spanning seven decades,' I say, as I look around at the shelves of forgotten toys. The only thing that hasn't forgotten them is the spiders, who are clearly quite happy in their undisturbed home. 'Also, if they ever make a sequel to *Arachnophobia*, I think we've found the set.'

Leo laughs as he picks up one of the soft toys lining the floor, a floppy-eared stuffed rabbit the size of a 5-year-old, and runs his hand over the handlebar of a child's bike, one of many lined up in a rack, still waiting for an owner. 'Dad bought me my first bike here.'

I step a bit closer to him because there's a wobble in his voice and I have a feeling this shop means more to him than he's letting on. 'Sorry, dark,' I mumble when my shoulder bumps into his back, not because it's dark, but because I get the feeling he needs a bit of human comfort.

He reaches down and takes my hand, locking his fingers between mine and squeezing.

I feel the sense of melancholy too as I look around. Toy shops are meant to be happy, enchanting places, but now, this magical place gives the same dismal feeling inside as you get from standing outside and peering in the window, taking in the lone cobweb-covered teddy sitting in the once-great display among a load of dead flies. This shop is the embodiment of what has happened to every other shop in Oakbarrow. The epitome of what was once loved and popular, something that drew crowds to the area, now left abandoned in time, exactly as it was on the day it shut down, ten years ago.

Near the entrance is a rack of 'try me' vehicles for children to ride around the shiny tiled floor on – scooters for older kids and ride-along ladybirds and ducks for littler ones, their only riders currently of the eight-legged variety. There's a hexagon-shaped cardboard arena for duels between remote controlled cars, the two battlers, now with broken plastic and missing wheels, lying in pools of battery acid leaked from their remotes. There are rows and rows of toys that I remember from my childhood – Tamagotchis, Furbies, action figures of Power Rangers and Teenage Mutant Ninja Turtles, Spirograph boxes, Sylvanian Families, and more Barbie dolls than you can shake a stick at.

'Wow, is that an original Game Boy?' Leo picks up a box and blows dust from it. 'That was one of the best presents I ever got back in the Nineties.'

'Me too.' I peer over his shoulder at the retro box. 'The year Mum and Dad got that for me, I accidentally saw it in a cupboard before Christmas and had to pretend I didn't know what I was getting on Christmas morning.'

'Accidentally, huh?'

'Yes!' I say indignantly.

He grins. 'Oh good, because I always used to go looking. I knew all the hiding places.'

'Your dad was Santa, Leo! That's against the rules for everyone but especially for you.'

'You know what I'm like when it comes to behaving. You

honestly think I was a perfect model child who brought good Christmas mojo on myself?' He waggles his eyebrows. 'Obviously that only started when I was 30. I'm all about good Christmas mojo now.'

We both dissolve into giggles and we're still laughing as we take in more shelves stacked with jigsaws, dolls from every generation dating back to the post-war years, train sets and toy car racing tracks, Scalextric sets, chemistry kits, skipping ropes and frisbees, and there are stands of choose-your-own marbles and rainbow spinning windmills, and the floor is packed with hula hoops leaning against the walls, kites, and gigantic dolls' houses.

Leo is still holding my hand as we go up the open-tread staircase to the second floor, even less modern than downstairs. Up here are the most popular toys of years gone by, from Rubik's Cubes, slinkys, and Space Hoppers to Hornby trains, Matchbox cars, Care Bears, and My Little Ponies.

The main part of the second floor is where Santa's grotto stood. I give Leo's hand a squeeze as we stand and look at the empty space in silence, and he lifts our joined hands and presses them against his chest, curling his fingers tight around mine.

I remember so clearly visiting Santa in his red-painted wooden shed with sheets of cotton-wool snow nailed to the roof. Beside it there was a lifesize empty sleigh pulled by plastic reindeer and a snowy path leading up to the door, lined by giant candy canes and populated by staff dressed as elves who used to manage the queues and take your picture when you sat on Santa's lap.

'Did you spend much time here as a kid?' I ask, my voice sounding like a shout in the silence of the shop.

'Yeah, loads when my dad was working as Santa.' His voice sounds hoarse from the dust and decay in the air. 'Mr Hawthorne, the man who owned it originally was an absolute legend. He was the heart and soul of the place. He opened in 1950 and worked here until he was 93. He's what you and I remember from when we were young. He was the kind of guy who went above and beyond for his customers. He'd often see children crying because they wanted something so badly but their parents couldn't afford it, and he'd slip a little note to the mum or dad saying to come back on Christmas Eve, and there it would be, waiting for them, free of charge just because he wanted to make children happy.'

'He sounds wonderful.'

'He was. He truly loved his job and did it solely because he loved it so much. It's probably a good thing that he died when he did because seeing it like this would've killed him. In those days, it seemed like it would be here forever.'

'So what happened? Someone else took over?'

'A son, I think. Someone who didn't understand that what kept it going for so many years was the personal touch and the absolute love that Hawthorne poured into it. It became all about stacking the shelves with cheap toys for expensive prices, and when the boom of the internet started, they didn't have a hope in hell of competing. They were out of business within a couple of years.'

'You know a lot about this place.'

'This is my childhood,' he says. 'This and the café that was next door. My sister and I used to hang out here after school and in the holidays when Mum got fed up of us under her feet and sent us to see Dad at work for a few hours. Mr Hawthorne gave us free run of the place. He let us play with anything we wanted. He never worried about us damaging anything, he just wanted us to enjoy ourselves,' he continues as we wander further around the floor. 'You only have to look at it now to see how much anyone cared after Mr Hawthorne died. No one's even bothered to clear it out or try selling it for retail value. Some of these things are probably valuable to collectors by now but they're just left here to rot.' He seems genuinely frustrated by it.

'This place was really important to you, wasn't it?'

'Yeah, in a weird way. My sister's older than me so she grew out of toys and wouldn't be seen dead here while I was still playing with Action Man and building every Lego kit I could get my hands on. I felt special here. Mr Hawthorne always asked my opinions on new things he was thinking of stocking. I think when you're a kid, no one really listens to your opinion because you're just a kid, and when someone does make you feel valued, it really sticks with you.'

'I think this place has probably stuck with a lot of people round here. It was a real treat when we got to come in here.'

'Exactly. That's the saddest thing. I genuinely think this place could've lived on. It might not have been able to compete with the internet giants, but I thought there would always be a place for it in Oakbarrow. You see people going retro more and more nowadays. I overhear a lot of talk in the coffee shop because people come here thinking it will still be open and stop in for a cuppa when they discover they've come all this way for nothing. Grandparents bring their screen-raised grandkids to get something they enjoyed when they were little. Parents desperate to break a kid of their iPad addiction. Anyone sick of toy cars that snap in half after three minutes.'

'I see it a lot too,' I say without thinking. 'People are always coming in looking for old toys of their generation. People's faces light up when they see something that reminds them of their childhood.'

His eyebrows knit together as his forehead furrows. 'In the bank?'

Bollocks. 'Where they come to get their money out so they can go to the places that sell these retro toys. Obviously.'

He shakes his head. 'Anyone would think debit cards had never been invented.'

'Oh, well, you know older people are a bit scared of technology, aren't they?' I say, sending up a silent apology for stereotyping an entire generation.

He knows I'm lying. Even in the darkness of the shop, I can almost hear the cogs turning in his mind, trying to work out how someone who works in a bank would see people's faces light up at the sight of retro toys.

'What was that?' I grab his arm like something has scared me. Now is the time to create a diversion. The less he thinks about me and my place of work, the better.

He shines the torch upwards. 'Probably just bats in the roof. Bat poo was definitely one of the many things we've waded through tonight.'

'How comforting,' I mutter.

'Don't worry, scaredy cat, I'll protect you.' The diversion works as he seems to forget all about my job. He slings an arm around my shoulder and squeezes me into his side and I snuggle as close as I can without it getting weird as we take the next set of stairs up to the third floor and come face to face with a wall full of board games. Classic red and white Monopoly boxes, Trivial Pursuit, Scrabble, Operation, Guess Who, Twister, Connect Four, Hungry Hippos, Cluedo, Snakes and Ladders, Buckaroo, Who Wants To Be A Millionaire, and those frustrating Magic Eye pictures that I could never see no matter how hard I tried.

Leo pulls out a Mouse Trap box and wipes dust off it. 'Wow. This was my favourite game when I was little. My friend had it and I never did, and every time I went over to his house, I wanted to play it, but he'd be bored because he'd played it loads.'

'Shall we have a game?'

He looks at me like a red frog has just appeared on my head.

'You know we're both in our thirties, right?'

'Oh, come on. We're in an abandoned toy shop. It would be wrong if we didn't play with something. Besides, you're never too old for a game of Mouse Trap.'

'The box says "six and up".'

'There you go then, we qualify.' I take his arm and pull him across to a soft-carpeted reading area stuffed with bean bags and little chairs, surrounded by shelves of books. I remember many a happy hour reading here, it was the perfect place for parents to leave their kids with the staff while they popped downstairs to buy surprise Christmas presents. The plush deep-red carpet is faded and threadbare now, worn away by customers and, more recently, probably something fun like cockroaches, and the array of books that used to delight are falling from the shelves, damp and stuck together.

Leo brushes off a space on the carpet big enough for both of us and sits on his knees, and I sit down next to him as we open the box and peer at the plastic pieces inside.

'Wow. I remember this like it was yesterday.' He reaches in and pulls out the red basket trap and turns it over in his hand, and a smile immediately breaks across his face. 'You always have such great ideas, George.'

He spreads the board in front of us and gleefully tips the plastic bits out. Neither of us can remember the rules or be bothered to read through the instruction leaflet, and even though you're meant to build the game up as you play, we just set the trap up and start.

We're basically just throwing the dice and moving the number of spaces, chasing each other around the board, shouting 'cheese!' a lot but never remembering to take any of cheese wedges you're supposed to collect, and setting the trap off for the sake of it even though none of our mice are in the cheese wheel space.

The trap was always the best bit anyway. The swinging foot that misses the bucket at least twice and finally connects, sending the little metal ball down the blue path and through the guttering to the pole that drops the other ball into the red bathtub, catapults the green diver upside down into the bowl, and finally brings down the trap. I remember the jerky movement of that basket coming down as one of the most satisfying moments a child ever experiences. As an adult, it's a bit bonkers, but I was never happier than the last day of each term at primary school when everyone would get to bring a board game in and Mouse Trap was always the firm favourite of everyone in the classroom, including the teacher.

Leo's laughing so much he's breathless, and there are tears of joy running down his face. I'm leaning against him, and we've regressed to throwing plastic mice and cardboard cheese at each other, and giggling so much that we're holding each other upright to save overbalancing and rolling around on this ancient carpet.

'Why didn't we realize how mad this game is when we were young?' he says in my ear. 'You basically spend the whole time resetting the trap. My mum always said it was a waste of time and now I'm the same age, I understand why.'

We give up on playing it pretty quickly. We've still got tonight's window to do and we've only made it up to the third floor of Hawthorne's four storeys, and we're not leaving without exploring properly. It's a responsibility of adulthood to explore every nook and cranny of an abandoned toy shop.

'Thanks, George,' he says as we poke all the plastic bits back into the box, set the folded board on top and put it back on the shelf.

'What for?'

'Another wonderful night.' He wipes tears of laughter from his eyes with the back of his hand. 'I've spent so much time in this shop but that was the most fun I've ever had here.'

I grin at him and he grins back and he looks so happy and buoyant and carefree that it's definitely been worth a little breaking and entering, and when I glance in one of the distorted funfair mirrors on the wall as we pass, I look as happy as him. Even with the warped glass making my head look all squiggly, my smile matches his, and I realize that I haven't felt this happy in forever either.

The toys on the fourth floor get even more vintage. It's stacked with old-fashioned boxes from Muffin the Mule marionettes and what must be the very first of the Easy-Bake ovens to James Bond Aston Martin cars and Troll dolls that date all the way back to the Sixties. We poke our heads into one of the rather unimpressive store rooms, so different from the Narnia-esque land of neverending toys that I'd always pictured. Once, they must've been meticulously organized and stacked floor to ceiling, but the shelving has collapsed over the years, and now there's just higgledy-piggledy mountains of unwanted toys that have stayed where they've fallen, buried in dust, their boxes nibbled by mice.

'Toy shops are meant to be magical places,' Leo says. 'They make adults feel like kids again and give kids a chance to enjoy being kids. Seeing it like this is just wrong.'

'I'd love to rescue this place,' I say. 'It'd be a hell of a project, but can you imagine seeing Hawthorne's open again? It would be incredible.'

'Me too.' He suddenly lights up. 'I'd love that. Wow.'

The idea of how amazing it would be to see Hawthorne's restored to its former glory floats into my mind. 'It would be impossible though, right? I mean, we both have jobs, and we have no idea who owns it now, and whoever they are, they clearly don't care about it very much …'

'Christmas is the one time of year to believe in impossible things,' he says, then takes a step back and looks at me in pretend shock. 'All right, what's gone wrong here? We've switched roles. You're meant to be the positive one. Either you've slipped me some of that potion or you're rubbing off on me. And whichever it is,' he takes my hand again, 'I'm enjoying it and I wouldn't mind it continuing.'

Oh, me too, Leo. I squeeze his hand with both of mine. 'I put extra wart of toad into the potion last night.'

He bursts out laughing and his laugh echoes around the shop, making the building seem more alive than it has in many, many years.

* * *

'Thanks for the push into criminality,' Leo says as we get back to the little landing we arrived on. 'It was awesome to see this place again. So much nostalgia.'

197

'A real blast from the past.' I look around, reluctant to end this yet.

'Look.' I nudge him with my elbow and point towards a red door down the next set of steps. It's got a metal label that says 'storage' on it, and underneath someone has stuck a white sticker with 'Christmas' scrawled across it in faded marker pen.

Leo does a sharp intake of breath. 'My father's grotto will be in there.'

I bite my lip and put my hand on his shoulder. 'Do you want to have a look?'

'No,' he snaps instantly. Then he swallows and turns away and I give his shoulder a squeeze. I hadn't realized how difficult coming in here might be for him.

'Sorry,' he mumbles under his breath. 'Yes. More than anything.'

Even after all these years, the first smell that hits me when we open the door is the metallic scent of tinsel. Christmas decorations always have the same scent to them. No matter how long they've been in a box in the attic, they always smell the same as they did when you put them away.

We're below the ground level of the building now and there's no chance of being seen from the outside so Leo pulls the cord hanging by the door, looking surprised when we hear the generator outside stir and the lightbulb flickers into life, still lighting up the room after all these years.

You could say that Christmas has thrown up in here, but that would be an understatement. It looks like someone's scooped the remains of a tinsel factory and a fairy light manufacturing plant into a room and thrown a few plastic reindeer in for good measure. If the North Pole existed, it would have less Christmas stuff than this room.

'Wow,' I say, not knowing where to start. I have no excuse to stay glued to Leo's side now we've got some light so I reluctantly pick my way across the room, sidestepping boxes of plastic snowman parts, jumping over great arches of lights, and waltzing around seven-foot-tall candy canes.

I stop and stare at a sign leaning against one wall. It's bigger than I am, and it reads 'Merry Christmas from Oakbarrow' in between two bells. I recognize it. 'Didn't this used to be up at the end of the high street as you walked out of town, past the church?'

'Yeah,' he replies without looking over.

I pull the sign forward and look at the one behind it. This one says 'Merry Christmas' with Santa in his sleigh being pulled by two reindeer. 'And this one used to be up near Woolworths as you get onto the high street.'

I delve further into the pile and pull out a stack of jingle bell shapes made of rope lights. 'And these are what used to hang from the lampposts. What on earth are they doing here?'

'Mr Hawthorne was responsible for the street decoration.' Leo sounds distracted.

'I thought it was the local council.'

'It was. They maintained it, but he bought the lights and paid for the running of it and stored them for the rest of the year.'

'We're always told that a festive-looking street is good for business. Head Office are always saying that decorating the outside helps business on the inside. Mr Hawthorne must've thought the same,' I say, instantly realizing it was a careless sentence and waiting for the inevitable, 'In a bank?' comment that will surely follow.

Leo's silent.

I've got so excited by the Christmas decorations that I remember from when I was little that I've temporarily forgotten how hard this must be for him, and I look back to see him trailing his fingers through the dust covering a candy-striped arrow sign reading 'North Pole'.

'Are you okay?' I ask softly.

'Mm,' he mumbles, and I get the feeling I could've asked him if he'd seen a giraffe waving from Saturn's rings and his response would've been the same.

I make another path through boxes of baubles as I go back

over to see what he's looking at when he drags a dustsheet off a pile of props: a gigantic sleigh turned upside down, an oversized display book for the naughty and nice list, a postbox for letters to Santa, and neatly wrapped giant presents.

'This was my father's chair,' he says, dropping down into a wooden seat he's just uncovered with a thunk so heavy that it reverberates through the room and reminds me how much weight he's carrying on his shoulders.

'You never told me what happened to your father,' I say, perching carefully on a knee-high resin reindeer next to him.

'Apart from my mum and sister, I've never told anyone what happened to my father.' His fingers rub over the arm of the bright red throne, cherry-coloured wood with curved arms and carved details painted in what was once white but has now faded to a dull magnolia. I remember the chair with Leo's father sitting in it. It was glittered back then and always had tinsel wrapped around the legs, with a dark burgundy velvet seat, shiny gold cushions, and sparkly holly leaves along the back.

I cock my head to the side, wondering what he means. 'What happened to your father?'

'I knew you were going to ask me that.'

'So tell me.' I lean down and try to catch his eyes but he refuses to look at me. 'It might help to talk about it.'

'Don't, Georgia, please.' His voice is low and shaking and he hasn't called me Georgia once since he found out who I was named after. 'I'm hanging on by a thread here and if I talk about it, I'm going to cry …' His voice cracks and he cuts himself off.

The plastic reindeer doesn't move easily so I squeeze it with my legs and try to jump it a bit nearer, in probably the most undignified move I've ever done in front of a man. Or any human in general. 'It's okay to cry, Leo.'

'No, it's not,' he snaps, sounding like he already is.

'Yes, it is. I know you're trying to be strong for your mum and sister but you don't have to do that with me.' I reach over and squeeze his knee. 'Talk to me, please. It's got to be better than bottling everything up inside and pretending you're okay when you're not.'

He finally looks up at me, his normally bright eyes red-rimmed and damp. It feels like he's searching my face for ridicule, like he's expecting me to make fun of him, and I hold his gaze until he sighs and drops his head, his curls flopping forward in defeat.

'We were fishing down by the river. You know, the Barrow that runs along the outer edge of town?' He says it so quietly that I have to lean in to hear him. I remember him saying something about his father dying on the river during the phone call.

'It was late autumn when the salmon are swimming upstream but we were both terrible fishermen and on the rare occasions we caught anything then neither of us would have the heart to kill it so we'd just put it back in the water and let it carry on with its day. We did it quite often but I think it was more an excuse to spend time together, just the two of us, than through any real love of fishing. Anyway, this one day everything was completely normal; we were sharing our flask of tea and eating the cake Mum always packed for us. We were laughing and joking as usual, and suddenly he went completely white, his face contorted in pain, he clutched his chest and fell out of his chair. He was dead before he hit the ground.'

Tears are rolling down his face and my chest is aching with how much I want to hug him but I also know that if I wrap my arms around him, he'll break down and stop talking, and above all else, I want him to keep talking. I settle for squeezing his knee a bit harder.

'I did everything I could. There was no phone signal so I had to leave him and run up the bank to call 999, then run back down. I did CPR, I did all the rescue breaths, everything I could think of, everything the operator was telling me down the phone, the paramedics had to drag me away when they got there, but it was too late.'

So that's what he meant when he said he couldn't save him the other day. 'Do they know what it was?'

'A massive heart attack. So severe that he was gone in seconds. It was just so quick, you know? One minute he was there, and literally thirty seconds later, he was never coming back.'

'God, I'm so sorry,' I say, blinking back tears of my own. 'I can't imagine how terrible that was.'

He shakes his head, his curls quivering with the movement, and I want to reach out and brush them back, stop him hiding his face behind his mass of hair.

'I've never told anyone that before,' he says, his voice sounding wrecked and broken. 'What is it about you? Why is talking to you so easy? You make me feel like I can say anything and it's somehow okay because I'm saying it to you.'

'You *can* say anything,' I say gently, at odds with how hard I'm squeezing his knee. He's going to be lucky if he doesn't need a replacement kneecap by the end of this. 'It's okay not to be okay, Leo. Bloody hell, you watched your father die in front of you. You can't just brush that under the carpet and pretend it didn't happen. You're allowed to have feelings too.'

'You don't understand. My mum and dad spent every day together for fifty years. My mum's life revolved around him and suddenly he was gone. Her life was empty. She stopped cooking because she didn't have anyone to cook for, she stopped cleaning because there was no one to appreciate it. For a long while, she stopped getting out of bed. The only thing that gave her life any meaning again was the idea of buying the coffee shop.' He lets out a sigh so deep that it sounds like he's been holding it in for a very long time. 'And my sister … he was her hero. She didn't cope with it at all. She lashed out, she blamed the doctors, the ambulance crew, the NHS, and mainly, she blamed me.'

'People do that in grief. That doesn't mean it was anyone's fault. It just means that life is unfair and desperately searching for someone to blame is part of coping with the unfairness of it.'

'Yeah, well, neither of them can deal with me falling apart too.'

'I'm sure they'd rather you fall apart than end up doing something stupid because you're trying to ignore your own grief and pretend everything's all right when it isn't.'

'It's better since you came along.' He glances up at me and presses his lips together, his mouth curving up into a sad smile. 'Everything's better since you came along.'

I blush at that, wanting to look away to hide my embarrassment, but determined not to turn away when he's so raw and laid bare, vulnerable in this moment. What I want to do more than anything is tell him how amazing he is, how inspiring it is that someone can go through that and still get up each morning with a smile and a joke for every customer.

All I've wanted to do since the moment I picked up that phone is make his life better – no, not even that. I wanted him to realize that life is wonderful, even when it doesn't seem like it. Above all things, it's always, *always* worth continuing to live.

And then there's the guilt. How much better would he think I made his life if he knew I've been lying to him since the day after the phone call? He's just shared something with me that he's never told anyone before, and I can see from the slump of his shoulders and the tremors going through his hands that it took a lot. How is he going to feel if he ever finds out that I'm not who he thinks I am?

He sniffs and rubs the heels of his hands into his eyes. 'I'm sorry, George. I didn't mean to say any of that –'

He goes to get up but I launch myself at him. Of course, I catch my foot on the leg of the reindeer and tumble into his arms rather than wrap him up in a protective hug, but you can't win 'em all.

'You okay, my lovely?' he murmurs as I struggle to get myself back into an upright position and slip my arms around his waist. A little thrill goes through me when he squishes me against his chest, his whole body closing around me as he hugs me back.

'It's been a while since you called me that,' I say, my red cheeks hidden against his soft jumper.

'Ah, it's just a generic pet name. I call all customers who look like they won't punch me that. There's only one I call George Bailey though, and she's a bit more special than anyone else.'

I giggle nervously and he holds his arm out. 'Here. You should hit me. I deserve to be slapped for how sickeningly sappy that was.'

I reach out and wrap my hand around his wrist instead, pulling it back to where it was resting on my hip so he's cuddling me again.

The movement of my fall has obviously jogged one of the Christmas decorations because a Santa on a shelf suddenly starts dancing and playing a tinny version of 'Auld Lang Syne', and it makes us both jump.

'And it just happens to be the song at the end of *It's a Wonderful Life*,' he whispers against my hair. 'Do you think the universe is trying to tell us something?'

'Mm,' I mumble, snuggling a bit further into his chest.

His breathing has that shuddery hitch you get after a long cry. It takes me right back to the phone call and hearing it down the line then too. If it's humanly possible to want to hug him tighter than I wanted to then, it's now.

He seems happier though. Lighter, somehow. Like sharing that has lifted a weight that even he didn't know he was carrying. And I feel privileged that he's opened up to me. The real me, not a random stranger on the phone, an actual friend. And he doesn't make any attempt to pull away, and it should probably be weirder than it is to just stand here hugging him, but it feels so natural with Leo.

'At least he was with you when he died,' I say after a few long minutes.

'Only you could try to make death into something positive.'

I pull my head back and look up at him with a sad smile.

'Even I can't put a positive spin on that. I just mean that at least he was with you at the end. He was happy, doing something he enjoyed with someone he loved. He could've been on his own doing his tax return or something like that. I know nothing ever makes it better, but …'

'In some ways it could've been worse?' he finishes for me and I nod.

'I'm trying so hard to be him, to run It's A Wonderful Latte as he would've run it, and I'm just … not. I never wanted this for my life and now it is, I feel like I'm failing at every turn.'

'You're not.' I squeeze his side and let my fingers rub his jumper for a minute. 'I promise you, Leo. Speaking as a customer, it makes such a difference to go there every morning and see a lovely face and a friendly smile, to have a two-minute chat with someone who makes the effort to know my name and remember how I like my coffee. That's you being you. It's nothing to do with what your father would've done. That's what's so great about high streets. The personal touch. The chat. The knowledge of your customers. I hate going into these huge busy shops where the cashiers don't even look up as they grunt the total in your general direction. You make people feel valued. Sometimes I go to order something in a coffee shop and I feel like an inconvenience for interrupting the staff chatting with their mates, which they carry on doing instead of answering something I've asked them.'

'So what you're telling me is that you cheat on me with other coffee shops?'

I burst out laughing and give his arm a light slap. 'Ah, it's not two-timing if I only go there to see how crap they are compared to you.'

'So we're a dysfunctional marriage where you have sex with other men to prove to me how good I am at sex?'

Leo and sex and having sex with Leo shouldn't be in the same sentence and my face heats up at the thought, but I can't help the grin spreading across my face when our eyes meet, his dancing with mischief that it's been a while since I've seen.

'And I call you my favourite customer.' He winks at me and pokes at a box of tangled fairy lights with his toe. 'Bit different to the fancy designer decorations at the soulless retail park, huh?'

I look around the basement at the decorations that once graced our high street, their boxes now discoloured beyond recognition and sporting some impressive damp stains, and the unboxed decorations half-covered by threadbare tarpaulin with corners chewed by God only knows what.

'Did you know that Oakbarrow won a best-decorated high street competition in the Eighties?' he says. 'Mr Hawthorne had an old newspaper clipping in a frame behind the counter.'

'Leo, that's it!' I grab his arm excitedly as an idea hits me.

'Do you know how nervous I get every time you say that?'

'Ha ha,' I mutter. 'Do you think it's still there?'

'What, the newspaper clipping?' He shrugs when I nod. 'I don't know. Why? What are you suggesting?'

I grin at him. 'I'm suggesting we break the law again, but properly this time.'

Chapter 14

'I can't believe we're doing this,' Leo calls over as he and my dad navigate a six-foot-tall nutcracker out of Hawthorne's tiny base-ment door, Leo walking backwards with the feet while my dad wraps his hands around the neck like he wants to throttle it. If someone doesn't start saying 'to me, to you' in a minute, it'll be a sign of an impending apocalypse. Quoting the Chuckle Brothers is the law when moving furniture, like shouting 'pivot!' when manoeuvring large items up a staircase. 'I've never been in trouble with the police, ever. I didn't intend to start at this point in my life.'

'You worry too much,' I tell him.

'We're stealing!'

'We're reclaiming. Borrowing, if it makes you feel better.'

'Your daughter has some kind of influence over me,' Leo turns to my dad. 'She makes me tell her all sorts of private things, she hypnotizes me into breaking and entering, and now she's bullied me into becoming a thief.'

My dad laughs. 'There's this little word called "no" …'

Leo looks over at me and grins, nearly losing his footing on a broken bit of concrete. 'Where would be the fun in that?'

'This is a good idea,' I protest, shivering at the sudden warmth that floods me at the affectionate look in his eyes. 'It's all just sitting there. It was for the street once, why shouldn't it be used for the street again?'

'Because the street itself hasn't broken into a building to nick it. No one's going to prise up its paving slabs and chuck them in prison. Us, on the other hand ...'

'You have customers now. We should give them a nice street to be on. Give them a reason to stay and shop at the other shops here. Do you know the old greengrocer? He popped in today to tell Mary he was thinking of coming back now the supermarket has gone. She hadn't seen him for a few years. Apparently he's got even more gorgeous in his retirement.'

'Mary?' Leo's ears visibly prick up. 'Doesn't Mary work at the –'

Bollocks. 'Mary. One of my colleagues at the bank. Very common name. That's right, isn't it, Case?' I raise my voice so she can hear me from the kitchen. 'The greengrocer popped into the bank to tell our colleague Mary that he was thinking of reopening with a skeleton stock next week to see how it goes, didn't he?'

'Sure.' Casey appears in the kitchen doorway, pushing thick blonde hair back. She points at the giant nutcracker. 'That was on the corner before Hawthorne's with a sign round its neck directing people in.'

'Anything else?' I ask.

'It's bloody difficult on this crappy old newspaper.' She waves around the frame of aged print that Leo and I rescued from the floor behind the counter of the toy shop where it had fallen down. 'It's too yellowed to make out anything except the big things.'

'I might be able to help seeing as I was the one who decorated most of it in the first place, even though it was a fair few decades ago now,' Dad says.

'It doesn't have to be exactly the same,' I say. 'I just thought it would be nice to make it as nostalgic as possible. From the very beginning of this, we've wanted to remind people of what these boarded-up old shops used to be. What better way than to decorate it as close as possible to how people remember it? We've got this amazing old picture of a prize-winning high street that Mr Hawthorne preserved all these years, we may as well try to follow it as closely as possible.'

'With the exact same crappy old decorations that look like they belong exactly where they came from – the Eighties. Except we get them with thirty years' worth of extra mould. Yay.' Casey pokes her tongue out at me. 'I don't know how you talked me into this.'

'Free coffee.' I stick my tongue out back at her. 'And because if we don't do something, this is probably going to be the last Christmas that any of us spend on this high street.'

'Yeah, because we'll all be in bloody prison.' Leo relieves my dad of the nutcracker and stands it up on the pavement, walking it one side at a time to where the alleyway joins the street.

'Still all clear,' Bernard calls from his position as lookout at the corner by the bank, a good spot because it gives a view right down to the churchyard and right the way up past Hawthorne's towards the old Woolworths and the start of the high street, just to be extra careful that we don't get caught.

Maybe Leo's got a point about prison after all.

'A nicely decorated street boosts morale,' I say when he comes back, panting from the effort, the slight sheen of sweat making him look even sexier than usual. 'It makes customers happy and it makes shop owners feel like the council cares about them.'

'They don't,' he interjects helpfully.

'No, but *we* do.' I sigh because Leo's being so negative about this since we discovered the old decorations. Even Casey is more positive than him and she's about as positive as Victor Meldrew having a bad day. 'You can't look out at Oakbarrow High Street now and pretend that anyone cares about it, can you? The closest thing we get to renovation is an estate agent popping out to replace a "for sale" sign that's aged so much it's now illegible. We need to remind people that there's still a high street here, because quite honestly, it's easy to miss, and since the windows thing took off, more and more people are walking down the street. We have to do something to make them want to stay. The windows have given us momentum, but it's up to us to keep pushing forward. No one else is going to help us.'

Leo sighs and inclines his head towards Hawthorne's door. 'Come and help me test some of these lights then. I bet all the bulbs are dead by now.'

* * *

'See?' I say, standing on a ladder outside the old chemist, Leo the same on the other side as we stretch a rope light banner of snowflakes across the road between us. 'What was it you said the other day? About a sentence in the English language that goes, "You were right, I was wrong"? You can give it a try if you like.'

He tries to frown at me but he's laughing too much and I smile at the sight of him looking so happy and getting involved in the decorating. All the fixtures and fittings for the decorations are still in place, albeit with a tad more rust than they had last time these lights went up, but they're all still strong and sturdy.

Leo gets off his ladder quicker than I get off mine, and as I climb down carefully, he's waiting at the bottom and holding his hand out to help me down. His hand stays on the small of my back as we stand on the pavement and look around, admiring everyone's handiwork. Each defunct streetlight has a hanging light-up bell attached to it, the posts are wrapped in a spiral of sparkling red and green tinsel and Casey is down by Aubergine, finishing each one off with a huge velour bow. Bernard is attaching a wreath of holly and mistletoe to every door, and my dad is using his old council privileges to wire our Christmas lights into the lampposts to power them.

'It looks amazing,' Leo says quietly. 'I can't believe they all came to help us. Even your dad. I bet he's not usually outside putting up Christmas decorations at eleven o'clock on a December night.'

'In all fairness, he's not usually putting them up on a July night either, that'd be far too early.'

'Ha ha,' he says. 'You know what I mean. It's late and it's cold and all three of them have come out to help anyway. Even your friend who hates Christmas.'

I laugh because Casey must have told us her feelings towards Christmas approximately 45,879 times tonight and I'm glad I'm not the only one who's noticed. 'She might hate Christmas but she doesn't hate the free drinks you're making for everyone.'

'Least I can do.'

'I know you're worried,' I say, squeezing the hand he inexplicably hasn't let go of yet.

'Just afraid of getting caught. The last thing I need is to be arrested, and I know we're doing it for the greater good, but there's no two ways around it – we've stolen these and we're undoubtedly breaching health and safety laws to put them up, and it's my key we've used. If there're any repercussions from this, it'll be on me.' He glances at me. 'Maybe I should just man up and stop being frightened of being alive.'

I freeze on the spot. It's exactly what we said on the phone. Is he testing me? Does he know? Or is he just sharing the same feelings with me as he shared with a stranger in a telephone call? 'Oh look, we've forgotten to put these hanging snowflakes up. I'll get on that immediately.'

I fold my ladder, hoist it under my arm, and hurry off down the pavement, hoping that's the end of that conversation. I want to talk to him so badly – when he said that on the phone, it genuinely was like someone had put into words how I've been feeling for years, but I can't have the same conversation as the real me to the real him because then there will be no hiding.

* * *

'It's a bit of a mess, isn't it?' Casey looks up at me from the bottom of the ladder, where I'm trying to wrangle a column of dangling snowflakes onto a bracket on the side of The Bum.

'You can say that again,' I mutter. 'It's a matter of time before he realizes who I am.'

'What?'

I glance down at her with a roll of thick red ribbon in her hand and look around to make sure no one's in earshot. 'Me. Leo. The bank.'

'Oh. Well, I'm sure he'll laugh when he finds out. It's just a little white lie.' She looks up the road to where Leo's untangling a row of reindeer to go up between the old pet shop and the newsagent.

'You know, I thought he was going to be a right stuck up prat who wouldn't be seen dead with someone who handles second-hand clothes for a living, but he actually seems very nice. Very *you*, despite the fact that your love life is so dire that the statue on the war memorial outside the church looks like a reasonable date prospect at the moment.' She points up the street towards Leo again. 'He's the kind of guy you'd date anyway. I can't for the life of me work out why you started this whole bank nonsense. Not the George Bailey connection, was it?'

I can't tell her. It's not the same as discussing it with Mary after Leo had basically told her himself. Casey doesn't know anything about the phone call and it's not my place to share more of Leo's private life than I have already.

'A moment of madness,' I say, because really, what else was it? Who tells someone they work somewhere they don't? Particularly when that person works on the same street and is likely to see them every single day?

She nods like this is a completely reasonable explanation. 'Well, the guy did name his coffee shop after your favourite film. I get similarly overexcited when I meet a hot guy with a six pack and no wedding ring.'

'Men can take wedding rings off, you know. Or can have long-term partners and babies without actually being married …'

She shrugs. 'If a guy wants to sleep with me, that's up to him. I'd rather shag a married guy than end up actually falling in love with someone and lying about where I work and getting into more of a tangle than you've got into with those bloody snow-flakes. Come here.'

'I'm not in love with him.' I step a few rungs down the ladder and hold the snowflakes out while Casey tries to untangle them from the bottom up.

'Well, you clearly have feelings for him. Ugly, messy feelings. And he clearly has ugly, messy feelings for you too.'

I go to protest but she interrupts me.

'He hasn't taken his eyes off you all night. And no one puts that much effort into a name on a coffee cup unless they want the recipient to notice them. And do you honestly think I didn't notice how long he kept his hand on your back when he helped you off that ladder earlier? Any man trying the chivalry thing with me would've had a boot to the bollocks.'

'It's sweet. *He's* sweet. I just wish it wasn't such a mess.'

She nods sagely. 'When I said it was a mess earlier, I meant the Christmas decorations, but it's nice to see what your mind is fixated on.'

'The Christmas decorations aren't a mess,' I say, choosing to ignore the last part of that sentence. Of course I'm fixated on it. I've thought of nothing but Leo since the moment I put that phone down.

Leo calls down the street before she has a chance to respond. 'Your dad's ready to switch on!'

Casey and I dump the snowflakes in a pile and make our way up towards the bank where Leo and Bernard are waiting at a spot that gives us a good view in either direction. We've tested the lights to make sure they all work, but this is the moment we find out if my dad has managed to get the wires for the biggest lights

213

connected to the council's outdoor generator like he used to.

'Three … two … one …' My dad shouts from somewhere behind Hawthorne's and Bernard starts doing a drumroll.

Lights all along the street ping into life, flickering a bit at first and settling down after a few seconds, filling the darkness with the multicoloured twinkling of Christmas cheer.

'Wow,' Leo utters from behind me, stepping a bit closer so his coat brushes against my back.

'It looks just like I remember it,' my dad says as he comes to join us, looking surprised when he sees that it actually worked.

'Me too,' Bernard says, sounding a bit emotional, and Leo reaches out to give his shoulder a squeeze.

It's not perfect, I know that. It doesn't exactly match the old picture because some of the decorations hadn't survived their decades of storage and rodent attackers, but it's the best Oakbarrow High Street has looked in a long time.

'It's just like I remember it when I was young,' Leo says.

'I reiterate, it's a mess,' Casey says, making us all groan.

'It's not a mess, it's festive. I don't think Christmas should be about designer colour schemes and what's on trend this year. It's meant to be a multicoloured, chaotic accumulation of all the decorations that mean something to a family, even if they clash. We all have little family traditions because Christmas is about remembering the Christmases that came before it. It doesn't matter if the retail park has got twenty-thousand twinkling lights in blue and gold. Our strength is in people's memories. We need to appeal to people like us who remember it when it was thriving.'

'She's right.' Leo is still standing behind me and he steps almost imperceptibly closer. 'I've been talking to a lot of customers who've come back lately and you'd be surprised by the number who've said how sad they've been to see it fall into disrepair and how nice it is to see someone doing something about it.'

I feel his warmth behind me, standing so close now that my

shoulder is pressing into his chest, his breath stirring my hair as he speaks.

'Every family has daft little things they do every Christmas because it reminds them of years gone by. My family always used to walk down Oakbarrow High Street on Christmas Eve and say Merry Christmas to all the shops. It's been a long time since we did it, and not all members of the family are still with us, but my stomach is full of butterflies at the thought that I can walk my mum home this year under these lights that we remember so well.'

His voice is shakier than usual and without thinking, I reach back until my fingers find his hand and give it a quick touch, but as I go to let go, he holds on, sliding his fingers between mine and squeezing.

'Even if this is the last year that Oakbarrow High Street exists as we know it, even if all the chatter and social media coverage disappears after there are no more Christmas windows, at least we've done something to make this year special.'

Bernard pats him on the shoulder in return, raising an unkempt grey eyebrow when he spots our joined hands. Thankfully, he keeps quiet about it but I quickly disentangle my fingers from Leo's. Casey would have kittens if she caught me holding hands with a guy. Not even kittens. She'd be so surprised that she'd spontaneously give birth to a litter of alpacas or something.

'Are you positive all this stuff is safe?' Leo asks my dad. 'It's all well and good making the street look pretty but it's not so great if we're going to electrocute the shoppers.'

Dad smiles at him. 'Like I said, I used to be an electrician. I can make sure it's safe but now I'm retired, I no longer have the accreditation to give out any official certificates. Safe and officially certified safe are two different things.'

I had no idea my dad was such a rule breaker. I thought he'd go mad when I told him about breaking into Hawthorne's and finding the old decs, but he offered to help wire them up before I'd had a chance to ask him.

'No one will know it was us who found them and put them up anyway. As far as anyone's concerned, it's a Christmas elf who comes in the night, just like the windows,' I say. 'We know they're safe, that's what matters.'

Leo's gaze levels with mine. 'It's a good job I trust you as much as I do.'

I gulp.

The church bell starts chiming for midnight and I turn to look down the high street towards the only working streetlamp near the churchyard.

'Every time a bell rings …' Dad says. No matter where we are, he still says it whenever we hear a bell chime to remind us of Mum and her favourite film.

Leo's eyes meet mine again. 'Bells have been doing that a lot lately …'

'Well, it is bloody Christmas,' Casey mutters, completely missing the softness in his voice and the shy smile as he ducks his head and looks at the pavement.

'What about a tree?' Dad asks. 'It's not Christmas in Oakbarrow without a tree, decorated by yours truly, of course.'

'Considering how many years it's been since *yours truly* retired and was fit enough to hop up and down ladders, decorated with *help*,' I say.

'We've got this far, we may as well do it properly,' Bernard adds. 'We haven't had a tree for a couple of years now, and do you remember the last time we did? It wasn't even a pine tree, it was a dead birch that had fallen down in the November storms, and they strung it with one string of battery-operated fairy lights and when the batteries went after three days, no one replaced them.'

'The old tree stand is still in Hawthorne's basement,' Dad says, and I'm still surprised by how much he's getting involved in this. 'We should get a tree and have a proper switch on, like we used to. Do you remember how all the shops stayed open, The Bum served hot mulled wine, and the café had all sorts of mince pies and stollen bites and mini puds laid out on tables for everyone to share? There were party poppers and crackers for the children, Santa did meet-and-greets, Hawthorne's speakers pumped Christmas carols out of their windows until the Salvation Army band arrived to play for us. It was the best night of the year.'

'We should do that again,' Bernard says. 'Get a tree and throw a big party on the day we light it up. You want to remind people of how our street used to be? There's no better way than that. We go all out. Invite everyone. You've made this much effort. If it's worth doing then it's worth *doing*.'

'It's only just over a week 'til Christmas,' I say, even though the idea has got my heart racing. I've often heard about the light switch-ons in Oakbarrow. They were almost a thing of the past when I was young, but they were even bigger in Mum and Dad's day. Every time we walked by the Christmas tree outside the church, Mum would mention them fondly.

'If we invite people, everyone will know it's us,' Leo says.

'Anonymous invites,' Dad says. 'Stack of them on your counter, stack of them in the shop, stack of them in the bank.' He points to Leo, then me, then Casey in turn.

'I'll take them around to the other shops,' Bernard says. 'If anyone does ask questions, I'll just say a stranger asked me to do it. I haven't got anything to lose.'

'Where are we going to get a tree of that size this close to Christmas?' Leo asks, surprising me again with his eagerness.

My dad thinks for a minute. 'You busy on Sunday?'

Leo shakes his head.

'There you go then. Georgia's not either. The pair of you can take my car because it's got a sturdy roof rack. There's a tree farm on the other side of Gloucester where the council always used to get their trees. They grow them onsite so they're unlikely to be out of stock, and it's only about an hour's drive each way.'

'Thanks, Dad,' I mutter. Is Casey right about my love life being so dire that even my pensioner dad is now playing matchmaker? You know things are bad when your father is setting up dates for you.

Casey gives him an approving look.

Not that going to get a tree with Leo is a date, of course.

Leo looks at me with both eyebrows raised and his eyes glinting with mischief and I can't help smiling again.

There are probably worse people to be stuck in a car for a couple of hours with.

Chapter 15

'What's that for?' I ask when Leo knocks on the door bright and early on Sunday morning, holding a tray of coffees in one hand and a potted Christmas rose in the other. The nervous tabby cat who never usually comes this close to the house is rubbing around his legs, and he's sporting sparkly tinsel reindeer antlers on his head.

'That's to say the florist has re-opened, the newsagent has sold out of his Sunday papers, I had a customer banging on my door asking if I was open this morning, and the people who used to run that little handmade gift shop are cleaning up to open tomorrow.' He grins. 'And good morning, and I'm sorry if these have gone cold in the time it's taken me to walk here.'

'That's a very talkative rose.'

'Decaf for your dad.' Leo hands me the tray of coffees he's carrying. 'He said he was watching his caffeine intake because of his heart.'

I smile at him, touched that he remembered such a small detail from a quick remark my dad made while we were decorating the other night. 'Thank you,' I say instead of anything else I want to say to him. 'Come in a minute – just going to grab a coat and check if Dad needs anything before we go.'

Leo's sitting on the sofa, deep in conversation with my dad by the time I get back from finding the rose a home on the kitchen window ledge and putting on an extra slick of mascara, as ordered by Casey in the endless texts she sent me last night. Wear a mini-skirt, straighten your hair, don't just hide it in a ponytail like you usually do, shave your legs. The mascara is the only one I've obeyed. Who *really* shaves their legs in December?

'George, why didn't you tell me what good coffee this man makes?' Dad asks, sipping from the cup Leo brought. 'I'd have toddled down there myself yonks ago. It's impossible to find a good decaf in the supermarkets. All my friends from the Old Codgers Club say the same. I'll send them in your direction, Leo.'

'Tell 'em to say you sent them and I'll chuck in a mince pie for free,' Leo says. 'We're always open, even on Sundays now.'

'You're not open today?' I say in surprise.

'Well, I opened the doors for that customer this morning and then another one followed, and another. I doubt we'll be very busy but it's not worth missing out on trade. I think people have come to see the lights. I took a picture last night and scanned in Hawthorne's old print and posted them side by side on Facebook, and the response was insane.'

'Oh, you don't have to come with me then –'

'Yes, he does,' Dad interjects.

He's clearly been taking lessons from Casey.

'But that means your mum's running the place on her own.'

'George, don't worry about it, I hesitated this morning and my mum physically pushed me out the door. My niece has come in to help for the day, and they're both under strict instructions to call me if they need to.'

'I might pop down myself later for another one of these.' Dad raises his cup and slurps from it again. 'I bet your mum remembers the old tree lighting ceremonies; it would be good to have a natter and see if she remembers anything I'm forgetting.'

'I was telling her all about what you'd said and she got so

excited, said it had been years since anyone had known what she was talking about when she mentioned the old tree and the ceremony that went into lighting it up. She'd love to talk to you.'

'There we go, that'll get me out of the house for a bit. Now you can stop worrying that I'll be here on my own all day, George.'

'Be careful. There might be ice patches. And wrap up warm.'

'Only if you stop fussing over me, take this gorgeous man and be gone before we're all still sitting here next April.'

Leo's cheeks have turned so adorably red that I don't even give my dad the reminder of his age that he usually gets when he tells me to stop fussing over him as he shoos us out the door.

'You worry about him too much, you know that, don't you?' Leo asks as we get in the car.

'Says you who worries yourself sick about your mum still working at her age.'

His forehead creases in confusion. 'When have I told you that?'

'Subtext,' I say quickly, focusing on starting up and pulling out of the street with the same concentration I'd need if a driving examiner was sitting next to me.

'You're not wrong.' He gives a slow nod of acceptance. 'Isn't your dad usually on his own all day when you're at work?'

'He has a carer come in for a couple of hours every weekday, and I run home at lunchtime to check on him. And a bus comes twice a week to take him to the community centre where he sits drinking tea with his elderly friends. They call it the Old Codgers Club and they talk about who's died this week.'

'I didn't realize he was that unwell. He seemed fine the other night.'

'It's easy to seem fine on the surface when you're suffering underneath.'

'I know that,' Leo says, developing a sudden interest in his cuticles.

'Maybe it's more …' I glance at Leo and then quickly back at the road, glad I've got driving as an excuse. I force myself to be

221

brave and say it. 'He's had a few scares with his heart. And I think they've scared me more than they've scared him.'

'I get it, believe me.' He reaches over and brushes the back of his fingers against my arm until my muscles, taut on the steering wheel, relax a bit. 'Losing my dad made me afraid of everything, and now I'm scared of being so scared that I forget to live my own life.'

Just like he did on the phone that night, he puts thoughts I've always been too scared to voice into words, and it's probably a good thing that driving is preventing me from dragging him into a hug and confessing everything, because I've never known anyone who understands me like he does, and he deserves better than this lie.

I swallow hard. 'I've always regretted not going to Paris. I pretend that I don't, but I do. And I could go there any time, I could get a couple of weeks off work and it's only a train ride or a short flight away, but I've never done it.'

'Why?'

It's such a simple question, but one that no one has ever asked me before. I don't think I know how to answer him but the words come out of my mouth before I've even thought about them. 'Because it's scarier than staying here. Everything's safe here. I know what to expect. I'd love to go to so many places but I'm not brave enough.'

I expect him to tell me to stop being so stupid, like anyone else would, but he reaches over and touches my arm again. 'I'm scared of losing the coffee shop because I don't know what I'd do afterwards. Like I said, I've never had a career, I've just moved from job to job doing whatever I could. I'm 37, I should have my life sorted by now. My sister's a hairdresser, her husband's a solicitor who's worked his way up since he started and now he will become a partner in the firm before he's 50. I feel like I'm still seventeen and figuring out what I want to do with my life. The coffee shop's been a convenient distraction but coming close to losing it has made me realize that everyone else seems to know what they're doing and have their lives completely together, and I just … don't.'

'You don't need to compare yourself to other people. To me, you're doing pretty damn well.' I glance at him and he ducks his head. 'You didn't give up, Leo. Many people would have.'

'See, that's the thing. *You* didn't give up. I did. I nearly …' he trails off, shaking his head.

Was he about to tell me about that night on the bridge? What the heck am I going to do if he does? Pretend that I don't know?

'And then you came along and brought me back to life,' he says instead of whatever he started to say. 'You're the one who didn't give up on the coffee shop. You're the one who pushed me into doing something rather than just sitting back and waiting for the county court judgements and the bailiffs to come. And I know that it's not safe yet. This level of custom is great, but after Christmas, it's going to tail off, and who knows if the other shops will disappear again, especially when they get a look at their new business rates, and Oakbarrow High Street will be back to square one, and …'

'There are things we can do. Other marketing gimmicks, more social media, we've got Valentine's Day, Mother's Day, and Easter not far off, and there's a way to fight the council if there are enough traders objecting to the business rates, and with more people back in the area …'

I look over at him when he doesn't respond. 'What?'

'Can we talk about something else? We're going to get a Christmas tree and I feel like I'm sucking all the joy out of Christmas. It should be more fun than this.'

It would be too sappy to say I'm just enjoying his company, right? I give myself a shake. 'Are you seriously playing cupid between your mum and my dad?'

'No! Well, maybe friendship cupid. My mum's still too attached to my father for anything like that, but they're the same generation, why shouldn't they be friends?' He puts on a baby voice. 'And if our parents are *fwiends* then you can come over to my house for tea and we can have playdates and sleepovers together.'

'Ha ha,' I say, thinking a sleepover with Leo shouldn't sound so appealing. It's probably wrong for something so innocent to bring to mind such steamy thoughts.

'I'm just embarrassing myself now, aren't I? There's only one thing for this.' He fumbles around in the pocket of his coat and eventually pulls out a CD, waving it around victoriously. 'Christmas music!'

I grin at his excitement. Leo loves Christmas music. He's got it playing in the shop from early November and usually starts some sort of countdown mid-October until the Christmas songs are back.

'I know you love it because I always see you singing along under your breath when you walk in.'

'I do.' I blush because he wasn't supposed to notice that. 'One of my favourite memories is being in the supermarket once and "A Wombling Merry Christmas" came on, and I was singing under my breath and there was an elderly woman looking at the marma-lade and she was singing along under her breath and we both looked at each other and had a jolly good sing along to *The Wombles* in the jam aisle. What other time of year would that be acceptable?'

'See? This is why I love Christmas.' He wiggles an antler with his fingers and the bells on the tip jingle. 'Christmas makes everything cool. Flashing neon lights? Cool in December. Glitter on everything? Cool in December. Tinsel recreations of animal body parts attached to your person? Cool in December.'

'I'm starting to wish I'd put my snowflake earrings and snowman deeley boppers on now.'

'You can borrow my antlers if you want?' I go to answer but he starts giggling. 'See, only in December is that a perfectly normal question. You'd probably be arrested for asking someone if they wanted to borrow your antlers the rest of the year. You'd at least get some weird looks.'

'You can keep your antlers. I've got my own collection of Christmas earrings.'

'I know, I always notice you wearing them to work near Christmas. I like the Christmas trees with the flashing star on top best.'

I blush, surprised that he pays that much attention to my festive jewellery choices. I've always thought I was just another customer to Leo, another face in the crowd of people he makes conversation with every day, but somehow he remembers a pair of earrings that I haven't worn since last year.

'You want to know an embarrassing secret? I've got a Christmas tie too. It's got Santa and some ho ho ho's on it, and when you press the bottom ho it starts flashing and playing Jingle Bells.'

'And there was me thinking that tinsel reindeer antlers were the height of your sophistication.'

He grins as he fiddles with the CD player and it whirrs into life, the first piano notes of 'Fairytale of New York' ping through the car, and Leo turns it up and immediately starts singing along with Shane MacGowan.

I clutch the steering wheel tighter because it's just wrong for a grown man in sparkly reindeer antlers to be so adorable and I'm smiling so widely at him that it's starting to hurt.

'Nearly time for your bit,' Leo shouts when there's a break in the music.

'I'm not singing! I have the voice of a dying hyena, that's why I only sing under my breath in supermarkets!'

'I sound like a reindeer with a flatulence problem, as you can tell!' he shouts back over the music. 'But Christmas songs are made to be sung along to and this is a duet! You can't leave me hanging!'

'The only time I sing aloud is when I'm hoovering and Dad's taken his hearing aids out!'

'You can't sound worse than me. Quick, your bit's starting!'

'Argh!' I shout because his grin is so big and he looks so care-free that I can't say no. As Kirsty MacColl starts singing, I throw caution to the wind and join in, crooning about rivers of gold.

Leo lets out a whoop and victory punches the roof of the car as we both shout along at the tops of our voices, probably scaring a few other drivers on the road. Our caterwauling is definitely loud enough to be heard from the International Space Station.

'Fairytale of New York' is one of those Christmas songs that you love but can't help getting a bit fed up with after you've heard it approximately six thousand times in the first three days of December, but singing it – if you could call it that – with Leo has made it suddenly become my favourite Christmas song.

'I can't believe I found someone with a voice as bad as mine,' he says, sounding hoarse when the song ends.

'I can't believe you got me to sing in front of you!'

'It only makes me like you more. If you had the voice of an opera singer, I'd feel all inadequate and rubbish, but I'm not embarrassed to be myself around you now. We can sing together in harmony.'

'I don't think the noise we were making could ever be classi-fied as harmony. Or singing.'

'Merry Christmas Everybody' by Slade starts up and I groan.

'I *hate* this song,' I shout at him over Noddy Holder's wailing. 'This is my most hated Christmas song!'

'Mine too!' he shouts back. 'That's what makes it so great! Everyone hates it but we play it every year constantly. I think all DJs are on some kind of mission to systematically make more people despise it every year.'

Despite that, we both start singing loudly when the chorus comes on. Maybe that's part of the joy of Christmas songs. We hear too much of them every year, but there's enough of a gap between one year and the next that we never get completely sick of them.

'Well, a couple of weeks ago, I wasn't feeling the Christmas spirit at all,' Leo says when the next song comes on. 'But it doesn't get much more festive than this – going to get a tree with Paul McCartney warbling about war in the background.'

'Oi! This is "Pipes of Peace", it's one of the most underrated Christmas songs.'

He holds his hands up. 'If you like it, that's good enough for me.'

He hums along and I sing, not even caring that we're not duetting this time, this is the kind of song you can't help but sing along to.

Gladly, Shakin' Stevens comes on next and we both go back to singing at the tops of our voices. Shaky's followed by Mariah Carey and we even tackle the warbling bits of the 'O Come All Ye Faithful' duet she sang with her mum. We're both giggling as we look at each other, despite the fact that it'll be a miracle if the windscreen glass doesn't start to split from the screechiness. Never mind sounding like strangled cats, if there were any cats around to hear us, they'd have started strangling themselves just to get away from our attempt at singing.

I bite my bottom lip as I look over at him because my mum always used to say that if you can attempt Mariah's warbling with someone, you know you've found a keeper.

We're both in fits of giggles by the time we turn off the motorway, and I've got tears of laughter blurring the road as we drive alongside fields of greenery, standing out in the countryside because everything else is brown at this time of year. It's the first time in forever that I've let myself go in front of someone. I used to sing while I painted if no one was home, but I can't remember the last time I did. I glance at Leo and he's looking unreservedly happy, smiling wide. Usually you can tell that he's self-conscious of his teeth, but I suppose you can't really be self-conscious of anything once you've attempted to reach Mariah Carey's high notes with someone.

'I can't remember the last time I felt this happy,' Leo says, once again putting into words exactly what I'm thinking.

'Me neither,' I say. He deserves that bit of honesty at least. I've never really thought about how happy or unhappy I am, but since I started spending time with Leo, I realize I've been happy. Happier than I can ever remember being before.

'We make a good team, don't we?'

I nod as the satnav directs us to take the next right, thinking about the pictures we've painted on windows and how creative he is with his ideas. I couldn't have done any of it without him. 'I think we do,' I say as the handpainted sign for a Christmas tree farm comes into view and satnav tells us we've reached our destination.

* * *

'I had no idea this place was here,' Leo says, as we stand in a yard area near the car park, waiting for a man to come back with our tree. Apparently my dad called ahead to tell them we were coming and exactly what type of tree we'd need, and they remembered him from his days of collecting the Oakbarrow Christmas tree, so were all too happy to find us the perfect one.

The smell of pine needles fills the air and the ground under-foot is damp and covered in soggy leaves leftover from autumn. It's peaceful here, despite the fact we're not far from the main road. The fields of trees surrounding us dull the sound of passing cars, and all we can hear is birds chirping and a radio playing 'Little Drummer Boy' coming from a trailer selling hot drinks and roasted chestnuts.

'Ooh, hot chocolate.' Leo grabs my hand and drags me towards the kiosk, which is stacked with paper cups and emanating the most gorgeous smell as well as Bing and Bowie's peaceful duet.

We're both wearing gloves and I wish we weren't. His fleece-covered fingers stay curled around mine until he orders two hot chocolates and fishes his wallet out to pay.

There's a display of Christmas hats next to the hot chocolate stand, from plain Santa hats, headbands with Christmas trees on top, to striped elf hats with ears and those ones with mistletoe dangling from the tip. Leo wanders over and examines them while we wait for our drinks. He holds up another pair of reindeer antlers, these ones with poinsettias along the headband and colourful bells hanging from every tip.

The woman at the stand pushes two hot chocolates towards me and when I turn back around, Leo is buying those antlers too.

'You've got a real thing for festive headwear, haven't you?' I say, waiting for him with a cup of hot chocolate in each hand.

He holds the bag out to me. 'For you.'

'Me? Why?'

He leans down so one of his own reindeer antlers taps against my hair, the bells on the tip jingling as he moves. 'So I'm not the only one who looks like an idiot in public.'

I grin. 'You don't look like an idiot.'

'I know. I look like a *complete* idiot, right?'

'In the best way possible,' I say, smiling wide so he knows I'm joking. I absolutely love that he's not afraid to throw himself into the season wholeheartedly. Casey wouldn't be caught dead wearing anything festive, and even Mary moans on Christmas jumper day, but Leo embraces it, just like me.

I couldn't stop myself putting them on if I wanted to. I make him take the cups as I pull them out of the bag and slip them onto my head, the fingers of my gloves instantly covered in glitter. 'Thank you.'

'You're welcome, my lovely. They suit you.'

I love that he chose them. Of all the festive headgear on that stand, they're exactly the ones I would've chosen myself, in all their glittery, jingly glory. He always seems to know what I'll like. It's a talent when it comes to making coffee, but it clearly stretches further than caffeine.

We stand under a tree sipping our hot chocolate. 'It's not as good as yours.'

He grins like he's trying not to be as proud as he is. 'Well, in all fairness, I've got a shop. She's got a towed trailer in the middle of the wilderness.'

'You can just take a compliment, you know.'

He leans to the side until our antlers clash and make both our bells jingle. 'Thank you for thinking this watery cup of pale dishwater is not as good as mine. This is an affront to hot chocolate, this is.'

'I was trying to be polite.'

'An affront to hot chocolate *is* polite. There's plenty of worse things I could call it.'

We smile at each other over our terrible cups of hot chocolate.

'What are we going to do about this Santa thing then?' Leo says. 'Your dad was saying they always had a Santa for children to meet at these tree lighting parties, and we've got all the props, we've just got no Santa.'

'I was thinking … what if we ask Bernard?'

He snorts.

'Why not? He'd be great at it.'

'How do I put this nicely? He's not the most … fragrant of gents, is he? I mean, I love the guy, he's great, but you don't want to stand downwind of him.'

'We could make him have a bath first.'

'I can't. I shower under a hosepipe balancing on the toilet rim.'

'He can come home with me – my dad won't mind. You can too, if you want.'

'Are you telling me I smell?'

I laugh because he does smell – absolutely delicious. His after-shave is cinnamon and wood, and the smell of roasting coffee and chai spice clings to his clothes, and whenever I'm with him, I always want to step a bit nearer because he smells so good. 'I still hate the idea of you alone in the shop. You're welcome to stay on our sofa.'

I expect him to refuse instantly, but he swallows another mouthful of the horrible hot chocolate. 'Thank you,' he says, his voice barely above a whisper as he disguises the shudder – hopefully from the hot chocolate and not the idea of staying with me.

He doesn't say anything else or give any hint that he's considering it.

'I'll tell you what you can help me with … I still haven't got a present for Izzy. What does a cool uncle get his 16-year-old niece for Christmas that makes him still be considered a cool uncle despite the fact he wears reindeer antlers in public?'

I can't help giggling at him because he's so painfully endearing sometimes. 'Gift voucher for whichever online music service she uses, one of those make your own phone case kits, and a selection box.'

'A selection box?' His face scrunches up. 'Don't you grow out of them at 7?'

I gasp in indignation. 'It is a truth universally acknowledged that all chocolate tastes better if it comes from a selection box. And it's better when you're an adult too. When you're a kid and you get a selection box, you've got your mum saying you can only have one bar before breakfast and telling you you'll spoil your lunch, but when you're an adult, you can eat the whole thing *for* breakfast and no one can tell you not to.' I clear my throat. 'I mean, not that I've ever done that or anything …'

'I'm going to have to test this theory.' He bumps his arm against mine. 'And thanks, I hadn't thought of any of those things. I was just going down the unimaginative cash route. You're really good at this.'

'You'd be surprised how often I get asked if I've got any gift ideas for people.'

'In the ban –'

'Yes, in the bank. People think about it when they're drawing money out, don't they?' I say swiftly, taking a sip of disgusting hot chocolate to save having to answer any more awkward questions.

* * *

'Mistletoe,' the tree guy says when he comes back, his arms around a Christmas tree in a net bag. He points upwards. 'Bad luck not to.'

Not to what? Kiss? I glance up at the tree we're standing under. I hadn't even realized there was a bunch of mistletoe hanging from it.

'I think we've had enough bad luck to last a lifetime lately. I don't think we can risk angering the mistletoe gods.' Leo grins at me. 'What d'ya say, George? Think we should obey the laws of Christmas?'

The smile that spreads across my face is obscenely wide. 'I think we probably should.'

I was hoping for a proper kiss, but he bends down and kisses my cheek, just a bit nearer to my mouth than could be classed as a friendly kiss, making me feel as jingly as the bells on both our antler headbands. I close my eyes as his lips curve into a smile against my skin and he lingers for much longer than a peck could reasonably last. It's a sweet, gentle kiss, and so *Leo* that it feels more intimate than a full-on snog would have.

When he pulls back, my cheek is burning like a glowing brand where his lips touched. He's smooth-shaven today – it's the first time in a while that Leo hasn't had scruff, and all I want to do is cup his cheek and sort of rub my face against his.

But that would be weird.

He's beaming when I look up at him. 'You didn't kiss me.'

'What?'

'I only kissed you. I think we both have to pay our dues to the mistletoe gods or we'll still get bad luck.'

He looks to the bloke with the tree for confirmation who does a shrug that quickly turns into a nod when he catches sight of the look on Leo's face.

I blush bright red even though the thought of kissing Leo again is not an unwelcome one. It's just that the kind of kiss I'd like to share with Leo is not the kind that can be done under a sprig of mistletoe while a bloke with a Christmas tree watches on.

'Oh, go on then.' I push myself up on my tiptoes and aim for the vague direction of his mouth, purposefully missing and getting a patch halfway up his chin that's bumpy with the first hint of stubble coming back. I do a big 'mwah' sound when my lips make contact, and Leo laughs as I pull away, wrapping his arms around me and pulling me against him in a hug.

'There, that wasn't so bad, was it?' he whispers against my ear.

I look up at him and grin. 'You're the one who directed us to this tree. I think you knew that mistletoe was there.'

'I didn't think you'd mind.'

'I don't.' I smile at him and he smiles at me until the bloke with the Christmas tree clears his throat.

'Well, there you go, you've both calmed the mistletoe gods and now you can be sure that your Christmas will go off without a hitch,' he says.

'We've got to get it there first,' I say to Leo as we watch two burly men trying to strap the tree to my dad's roof rack. 'Have you seen the beginning of *National Lampoon's Christmas Vacation* where the tree's too big and they can't see to drive home?'

'Best Christmas film ever, apart from *It's a Wonderful Life*, of course.'

I grin at him because agreeing on Christmas films is another thing we have in common. 'Well, it's a good thing we both love it because I think we're about to re-enact it.'

'Maybe we should offer a better sacrificial kiss to the mistletoe gods?' He waggles his eyebrows.

'I would not be opposed to that.' I grin as he leans down to kiss me again.

Chapter 16

'Is Leo okay?' I ask as the bell tinkles above the door when I walk into It's A Wonderful Latte on Monday morning and see Maggie behind the counter. My heart is instantly in my throat and my mind goes to all the things that could've happened to him. He's *always* here in the mornings.

Maybe the Mariah warbling really did scare him off?

Maggie's greeting is cut off and her smile goes from welcoming to troubled. 'Of course, lovey. The invitations for Saturday are done and he's just popped out to collect them from the printers before the morning rush starts. Isn't it wonderful to be throwing around words like "morning rush"? A few weeks back, it seemed unlikely we'd ever have a rush again, morning or otherwise.'

I breathe a sigh of relief, and I can hear Leo's voice in my head telling me I worry too much, but I can't help it sometimes.

'I can make you a coffee if you're in a hurry,' she says. 'Or have you got time to wait for him? He knew you'd be in and he didn't want to miss you. I'm sure he won't be long.'

'I can wait,' I say, not bothering to glance at my watch. I've been leaving home earlier than usual in the past few weeks just to make sure I had a bit of time to spend with Leo without leaving

Mary to freeze outside for too long. 'It would be … weird … not to see him in the morning.' I struggle to think of the right word. Other than Sundays when One Light is shut, I can barely remember the last time my day started without seeing Leo.

I can sense Maggie's eyes on me and I get the feeling she's trying to read me. I look around instead, hoping to ward off any awkward conversation. Fairy lights are twinkling along the garland at the base of the window, the fire is roaring away in the hearth and there's a customer sitting in front of it leaning over a laptop. The green artificial tree Leo's put up in the corner is strung with white tinsel, glittering fairy lights, and an array of red baubles. Instead of an angel, there's a Santa hat on top, a fitting tribute to his father.

'Yes, I've lost track of how long you've been coming in here. Every day for, oh, it's got to be a couple of years now, hasn't it?'

I blush that even his mum is hinting at how big my crush is. 'I really like coffee.'

'He likes you too,' she says with a knowing smile as I wander over to the cake display unit near the till.

'You've been busy this morning,' I say, attempting a quick subject change and nodding to the selection of muffins, cakes, and biscuits laid out under glass. It's not the first time she's said it, but it never gets any less awkward.

'I've been hoping to catch you alone, actually.'

Please be financial advice. Please be financial advice. I'm nowhere near as out of my depth with financial advice as I am with Leo.

'And the fact that your first question this morning was "Is Leo okay?" and not "Where's Leo?" speaks volumes.'

'Oh, that's just me, I worry too much. Ask Leo, he'll tell you.' I wave a nonchalant hand, wondering if she'd prefer to talk about premium bonds and credit ratings.

'You confirmed my fear that he's not okay.'

'He is,' I say, torn between wanting to protect her in the way

235

Leo does and wanting someone else to know how bad things have been for him. 'I think. He's better than he was, anyway.'

'Since he started spending time with you.' I go to protest but she stops me. 'I'm glad he met you. He won't ever admit it but he needs help and he seems to have accepted it from you, whereas with me, he's always trying to be strong and invincible so he can look after me.'

'But you help him too. You bring him meals every day and you're always working here even though I'm sure you'd rather be at home with your feet up.'

'I feel close to my husband here. At home, I'd be sat there all day staring at his empty armchair. It feels better to be here. He had his regular table in the corner by the window and I forbade Leo from ever moving it. He used to sit there and watch the world go by and he was truly happy in those moments.'

I think of the smiling old man I remember sitting in that corner, always eager to help anyone with anything. I remember people asking him for directions, and he was always the first to jump up and help people with heavy shopping bags or awkward pushchairs.

'He'd love Oakbarrow coming back to life like this. He'd be incredibly proud of what you two have done here.'

'I loved Oakbarrow as it was too. I can't take credit for any of this, it's Leo's creativity and your inventive use of social media that's brought people in. I just wave a paintbrush around.'

'It's been nice to see Leo getting involved in something. He hates this town. He's always wanted to get away. My husband left the money to buy this place, but Leo never wanted to stay here. I was happy to divide the money between my two children and let them use it for whatever they wanted to make their own lives better. It often felt that buying this place would be like clinging onto the past. When someone dies, I think the best way you can honour them is by continuing to live, but that doesn't always mean living the life they wanted for you.'

'He blames himself, doesn't he?' I take a deep breath and exhale slowly. I feel a bit guilty for talking about Leo behind his back, but his mum is never going to tell me any of this stuff in front of him, and the lure of getting to the bottom of the depths I see in his eyes is just too much.

'He's told you what happened.' It's a statement, not a question. 'I didn't think he'd ever told anyone what happened.'

She doesn't hide the look of surprise on her face and it makes me feel warm inside that he really does trust me enough to open up to me. This is what I wanted from the moment I realized who had been on the other end of that phone. I wanted Leo to know he had someone he could talk to rather than keeping everything bottled up inside. It also makes the pong of betrayal a bit stinkier. I don't think Leo trusts many people in his life, but he *trusts* me, and I've been lying to him all along.

'I think …' Maggie continues, talking slowly and carefully, considering what she's saying before she speaks, 'he's tied himself here as some form of penance. I doubt even he sees it like that, but he did blame himself entirely, and I think living the life his dad wanted is the next best thing he could do for him. He couldn't save him but he could do what he never got the chance to.'

'But he does love this place. It might not be what he had planned but he loves experimenting with coffee and talking to customers and all the nostalgia and memories he's got here, and he's been amazing with the windows …'

'I think he likes Oakbarrow a lot more since he got to know you,' she says, still considering each word. 'But this wasn't his choice; it was just one of those hands that life deals you that leave you stuck between a rock, a hard place, and another rock. Leo didn't want to run a coffee shop but he felt he owed it to me, Becky, and the memory of his father. I saw him at the hospital. I'd never seen Leo in such a state and I never will again. He was covered in mud from where he'd scrambled up the river bank to get a phone signal. His jeans were ripped and bloodied where he'd torn his leg on something and he hadn't even noticed. He'd broken a bone in his hand and didn't realize it until two days later when we went to collect my husband's things and a doctor noticed how swollen it was and sent him for an x-ray. He'd done *everything* humanly possible to do, and I think he feels that it wasn't enough. Docs told us there was nothing that could've been done. It was a heart attack, sometimes these things just happen, there's no warning, no way to prevent it, but …'

'Sometimes that's not enough,' I say, thinking about my own mother's battle with cancer and my dad's heart scares, the few things Leo has said over the past few weeks about his guilt, and just that general 'what if I could've done more' feeling we all get when something bad happens.

I bite my lip so hard that I taste blood and screw my toes up inside my shoes to give me something to focus on as opposed to bursting into tears in the middle of the shop while Maggie is sharing her worries with me. The thought of Leo being so broken makes me want to hug him until the end of time, and I still find it so hard to imagine the sunny, happy guy I knew before, ever going through something like that.

'None of that means he's not happy here now,' I say after I'm sure my voice isn't going to crack. 'No matter how the hand was dealt, he does love this place, not just because his father loved it.'

'Oh, I know. He's willing to give up everything to save it.' She fixes me with a steely look. 'And yes, I know he's living here. I know he's in trouble, Georgia. I know the business is failing and I know he sold his house to try to keep it afloat, and I know you already know all this, and I'd appreciate it if you didn't tell him I know.'

'How do you know I know?' I ask, stupidly. There are far too many 'knows' to keep up with.

'Because of your complete lack of surprise, and because you know about his dad. Apart from the very first moments when I arrived at the hospital, Leo has never spoken about that day again.

If he's told you that, he's told you everything. And I'm glad he has. Keeping that sort of thing inside damages a person.'

Oh, you have no idea, I think, wondering how much else she knows. Mothers know everything. You can't hide things from a mum, mine was exactly the same. I just wish I'd appreciated it more in my teenage years.

'I don't know if all these customers will carry on coming after Christmas. I don't know if the traders coming back will really bring Oakbarrow back to life in the long run, if the council will drop our business rates again or if we'll carry on earning enough to pay the new rates, but when Leo finally plucks up the courage to admit how bad things are, I have the means to help. My husband and I had some savings and I'm not going to let this place go without a fight, especially when *you've* fought so hard to save it. Do you mind me asking why?'

I start the age-old excuse of how much I like coffee and how I don't know where I'd get my fix if It's A Wonderful Latte wasn't here but she stops me.

'Bearing in mind that I already know what you're going to say because I know where you work, Georgia.'

'At the …'

'Where you *really* work. I've admired your windows for years and I went in when you had an autumn display up about a year and a half ago and I asked the lady at the till who painted the leaves and squirrels and if they were available for hire, and she told me that your Head Office liked your windows to have something different and would never stand for their manager – Georgia – painting other windows in the street.'

I have a well-rehearsed list of excuses for this situation. It's a common name, Mary is old and might have got confused. Apparently other people's senility is my number one excuse for everything lately. Isn't there someone called Georgina working nearby, that must be who she means. I used to work there but I moved next door … All the excuses suddenly seem pointless. She knows the truth and there's no getting around it, and as she stands there and blinks watery eyes, steel grey in colour hinting at the strength behind them, I don't want to lie to her. I take a deep breath. 'You've known all along?'

She nods. 'I'm not going to tell him. I think there's a very good reason that you haven't told him. I also think there's a very good reason that one day, about two and a half weeks ago, you started trying to save our shop.'

I get the feeling that she already knows what happened – if not exactly then she's certainly got a good idea – and lying would be futile. 'It wasn't the shop I was trying to save.' My voice breaks on the last word and my nose starts burning.

She blinks back tears of her own and gives me a nod of understanding.

'He's helped me too,' I say quickly. 'He's made me believe in myself. He's made my life exciting again. He's reminded me of how much I love Oakbarrow and this time of year.'

'And I think you've reminded him of what a wonderful life we all truly have, because I know he forgot that for a long while.'

* * *

'Usually the sight of my two favourite ladies would make a guy happy, but my ears are suddenly feeling very warm. One could say they were on fire,' Leo says, the bell jingling as he comes in.

The urge to hug him is too strong to ignore. I cross the shop, slide my arms around his shoulders and drag him down into a bear hug.

He hugs me back without hesitation, his arms encircling me, the bag he's holding bumping against my back. 'You okay?' he whispers.

'Mm,' I mumble, holding him a bit tighter, constantly surprised at how thoughtful he is. He's the kind of guy who, if I had

240

answered no to that question, would drop everything and make me sit and tell him what was wrong.

I don't let go until another customer tries to push the door open and I realize we're blocking the doorway.

'What was that for?' Leo asks after we've shuffled over to the side and he pulls back to look at me. 'And if my ears weren't already burning, they are now. Have you been crying?'

'No,' I lie as Maggie makes the new customer a drink in the background. 'Just a late night, as you know, because I was with you painting Santa buying reindeer food on the old pet shop window.'

'It wasn't that late. I had you home feeding cats by eleven. We were both knackered after unloading that mammoth tree.'

'Must be a pine needle allergy then,' I lie again.

He raises an eyebrow. 'Thank you for yesterday. I had the best time, even though I'll probably have pine needles embedded in my skin until at least July.'

'You bought me a Christmas rose, a reindeer antler headband, and the worst hot chocolate known to mankind, and you're thanking *me*?'

'You sang along to "Fairytale of New York" with me,' he says with a shrug. 'Fair's fair.'

I shake my head fondly.

'Look, I got the invitations printed out at the old stationery shop.' He rustles around in the bag he's holding and shoves a stack of them into my hand, looking like a kid who's just opened his first Christmas present. 'Aren't they fantastic?'

'They look amazing.' I run my fingers over the glossy postcards. Casey has done a fantastic job of putting them together, using a copy of Mr Hawthorne's old photo framed by my trees from the Bedford Falls window, with the words 'Let's take Oakbarrow back in time' across the top, and underneath inviting everyone to come and watch the Christmas tree switch on, where there'll be hot drinks from Leo, hot mulled wine from the manager at The Bum who's still got his premises license and is opening up again for the night, Santa in his sleigh for the kids, and late-night shopping for any last-minute Christmas essentials.

Maggie holds her hand out for one when the customer leaves. 'Just like things used to be,' she says, sounding nostalgic as she stares down at the invitation.

'And do you want the fantastic news or the fantastic news?'

'Either as long as it's fantastic,' I say, laughing at the brightness in his blue eyes.

'The market's coming back. All Christmas stalls open on Saturday and Sunday morning, and from January, they've got the space weekly again for the craft market on Saturdays and the farmer's market on Sundays.'

'For real?' I say in surprise. 'When you say fantastic news, you really mean fantastic news, don't you?'

'Wow,' Maggie says. 'That market was probably the biggest loss for Oakbarrow. It brought so many people into town every weekend. I worked there myself when I was younger and needed extra cash.'

'I sold a couple of paintings there when I first left college,' I say.

'You should do that again,' he says. 'You're more than good enough.'

I blush even though it's a nice thought. It's something I never thought I'd do again but painting the windows, and Leo's constant encouragement and belief in me has made me think about getting out an easel and a blank canvas again. 'Our customers always got so excited about it. It was known for miles and had a massive following in the online crafter community. Do you know how they got the space back?'

'According to the bloke in the stationery shop, the council were willing to negotiate on the new rent price due to what they bring to the area. If the council are willing to negotiate at all, it's got to be a good thing. Maybe we won't always be stuck with such ridiculous business rates.'

Maggie looks like she's going to cry again as she looks across the counter at us both. 'I think you two might've done it, you know. The market coming back might be the one thing that saves Oakbarrow. Losing it was definitely the final blow for this town. I'm so proud of you two,' she says, looking like she might simultaneously burst and pinch our cheeks.

'It was all George,' Leo says.

'It was all Leo,' I say at the same time and we both start laughing.

'Maybe you just make a very good team,' she says.

'That's not the first time I've heard that,' he says, making me giggle at the memory of the tree lot yesterday.

'Well, your dad decorated the tree and your dad was Santa,' Maggie says to us both. 'You were definitely meant to meet. Maybe there is a bit of Christmas magic in the air this year after all.'

Chapter 17

'Where did all these people come from?' Casey asks as we walk down Oakbarrow High Street at 6 p.m. on Saturday evening.

She's wearing a skirt that's way too short for this time of year with slim, golden tanned legs that go on for a mile and make me feel like I'm walking about on a pair of tree trunks. Her arm is hooked through mine because heels that high and any lingering patches of ice that Bernard might not have caught when he salted the road earlier don't mix. My jeans, trainers, thick-knit cowl-neck jumper and coat make me feel like a festive frump next to my blonde bombshell friend, who screwed her nose up in dismay when she realized she'd have to be seen in public with me wearing the reindeer antlers that Leo bought me and the Christmas tree earrings he mentioned liking.

'Maggie put the invitation on their Facebook page,' I say. 'I'm not sure if people are following because of the windows or because she's a lovable pensioner learning new technology for the first time, but she posted her first selfie with yesterday's picture of Santa getting his nails done on the nail bar and got more likes in an hour than I've ever had on all my posts combined. And I post cat pictures – everyone loves cat pictures.'

'I don't. You could post pictures of hot naked men instead.'

I do a comedy shudder. 'No thanks, I prefer cats.'

'*Who* doesn't like hot naked men?' Casey sounds so incredulous that I might as well have told her I don't like chocolate. 'Besides, I know you like one not-very-hot man who you'd like to see naked.'

'Leo's hot.'

'Eh, Leo was hot but now he's my best friend's boyfriend. I can no longer make any judgements on his hotness.'

'Trust me, Leo is *not* my boyfriend and he never will be at the rate I'm going.'

'What do you mean? He's got it bad for you.'

I shake my head. 'I can't keep this up much longer, Case. Even his mum knows I work at One Light. It's a matter of time until he finds out, and then what?'

'Buy him a drink up The Bum and have a laugh about it?' She looks at me and sighs when I don't laugh. 'I don't know what it is you're not telling me that makes this such a big deal but I assume there *is* something that you can't tell me, so just strip off in front of him and offer him your body. Stop making sex more complicated than it is.'

'That doesn't actually work, does it?'

She shrugs. 'Depends on the guy.'

She doesn't sound as nonchalant as usual when she says it and I glance at her but her gaze remains stubbornly on the road ahead.

'Not every guy would break your heart if you offered someone more than your body,' I say quietly.

'Been there, done that, got several of my ex-fiancé's T-shirts that I now wear for bed. Some slightly torn after I cut them up.' She glances at me and looks away quickly. 'Maybe one day I'll be like you and want love with all the hearts and flowers, but for now, I like using men the way a man used me. I like turning heads as I walk past. I like sex and lots of it – the amount I missed out on when I was engaged because my fiancé was getting his fill elsewhere. Many elsewheres.'

245

I hug her arm. 'I know. I just meant –'

'Look, there are people literally queuing up to take a picture of your Bedford Falls window. Your art has taken off in the weirdest way possible.'

I know she hates talking about anything to do with her ex so I let her get away with the subject change. 'Got to admit I never thought my best canvas would be a coffee shop window, but it is kind of a special coffee shop.'

'I've got to admit the street looks kind of special too, George.' She laughs and gives me a nudge. 'It reminds me of when I was little. And you might want to record that for posterity because, as Oakbarrow's self-appointed grinch, I'll probably never say it again, but it makes me feel all Christmassy.'

I know the street's looking good, but it must be even better than I thought if it can make even Casey feel festive. Over the course of the week, Bernard, Leo, and I have got the tree up and secure in the old stand outside the churchyard, and decorated it under my dad's instructions, but the lights won't be lit until tonight. The bells hanging from streetlamps are twinkling with orange lights, and all the shops that have returned to the high street are open late so their lights illuminate the darkness. The rows of Santas and reindeer strung across the road between either side of the street above our heads are twinkling white, red and white glittering snowflakes dangle from the side of each building, and we found more giant nutcrackers that are standing like sentries at intervals along the pavement, and garlands of lights are arranged across shop fronts.

Mainly it's been a week of ducking behind the counter or into a clothes rail whenever Leo walks by and emergency runs into the bank when he comes in to tell me something. He's been in and out more times than the cuckoo on a cuckoo clock this week to go over plans and run-throughs of tonight with me or Bernard, and I'm a little bit exhausted from being on constant Leo-watch. What started as a tiny white lie is now too ridiculous for words, and I'm convinced that it's only a matter of time until he catches me out.

I have to stop thinking about it.

Casey heads off in the direction of The Bum in search of mulled wine as I push open the door of It's A Wonderful Latte, barely able to hear the bell jingling over the din of people. Every table is full, and more people are milling around on their feet, all holding coffee cups. It's the busiest I've ever seen it by a country mile, even when it first opened.

Maggie's got her arms in the cake display case, dishing up slices of peppermint brownie, orange and clove muffins, ginger-bread biscuits, and mini mince pies faster than her tongs can carry them. There's a woman I don't recognize making drinks, and a teenage girl manning the till.

I duck past a man with a cup of coffee in each hand and edge my way around a woman stood stock still in the middle of the shop who looks like she's been browsing the menu for at least half an hour.

'Leo's niece?' I ask the girl when I finally find an inch of space near the counter.

'Georgia?'

'Yes,' I say, surprised that she'd know. He must've told her about me. I feel all warm inside at the thought. I know he's got a strained relationship with his sister's side of the family and I can't believe he'd bother to tell them anything about me. 'Izzy, right?'

'Yes.' She looks pleased that I know her too, even though being behind the counter of the coffee shop kind of gives it away.

I wait for a moment as she takes money from a customer and hands him change, a receipt, and his drink in one swift move, not forgetting the warm smile, and I'm impressed by how easy she makes it look. Teenagers aren't fazed by anything. 'You're a pro at that. I'd be a shaking wreck on the floor by now. I get in such a muddle when there are too many customers at once.' Of course, too many customers are a thing of the past in Oakbarrow, but tonight, it doesn't feel like such a distant memory after all.

'Ah, this is easy.' She waves a hand and smoothly passes another customer the bag of brownies that Maggie has just sent over. 'Your pictures are incredible. I wish I could do that.'

'Thanks,' I say, blushing that not only has Leo told his niece about me, but that anything I've painted is modern enough to appeal to a teenager. I thought comedy Santas and Bedford Falls would've been as unfashionable as I am.

'Mum, Georgia's here!' Izzy calls when there's a brief lull in customers as the woman at the espresso machine finishes a line of purple cups and Izzy calls out names and hands them out to waiting people.

'Mum?' I repeat, thinking I must've misheard as the woman makes her way over, smiling at me. 'You're Leo's sister. You're … here.'

I try not to look as surprised as I am. After everything Leo's said about his sister's grief and the way she's avoided anything that reminds her of their father, she's the last person I expected to see in It's A Wonderful Latte, never mind working here, but there's no doubt about who she is. She's got the same light brown hair, the same curls, the same chin, the same nose. 'Becky, right?'

'It's so good to meet you,' she says. 'Leo's told us so much about you. I think my mum's already buying a hat.'

I gulp. Not at the wedding bit, but at the thought that Leo thinks I'm important enough to mention to his family. Surely he's got better things to talk to his sister about?

'I've been following the posts on Instagram. I decided I couldn't let another Christmas pass without seeing Oakbarrow, especially after all the work you and my brother have put in. Even if it's painful in some ways… I've been smiling more than I've been crying, which is progress from the last time I was here.'

'We watched *It's a Wonderful Life*,' Izzy says. 'I'd never seen it before but it was brilliant, even for something so ancient.'

An unexpected laugh bursts out of my mouth. 'See, Casey?' I say despite the fact that she's not here. She's always moaning about how old it is. 'It's a film that crosses generations.'

'I bawled like a baby the whole way through,' Becky says. 'It was the first time I'd seen it since my dad died, but it was cathartic too. Maybe enough years have passed now that it was therapeutic instead of heartbreaking.'

'It was my mum's favourite film when she was alive too,' I say. 'Believe me, I understand.'

She smiles at me, revealing teeth so much like Leo's that I automatically smile back. 'You've certainly got the hang of those machines. You're even quicker than Leo.'

'This place is amazing. I should've come a lot sooner.' Her eyes flick to Maggie and back to me. 'It was always my plan to help Dad out in the shop when he bought it. Coming back tonight has reminded me of how much I loved it here. It's exactly how he would've had it. It feels all warm and homely. He'd be proud of what Leo and Mum have done. Even the name. We never discussed it but I have absolutely no doubt that he would've used It's A Wonderful Latte too. Even that blimmin' bell above the door that's been driving me batty every time someone comes in or out.'

'I like it,' Izzy says. 'It makes me think of angels getting their wings now.'

'Me too,' I say. I've always had a soft spot for that bell. It's never jingled as much as it has tonight with so many customers though. No sooner than the thought crosses my mind, a man barges in near the till and orders a 'wonderful latte', elbowing the mate with him to make sure he appreciates the display of superior wit. Becky looks at me and rolls her eyes. 'That pun gets old very quickly.'

'You look rushed off your feet; do you need any help? I ask as she goes to make the aforementioned latte.

'No, I'm having a great time. Mum said things were slow so

249

it's fab to see it so busy again. And Leo's down by the Christmas tree somewhere.' She looks over her shoulder and winks at me.

Why does everyone think there's something going on between me and Leo? Even though it's a ridiculous notion, I can't wait to see him so I inch my way out of the packed shop and back into the cold December air.

I hear my name as I step out of the door and look up to see Mary hurrying towards me, a glass of mulled wine in one hand, the greengrocer in the other. I look pointedly at where her arm is hooked through his, but she ignores me. 'Have you *seen* this place? Doesn't it look incredible?'

'Just like it used to,' I say, bending down for a quick hug. 'You two look like you're having fun.'

'Patrick's just making sure I stay on my feet,' Mary says, despite the fact she watched Bernard up and down with the road salt this afternoon and is wearing sensible flats so doesn't even have the excuse Casey has got with her stilettos.

'How's trade going now you're back?' I ask Patrick.

'Brilliant,' he says. 'I can't believe it took me until now to try it again. I plan on seeing how January goes and then expanding my stock in February. Without that mini-supermarket stealing my customers, things are selling even faster than they used to.'

'Fantastic.'

'Not as fantastic as you folks have made this street look. It was like this in its heyday, although I never remember it being this busy. And that picture –' he nods towards the coffee shop's window, 'I've never seen *It's a Wonderful Life*, and even I recognize it.'

'I'll fix his movie choices before the weekend is out,' Mary says, well-versed in my usual response to anyone who's never seen *It's a Wonderful Life*.

'You've got the DVD, maybe you could get together and watch it,' I say, grinning at the thought. 'It is Christmas after all, it'll be a bit late if you don't get on it soon.'

'George!' Mary says, blushing.

Patrick doesn't look like he objects to the idea.

'Oh, I meant to tell you,' Mary says as I go to walk away. 'Head Office phoned earlier wanting to know why we'd had such a sudden spike in sales. I told them there'd been a bit of a street makeover, but you will be careful they don't find out you're involved, won't you?' She nods at the coffee shop. 'He's got more customers than we have. If Head Office discover that you've put all this effort into helping him, they're not going to be happy. They're going to be wondering why you didn't paint Bedford Falls on our window and offer a raffle prize at One Light.'

'I don't think it matters too much. Bringing people back to the street is what's important. If they come to one place, we all benefit.'

'But he's got young Instagrammy people taking those selfie thingys with the window. Not the sort of people who shop in charity shops. Head Office won't see that it benefits us – they'll see it as their manager helping a competitor.'

'We've seen an increase in customers. Our shelves are looking emptier and our donations have gone up. Our take-offs have been much less than they were because people have bought things. Charity shops suffer at this time of year anyway because people are buying presents and want new things, not second-hand. We have no possible competition with Leo, he sells coffee, we're a charity shop. Don't worry so much,' I say, worrying. 'Enjoy the night. It's not long until the light switch on now.'

I watch as Mary and Patrick wander up the street arm in arm, knowing she's got a point, and wondering how much Leo would laugh at the irony of me telling someone not to worry.

* * *

If possible, it's even busier down by the Christmas tree. Bernard is there in full Santa costume, sitting in the sleigh we rescued

251

from Hawthorne's basement, while children sit next to him and tell him their Christmas wishes. I stand back and watch for a moment, trying to work out who looks happier – Bernard or the children who are going up to meet him. Bernard was so touched when we asked him to play Santa that he actually got emotional, something I've never seen Bernard do before, no matter how hard times have been for him.

My dad is still supervising the last of the Christmas lights, standing and directing one of Bernard's friends on where to put the finishing touches. He seems younger than he has for years, buoyed up doing something he loves again.

It's cold and crisp tonight, and the Salvation Army band that Bernard organized are tuning up with a brass version of 'Wonderful Christmastime'.

'Paul McCartney, good choice,' I say, sidling over to where Leo's standing in the little clearing in front of the tree.

He seems to be supervising in general, directing kids into a line to meet Santa-Bernard, answering questions, directing people towards the coffee shop or The Bum, even giving one woman the time despite the fact there's a clock on the church tower above our heads.

He tips a reindeer antler towards me and his grin doesn't fade. 'I had some solid advice on the merits of Macca at the weekend.'

I look over at my dad again, currently waxing lyrical about the tautness needed to get the perfect drape of tinsel, and Leo follows my gaze. 'I'm keeping an eye on him.'

'I know,' I say, realizing I do know. I trust Leo. He knows I worry and I know without even asking that Leo's watching him out of the corner of his eye. 'Thanks.'

He smiles.

'Nice jumper. I was expecting your Christmas tie but this is a real step up.'

'I thought you'd like it. I was getting dressed earlier and as I pulled this over my head, my first thought was that you'd think

I'm the epitome of cool sophistication. I'm one step away from the London catwalks, right?' He strikes a pose and throws me his best *blue steel* smoulder.

The jumper is the deepest maroon colour with a white Fair Isle pattern and a bright green Christmas tree on the front, starting from the trunk at the waistband and covering the whole front until the star at the top which fits nicely in the dip of his collarbone, complete with 3D baubles and actual fairy lights that flash. Although, thoughts of Leo getting dressed lead to thoughts of Leo undressed, and my face heats up as I imagine that awful jumper sliding over smooth naked skin …

'Oh, definitely.' I couldn't stop myself giggling even if I wanted to because I love that he's not afraid to really get behind Christmas. I love this time of year and all the sparkly, tacky goodness that goes with it, but no one should be able to look that good wearing a Christmas jumper. It's quite unfair, actually. Most people wearing that would look like they'd just failed an elf audition. How can he still be sexy?

'Well, it's only once a year. If you can't fully embrace looking like a prat at Christmas, when can you? Nice earrings and antlers.' He beams at me and then looks worried. 'And I've just realized the juxtaposition of those sentences made that sound like an insult. Sorry. I meant that *I* look like a prat, not you. You look gorgeous.'

'Thank you,' I say, loving how nervous and rambly he gets sometimes. 'I'm utterly sure I do look like a prat, but at least we can be prats together. You're making me wish I'd worn a Christmas jumper now but Casey would've disowned me.'

He smiles as he helps another child out of the sleigh, hands them a candy cane and thanks them for coming.

'You're good at this.' I watch Leo direct the next child in the queue to sit next to Bernard in the sleigh but she's too busy already babbling at him to hear.

He shrugs. 'I grew up around Santa's grotto. I often donned an elf hat and stood in for the store elves when they ran out to do their Christmas shopping. Until I realized how desperately uncool it was and all my friends made fun of me.'

'And then you carried on anyway because you love Christmas?'

'Pretty much.' He leans closer and whispers, antlers jingling. 'It might surprise you but I have no problem looking like an idiot in public.'

'You don't look like an idiot,' I say, fighting the urge to kiss his cheek. His skin is so near, his face reddened from the cold, and he smells completely delicious. He's got a different aftershave on and he smells of dark pine, burning wood, and clove. I force myself to take a step back and put on a jovial tone. 'Just a bit of a wally.'

He laughs. 'I am fully accepting of that fact.'

'If your mum has a picture from when you were younger, I'm going to make her dig it out.'

'I'm going to make sure Santa leaves coal in your stocking if you do. And my mum has many pictures of me looking desperately uncool at Christmastime. I'm surprised she hasn't had them made into cards and distributed them to the whole town by now.'

'Speaking of family, I've just met your sister …'

'Yeah,' he says. 'I didn't expect to see her. Apparently Izzy really wanted to see Oakbarrow like this and between her and my mum's … let's call it gentle persuasion as opposed to persistent battering … Becky decided to come. She said she's been having grief counselling and that's been helping her to enjoy the happy memories rather than try to avoid them. It's good, I think.'

'She seemed to be loving it in the shop.'

'She always did love it there.' he nods. 'Hopefully this'll be a turning point for her. I've got enough customers that Izzy can come back to her Saturday job, especially with the craft market reopening, so I'm hoping Becky will start dropping her off and picking her up, and maybe start to see that It's A Wonderful Latte is a way of honouring our father rather than a painful reminder of what we've lost.'

254

'Spoken with expertise by a man who's spent the past two years brushing his own grief under the carpet and pretending to be fine when he's not?'

I realize that was maybe a bit too harsh when he winces. 'I'm okay, George. You've made me face the things I hadn't dealt with. There's no getting over it, there's only accepting life as it is now and learning to carry on because there's *no* other option. I'm not going to end up where I did before.'

What does that mean? As me, I'm not supposed to know where he ended up before. Is he trying to tell me something?

I don't have a chance to push it because the church bell rings seven times to mark seven o'clock. The crowd gathered around the tree has gradually grown and people are filling the road, more people than I ever thought I'd see on Oakbarrow High Street again, even more than I remember from the busiest times in days gone by. Everyone has It's A Wonderful Latte cups or beakers of mulled wine from The Bum in their hands, there are Christmas jumpers as far as the eye can see, and the decorations lighting the street are amplified by hundreds of flashing Christmas earrings, headbands, ties, and otherwise. It's amazing to see people getting into the Christmas spirit.

Leo and I have got a spot at the front and I'm hyperaware of him next to me, slightly behind and to the side, his shoulder and arm pressed against my back. Casey's somewhere in the crowd with a newly-single guy she had a crush on in school. Maggie, Becky, and Izzy are outside It's A Wonderful Latte, which has closed its doors for the big switch-on. Mary and Patrick are on the sidelines near the tree too, and my dad has finally sat down in a chair Leo got for him.

Bernard stands up in the sleigh after the church bell has finished chiming, the switch my dad has wired up to the tree lights in his hand. 'Thank you all for coming,' he starts, addressing the crowd. 'I can't tell you how much joy it brings me to see Oakbarrow High Street so busy after all these years. I want to dedicate this tree, this street, and the community spirit that's abundant tonight to a man who is no longer with us. A man who I'm sure we all remember in our own special way, whether as the Santa we used to visit at Hawthorne's toy shop when we were little, or the man who was an almost permanent fixture in the corner of the café up the road there.'

Leo sucks in a breath beside me and I reach back until I find his hand and slot my fingers through his.

'To Derek Summers.'

The crowd echoes Bernard's words, clinking cups with the people standing next to them, and I squeeze Leo's hand tighter.

I think Bernard is done but he carries on. 'Derek may no longer be with us, but his son is continuing his legacy. Derek's son is partially responsible for everything you see around you tonight, along with help from a little guardian angel I like to call Clarence. It is their dedication, their love of Oakbarrow, their creativity, and their belief in Christmas magic that has made this quiet little street come back to life in the past few weeks.'

His eyes are on me and Leo now, ignoring the rest of the crowd, like he's speaking only to us. 'Derek's son doesn't know that I was one of his father's best friends, that Derek and I actually built this very sleigh by hand in my garage when you were too young to remember.' He bends down and pats the smooth side of the red wooden prop.

When I look up at Leo, he's focused completely on Bernard, but there are silent tears sliding down his face. I reach up and brush them away, and let my hand linger, tucking his hair back and sliding down to wrap around his arm and hold him against me.

'And I can speak here with his voice. Your father would be *exceptionally* proud of you, Leo. You, your family, and the shop he loved so much are a credit to him and this town. Don't ever forget that, even when times are hard. If a man has friends, he truly has a wonderful life.'

Even Bernard is getting choked up and he stops to compose himself.

I had no idea Bernard knew Leo's father, and by the complete surprise clear on Leo's face, he didn't either.

Bernard clears his throat and picks up a coffee cup, raising it in a toast.

'To Leo and Clarence, who would've made an old Santa very proud on this wonderful night.'

I blush as every pair of eyes in the crowd swivels to us and Leo edges minutely closer, clutching my hand almost hard enough to hurt.

Thankfully, Bernard chooses that moment to start the count-down and the tree bursts into light, drawing the attention away from us.

The lights ping into life row by row from bottom to top, lines of twinkling fairy lights spiralling around the tree until the star on top lights with a burst of orange.

It's a much smaller tree than the ones Oakbarrow used to have and some of the sets of lights we found had given up the ghost after so much time, but it looks stunning. The tree might not be a giant but it's over nine foot and it's the best tree anyone's seen in Oakbarrow for many years. A hush falls across the crowd as everyone just stands there admiring it.

I can feel Leo breathing, each breath slow and considered, a short inhale and long exhale, like he's focusing intently on it. There are tremors running through him, where his body is pressed against mine, and my fingers tighten automatically around his hands.

He puts an arm around my chest and leans against me, his chin on my shoulder, his head resting against mine, and although I'm desperate to turn around and pull him into a hug, I get the feeling he just needs to be still and quiet for a few moments.

The Salvation Army band strikes up again with 'Fairytale of

New York', and Leo's arms slide down to my waist and tighten around me, pulling me closer against him.

People start to stir, chatting to their neighbours again, wandering away from the clearing around the tree, the kids who were queuing to see Santa swarm back towards the line they were in, but Leo doesn't move.

'Thank you,' he murmurs in my ear, his voice rough and muffled.

'That was all Bernard. I didn't know what he was going to say.'

'I don't mean for that. I mean for everything. You brought me back to life, George.'

My hands are still covering his where they're around me and I flex them, letting my fingers rub across the back of his hands.

'I don't want this to end,' he says, even quieter than before. 'You, me, this. Christmas. I don't want you to go back to being just a customer. I don't want you to go back to being just a friend. For the first time, I like living here. I'm excited about what the new year is going to bring for Oakbarrow and I want to share that with you.'

His hands are clasped together on my stomach and I have to prise them apart with my fingers before I can turn around, almost like he doesn't want me to move in case it breaks the spell.

Everything feels a bit more twinkly and magical tonight than it does usually, like anything could happen, and when I do manage to pull back and turn around in his arms, his face is pure nervousness, like he's said something so wrong that he's honestly expecting me to slap him, and my whole insides melt at how he could possibly be that nervous. Doesn't he realize that I'm head-over-flipping-heels in love with him?

I go to speak but my voice comes out cracked and I have to wet my lips and try again. 'I'd like that,' I say, barely above a whisper.

His face slowly spreads into the widest smile I've ever seen, and I am powerless not to smile in return.

He looks happy, and a few weeks ago, I never thought I'd see him happy again. No matter what happens now, if he's happy, it's all been worth it.

His eyes are dark with desire, centred on my lips, and I know he's going to kiss me. My eyes close and my fingers automatically find their way into his hair and I nearly do a squeal of joy at finally getting to wind my fingers in his mass of curls because I've wanted to do it since the first time I saw him.

But squeals of joy in the middle of kissing would be undignified. Instead our tinsel reindeer antlers clash in midair and my flashing Christmas tree earrings get caught on his flashing Christmas tree jumper.

So not undignified at all, obviously.

I melt as Leo's lips touch mine. It's only a peck at first, soft and sweet, and everything Leo is wrapped up into one simple touch. He breathes a sigh of contentment against my mouth and it sets something in me on fire. My fingers tighten in his hair and pull him closer, and the kiss turns more intense for a few moments, his fingers clutching my jacket, my hair, anything, like he can't pull me close enough, and I can't breathe because I've imagined kissing Leo more times than is probably normal but the reality is so much better than my imagination.

His sigh of contentment turns into a moan of need and we both suddenly realize where we are.

In public, with plenty of people still nearby, Bernard's eyes flicking towards us every time there's a break between children in the sleigh, the vague sound of Casey's cheering, and my dad looking deliberately in the other direction.

I meet Leo's eyes and we both start giggling.

'Hold that thought,' he whispers, wrapping his arms around me and pulling me against him again.

His smile is so full of joy and he sounds so happy that it spreads through me too. We did this. We brought Oakbarrow back from the brink, just the two of us, and if we can do that, we can overcome anything.

I forget about the people around us, the band playing, the chill in the air, and a sense of contentment settles over me – everything will be all right. He will understand.

I reach up to straighten his tinsel antlers and take a deep breath. 'Leo, there's something I need to tell –'

'Excuse me,' someone says before I have a chance to finish the sentence.

A policeman pushes past us and approaches Bernard. 'Are you in charge here?'

'Depends on who's asking,' Bernard says, his eyes flicking towards us.

The policeman holds up a badge and shows it to Bernard. 'I would've thought that fairly obvious.'

'Hmm.' Bernard takes much longer to examine the badge than necessary. 'I am and I'm not. What seems to be the problem?'

'I would've thought that fairly obvious too.' The policeman gestures to the huge sparkling tree behind him. 'I've been sent as an enforcement officer by Gloucestershire county council as they've noticed you're holding an unlicensed public gathering tonight. They also seem to be missing a record of your planning permission for these decorations, and your health and safety certificates appear to have gone amiss too. Are you the man responsible? If not, could you point me in the correct direction, please?'

'I am,' Bernard says, folding his arms across his red Santa coat and puffing his chest out.

The police officer *really* doesn't look impressed. This cannot end well.

'He's not,' Leo says instantly, pulling away from my side and striding towards them. 'I am. This is nothing to do with him, it's solely my responsibility.'

'No, it's not,' I say before I've even thought it through. 'You're the one who tried to talk me out of it. This was my idea. I'm responsible.'

'She's not,' Leo says.

'Neither of them are,' Bernard says. 'I'm the oldest, I'm the one in charge.'

The police officer looks between us. 'I'm going to have to fine all three of you then. You've hooked into the council's electricity supply without permission, we have no health and safety certificates for this display, and you're holding this public gathering without public liability insurance … Unless you can show me your documentation for all of those things right this second, I have no choice but to issue you with a fixed penalty notice, and instruct you to begin the process of removal immediately.'

A gasp of misery echoes through the crowd and I feel the same hollowness knocking around inside me. All this effort, all these people who have come out tonight to see Oakbarrow like it used to be, and it's all over already. *Of course* the council have found out – we were naive to think they wouldn't.

'If these decorations are not removed within twenty-four hours, court proceedings will follow.' He points a pen towards Bernard. 'I'm going to need your names and addresses. We'll start with you.'

Bernard manages to look pleased about this. 'My address is that bench in the churchyard, and my name is Santa Claus, of course. Ask any of these people if you don't believe me.'

'Hilarious, my friend. If only I had a pound for every time I hear that in December.' He turns to me and Leo. 'And I suppose you two are the Easter Bunny and the Tooth Fairy?'

'No, that's my head elf and my wingless angel, Clarence,' Bernard says.

The police officer looks like he's running out of patience faster than a cheetah on rollerblades. When he speaks, it's through gritted teeth. 'I'm sure you think you're all stand-up comedians, but this is a serious matter. If you refuse to give me your names and addresses, or if I suspect you're giving me false information, I will call for back-up and you will be taken into custody and charged with wasting police time, as well as everything else you're getting up to here.'

I'd be lying if I said I didn't feel a spike of panic. Fixed penalty fines, being arrested and charged, enforcement officers … I've never been on the wrong side of the law before and my knees feel unstable and my hands have started shaking. So much for that sense of contentment, eh?

'You can't issue a fine to Santa Claus,' a woman in the crowd says.

The policeman falters for a second as his eyes shift towards the young girl standing with her, obviously reconsidering destroying the Christmas magic of her childhood. 'I'm not issuing a fine to Santa Claus, I'm issuing a fine to this gentleman and his friends.'

'Mr Scrooge, is that you?' a man shouts from a few people back. 'You're looking remarkably well for someone first written about in 1843!'

The policeman half-stifles a laugh and actually looks ashamed for a moment. 'Look, I'm just doing my job. These people are in breach of multiple rules and regulations. They don't have planning consent or insurance, they don't have the specific approval required to attach to street furniture and lighting columns, they're interfering with the streetlights, and they're causing a public nuisance.'

'*You're* causing a public nuisance!' someone shouts.

'Interfering with the streetlights,' another man scoffs. 'There have been dodos seen more recently than a fresh bulb in any of those lamps!'

'What if it wasn't just them who did it?' someone else in the crowd calls out.

'Yes!' My dad suddenly jumps up and hobbles across to us. 'It was me too!'

'And me!' Mary steps forward.

'Me too.' Patrick doesn't have much choice as she practically drags him with her.

'Same!' Casey shouts.

'Us too,' an elderly woman's voice calls from outside It's A Wonderful Latte, and I turn around to see Maggie waving her hand like she's trying to attract attention, Becky and Izzy at her side.

They're echoed by a chorus of people claiming responsibility for what we did. Shopkeepers I recognize, people I've never seen before, customers I know from One Light. One by one, people say it was them even though it wasn't. There are so many people stepping up that eventually the policeman has to interrupt them.

'Someone has organized this. One or two people.' He glances at me, Leo, and Bernard again. 'Or a few. But not every one of the few hundred people here have put up decorations that you do not have permission to display.'

'You don't know that. You weren't here when we put them up,' someone else challenges him.

'If it was every single one of us, you can't fine us all,' says a man I recognize from the florist's shop. 'If the council have a problem with this, maybe they should have done it themselves. Gloucestershire council have turned their backs on us so the residents have decided to do something about it themselves. It's not a crime to want your town to look festive.'

'The council's budget is limited.'

'So is ours. So is everyone's. You want to fine us, go ahead. Fine Oakbarrow High Street as a whole. We'll all chip in to pay it. I will, I know many of the shopkeepers who have come back here in the past few weeks would think that it's worth a little contribution to see their high street looking like this again. Do your worst, matey. It's Christmas and this is the most festive I've felt in years because these people have done what should have been done years ago.'

The crowd murmur agreements like the rumbling of an approaching thunderstorm.

'All of us have had a hand in our high street declining.' This

263

time the newsagent joins in. 'We are the people who stopped shopping here because the shops we liked could no longer afford to stay in business, we are the ones who have chosen to go elsewhere because it's more convenient, and now we are the ones who have a chance to turn back the clock. It's worth more than money.'

'Impose whatever fine you want,' Patrick says. 'It will be paid – by all of us, for all of us. And I sincerely hope that next year, everyone will get together and do exactly the same again, fine or no fine.'

The police officer looks like he's wavering and I actually feel a bit sorry for him. I doubt he expected to find a couple of hundred people knee deep in festive spirit on Oakbarrow High Street tonight.

My dad takes pity on him. 'Did you grow up here?'

'Well, yes, nearby,' he says, his voice sounding stuttery and nervous.

'Don't you remember it looking like this?'

'I remember coming to Hawthorne's. My father bought me a toy police car that you rode around in. It was my favourite for years. When I got too big to fit in it, I put my teddies in and gave them rides instead.' He smiles, his eyes wandering up the street to where you can see the upper parts of the redbrick building towering above its neighbours. 'That was the moment I decided I wanted to join the police force. I loved that shop.'

'Do you remember how the street used to look? The snow in Hawthorne's doorway?' Leo gestures towards the sleigh Bernard is still standing in. 'Santa's grotto? The carol services at the tree by the church?'

'Everything's been installed by an electrician,' Bernard says. 'Everything's safe, and people are enjoying it. Oakbarrow High Street is different – better – because of this. Where's your Christmas spirit?'

'Well, I …' the officer stutters, not looking half as steadfast as he did when he arrived.

'Look at how many people we've made happy. When was the last time you saw this amount of joy in our little town? It'll be Christmas Eve in two days. The elves and I will have everything down by Boxing Day. Can't you just tell your bosses that you couldn't find who was responsible?' Bernard taps his nose. 'I'll make sure you're on the nice list ...'

The police officer smiles. 'I suppose I can't really say no to Santa, can I?'

The crowd cheers, the Salvation Army strikes up with 'Hark the Herald Angels Sing', and the policeman goes to The Bum for a well-deserved mulled wine.

Leo drops his arm around my shoulder and breathes an exaggerated sigh of relief.

'Times like this remind me of why I love Oakbarrow so much. Even strangers will step in to help when you need it. If a man has friends, he truly has a wonderful life,' Bernard says, repeating the toast he made earlier that seems even more significant now.

* * *

It's eleven o'clock before the last of the stragglers have left and all the shops have shut. Maggie, Becky, and Izzy have taken my dad home, Casey's taken her new old-crush's phone number as opposed to his condom size, Mary and Patrick have made plans to spend the day together tomorrow and gone their separate ways for tonight, and Leo and I are still picking up empty coffee cups from the pavement.

'Well, that was a wonderful night.' Bernard flops down onto the bench in the sleigh and picks up the cup of tea that Leo's brought him.

'Thanks for all you've done,' I say, standing upright and putting my hands on my lower back which is definitely telling me I've been on my feet for too long.

265

'This was all you two,' Bernard says. 'Everyone else in Oakbarrow had given up on ever making this town better, apart from you two. And you did it. You brought the community together again. You reminded us all of Christmases past. That won't just disappear now. People will hold onto it for the rest of the year too.'

'I think we might not have been alone.' Leo stands upright too and grunts at the movement. He points upwards. 'If my dad was here, and Georgia's mum, they'd have loved it.'

'They'd have been very proud,' Bernard says. 'Why don't you two take the weight off for a minute?' He pats the red sleigh bench, and the temptation of sitting down is just too much.

I squeeze in on one side of Bernard and Leo squeezes in on the other. He groans and pushes his back against the wooden bench to straighten it. 'Next year, we hire litter pickers.'

'Next year, hopefully the council will listen to demand and do it themselves,' I say.

'There's a very good chance that they will. Look at what happened tonight. We all showed them how much love we still have for this town. I'm proud of you two, you know that?' He drops an arm around both of our shoulders. 'And for once I'm not afraid to put my arms around you because my lovely Clarence here let me use that fancy shower gel.'

We all sit there in silence for a while, looking at the now empty street, completely still, apart from the twinkling of Christmas lights.

'Come on then,' Bernard says. 'Tell an old Santa standing in for another old Santa who'd have boiled over with delight at the sight of a certain kiss earlier … what's your Christmas wish?'

I look at Leo over the top of Bernard's Santa hat. *You*.

'I think I've already got mine,' Leo says, not taking his eyes off me.

I smile at him, feeling so happy I might burst. I can't remember the last time things felt this right. For the first time in years, I don't feel like I'm missing out on anything by staying in

Oakbarrow. Sometimes the best things are the things that have been in front of you all along.

'Actually, there is one thing, Bernard. Tell me something.' Leo nods towards me. 'Why do you call her Clarence? Because she's some kind of angel?'

I mime sticking my fingers down my throat and Leo laughs.

Bernard looks at me and my smile stops in its tracks as I feel the blood drain from my face. I suddenly know exactly what he's going to say.

'Because Clarence stops people jumping off bridges.'

Chapter 18

If Leo got the hidden meaning, he was too polite to mention it. He was quiet as he walked me home, tired after the long day, but he didn't kiss me again.

I didn't go into town yesterday as it was Sunday, and this morning, he and Maggie are rushed off their feet. The queue is long and it's Maggie who serves me, taking my money and handing me a cup without my name written on it. Leo gave me a tight smile when the bell jingled as I came in but hasn't looked round from the coffee machines since.

I overthink it as I walk down the road towards One Light, sipping my coffee that doesn't put as much of a spring in my step as it usually does.

Does he know? It doesn't get much more obvious than 'Clarence stops people jumping off bridges', does it? Is he expecting me to explain myself? Does he realize I've been lying to him and can't bear to look at me? Is he just really busy? Maybe his phone is out of battery and that's why he didn't text yesterday? Or because we've been texting about the windows and the tree and stuff and now tomorrow is Christmas Eve, there's nothing left to organize. Maybe that's it …

'Hi!' I nearly have a heart attack on the spot as I turn the corner at the bank and find our two most senior managing directors waiting outside One Light's door, both in smart suits carrying posh briefcases, and both looking like they've been waiting a long while.

The lady, who I met years ago during training and now can't remember the name of, is rubbing her hands together to generate heat, and the man who I've never met is checking his wrist in a way that says he hasn't read the time once but can somehow prompt my arrival by glaring his watch into submission.

'What are you doing here? I didn't know you were due today!' My voice is so unstable it sounds like a 4-year-old picking up an untuned violin for the first time, and if they can't tell that the smile I've forced onto my face is hiding a litany of silent swear words, they're due an appointment at Specsavers.

All thoughts of my usual shortcut through the bank are forgotten and I'm suddenly thanking whatever lingering Christmas magic it was that made Leo busy this morning so he's unlikely to be watching. What a mess it would've been if he'd walked me to work today.

'We just popped down as it's nearly Christmas and we wanted to see the seasonal displays for ourselves and watch how they're performing,' the lady says, and I wish I could remember her name. I can't ask because she'll know I wasn't paying attention in those training weeks, and both of them seem to know me well enough to be in no mind for introducing themselves.

'And it wouldn't be a spot check if you knew we were coming,' the man says.

'Oh, marvellous,' I squeak. 'What a wonderful festive surprise.'

'Things have really picked up lately so you must be doing something right.'

Oh, if you only knew. I realize the noise I can hear is the coffee sloshing inside my latte cup as I wave it around. 'Oh, sorry! I'd have got you both one if I'd known you were coming.'

'Well, maybe you can let us in and get the heating on,' the

269

man says. 'It's five to nine. Customers might be along in a few minutes and we don't want them walking into a cold shop. People spend less when they're cold, and we don't want that, do we?'

'Of course we don't,' I say through gritted teeth, debating telling him that we're trialling a new Arctic experiment so customers come in, realize they're freezing, and buy all the coats in a mass coat exodus.

'So...' he says.

'Oh, right! Keys!' I fumble through my bag, wondering if the keys have gone to bloody Narnia via the pocket at the back where you keep a spare tampon.

'I hope there aren't any staff waiting around the back. They'll be frozen into icicles by now,' the woman says. 'Staff-cicles!'

I giggle like it's the funniest thing I've heard all year, trying not to think about Mary, who will undoubtedly be waiting patiently in the car park. Volunteers will be off with their families because it's Christmas week, but Mary's still in today.

This must look so unprofessional. I'm late, my keys have made a break for freedom, Mary's probably lost at least one toe to frostbite by now, but I've still found the time to nonchalantly stroll down the road with my all-important latte.

'Keys!' I screech as my fingers close around cold metal, yank them out in victory, get my glove caught on the bag zipper, and promptly drop said keys onto a frozen puddle, where they slip and slide away from me and straight into the shiny toe of the nameless man's smart shoes.

He lifts his toe and stops them, pressing them down into the frozen pavement until I've managed to free my glove from the bag and skid across to retrieve them. He gives me a look that says he's seen a more competent shop manager showing its bum to visitors in the baboon enclosure of the local zoo.

My hands are shaking as I try to fit the key into the frozen lock and end up having to crouch down and blow on it in an attempt to defrost it. A customer walking past stops to look in the window, but takes one look at us gathered around the door and walks away.

The man clicks his tongue. 'Lost trade. Do you realize it's gone nine?'

'No, the church bell chiming nine times didn't give it away,' I mutter, momentarily forgetting who I'm talking to.

I wish I could momentarily forget the appalled look on his face too.

The key finally crunches through the last of the ice in the lock and turns. 'Ah, here we are. Just let me go and rescue Mary from the car park and I'll be with you. Cup of tea?'

Both give me two orders for varying amounts of milk and sugar, which I immediately forget.

Thankfully, Mary has got a bit more experience of managing directors and shakes hands with the man – who loudly laments about how cold she is – and embraces the woman like an old friend. Still no names though.

She saves my life by offering to make the teas and takes their orders again without showing me up for the nervous idiot I am. With Mary upstairs, I can't leave the shop floor in case a customer comes in, so I stand there like a plum, still in my coat, bag over my arm, coffee cup in hand.

The managers take the opportunity to wander around inspecting everything. I watch the lady pull out a blouse that wasn't hung properly, tut, undo the buttons and redo them so it sits nicely on the hanger. I want to tell her that I didn't put it out like that, someone's obviously tried it on and put it back wonky, and we closed up in a hurry on Saturday for the tree lighting and we clearly didn't catch it. I keep my mouth shut. The man swipes his fingertip across the top of the rails, inspects it, and clicks his tongue.

The usual Christmas radio station I have playing quietly in one corner is replaced by a cacophony of tuts and tongue clicks.

I sip my coffee and tell myself to calm down. I have nothing

271

to worry about. Sales are stronger this month than they've been for years, even a stray dust bunny lurking under the men's trousers that I must've missed when hoovering isn't enough cause for them to complain. Our double window display is striking, with all the mannequins standing around a Christmas tree, surrounded by balled-up wrapping paper to make it look like they've just unwrapped the gifts on show, the selection of clothing is good because our donations have increased as more people have come back to the high street, and the bric-a-brac shelves are miraculously tidy. There's nothing for them to find fault with.

The man strides past me and stops to give my latte a death glare. 'Coffee cup on the shop floor. Unhygienic and unprofessional.'

'There's no one here!'

His frown doesn't let up. I'm tempted to mention something about the consequences of the wind changing but I sigh instead. 'I'll stash it under the counter if anyone comes in.'

'You know the rules. You're meant to be the one enforcing them. If you have drinks on the shop floor then the volunteers have probably got cups of tea and biscuits and God knows what else out here. I fired a volunteer at another branch for eating a pasty on the shop floor last week. A pasty!'

'Crime of the century,' I mutter, thinking I just fancy a pasty. I wonder if there's any hope of the bakery coming back to Oakbarrow, they used to do a gorgeous pasty.

The woman comes to join the man near the counter. 'We were admiring the artwork on that coffee shop up the street. Looks a bit like the sort of thing you usually do on these windows. Your handiwork?'

'Me?' I squeak. 'What shop was this again?'

She nods to the latte cup in my hand. 'That shop.'

'Oh!' I give the cup an offended look, like it has somehow placed itself in my hand without express permission. 'No, I don't know anything about that.'

'Only it is Bedford Falls, isn't it? And you are, of course, Georgia Bailey. I thought there might be a connection.'

'Not at all.' I give her a smile so falsely sweet that a child would only have to look at me for their teeth to fall out. 'I only work on our windows. Gotta have something to make us stand out,' I trill, wondering if the cereal I had for breakfast was actually budgie food by mistake.

Mary rescues me once more by choosing that moment to pop her head round from the back room. 'Two cups of tea and a packet of choccie biccies we were saving for a special occasion,' she says, thankfully having the sense not to bring their drinks onto the shop floor like I would have. 'Shall I take over on the till and you can all go through?'

'Thanks,' I mouth to her as they file out the back, only to be met with half the room buried under unsorted black plastic bags full of donations.

'Not many of the volunteers have been in this week because it's nearly Christmas,' I say by way of explanation.

'Volunteers or not, this is a hazard.' The man nudges one of the bags with the toe of his polished shoe. 'I suppose you were just going to leave it all here over Christmas? There could be anything in those bags. If you don't have volunteers, you do the sorting yourself. You are paid staff, are you not?'

'I was going to do it today,' I lie.

'With only yourself and Mary to cover the shop floor? Who was going to do the take-offs? Who would steam the clothes? Perhaps you were planning to open the door and invite customers to help themselves and pop their own money in the till as a goodwill gesture?'

'Look, there was this thing on Saturday night for the street, and we left early and –'

The man's head whips round so fast I'm surprised he won't need a chiropractor to sort his neck out. 'Early?'

'In a hurry!' I should've just given him a shovel and saved

myself the trouble of digging this hole. 'Not early. In a hurry. To get to this Christmas street thing, for community spirit, you know? We were both there, um, promoting the shop.'

'Did you hand out leaflets?'

'Er, some,' I lie again. I try for a swift subject change before they question me any further. 'Would you like to go upstairs to the office?'

'No, I think I'll stay here by this nice warm radiator,' the lady says, warming her hands above it.

I silently thank Mary for thinking to put the heating on. I had not.

'Can you bring your paperwork downstairs and we'll check it over?' she says. 'We need to confirm your figures against the ones being reported as there's been such a spike in sales.'

'Of course, won't be a tick,' I say as I go up the stairs to get it, trying not to watch the man pushing aside piles of unsorted bric-a-brac to make a space on the workbench.

When I get back downstairs with the file of this month's sales figures and takings, amazingly without dropping the pages all over the place, the woman is still trying to warm her hands up on the radiator and the man is peering critically at the rail of clothes next in line to go out to the shop floor. They've both ignored their tea and they haven't even touched the chocolate biscuits. What is *wrong* with these people?

'Here we go,' I say breezily, putting the file down and opening it out in the empty space that was once my organized chaos workbench. I see an opportunity to find out their names while they're distracted. 'I'll just check Mary's okay out there. Won't be a tick.'

Except I don't get a chance.

'George!' Casey bellows, letting herself in the back door.

I flinch at the look the managers' exchange. It's easy to see what they're thinking: security issue.

'Another Leo situation has arisen in the bank!' she yells, stopping in her tracks when she comes into the back room and sees the two official-looking people. 'Oh! I'm sorry, I didn't realize there was anyone here. I mean, um …'

'A Leo situation?'

Casey's eyes meet mine over the rack of clothes, looking for help with an explanation. I wrack my brain trying to think of something. A star sign emergency? An escaped lion?

'A bloke who brings us regular donations,' I say in a flurry of inspiration. 'He gets confused and takes them next door by mistake. Such a silly man!' I titter. When have I ever tittered in my life?

'I'll just go and collect them. Won't be a tick!' I've lost count of how many times I've told them I won't be a tick now. They're going to get a complex that I'm trying to get away from them. Would they notice if I left them with the paperwork and just disappeared into the bank until they leave?

'You're very squeaky this morning,' Casey says as I bundle her out the door and shut it behind us. 'Who are they? Why are there birds outside tweeting in lower pitches than you?'

'Managing directors,' I say, trying to regain my normal voice. 'Unannounced spot check. Did Leo say what he wants?'

'No, but speaking of managers, Jerry's off sick and –'

I barely hear her over the rushing in my head. Leo's come looking for me. Is it to confront me? To say good morning because he didn't have time earlier? That's the sort of thing Leo would do – wander down when the shop's emptier because he was busy before? Maybe all my worrying has been for nothing. Maybe Bernard's comment on Saturday wasn't as obvious as I thought.

I yank the back door of the bank open and run headfirst into a man. A very large man. In a very posh suit. Who is glaring at Casey. 'I was just coming to find out where you'd disappeared to,' he barks. 'What is going on in this place? Why am I like a bloody sheepdog having to round up my staff?'

He turns his beady eyes to me. 'And who the hell are you? You don't work here.'

'Who the hell are *you*? *You* don't work here!' I snap at him, regretting it instantly. What was Casey just saying about managers? His dark blue suit over the familiar light blue shirt of the bank's uniform says he clearly does work here. Me, on the other hand …

His eyes narrow even further and I do the only thing I can think of. I reach up and pat his shoulder. 'It's fine, I have security clearance, I work next door. Won't be a tick!'

Apparently when in a pickle, telling people you 'won't be a tick' is guaranteed to work.

'It is not fine!' the man shouts as I hurry away from him. 'Call the police! We've got a security breach!'

'It's honestly fine.' I hear Casey trying to reason with him. 'She's my friend, everyone knows her …'

All I can think about is Leo. Or, more specifically, grabbing Leo by the arm and dragging him halfway up the street before that man shouts any louder.

'Leo!' I sound more than a bit hysterical as I barrel headfirst out of the staff door and into the surprisingly crowded bank.

Leo smiles when he sees me and holds a cup of hot chocolate out. 'My favourite Georgia' is scrawled on the cup in his looping handwriting. 'Thought it might be too soon for another coffee, but I wanted to see you. I should've said hello to you this morning. Properly.' He waggles his eyebrows suggestively and no matter what else is going on, my knees still feel a bit jelly-like at the thought of kissing Leo.

'Who the hell are you?' the man bellows, the security door slamming as he storms out behind me. 'What the hell is this about non-staff members having security codes? That's the most ridiculous thing I've ever heard!'

'Everything all right?' Leo asks me.

'Oh, fine!' I say, even though I can basically hear the boom of my lies imploding. 'Utterly fine! Why don't we go outside for a minute?'

'Excuse me, Georgia?' The lady boss from One Light pops her head round the front door of the bank before I have a chance to push Leo through it. 'If someone's bringing donations here by mistake, you really must direct them to the correct place. Donations here would be a serious security issue.'

'*She's* a serious security issue,' the new man yells at her before turning back to me. 'Who the bloody hell are you and what are you doing in the staff-only area of my bank?'

My eyes flick to Leo as I turn to face the new man. 'I work here,' I try, my voice shaking as much as my confidence in this ridiculous plan is.

'You've *just* told me you work next door. If you work here, why aren't you on any of the staff rosters? Where's your staff ID? Why weren't you here at nine o'clock this morning?'

'Who are you?' I counter. 'You're the intruder. Why have I never seen you before? Where's *your* staff ID?'

He swiftly produces it from his pocket. Hmpf.

All the customers in the bank have turned to look at the source of the yelling, and joy of joys, my managing director didn't stop at putting her head round the door of the bank but has now come to stand inside, closely followed by the nameless man. They look at each other like they should've brought a bucket of popcorn and a large Coke.

'I was trying to tell you that Jerry's been signed off for two weeks with tonsillitis,' Casey says. 'This is his temporary replacement from another branch, Mr Atherley.'

'Do you think I don't know a bank robber when I see one?' Mr Atherley demands.

'A bank robber?' I splutter. 'Oh, come on. Seriously?'

He crosses his arms and glares at me a bit harder. 'Behind the counter is strictly off limits to the general public and you're running around in there willy nilly! What exactly are you doing if not trying to rob the joint? There's no point playing innocent now you've been caught!'

Leo looks like he walked into a bank and ended up in a fridge-freezer.

I give him a smile through gritted teeth. 'The world has gone nuts. How strong was the mulled wine from The Bum on Saturday? I think people are still drunk!'

'I've clearly come at a bad time,' he says, gesturing towards the door. 'I'd best leave you to it.'

Even in the midst of all this, it strikes me how sweet he is. He *must* have realized what's going on by now. The replacement manager has just yelled that I'm not staff about twenty times and he's mentioned me working next door. He knows what's going on – he's just making things less awkward for me by disappearing.

Again, I realize how much better he deserves than this.

'Leo, wait!' I lean forward to grab his arm just as Mr Atherley grabs mine and curls his fingers around my wrist.

'Oh no, you're not going anywhere, Little Miss Thief.'

Leo stops and turns back, half-looking like he wants to run away and half-looking like he wants to lamp Mr Atherley for hurting me.

Which is quite sweet, given the circumstances.

It's a perfect storm of everything you don't want to happen happening all at once. All the people you hoped would never be in the same place at the same time are all right there. I can almost hear the *Jaws* music.

Oh, wait. No, that's just the police sirens.

'Yes, you can look worried, girl. "I work next door and someone gave me security codes,"' Mr Atherley says, putting on a high voice to imitate me. 'What a lot of nonsense. Casing the joint, more like. The police are on their way. I'm sure they'll be happy I caught you so early – attempted robbery, trespassing, fraud, and there are many other charges relating to being in the staff-only area of a bank without permission.'

'This is really just a big misunderstanding. I have permission. This was fine with –' I cut myself off before I drop Jerry in it. He *shouldn't* have ever let me in here, I know that, and I can't throw him under a bus to save my own skin.

'I don't want to hear your excuses. You can explain to the police. Honestly, I don't know how you ever thought you were going to get away with it.'

'Me neither,' I mutter, although I'm not talking about robbing a bank.

'George …' Leo starts, but he's cut off by the flash of blue lights and the slamming of car doors outside.

* * *

Handcuffs are tight, aren't they?

I've been dragged outside into the street to save making a scene in the bank, as if the angry man pacing up and down outside shouting about robberies while a policeman tries to calm him down is making any less of a scene. Except now we've got an even bigger audience.

Casey has thrown herself against the door of the police car to stop them taking me away.

'Oh, come on,' I say for the millionth time. 'I'm not a bank robber.'

'If I had a penny for every time I've heard a bank robber say that,' Mr Atherley scoffs.

'This is ridiculous.' I turn to the other policeman who is standing close to me in case I make a run for it despite the handcuffs. 'Everyone there will vouch for me. I've worked next door for years. I know all your staff.'

'So you've used your connections to gain access,' Mr Atherley sneers.

'I wasn't doing any harm. I popped in to see my friend.' I nod towards Casey who nods emphatically in agreement.

Everyone is looking. The two managing directors are watching with extreme interest, and from the corner by the bank I can see Maggie standing in the doorway of It's A Wonderful Latte. Mary is in the doorway of One Light, along with every other shop owner standing in their own doorways, and there's a crowd of people gathered around. But mainly there's Leo.

He stands out because he's the only part of this I truly care about.

'She's not doing anything wrong,' Casey says.

'There's an innocent, completely reasonable explanation for this,' I say, hoping no one will actually ask me for it.

The two policemen seem thoroughly bemused by all this. One I recognize from when our charity box was stolen last year; he sat in my office with a cup of tea and did his incident report, and I know he remembers me too. He's probably trying to work out how I went from charity shop manager to bank robber.

'I'd *love* to hear it,' he says, standing next to Mr Atherley, who is *still* ranting.

I wonder if distracting them by suggesting anger management therapy for him would help?

I can't avoid it, can I? There is nothing I can say now except the truth.

I look at Leo, his eyes holding mine across the crowd.

This is it. The truth has to come out. In the most public way possible. I should have been brave enough to tell him before, at least it would've been private then.

I go to speak but Leo steps forward before I have a chance.

'This is all my fault,' he says. 'She's not trying to rob the place.'

'Maybe you could enlighten us on what exactly is going on here then?' the policeman next to me asks.

Leo's eyes don't leave mine as he speaks. Burning and intense, impossible to look away from no matter how much I want to sink into the ground and never have to face him again.

'She's pretending to work there so I don't find out that she's the girl who saved my life on the night I tried to kill myself.'

My breath catches in my throat. He knows. I've gone from angry at the mistaken robbery accusation to blinking back tears. His eyes still don't leave mine as he continues.

'This isn't a robbery attempt. She isn't casing the bank. I phoned the charity shop instead of the suicide prevention helpline by mistake, and instead of telling me I was an idiot, she made me want to live again.'

He swallows and I think I'd be able to rip these handcuffs off with the sheer force of how much I want to hug him, but I stay still because Leo would probably rather have a hug from a pissed-off porcupine at the moment.

'I was a mess, and I opened up to someone I thought was a complete stranger *because* I thought they were an anonymous stranger,' he continues. 'And when she realized, she didn't want to embarrass me by admitting we knew each other. I wouldn't mind betting that she told me she worked at the bank on the spur of the moment because she realized I'd figure it out if I knew she worked at One Light, but once it was out there, she couldn't take it back.'

His mouth curves up into a sad smile and his eyes still haven't left mine. Everyone else fades away as he speaks. Despite the crowd of onlookers, it's like me and Leo are the only people here.

'And I think she's been hopping back and forth for the past few weeks, pretending to be on a break while someone runs through the back way and tells her I'm waiting in the bank.'

His beautiful blue eyes are earnest now, like he's waiting for some sort of confirmation from me.

I nod and he nods back, and I can almost see the light go out in his eyes. Maybe it wasn't confirmation he was looking for. Maybe it was denial. Maybe he wanted me to say he's got it all wrong.

'True?' the policeman next to me asks.

'Unfortunately,' I mutter.

'There we go then. Problem solved. No bank robbers here, Mr Atherley.'

'You're not telling me you actually believe that?' Mr Atherley splutters.

The policeman next to him looks between me and Leo. 'Oddly enough, I do.'

The other one undoes my handcuffs and gives me a pat on the shoulder. 'Do yourself a favour, Miss Bailey – stay out of the bank until the other guy comes back. I don't think this one likes you very much. Can't imagine why.'

It's over in a flash. It feels huge and monumental, like there should've been a clap of thunder and a strike of lightning or something, but there's just … emptiness. The police car drives away and everyone disperses. Mr Atherley goes back into the bank and makes the 'I'm watching you' gesture at me, before telling Casey she'll be fired if she doesn't get back to work immediately. Maggie has disappeared back inside It's A Wonderful Latte, while some of the gathered crowd have gone into One Light so Mary's followed them back in. Within a few minutes, the only people still outside are the two nameless managing directors, who are looking aghast and having a hushed conversation with each other.

And Leo.

Who's just standing there staring at the pavement.

I rub my wrists as I approach him. 'Leo, I'm so sorr –'

'Don't, George. I get it. If you'd said you worked at One Light, I'd have known it was you. I understand why it came to this.'

'How long have you known?'

He does a self-deprecating laugh that doesn't sound like he finds anything remotely funny. 'If I'm honest with myself? Since the day after. You came into the shop and your voice sounded so familiar, and you asked me what I'd done the night before and you bought me a coffee, and I was sure it was you. I *saw* the moment you realized it was me cross your face, and I've only just

282

understood what that look meant. I thought I must be imagining it. Projecting. Wishful thinking. I wanted it to be you, George.' He kicks at a piece of broken concrete edging. 'And then we started spending time together and you said so many things that you'd said on the phone, and I kept thinking it was you and then telling myself how stupid I was being, it couldn't possibly be you.'

I want to say something, do something, march over and pull him into my arms, but he's tense, his shoulders drawn up, his back hunched over in a harsh curve. He'd look more approachable if he was surrounded by barbed wire and holding a 'leave me alone' sign.

'And, well, we've established before that you're a terrible liar. I knew something was going on with the bank. No one has that many breaks. You don't know the first thing about banking. Everyone else in the bank wears a uniform. And mainly, I once said to you that someone saved my life, and you didn't ask me about it. I know you well enough to know that you would've pounced on that and not let go until you had an answer – unless you already knew. Bernard calling you Clarence suddenly started to make blinding sense in a way that I understood on some level but I still didn't make the connection. It was only on Saturday night that I understood what I didn't know I didn't understand until then.'

'Why didn't you say anything?'

'I didn't want to know. I meant what I said on Saturday. I didn't want this to end. If I knew what I didn't know then I'd know.'

'In any other context, that would probably be the strangest sentence you've ever uttered.'

He doesn't smile like I was hoping he would, and I sigh, feeling like the few feet between us on the pavement is six miles wide. 'I am sorry, Leo. I know you don't want to hear it but I never meant for it to come to this.'

He goes to speak but nothing comes out. He shakes his head and looks the other way.

283

I want to touch him. He looks like he always looks when he needs a hug, and every inch of me wants to cross the few steps between us and, at the very least, slide my hand across his shoulder and squeeze. But I know Leo. Sometimes you can get away with pushing him and sometimes you will only succeed in pushing him further away, and I know that if I touch him now, it will be the latter.

'It's fine,' he says eventually. 'Like I said, I understand why it did. You don't have to explain yourself.'

This is all so wrong. Everything feels wrong. He says it's fine but nothing has ever felt less fine than this.

'Thank you for what you did that night.' When he turns around again, he's biting his lip so hard it looks like he's trying to give himself a new piercing with his teeth. 'You saved my life. I shouldn't have asked you not to hang up, but I don't know what I would have done if you had. You made me feel normal. I'd been feeling alone for a long time and for the first time, I wasn't alone that night. And I haven't been since because you made sure I wasn't.'

He doesn't seem angry, or hurt, or ... anything. His voice is low and monotone, and his face is expressionless.

He looks at my two managers who are now standing to one side and furiously consulting between themselves and a conference call with someone else on a phone the man is holding up. 'You've got the best manager in the business here. Above and beyond. I get that she's probably going to be in a bit of trouble for all this, but don't be too harsh. It was my fault, not hers. I phoned the wrong number and begged her not to hang up on me. She saved my life and she's been working night and day to save my livelihood because of what I told her. She should be rewarded, not punished.'

'Are you seriously trying to save my job?' I say in surprise. 'You must hate my guts right now.'

'I could never hate you, George. And you saved mine, so tit for tat.'

'Tit for tat?' I don't try to hide the confusion on my face. 'We've come to that now?'

He shrugs.

This is so unlike Leo. He's cold and emotionless and his smile seems like a distant memory.

'I don't care about my job, Leo. I don't care about the bank or nearly getting arrested. I only care about you. This all got so out of hand. I never meant –'

'Okay, thanks for all you've done.' He looks me straight in the eyes again and his gaze lingers for so long that I think he'd take less time if one of us was off to the electric chair. 'Have a nice life.'

Have a nice life?

I don't think there's much life left given the way it feels like my heart actually stops beating.

'That's it? You're just going to walk away?' I shout after him.

He comes back. 'What did you expect me to do, George? I trusted you more than I've ever trusted anyone in my life. I have *never* opened up to anyone the way I did to you.'

'But I didn't use anything you told me. Everything you said on that phone is completely confidential, I didn't –'

'I'm not talking about the phone call. I'm talking about you. I held back on the phone. I didn't hold back with you. I've been feeling things for you that I've always thought were never going to happen for me. And now I feel like I've been conned. You've been lying to me for weeks. I thought I felt something special with the girl on the phone but even that was a lie.'

'How could I tell you I was ten minutes down the road? I wanted you to talk, you *needed* to talk, and you'd have stopped if I'd said that.'

'Yeah, and I suppose everything else was just a token agreement too? All that stuff about feeling trapped and being frightened of being alive? Feeling like I felt? Hollow words to prevent another loser on another bridge becoming yet another statistic.'

285

'No! My God, Leo, for the first time in my life, someone put into words the feelings I'd had for years and had never had the courage to confront before.'

'Forgive me for not believing you.'

My breath is coming out in fast, sharp pants, and I can feel myself panicking because he's going to walk away and there's nothing I can do about it.

'This whole thing is an elaborate con. Everyone who I felt comfortable with, people I thought were my friends, *our* friends who helped us decorate the other night, and everyone knew except me. Everyone was lying for you. Bernard, your dad, Casey, the bank manager, Mary from the shop.' He glances up towards It's A Wonderful Latte. 'I bet even my mum knows, doesn't she?'

I can't answer without giving him the answer he doesn't want to hear.

'Your silence is enough of an answer.'

I can feel myself losing him and I don't know what to say to make this better. 'But no one knew why. I never told anyone that.'

'I don't care about that. Let everyone know. Talk about mental health. Suicide is the biggest killer of men under 50. Someone attempts it every forty-three seconds. Even people who are happy and friendly on the surface can be suffering. Anyone can smile in public and in their heads, they're mapping out where the nearest bridge is. I'm not embarrassed about that. I'm not trying to hide what I nearly did. We shouldn't be acting like mental health is something to be ashamed of. It affects everyone. No one is immune. Everyone is fighting a battle that we know nothing about.' He pushes a hand through his hair. 'I'm not embarrassed because I tried to kill myself. I hope that what happened this morning gets put up online and goes viral so other people see that this can affect anyone. Even people who seem happy on the surface. I hope others see it and know they don't have to suffer in silence, that there are helplines like yours, that there are people who care, people like you out there who'd go to such extreme lengths to help someone. To save someone.'

'I didn't stop you jumping off that bridge, Leo. You stopped yourself. You called me *because* you wanted to live. I didn't do that.'

'You've done it every day since. Don't you get that? You saved my life because I could suddenly picture a future with you. You gave me something to live for, George. Something to look forward to every morning. And I don't just mean since the phone call. I've looked forward to seeing you every day since I opened. For years, I've *hated* Sundays because I don't get to see you.'

'Me too,' I say, feeling abnormally tearful. That's the kind of thing I've *wished* I could hear Leo saying to me for years, but it's all so wrong now.

'I've always liked you, and I've never had the courage to say anything, and then I got to know you and you were not just my favourite customer, you were my perfect person. I thought you understood me, but it's easy to "understand" someone when they've already told you exactly what they want to hear.'

The tears pooling in my eyes spill over. I try to speak but the only thing that escapes is a huge sob.

'I understand why you did it,' he says gently, looking like he's about to cry himself. 'But how can I ever trust you again?'

And that says it all, doesn't it? I know Leo well enough to know that betraying his trust is one of the worst things anyone can do to him. I know he's shared things with me that he's never had the courage to tell anyone before, and I've just undone all of that.

'Once again, your silence is answer enough.' His voice breaks on the final words and he turns around and walks away.

And I don't know how to stop him. It's like I'm outside of myself, watching on, unable to do anything to stop it happening. There is nothing I can say to make this better.

No matter the intention, nothing changes the fact that I have broken his heart as much as I've broken my own.

Chapter 19

I feel empty when I get back inside One Light. Desolate. Stupid. Why didn't I see this coming? Did I honestly think I could keep up the pretence forever without him finding out? I care about him more than the momentary embarrassment that telling him it was me would've caused, and now what? He'll never trust me again. I doubt he'll ever even speak to me again. He'll probably never trust anybody again. Next time he needs to talk to someone, what's he going to do? Because I know one thing for sure – he won't phone One Light again.

'You okay?' Mary asks as I traipse through the shop, aware of all the eyes on me. For once, I'm not exactly pleased at the number of customers we've got.

I shake my head, knowing I'm going to break down in tears if she looks at me too kindly.

'I hate to say it but both managers are waiting for you upstairs in the office, and they don't look happy.'

Of course they don't look happy. I trudge up the stairs feeling drained, each foot taking too much energy to lift. As if everything they've just heard wasn't bad enough *without* adding the almost arrest, the handcuffs, and the very big, very public spectacle. It doesn't exactly reflect well on the charity, does it?

In the office, the man is doing something on his tablet and the lady is sitting in my desk chair with her hands folded in her lap, waiting.

There are no spare chairs and I can't be bothered to drag one out of the kitchen, so I sit down on a plastic bag full of rags that haven't been collected yet. It's probably the most informal spot for what I'm sure is going to be a formal firing.

'I don't know where to start,' she shakes her head. 'Answered a critical call, pretended to be someone else, disobeyed the fundamental rules this charity exists on, used a brilliant marketing strategy to help a competitor rather than benefit the charity you work for. The list is endless.'

'Leo's *not* a competitor. Between us, we've been helping the whole street so everyone benefits,' I sigh. 'And I didn't pretend to be someone else. He knew he'd phoned the wrong number. I just didn't tell him when I realized it was him. I told a little white lie that got out of hand.'

'Georgia, you answered a call meant for the helpline. The people there are trained in dealing with those calls. They know what to say, how to act, how to handle those sorts of issues. You do not. You could've said the wrong thing and pushed a suicidal person over the edge.'

'But I didn't.' I know my response is half-hearted at best, but I've given up trying to defend myself.

'What about you?' she asks. 'Training is in place to help *both* staff and the people who use our service. How would you have felt if he had jumped? You can't save every person who phones. How would you have handled it if you had heard him take his last breath and drown?'

Tears fill my eyes at the thought and the look on her face softens for a moment. 'I've worked on the phones, Georgia. There are some things that you can never un-hear. It might seem harsh to you, but our rules are in place to protect everyone – our staff *and* the suicidal people.'

'You know what, maybe you shouldn't class them as suicidal people like there's something wrong with them, like they're different to other people, a race all of their own. Everyone is individual. Everyone can hit hard times and end up in a place where they never thought they'd be. Sometimes the only thing anyone needs is a friend.' If I'm not well on my way to being fired here, snapping at the managing director will certainly speed up the process. 'And you know what, if he had jumped, I'd still be glad I'd answered that phone because at least he'd have known in his final breath that someone cared about him.'

'We can't be emotionally involved. Part of the training procedure for staff on the helpline is learning to distance themselves. It's a heavy, emotional job that takes its toll. You're a retail manager, you don't know how to cope or what to say, and the … *mess* … you seem to have got yourself into over that phone call is proof of that.' She struggles to find an accurate word for the current situation and I know exactly how she feels.

'Look, it happened once.' I try to tamp down my annoyance. I understand what she's saying but it's done now. I can't change it. 'I've asked you repeatedly to get the leaflets reprinted with more space between the two phone numbers. It's never happened before –'

'And it won't again?' She phrases it as a question but uses a tone that suggests there's only one answer.

I don't reply. Because honestly? If I picked up the phone again and someone on the other end asked me what it would feel like if they jumped, I *still* wouldn't be able to hang up. 'I answered that call because that's what anyone would've done. What came after that was because I saw a way to help someone and I took it.'

'We have no choice but to terminate your employment,' the man says, finally glancing up from his tablet. 'Taking that call and not *immediately* telling the caller they had the wrong number and giving them the right one, using the information he'd told you in confidence to gain access to his life, trying to fix the problems he'd shared with you in private, forming a relationship with him, and then there's all this nonsense of getting the bank involved, pretending to work there … we don't even know what to do with that. All followed by this scene with the police this morning. It falls far below the professional standards we expect from our staff. You are the face of our charity in the community. We are supposed to present a solid, strong, and steady base from which we help people.'

'And yet, when someone actually turns to me for help, I get sacked for it.'

'Actually, you would probably have only got a warning for taking the call. It's everything that seems to have followed that's grounds for dismissal.'

'Great,' I mutter.

'I've just heard you tell that man that you don't care about your job,' the lady says.

'That's not true. I was just saying that … well, not just saying it, I do care about my job, I love working here … but I love him more.' I pause as the words themselves hit me. *Really* hit me. Because what started off as a crush has turned into so much more as I've got to know him. 'He needed to talk that night and if it means losing my job because I talked to him then so be it. I'd do it again in a heartbeat. I'd do all of it again because we've made a difference to this street. Because of Leo's call, we managed to do something good here that has brought people and businesses back. Our sales this month have almost tripled from what they were last December. Our donations are up. Our high street feels alive again. People are happy. People are doing their last-minute Christmas shopping here rather than rushing through as quickly as possible to get to the retail park. But mainly, I would answer that call again because Leo is still alive, and if I had any part of that then it was all worth it.'

The man tuts.

'What if he was your son? Your husband, your brother, your uncle, your nephew, your cousin, your friend? Anyone you loved? Would you say the same then?'

'Rules are there for a reason,' the lady says, not answering my question.

'Sometimes rules have to be broken.'

The man gives a nod of acquiescence. 'Your final pay cheque will be in your bank next week.'

'We don't have an option here, Georgia,' she says. 'Everyone understands that you were trying to do the right thing. Mary has been pleading your case while you were still outside. Even the girl from the bank came in and tried to take the blame, but ultimately, you are in a position of responsibility and we can't have a manager behaving like this and let it go.'

'It's fine,' I say, because I do get it. How many times has the thought of being fired crossed my mind in the last few weeks? I knew the consequences. I just convinced myself that I'd never be found out, not by them and not by Leo.

I collect my bag from my locker and hand her my set of keys. I never did find out their names.

I trudge home the long way round to avoid walking past It's A Wonderful Latte.

Maybe it's for the best that I don't work on Oakbarrow High Street anymore. I'll never be able to set foot in It's A Wonderful Latte again, and that's always been the highlight of my day.

Chapter 20

It's Christmas Eve and even thinking that reminds me of the first line of 'Fairytale of New York' and singing along with Leo in the car, and that sends me down a spiral of memories I'd be better off forgetting. I should be working today. I always work Christmas Eve and Mary always has the day off, and volunteers don't come in this close to Christmas. It's usually just me in the shop, which is fine because it's always absolutely dead on the high street on Christmas Eve, so it doesn't matter if I close up for two minutes while I pop to the loo or make a cup of tea. I was looking forward to it this year because Oakbarrow High Street is so much more lively now, I thought the Christmas Eve atmosphere might feel like it did when Mum and I walked home from getting last minute Christmas dinner supplies when I was young.

In reality, I haven't got out of my pyjamas all day and the closest I've ventured to Oakbarrow High Street is the bottom of the garden to put food out for the cats, and the most interaction I've had is sitting on the step with the nervous little tabby who usually hides under the hedge on my lap while I cried into her fur.

Now it's ten o'clock and I'm in the kitchen peeling potatoes in preparation for tomorrow's lunch that I always try to do just like Mum would've made it. All I can see is the Christmas rose Leo bought me, taunting me with its creamy white petals from the window ledge.

I've wanted to call him so many times today, but I haven't. I didn't think I'd be able to cope with him putting the phone down on me, as he undoubtedly would. I just want to make sure he's all right because he seemed so broken as he walked away yesterday and it was all because of me. I did that to him. Maybe I'll try again after Christmas. Maggie will know what happened by now and she'll look after him. She'll make sure he's oka –

A sudden hammering on the door makes me jump out of my skin.

'Who on earth's knocking like that at this time of night?' my dd asks from the living room.

He starts to get up out of his chair but I stop him. 'I'll get it.'

When I pull the door open, I'd be less surprised to see a sentient snowman than the sight that actually greets me.

'Oh, George, I'm so glad I've caught you!' Bernard pants, sweat beading on his forehead. He's bending over trying to catch his breath and looking like he ran all the way here. 'It's Leo. He's on the bridge again and he needs to talk to you, can you come right now?'

My dad has appeared behind me, and he grabs a coat and thrusts it into my hands. 'Go! I'll defrost the car and be right behind you!'

'Bloody hell, Bernard!' I say, shrugging my arms into my coat as we run down the icy garden path and out onto the street. 'What's he doing up there again?'

'I don't know,' he wheezes. 'He wouldn't tell me anything. You're the only person he'll talk to.'

'I don't think it's me he wants to talk to,' I shout over the noise of our feet hitting the pavement. 'You must've heard what happened?'

'I don't think there's anyone within a hundred-mile radius who didn't hear what happened.'

'Brilliant,' I mutter. Small town gossip spreads faster than superglue you've accidentally got on your fingers and this must've been the zenith of small town gossip. 'How did Leo seem? What if he jumps before we get there, Bernard?'

'George, I don't think …'

'This is all my fault,' I say as we pass the magnolia tree that Leo and I stood under, and turn out of the residential streets and onto the upper end of the high street. The pavements are gritted and I feel a flash of satisfaction that the council have sat up and taken notice. This is the first time in many winters that Oakbarrow has been gritted.

'It's my fault,' Bernard says. 'I said too much on Saturday night.'

I shake my head even though he's concentrating on where he's going rather than looking at me. 'I did it, Bernard. I asked everyone to lie for me. Even you. You love Leo, you didn't want to lie to him, but I gave everyone no choice.'

Bernard makes a noncommittal grunt. 'But I understand why.'

'How did you know, anyway?'

'I was around that night. Doing my nightly patrols, as usual. I saw him up there, was on my way to go and talk to him when I heard him on the phone. I didn't mean to eavesdrop or anything but when I realized what was going on, I thought I'd better stay nearby in case he tried to jump again. I put two and two together after that. After he went home, I walked over the bridge and saw the little pile of leaflets you leave there. I'd seen your light on in the shop. The next night, I caught you painting his window and telling him you worked for the bank. He asked me if I knew anyone from the charity shop because he'd talked to someone on the phone and couldn't find her. Things started to add up.'

I nod because I'd guessed as much already.

'I love that boy like a son. Derek was one of my greatest friends and he'd be so proud of the man Leo's become. I care for you too, Georgia, but you both needed a shove in the right direction. How much longer did you think you could pretend to work in the bank? He was already suspecting. I was trying to give you the opportunity to tell him before it turned out worse than it was.'

'How come we didn't know you were friends with his father?'

'I didn't want him to feel some sense of responsibility towards me. If the old man had bought the café as planned, he would've brought me food and drink every day, I know he would. I didn't want Leo to think he had to do the same. But it turns out he does the same anyway because that's the kind of person he is. He's a good lad, Georgia, and the closer you two got, the worse this was going to turn out for both of you.'

'I know,' I pant as we race past the war memorial and the Christmas tree, and turn right at the church, onto the main traffic road out of Oakbarrow.

Water is running down my face and I'm not sure if it's sweat or tears. Pure panic at the thought that we might be too late. I cannot let Leo go after all of this. Especially when the way he's feeling now is my fault.

The adrenaline is making everything numb. My muscles are burning in my legs, my feet are screaming, and even with the road salt, I've been doing a good *Dancing on Ice* impression on the more slippery spots.

The bridge is in sight. I can see the superstructures overhead, and I somehow manage to run even faster, despite the fact that the bottoms of my pyjama trousers are wet from the road and flapping around my feet, doing their best to trip me up.

And then he's there, standing on the patch of grass at the side of the bridge, between the bollards, and I launch myself at him, wrapping my arms around him and holding on so tight that he's going to have difficulty breathing.

'I know you hate me but I'm not letting go. I love you too much to let you jump, Leo.'

He … laughs? A gentle, bemused chuckle. Why is he laughing? I squeeze him tighter just in case he's lost it completely.

'I'm not jumping off this bridge.' His lips press against the side of my neck. 'And I love you too, George.'

'What?' My eyes spring open in surprise as I suddenly realize we're at the side of the bridge – there's a six-foot-high barrier wall at this part. We're nowhere near the broken rail where it would be easy to climb over.

'I am, however, going to die of a punctured lung if you don't loosen your grip a bit.'

I mumble an apology as he sets my feet down on the grass and I scrunch my hand in the sleeve of his coat, determined not to let him go, even though I suddenly get the feeling that this isn't as straightforward as I thought it was.

'If I had any doubt that you love me, at least now I've got the bruised ribs to remind me.'

'What?' I ask as my eyes adjust to the darkness and I realize what I'm looking at on the bridge.

Maggie is standing there.

And Mary and Patrick are holding hands.

And Casey is standing with my dad. How did he get here without us seeing him?

Bernard is limping over to join them.

Have they all come to stop Leo jumping?

Have they come to push me off?

'What's going on?' I ask as some of the unexpected exercise haze clears and I can think over the blood rushing in my head to realize what he said. 'Did you just say you loved me?'

'I did. I do. It's Christmas Eve and I wanted to see you at the place where we first "met".'

'We first met in the coffee shop a couple of years ago. It's a lot warmer and a lot less … bridge-y … than this. What are you doing up here, Leo? From the audience, I take it you're not jumping?' I gesture to said audience. Dad's car is parked on the pavement and they're standing in the beam from the headlights facing us. He must've gone the other way round to get here before me and Bernard.

He shakes his head. 'No. I'm apologising. I overreacted yesterday.'

'Well, thanks for the heart attack.' I still won't let go of his sleeve but I put my other hand on my chest to try to stop my heart bursting through. It's pounding so hard that it might be a very real possibility. 'You couldn't have just phoned and said "meet me on the bridge"? What is this, some sort of revenge? Nearly kill me with worry?'

'Who said I was jumping off the bridge?'

'Well, Bernard …' I go to point at him but stop in midair, feeling sheepish as I realize he didn't actually say that. 'He said you were on the bridge and you wanted to see me. I kind of jumped to conclusions.'

He smiles. 'You worry too much.'

There's no disputing that. I feel overwhelmed and elated and excited because Leo's just said he loves me, despite everything that's happened since that phone call. Even when I'm standing here in tatty pyjamas that I've been wearing since last night, damp from the melting ice and covered in road salt, and my dad's old coat that's baggy enough to wrap around me twice.

'But you came anyway,' he continues. 'Even after everything I said yesterday, how harsh I was to you, you still ran the entire length of Oakbarrow on a glacial Christmas Eve because you thought I needed you.'

'I needed *you*, Leo. All I care about is you being okay.'

'I am, because of you. *Because* you lied to me. Because you were right, I wouldn't have talked to you that night if I'd known you were someone I'd see the next day. If you'd told me afterwards, I'd have clammed up and avoided you because I'd have been embarrassed. I really do get it, George. I know why you said you worked in the bank and that once you'd said it, you couldn't do anything but go along with it.'

'Well, you knew that yesterday. What's changed?'

'Time to think about it. And Mary can be really vicious when she's angry.'

'Mary talked to you?' I ask, my eyes flicking up to the row of people on the bridge.

'Mary threatened to cut my toes off and feed them to the pigeons. But yeah, she talked to me. Casey too. And Bernard. Your dad was a little more polite but the implication was the same.' He gives me a tight smile. 'I'm sorry about your job. I didn't mean you to get fired because of me.'

'It's not because of you. It's because I'm an idiot, and because I couldn't promise them I'd never take a call like that again. I couldn't tell them I regretted it because I don't. Oh, and the whole population of Oakbarrow watched me get arrested for trying to rob a bank. That might've had something to do with it.' I look over at our audience again. 'I can't believe they all talked to you. No wonder my dad was so keen to go and wish our neighbour a happy Christmas today, he was finding an excuse to phone you without me hearing, right?'

'In all fairness, it made a nice change from my mum's constant scolding over how badly I treated you yesterday.'

'Leo, it's fine. You were shocked and –'

'It's not fine. Everything you did was to help me. And between us, I think we achieved something pretty damn special. I *still* mean what I said on Saturday. I don't want this to end. You've made me love this place again because you're in it. I've spent so many years desperate to get out of here, but when I'm with you, I can't remember why I ever wanted to be anywhere else. I've spent years resenting this town, and all of that disappeared when I met you. Spending this month with you, running around the streets in the dark, making our town better … it's felt like home. When I'm with you, there's no place I'd rather be than right here.'

'Me neither.' My voice catches in my throat, unable to believe this is happening.

'Except Paris.' He reaches into his back pocket and pulls out an envelope and holds it out to me. 'Two weeks in January. Just you and me. And before you start worrying, every single one of those people up there have volunteered to look in on your dad multiple times a day and make sure your cats are well fed.'

Tears are pooling in my eyes and blurring the tickets in my hand. It's not even the tickets that are making me cry, it's the fact that Leo knows me well enough to know all the excuses I'd find not to go and has already taken care of them.

'Leo, I …' I'm at a loss for what to say to get across how much that simple thing means. 'How can you afford this?' My words come out in a stuttery jumbled mess. I'm terrified of the idea of leaving here but exhilarated at the idea of finally going somewhere and seeing a bit of the world, with him.

'Because *someone* did something that's made coffee very popular in Oakbarrow again.'

'Yeah, it was mainly your mum with the social media, wasn't it?'

He drops his arm around my shoulder and squeezes me into his side. 'You know exactly who I mean.'

'What about It's A Wonderful Latte? You're there every day, you can't just disappear for two weeks.' The grin he gives me is cheeky and just a little bit smug. 'Can you?'

'My sister's going to step in for a while when we're away, and on busy days like when the craft market is in town. Paris won't be our last trip and Becky and Izzy are ready and waiting. Becky actually wants to do it. She knew a lot about what my father wanted to do with the place and now she's confronted the emotions that come with it, she wants to run it with me and Mum and honour him as a family.'

'He'd love that.'

'He would. And he'd love you for what you've done for all of us … That's why they're here.' He nods to our friends and family on the bridge. 'It seemed right that we all spend Christmas Eve together. And Mum and Becky are doing dinner tomorrow, Mary's spending it with Patrick, and Casey's going to her own family, but Bernard's coming, and you and your dad are invited too. Please say you'll come. After everything we've done for Christmas in the past few weeks, I can't imagine spending it without you.'

'Are you sure?'

He steps minutely closer and tucks the strands of hair that have escaped from my ponytail back behind my ear, letting his thumb linger on my earlobe, brushing one of the plain silver studs that I haven't even changed for Christmas earrings today. His eyes are holding mine, shining in the dark night, the passionate look in them leaving me with no doubt about what's coming.

My breath catches as he angles his head, not dropping eye contact until the very last moment when our lips finally meet. It feels like the first time I've ever kissed him, at least the first time with no secrets between us, and the kiss turns deeper, more desperate, as I let go of everything that's happened in the past twenty-four hours, all the weeks leading up to it, the pain of yesterday, the sheer dread that took over when Bernard knocked earlier, the panic and fear of losing Leo.

I melt against him as his hands clutch my jaw, and he kisses me like he's drowning. My fingers wind in his hair and pull him impossibly closer as everything else fades away. We could be hit by a low-flying sleigh carrying Father Christmas and I wouldn't notice.

It's an embarrassingly long time before we remember we've got an audience, but instead of jumping back awkwardly like I expected him to, Leo rests his forehead against mine.

'Does that answer your question?' he whispers, his breath warm against my cheek.

I'm incapable of words so I just nod, not wanting to pull away – mainly because I like being this close to him, and also because I'm not sure my knees won't buckle after that kiss.

'There's something else,' Leo says when he does inch back a little. 'I got in touch with the owner of Hawthorne's today. It's the grandson now. He's younger than us, grew up playing virtual games on screens small enough to fit on a matchbox. Never knew granddad's old shop in its heyday, didn't think it had any value now. I explained a bit about what's been going on here, about

301

the street and trying to take things back to how they used to be. He put his father on who's a bit older than us and remembers it like we do. We had a really good chat, he remembered me and my father, and the upshot of it is that they've arranged a structural engineer to come out in January and make sure it's safe, and then they need a clean-up team and a new manager before they re-open. I said I knew an amazing retail manager who happens to be at a loose end at the moment.'

'You did not!' I slap at him but instead of hitting him I scrunch my fingers in his coat and squeeze his arm.

'Hawthorne Junior can't wait to meet you. I told him everything and he loved it. He looked up our stories online while we were talking. Said we clearly made a great team and as long as you'd be the manager, offered us both an additional job doing weekly window designs like his father used to do.'

'Us? How are you going to manage that? You're rushed off your feet as it is. Even your sister getting more involved won't change that.'

He smiles that 'I know something you don't know' grin again. 'Well, my new assistant manager was delegated his first job tonight – to go and collect my favourite Georgia and fetch her here. Admittedly his jobs will probably be more coffee-related in the future, but –'

'Bernard's your new assistant manager?'

'I've always said I'd employ him if I had the work, and now I do. Because you didn't give up.'

'*You* didn't give up, Leo. You reached out for help when you needed it. That's the bravest thing anyone can do.'

'And I'm so glad I did.' He's blushing as he speaks. 'I know that we haven't waved a magic wand over Oakbarrow and made all its problems go away. All the shopkeepers who've come back might not stay, customers might stop coming, not all the empty shops will sell to new retailers, but things are better than they have been for years, and as long as you're with me, some of your

302

positivity might rub off. And if it doesn't then you'll just have to brew an extra batch of that potion.'

'We do make a pretty good team, after all.'

He grins. 'And we know that Bernard makes a great Santa for when you re-open Santa's grotto next year.'

I grin at the thought, fully expecting my face to actually start splitting in a minute. I'm overwhelmed at the idea of working at Hawthorne's, running a toy shop and all the possibilities it holds. Reviving a place that I loved so much when I was little for a new generation. Recreating that feeling I had as a child, the feeling of magic that's never the same once you're an adult.

'I can't believe you did all this,' I say, my voice shaky from excitement and sheer disbelief. 'You've certainly been busy.'

'Didn't sleep a wink last night,' he whispers, leaning in close. 'I can't put into words how much these past few weeks have meant to me and I hated myself for walking away yesterday. I was trying to protect myself from this lie when I knew you'd only been trying to protect me from the very beginning. Figured anyone who'd go that far for me deserved more than a quick apology.'

He reaches down to retrieve a paper bag from Patrick's shop that I hadn't even noticed leaning against the wall. 'And this.'

'What's th –' I burst out laughing when I see the purple cardboard of a selection box peeking out. 'You remembered!'

'Someone once told me that all chocolate tastes better from a selection box, but only if you eat it for breakfast.'

'Thank you,' I mouth at him, because it's such a silly little thing but he remembered something so trivial and did it anyway.

He smiles wide and uninhibited. 'I love you, George. I promise to get you a selection box for Christmas morning breakfast every year from now on.'

'That'll be pretty weird after you've broken up and are both married to other people!' Casey shouts over.

'Thanks, Case,' I shout back. 'Always the voice of reason at key romantic moments.'

'It's better than the usual Christmas Eve tradition of watching that bloody old film you've made me watch a hundred and seventy-nine times!'

'Oh, I think *It's a Wonderful Life* might have to become one of our Christmas Eve traditions too.' Leo leans over and kisses my cheek. 'It's more than just a Christmas film. I think it's brought a little magic into all our lives.'

* * *

The frosty grass of the verge crunches underfoot as we lean on the lower part of the wall and look out at the river racing along, reflecting the icicles hanging down from the underside of the bridge as they glisten in the moonlight.

Leo's arm is around me, one hand resting on the back of my neck and rubbing absentmindedly, the other intertwined with my fingers, his head leaning against mine. Dad and Maggie are chatting quietly, Casey's texting her new crush and the fact she's even bothering speaks volumes about how much she likes him, Mary and Patrick are holding hands, and Bernard looks happy and relaxed as he takes it all in.

The stars twinkling in the sky make me think of Leo's dad and my mum. Memories always feel closer at this time of year, but tonight it's like they're here with us, smiling down on Oakbarrow.

'It's another wonderful night,' Leo whispers in my ear. 'I seem to have had a lot of those since I met you.'

I look up at him and smile. 'It's the most perfect Christmas Eve I've ever had.'

He kisses me again as the church bell chimes for midnight and I wonder if maybe the sound of a bell ringing doesn't just mean that angels get their wings – maybe it means that people get their wishes too.

Acknowledgements

Mum, this line never changes because you're always there for me. Thank you for the constant patience, support, encouragement, and for always believing in me. Love you lots.

Bill, Toby, Cathie – thank you for always being supportive and enthusiastic.

An extra special thank you to Bev for always being so kind and encouraging, and for all the lovely letters this year.

Special thanks to two great friends and supportive cheerleaders – Charlotte McFall and Marie Landry.

The lovely and talented fellow HQ authors – I don't know what I'd do without all of you.

All the lovely authors and bloggers I know on Twitter. You've all been so supportive since the very first book, and I want to mention you all by name, but I know I'll forget someone and I don't want to leave anyone out, so to everyone I chat to on Twitter or Facebook – thank you.

The little writing group that doesn't have a name – Sharon Sant, Sharon Atkinson, Dan Thompson, Jack Croxall, Holly Martin, Jane Yates. I can always turn to you guys!

Thank you to Josh, the happiest guy I know, whose unflinching honesty inspired Leo.

Thank you to the team at HQ and especially my fantastic editor, Charlotte Mursell, for all the hard work and support, and for never complaining no matter how bad my first drafts are!

And finally, a massive thank you to *you* for reading!

Dear Reader,

Thank you so much for reading *It's a Wonderful Night*, I hope you enjoyed reading Georgia and Leo's story as much as I enjoyed writing it!

I loved creating the little town of Oakbarrow and watching it slowly come back to life with the joys of Christmas. Winter is my favourite time of year, and as I wrote most of this book in the spring and edited it during the summer heatwave, it was lovely to feel a bit cooler! Watching *It's a Wonderful Life* (for the millionth time!) was quite a surreal experience on a sweltering July night!

If you enjoyed *It's a Wonderful Night*, please consider leaving a review on Amazon. It only has to be a line or two, and it makes such a difference in helping other readers decide whether to pick up the book or not, and it would mean so much to me to know what you think! Did it make you smile, laugh, or cry? It definitely made me cry while writing it!

If you've been affected by any of the themes in this book, please reach out for help. The Samaritans are a 24-hour free service that you can phone on 116 123, and if you're reading this from outside the UK, there are helplines in every country.

Thank you again for reading. If you want to get in touch, you can find me on Twitter – usually when I should be writing – @be_the_spark. I would love to hear from you!

Hope to see you again soon in a future book!

Lots of love,

Jaimie

Turn the page for an exclusive extract from *The Little Wedding Island*, another charmingly romantic read from Jaimie Admans…

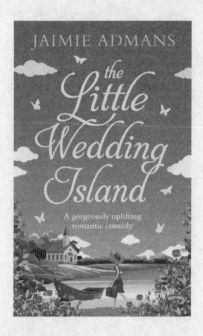

Chapter 1

'Bonnie, you can't argue with people on Twitter just because you don't agree with something they say.' My boss, Oliver, pinches the bridge of his nose like he's trying to stifle his fortieth headache since I got into his office five minutes ago.

I sigh. I *knew* I was going to get in trouble for this. 'But did you see what he said about that lovely couple's beautiful wedding? I couldn't ignore his delusional twuntery – someone had to say something.'

'He works for *The Man Land*. We're in direct competition with them and you know it. By arguing with him, you've given him more publicity. Thanks to that little stunt on Twitter over the weekend, he's gained *another* few thousand followers who are all laughing at his column *with* him while laughing *at* you and our magazine.'

'Someone needed to call him out. He can't just go around writing such horrible things about people's wedding days.'

'But not someone who works for the *other* magazine in this battle of the mags thing that Hambridge Publishing have got us embroiled in. Everyone knows it's them versus us, but it's meant to be in a professional way. It's not meant to degenerate into petty insults and name-calling. How you conduct yourself online, even outside of work, reflects back on our magazine.'

'I use an icon on Twitter. No one knows it's me.'

Oliver rubs his temples. 'You use a random photo of a wedding dress, your real name, and your bio says you write for *Two Gold Rings* magazine.'

'It's not a random photo – it'll be *my* wedding dress one day,' I mutter.

I don't know why I'm trying to defend myself. He's right. I love writing for a bridal magazine and I do mention it in my Twitter bio. The thousands of people who retweeted my argument with Mr R.C. Art over the weekend know exactly who I work for and the very public battle between us and *The Man Land*.

I try again. 'He called the bride a 21-year-old sentient boob job fake-tanned to the colour of an overcooked Wotsit and the groom a 70-year-old walking bank account sponsored by Viagra!'

Oliver lets out a snort and I frown at him. 'It's not funny. He has no right to make fun of their wedding day and publicly humiliate them online. He called it the unholy union of a cross-dressing scarecrow and a taffeta loo roll holder, and I'm still not sure which one was which. It was totally unfair. It looked like a beautiful wedding.' I scroll through my phone and hold it out to show him a picture. 'See?'

Oliver glances at it and stifles a laugh. 'Well, I've got to admit I admire the man for his way with words. He's really hit the nail on the head this time.'

'Their wedding day is *their* wedding day. Nothing about it has anything to do with him,' I snap, yanking my phone back across the desk towards me.

'Bonnie, you don't even know these people. It's not up to you to stick up for them. If they take offence at what he said, let them sue him for libel. Everyone knows this R.C. Art guy writes horrible stuff in his monthly column. It's tongue in cheek, designed to get a laugh at someone else's expense. He's like the Katie Hopkins of weddings. He says controversial things to get a reaction out of the public. *The Man Land* don't pay him for his writing, they

312

pay him for the amount of press he gets them. The best thing anyone can do is ignore him, which is not what you did.'

'He deserved putting in his place. It didn't matter who he worked for.'

'But you didn't put him in his place. All you did was give him a petty, childish argument that he could use as an example of how crazed brides get.'

'I'm not a bride.'

'Well, for whatever reason, you have a picture of a wedding dress as your profile photo …'

'Which is better than him. His profile photo is just two engagement rings with a big 'no entry' road sign over them.'

Oliver slams his hand down on the desk. 'Bonnie, you don't seem to realize how serious this is. I've had the owner of Hambridge Publishing on the phone this morning and to say he's not impressed would be an understatement. It looks like you were deliberately baiting R.C. Art and trying to draw him into an argument so *The Man Land* would come off looking worse than us.'

'That's ridiculous. If anything, he did it on purpose to make me look bad. He screencapped my tweets and posted them for all to see, and conveniently cut off his original post where he thought it was okay to compare a bride's make up to the zombies from Michael Jackson's *Thriller* video and the wedding guests to *Night of the Living Dead*. He made it look like I was randomly attacking him by taking out what I was responding to.'

'You shouldn't be responding to anything in this situation. This thing between our magazines is a well-known publicity stunt and people are watching what we do.' Oliver's face is red and he looks like he's one step away from banging his head, or more likely mine, on the desk. 'I don't care if you stood up for that couple with the best of intentions. You can't keep fixating on other people's weddings to detract from your own loneliness, and getting into a slanging match with *The Man Land*'s high-profile anti-marriage columnist is asking for trouble. Quoting his column and trying to incite your followers against him reflects badly on our whole magazine.'

'I didn't try to incite anyone! I just pointed out that there are some twats in the world and most of them have a Twitter account. And what about him? Have Hambridge been on the phone to his boss this morning yelling at him too? *He* posted screencaps of my tweets and told his followers that I'm the kind of idiot he has to deal with on a daily basis.'

'So you react with dignity, poise, and silence. Trolls go away if you don't feed them. You served him a seven-course meal with extra dessert. You may as well have called him a poo-poo head, blown a raspberry at him, and ran and told your favourite teddy bear. Actually, on second thoughts, that might have been a more mature way to deal with it.'

'R.C. Art,' I grumble. 'What kind of a stupid pseudonym is that? It sounds like a school class, which is fitting given his level of maturity. He probably looks like the offspring of a flying monkey and Yoda. No wonder he hides behind a picture and uses an alias. He's probably a bitter and twisted old man who's so bitter and twisted because he's too horrible to have ever found anyone to marry him. He wouldn't be so nasty if anyone loved him, would he?'

Oliver pinches the bridge of his nose. Again. 'Says the woman who has a wedding dress but doesn't have a groom to go with it.'

'I don't *have* the wedding dress. I've only paid a deposit and it's on hold for me at Snowdrop – you know the little bridal boutique tucked away near Marble Arch?'

'No. I've been divorced for four years. Oddly enough, I have no knowledge of bridal shops and nor do I want any.'

'You run a wedding magazine!' I say, wondering why I expect anything different from a man who has the Ambrose Bierce quote *'Love is a temporary insanity curable only by marriage'* printed on the wall above his desk.

'I edit a wedding magazine. I rely on you and your colleagues to provide the content. I'm just counting down the days until I retire and never have to read another comparison between napkin rings or essay on wedding favours ever again. Only three years and ninety-three days to go now. What I really don't need is to have to find another job at this time of my life if we lose *Two Gold Rings*, which we *are* going to at this rate.'

'We won't. *The Man Land* prints nothing but sexist, unfunny drivel. *Two Gold Rings* has been going for decades and thousands of brides have turned to us for all their wedding-planning needs. It's good versus evil. Love versus misogynistic sarcasm. There's no way they're going to win.'

'They have a much bigger online following than us, and a *lot* of men agree with their views. I'm one of them. I completely agree with R.C. Art when it comes to marriage. It's the worst mistake anyone can ever make. People spend thousands of pounds on a day that will ultimately end up destroying their lives. If he wants to make fun of that, well, good on him. Obviously we couldn't publish that kind of thing in *Two Gold Rings*, but I always thoroughly enjoy a sneaky read of his column. He's very funny.'

'He's rude and cold hearted. People's wedding days are special. They're in love. They're happy. It's the best day of their lives. How can anyone be so cynical that they agree with that anti-marriage idiot?'

'Bonnie, you're a sweet, naive, hopeless romantic. You've never been married, and judging by the soppy things you write, you still think Prince Charming is going to ride around the next corner on a big white horse. When you've come out the other side of a messy divorce, your opinion might change. To me, R.C. Art sounds like a guy who's been burnt by love and now uses his column to help other men avoid the same fate … Which brings me nicely back to why I called you in here.'

Back to the Twitter spat. I should've known my boss wouldn't let me get away with it. I stupidly believed he might be pleased with me for sticking up for a couple who didn't deserve to have their beautiful wedding day lampooned by a deluded prat for his own entertainment.

'I've got a very angry boss, Bonnie. You know what Hambridge have done with this stupid battle of the mags thing. Pitted their two worst-performing publications against each other in what they hoped would provoke a spirited public reaction to save their favourite, and they've been met with, well, mild indifference would be putting it kindly. There are no public petitions, no protests, no Twitter hashtags to save *Two Gold Rings*. It's up to us. We have to sell more copies than *The Man Land* this quarter and bring in more revenue, and if we don't then we can all kiss our jobs goodbye, and *Two Gold Rings* will be no more. Two advertisers have already pulled full-page ads from next month's issue because they don't want the association with us. Over twenty thousand people have RT-ed the screencaps of your argument that he posted. I have no doubt that more advertisers will pull out and more readers will go to pick up a copy and remember what they saw on Twitter and put it down again.'

'I was only doing what I thought was right,' I say, wondering just how much trouble I might be in here. The magazine is teetering on the edge of destruction, and I've made it worse. I *should* have just ignored R.C. Art – I know that – and now I'm, what, the 'troublesome' reporter? I feel sick. I've never been troublesome in my life.

'I know.' He pushes his hand through his curly grey hair with a sigh. 'But I think that, given the circumstances, it might be a good idea if you just… weren't here for a while.'

'For a while …' I repeat. 'You're suspending me?'

'Oh, good Lord, no.' He laughs. 'And give you a paid holiday as a reward for dragging our name through the mud of the Twittersphere? No chance, especially now that we need all hands on deck to outdo *The Man Land* next month.'

'What, then? Work from home?'

He rifles through his in-tray, suddenly looking positively gleeful. 'Have you ever heard of Edelweiss Island?'

'Like the song in *The Sound of Music*?' I ask, feeling my ears perk up. 'No, but it sounds nice. Should I have heard of it?'

'It's an island off the south coast of Britain, not far past the Isle of Wight. Calls itself The Little Wedding Island. It's been a wedding venue for years now, but not a hugely popular one, until recently. A story has leaked about the church on the island – apparently no marriage that's ever taken place there has ended in divorce. It sounds like a load of old codswallop to me, but people are talking about it, and the talk isn't going away. Some of the major newspapers have sent journalists there but they've all come back empty-handed, so no one's ever got to the bottom of it.'

'Oh, that's so romantic!' I gasp in delight. 'A church with no divorces! It must be the most amazing place.'

'That's exactly why you're going there,' Oliver says with a false grin that's probably as wide as my genuine one. 'I can't be seen to be doing nothing in light of the nonsense on Twitter, Bonnie.'

'So you're exiling me?'

'Only for a little while, and let's not call it exile. Let's call it 'a sabbatical' with a job to do. Edelweiss Island is the story everyone wants and no one's managed to get yet. If we get it, we'll win the battle. This is literally life and death for *Two Gold Rings*. You don't have to worry about being suspended or fired, because if you don't get that article, there won't be a job to lose by the summer.'

'I still don't understand how they can pit us against each other. Our readerships are a totally different demographic and we've already got the advantage because women buy more magazines than men.'

'They don't care. Hambridge wanted something to drum up public interest. It's backfired. It's not the massive boys versus girls publicity stunt they hoped for. Our market is too niche. People buy our magazine when they're planning their wedding, they get

317

married, and they stop buying it, whereas *The Man Land* cover everything from controversial news stories, fitness, and DIY projects to book, film, and game reviews. *They* cater for all types of men with all types of interests. We cater for a very specific group of women who lose interest once a specific date has passed. We're actually at a disadvantage, which brings me back to Edelweiss Island. *Everyone* will read an article that really, truly gets to the bottom of these stories about the no-divorce church. Demographic, gender, what pretty wedding dress is on the cover all goes out the window. Getting it will wipe *The Man Land* out. It will give us respect within the industry no matter how poor our sales are. It will give you major attention with your name on the by-line. Everyone from the head honcho at Hambridge to household-name tabloids want this story. And *you* are going to Edelweiss Island to get it.'

My stomach ties itself in an even bigger knot than it's been in since I saw his angry face waiting for me when I got off the elevator this morning. 'What exactly do you want me to do there?'

'According to my friend from a newspaper who's been trying to get the vicar to do a phone interview to no avail, the locals are quite a tight-lipped bunch. You'd think they'd be keen to push this story about the church of no-divorces, but apparently it's the opposite. With a bit of luck, they'll be more open to a writer from a bridal magazine than they would to a reporter from a tabloid newspaper. I want you to go there and find out what's going on. Is the story true? Has the church really never had a marriage that ended in divorce? How do they know? What exactly are the numbers? If it's true, it could be that they've only had two or three weddings there, which doesn't make it a difficult record to keep. Or is it just a story designed to drum up tourism?'

'Aw, it must be true. They wouldn't make that up, would they?'

'They would if they were selling something. Apparently they

offer package deals, like a wedding and honeymoon in one, and according to the only review on TripAdvisor that has since been taken down, you can get your wedding dress and your cake and stuff like that on the island, and they do a discount for getting it all in one place.'

'It sounds perfect,' I say, smiling at the thought.

'It sounds like a business that's failing,' he says with a frown. 'And whoever's running the joint has invented this story to dredge up customers and increase tourism. You go there and find out if the no-divorce thing is true or not – if it's real then you can write a lovely story about how romantic it is and our readers will lap it up, and if it's fake, you can write an exposé about this scam island and we'll be the first press to reveal the truth about it.'

'It must be real. They wouldn't make up something like that. There are records, I bet it could be checked out easily enough.'

'Do it, then. Check everything out. And for God's sake, bring me *something* that the other reporters haven't been able to find out. Something real. And don't come back until you've got something, either. I want the article on my desk in four weeks. No extensions.'

'It sounds wonderful to me. I can't think of a nicer place to be banished to.'

Oliver rolls his eyes and I'm sure the look he gives me is one of pity. 'Well, I can't think of anything worse than a whole island of weddings. It sounds tragic. Apparently there are loads of desperate women trying to get married there now, couples travelling from all over the world, convinced the church will somehow stop their marriage ending in divorce. And you had better make this article a good one, Bonnie. At least R.C. Art makes people care. Whether they care because they agree with him or because they vehemently disagree, people respond to him. Write me something that people will respond to, enough people to make copies of our magazine fly off the shelves. Think of how good it will feel when you can say you're solely responsible for putting R.C. Art out of a job.'

'Don't worry, I've blocked the prat now,' I say. 'Believe me, if I never see, hear, or think about R.C. Art ever again, it'll be too soon.'

Don't miss the next book from Jaimie Admans, *The Vintage Carousel by the Sea*, coming in 2019!

DIGITAL
H Q

If you enjoyed *It's A Wonderful Night*, then why not try another delightfully uplifting romance from HQ Digital?